# Also by Richard Harbroe Wright

## The Island and the Town

Continuing from the end of *Loft Island,* Stephen's friend Martin wonders why he has heard nothing from Bronwen. His visit to Chepstow starts a chain of events that disturbs life there, in Loft Island and the mainland home of a solicitor. Then Martin's father is found dead, and a home is needed for his two younger brothers as well.

At last, though, compensation for the losses suffered in the flood that started Loft Island is made, and plans for their joint futures are planned, with some surprising twists and turns.

## The Suspects

A light-hearted story with spikes. Faced with little to do over the summer, six mid-teen mates camp illegally. Evicted back to their home town, they soon find they have to return to camp to keep out of the way. A dog, a Dutch recluse, a town gang of adults, parents, maps and a hospital all play their part. There are brambles, nettles, blackthorns, wild swimming, self-sufficiency, fires, friendships and of course the dog. And those truffles…

## Change at Tide Mills

Near Seaford, 1963: a chance, fleeting glimpse of a girl from a train brings Owen running back from Seaford to Bishopstone Tide Mills. His interest is matched by his father's interest in the failing Mill. For the Tide Mills in the story is still fully built.

The youngsters explore, finding evidence of the past which leads to a search for the past inhabitants. It unearths a story of lost love, a tyrannical husband and his mistreatment of a wife and the child.

Gradually the site is restored and ready for its next chapter. The characters of the old story are brought together and find surprise after surprise. This is a tale of families, of the ups and downs of life, of some little adventure. But it's also a tale of the real Sussex of the time, with its old customs, its history, and some of its Characters.

**Available online at rw2.co.uk, or at Amazon.**

# LOFT ISLAND

**Richard Harbroe Wright**

Published by Richard Wright
Seaford, Sussex, UK

Richard@rw2.co.uk

First published 2018

This second Edition 2020


ISBN: 979 8 571791 74 8

Dedicated to my wife Judy in thanks for support, multiple re-reads and copious editing, and for saying that she found *Loft Island* absorbing but asked for a map.
There is a map.

While I'm at it, thank you to my parents for allowing a 12 year old to venture onto the Salcombe estuary in a variety of motor boats and sailing dinghies, all without a lifejacket. Thanks to my father, to Arthur Ransome and to the 1939 Manual of Seamanship for teaching me to sail, to the 16th and 17th Hove Scout Groups, and to *Ashley Book of Knots;* all of whom taught me the knots enabling me both to prepare and sail a dinghy and to stop sailing and moor when necessary.

I was not a duffer: I didn't drown (See Swallows & Amazons, Arthur Ransome, for details). At times it was a close thing, but we don't talk about that.

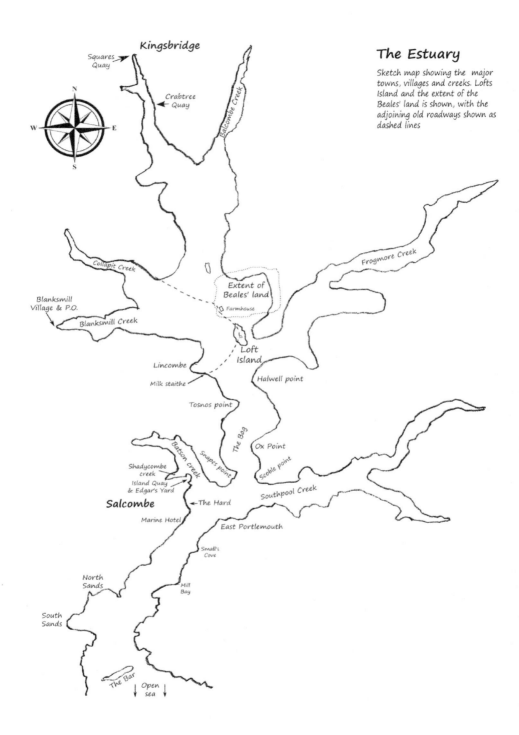

Kingsbridge

Squares
Quay

Crabtree
Quay

Balcombe Creek

# The Estuary

Sketch map showing the major
towns, villages and creeks. Lofts
Island and the extent of the
Beales' land is shown, with the
adjoining old roadways shown as
dashed lines

N
W        E
S

Collapit Creek

Frogmore Creek

Extent of
Beales' land

Blanksmill
Village & P.O.

Blanksmill Creek

Farmhouse

Loft
Island

Lincombe

Halwell point

Milk staithe

Tosnos point

The Bag

Batson creek

Ox Point

Snapes point

Shadycombe
creek

Scoble point

Island Quay
& Edgar's Yard

Southpool Creek

**Salcombe**

The Hard

Marine Hotel

East Portlemouth

Small's
Cove

North
Sands

Mill
Bay

South
Sands

The Bar

Open
sea

# By way of explanation:

### Salcombe

The Estuary has been adjusted for the sake of the story a little. Salt Stone has grown extensively into a verdant island with a farmhouse and become Loft Island. Blanksmill Bridge has grown a village. Water levels have been adjusted – but that's part of the story.

The rest of the area is as accurate to 1950s-60s South Hams as my memories of it from many years' childhood holidays allow. There may be one or two alterations to geography that I've forgotten.

### The 1950s

"The past is a foreign country: they do things differently there." (L.P. Hartley, *The Go-Between*). Some behaviours described in this story are so out of place with 21st century practices and sensitivities that it's difficult to realise they were normal in the 1950s. Who now would believe the existence still of people for whom Victorian 'high class' standards (double standards?) were still *de rigeur?* Who would now countenance even young children of different genders sharing a bed in emergency situations? Kids skinny-dipping in Britain nowadays? Probably not. Also let's not forget that in the 1950s a boy of 14 was likely still to have a child's voice and wear shorts to school; yet in another year could leave it and enter an adult job with sometimes adult responsibilities.

Yes, a foreign country to us, now, despite being 'only' 60-70 years ago.

### Names and people

I am proud to use the Loft and Beale surnames as they belong to my family. Otherwise I have tried to use Devon surnames in many cases. With the exception of Alvar Lidell, then a BBC newsreader, none of the people in the story genuinely depicts any actual person, living or dead.

However, I wanted to hint – no more – at the old and respected but alas now gone business of Edgar Cove, Boatbuilders, of Island Quay, Salcombe. They were never undertakers, so far as I know, though many other craftsmen in wood did also fulfil that role. The owner and staff in the 1960s when we hired boats from them were delightful people and deserve to be recognised and remembered with fondness, even this late in the day.

# Contents

1 - Floods.................................................................................1

2 - Tragedy .............................................................................14

3 - Help..................................................................................24

4 - Police ...............................................................................34

5 - Boat.................................................................................43

6 — Milk and Town...............................................................52

7 - Statements .......................................................................62

8 - Arrangements ..................................................................71

9 — Church, Susan, Peter ......................................................79

10 - Dinghy ............................................................................90

11 — Mr Merryweather ........................................................100

12 — Learning to sail ...........................................................111

13 — Sailing lessons.............................................................123

14 - Rehearsal......................................................................135

15 - Inquest.........................................................................144

16 — Inquest continued (1) ..................................................158

17 — Inquest continued (2) ..................................................167

18 - Funerals.......................................................................175

19 — Life, Susan, sailing, school .........................................187

20 — Doctor .........................................................................199

21 — The moment ................................................................208

22 - Disappearance .............................................................220

23 - Journey........................................................................227

24 - Confusions ..................................................................236

25 — Arrest, and Martin ......................................................246

26 — Café, return, Peter, Dot ..............................................256

27 - Flight...........................................................................264

28 - Return..........................................................................277

29 - Injury...........................................................................288

30 — Court case...................................................................299

31 - Weddings .....................................................................313

32 — Christmas and more .....................................................328

# 1 - Floods

The dark puddle of rainwater beckoned. The small lad's eyes lit up. He gathered himself as if a pouncing cat and launched himself to land in it…

…soaking the socks and bare legs of the older lad in front of him. Stephen swung round in shock and anger.

"You little… *pig*!" Fortunately he had remembered who might be listening.

The boy looked at him, suddenly scared, and made a wellington-boot clad rush for the Juniors' entrance.

The long, kindly summer of 1954 had enabled three friends, both farmers' children, to walk, swim, and camp all the time once their farm jobs were completed. Greg Beale's young sister, Mary, wasn't able to camp, as there was just the one tent. But she knew where they would be and would often leave home early to join them. She would track them, often arriving in time to see them struggle from the tent and dive straight into the nearby sheltered stream or pool, unashamed, before running back to dry off outside the tent, and to dress and have breakfast.

That would be the point at which she would join them, and spend the days doing what they did.

The spectacular summer had eased away to the return to school and the cooler temperatures of September. The attractions of sleeping in a tent lessened. But even in the cooler air the streams that ran from the still-warm land were comfortable to swim in.

After a grey Christmas and New Year the rains started, at first subtly, but as February approached there was an increasingly noticeable malice in them. Land grew soggy. Water lay on low lying fields and reflect the sky. Walking became an effort and boots were essential. By March, conditions for walking and driving were becoming hazardous, with so many stretches of path and road covered by water. Finding solid ground for foot or tyre was chancy.

Shaking his arms uselessly, Stephen wished he had a larger oilskin, his having been new when he'd been eleven. It was tight everywhere and allowed rain in. Also he was wearing shoes because his journey started with a cycle ride from his farm to the nearest bus stop.

Trudging in annoyance into the school's lobby, he dried himself as well as he could with his spare towel, and made his way to their classroom where he knew there would be a gas fire.

His friend and neighbour from the adjoining farm joined him and the pair stood, steaming gently as a little comfort returned.

"Cold too, isn't it?" Greg remarked.

"Freezing. Specially after that little pig sprayed my legs."

Greg nodded. Silence reigned. Steam rose.

"You were part of a dream I had last night," Greg announced suddenly as if glad to rid himself of the memory.

Stephen's eyebrows raised. "I am privileged!"

"Not really. It was a nightmare."

"Oh, thanks!"

"No, I don't mean *you* were the nightmare. That's just the sort of dream it was."

"Oh. Well, that's better."

"Not really." Greg shuddered, surprising Stephen even more. Greg was normally as down-to-earth as himself.

"What happened?" he asked, quieter now.

"We were climbing Everest. Well, I think it was Everest. It was a real mountain, anyway."

"Who was Hillary and who was Tensing?"

"Ha ha. Actually, you must have been Hillary. You were leading up and I was on the end of the rope."

"Just as well. I don't talk Nepalese. Go on."

Greg gave a half smile. "You got up to the top and I was coming up to join you when the rope started to fray. I could see it but you couldn't. And I could barely talk, let alone shout, so I couldn't make you understand."

Stephen said nothing, but grew more serious.

"At last you looked over and saw what was happening, and started letting down another rope . But before I could get to it the main rope broke."

He stopped. Stephen looked at him, allowing the silence to continue and wondering whether to ask him what happened next. Greg's face was enough to still any question.

"That's when I woke," said Greg in a grim voice. "I was sweating and breathing so fast it almost felt real. Took me ages to recover, too. Mum looked in and asked if I was all right; she said she'd heard a shout or something."

The door opened and the teacher came in.

"You're okay now, though?" Stephen was still speaking quietly. Greg nodded as they walked to their desks.

After the first two lessons of the day Stephen's legs were just about dry, helped by exposure to the gas fire whose attentions to his socks whilst he was chatting had nearly scalded him. At five to eleven, as they filtered back into the classroom, there was a surprise. The teacher had brought in a small radio which he proceeded to plug in and switch on. Whilst they waited for its valves to warm up it was explained that there were good reasons for the radio, as they should soon discover. At the start of the BBC News he turned up the volume.

*"Here is the eleven o'clock news, and this is Alvar Lidell reading it..."*

Why, wondered Stephen, should he bother with the radio news?

*"The persistent rain from the Atlantic which has been affecting the south of England shows no sign of abating. The London Meteorological Office announced that the depression which is now stationary some miles from the coast of Cornwall is deepening further, and that a further prolonged period of rain and wind can be expected. The effect on ground water levels in most of Somerset, Devon and Cornwall, and over parts of South Wales, has been marked, and officials have taken steps to ensure that those most at risk in areas prone to flooding are warned."*

More? Not more! They were fed up with it, thought Stephen. Official warnings? No one had warned any of *them.* The news reader droned on, talking about rivers and lakes and ponds and their bursting banks... but then the entire class pricked up its ears. *"Near Kingsbridge in South Devon authorities are concerned about the security of two reservoirs. It is reported that their retaining dams have been requiring maintenance since before the war, and could now be approaching a dangerous condition because of the excessive weight of water bearing on them. The situation will be continually monitored, and warnings given if there is cause for immediate alarm."*

"Oh well, that's all right then," Stephen muttered to himself. The teacher looked at him sharply. The news went on to a different topic, and the radio was switched off.

"I thought it would be as well to play that to you, children, so that you could experience geography in action. It is a subject which is not restricted to dry books..." (or even wet ones: Stephen's brain couldn't help but add) "...but is a living, breathing matter that concerns us all." He continued droning on as if there was nothing depressing or dangerous about the weather they were living through, with its possibly disastrous local consequences. The teacher was not the sort who welcomed questions, so Stephen's remained unasked. He was uneasy about what he had heard, worried that the valley he lived in, and their farm, could be flooded.

"Hey, Stephen?" called Greg. It was late afternoon, and school was mercifully over. Stephen was thankful that his friend seemed to have recovered.

"What d'you think about that news he played, then? Is it really that bad?"

Stephen thought. "It must be if they say it looks dangerous. And they said they were going to warn us."

"But what do we do? And who's going to warn us?"

"Radio? Police? Air raid wardens? Dunno."

There was nothing else to say. Stephen wasn't really in the mood to joke, even with Greg. He'd seen too much rain by then and was depressed. If anything the rain had actually worsened. Now there was an evil, chill wind too. The grey, featureless sky lowered over them, interrupted only by the occasional windblown cloud which increased the misery of the downpour.

They left the school buildings and ran to the waiting bus. Even over that short distance the rain once again penetrated still-damp raincoats and found unintended gaps in others' more practical waterproofs and oilskins.

From his favourite seat across the gangway from the driver, Stephen watched anxiously the man fought the wild weather that scoured his familiar landscape. The road resembled a dark river.

The driver was as familiar to his passengers as were the buildings they had just left. A Devonshire man with years of experience, Stan had first met each of them when he or she started at the Kingsbridge school. He had become a friend, and at times a confidant. He was as concerned with their welfare as any of their teachers, and was determined on maintaining the safety of them all on the journey.

As the bus crawled down the last steep hill before the village nearest his home, Stephen had a grandstand view of Stan's fight with the controls. The steering wheel was alive. The bus swayed with every gust of wind, with every pothole. The constant batter of rain on the windscreen frequently defeated the wipers, especially when the bus was heading downhill or braking, when water sluiced off its roof. Stan's skill and the grip of the tyres on the near-liquid road surface were being tested to the full.

The passengers were normally a noisy but good-natured bunch. This evening they were depressed, overawed by the weather. Many

4

of them were farmers' children; others lived in the villages between Kingsbridge and Salcombe, or in Salcombe itself. Greg and Mary lived on their family farm, as Stephen did on his. As farm dwellers they all knew the swings of the seasons but none had encountered weather as severe or as prolonged as this.

They arrived at last at the comparative safety of the cluster of houses at Blanksmill. A muted cheer rang out, and Stan heaved a sigh of relief as he came to a halt by the little bridge, which now had water flowing over it as well as under. The ford at its side, unused by traffic for years, would have been impassable, even for a bus.

"Well, we made 'un!" he said, as cheerfully as possible. "Sorry you're late, look, but you're here and safe, and that's about it, me dears."

Stephen, Mary and Greg now faced a wet cycle ride to their homes over roads exposed to the worst of the weather. They lived in the flat bottom of the main valley. Once it had been an extensive river estuary stretching from the sea between Start Point and Bolt Head, past the town of Salcombe, and right up to Kingsbridge with its railway. The expanse of many square miles of water had become more and more shallow over the centuries until at last the local landowners, eager to expand their small empires, had artificially blocked it with a sea wall at the narrows above Salcombe. A system of lakes and locks kept sweet and salt water apart whilst still providing a course for the many streams which still flowed into what had become sweet valleys of pasture . Their banks had been built up to avoid regular flooding. Many of the banks now had tracks and roads built on them. These served settlements which had gradually been built on the fertile land of the valleys.

Stephen lived on one of the two 'islands' left in the valley. Although they had been deserted by water for a century they were still named as such. The northernmost was too small to be of much use, but Loft Island with its farmhouse had land stretching almost to the steep sides of the original estuary. The house itself was ancient, and comfortable. Stephen's grandfather used to say he was glad it was there because the sea would one day reclaim its own and flood out all those who were silly enough, in his words, to build on the sea bed.

The Beale farm was further north. It had been built on only slightly raised ground above the old estuary's bed. The Beales' and the Lofts' boundaries marched together, meaning that co-operation between the families was as natural as night after day.

As the group of friends was   leaving his bus Stan suddenly called after them.

"Yere! Just a mo. I dunno 'bout tomorrow, see. If this keeps falling fit to bust mebbe I shan't get through. You'd best get your mums to check with the depot. Ok?"

They assured him they would do that, suddenly hopeful of a day's freedom if the roads were blocked. Or perhaps even more time off if the weather stayed bad. "Although what good would that be, if it's raining like this?" thought Stephen.

They went their separate ways with depressed goodbyes. The three cyclists struggled their way to a small shelter at the back of Blanksmill's only shop where their bikes were stored and were about to retrieve them when old Mrs Luscombe appeared at her back door. "You 'ain't cycling home today, surely? 'Tis worse than ever. You'll be blown off the road as sure is I'm standing 'ere!"

"We've got to get home, Mrs Luscombe," said Greg. "Walking is going to be as bad. Worse, if anything. It'll take longer."

"Well, why don't I phone your homes and get them to come for yer? They was 'ere an hour back, but that good fer nowt Stan took so long to get his owd crate 'ere they've gorn again."

"You mean they'd come to collect us?"

"Well, issen that what I'm saying? They was all frettin about the bus, but med sure you'd have started walking, so they've gorn looking."

"Well, if they've come for us once, I suppose they could do the same again," said Greg doubtfully. "But I know mum and dad are busy on the farm this weather."

"An' would they see their young-uns catch their death, then? No, you get yoursel' on my phone. I'll not be chargin' you!"

They were about to troop into her shop when the bell on her front door jangled. "Oh, drat and botheration," she mumbled. "Just you wait there. I won't be two shakes."

She struggled her way through the crowded store room, Stephen, Mary and Greg were looking around this Aladdin's cave full of years of unsold stock when Mrs Luscombe's call of "come through 'ere, you!" brought them running through to the back of her counter. And there, dripping and anxious, was Stephen's father. As his son appeared his face cleared.

"Thank God," he said. "I've been worried sick. The forecast is for still harder rain this evening and I was worried in case the bus got stuck and couldn't get through. Anyway, I've come to take you all back – yes, you two as well. I've spoken to your parents and suggested it, as they're trying their hardest to keep the water where it should be and can't really leave the place."

"Thanks, Mr Loft," said Mary. "It's kind of you. But what do you mean about the water?"

"At the moment, Mary, it's threatening to burst the bank of the stream that skirts your land, and they're trying to persuade it not to. I'm afraid if it does rain harder tonight they won't be able to stop it. We've got to keep a careful eye open - in between trying to keep our own farm running still."

"Is it really that bad? I know there's been an awful lot of rain and the valley looks like a sea. And I suppose the stream was very high this morning, but would it really burst its bank? It's awfully thick!"

"You wait 'til you see it, Mary. You'd not recognise the gentle little stream of summer at all. Think how high Blanksmill's is at the moment, and that's already over the bridge. No, we're worried about your family, you and Greg; it looks as though we may have you as visitors later this evening."

"Couldn't we just live in the upstairs?" asked Greg. "We wouldn't get flooded there."

"And where do you cook? How do you run the farm? No, I'm afraid there's just no choice. We're not leaving you to drown! Anyway, you come over to us often enough. Don't you want to, suddenly?"

"I didn't mean …. Oh, you know." He'd seen the grin in Henry's eyes.

"The farm'll be OK, I hope, Greg. Your cattle are still safe up on the hills, I'm told, and that's where they can stay until we've got grazing again for them where they belong. It's just the chickens and pigs that are confused at the moment, and it looks as though they'll be coming to us on the way through."

Like all the streams in what had been the estuary, that which passed the Beales' farm on its way to the main watercourse had been banked up to prevent flooding. It was this bank which was now in danger. The 'island' from which Stephen and his father ran the farm was further down the same stream, but as it was mostly over 30 feet high it should be in no danger.

They ferried the three cycles round to the Lofts' small farm truck. Inside the cab was quite a squeeze, with Greg and Stephen squashed onto a seat for one. Rather than sit on her brother's lap Mary elected to sit on Stephen's, to his father's amusement, but he wisely said nothing.

Their truck splashed across the flooded Blanksmill bridge and took the left fork downhill toward Lincombe and the open valley. Stephen was watching the water level as they followed the stream downwards. What he had seen at the bridge prepared him little for the turbulent, muddy water that now scoured out the bed of the stream and was fretting at its banks.

As they dropped down from the wooded part of the road at Lincombe, entering the exposed main valley and setting off along the road, they could see what Stephen's father meant. All the extensive, valuable pasture belonging to the two farms, and the land of others' farms, were completely covered with water as far as the eye could see. Winter floods there were fairly normal, but he had never seen the sheet of water stretch all the way to the shoreline of a century earlier.

The road turned north east, bringing the remainder of the low land up to Kingsbridge into sight. It appeared increasingly as if they were motoring in the centre of a windblown, inland sea. They climbed up to their own island and down again heading north west towards Beales. Stephen saw in detail what his father had meant. The flood was just two feet from the raised level of the road, way above the flat lands around it. The wind was already blowing great spurts of water onto the surface, to the peril of car drivers. The further north they struggled the more vistas of water opened up. The young passengers were speechless.

The rain thinned for a moment and they could again see the western side of the main channel, near the end of what was still called Collapit Creek, though in their memories until today it had borne just a small stream. Even as they watched, water crept across the lush pastures at its western end, as the stream over-topped the bank and spewed its contents over the road that led from it into the valley.

It was a depressed and worried party which reached Beales' Farm. Henry took two cycles from the back and Mary and Greg wheeled them through their muddy front gate. John Beale appeared, and greetings were exchanged.

"We've got the chickens crated up," he said, "but the pigs are being obstinate as usual. I'll have to bring them over later, if that's all right?"

"All right by me, John, but don't leave it too late or they'll get drowned!"

He waved his agreement and turned to the barn to retrieve the family's poultry which were to be the first of the Beale guests at Loft Island that night. Mary and Greg followed to bring the other crates which would adapt into temporary coops once on the island. With them in the truck Henry made ready to set off south again.

"Tell your father not to chance it if the level gets any higher," he called after Mary and Greg. "I know I've told him once but he's as obstinate as I am. We've not got much room at Lofts' but at least you'll be safe there."

"We'll tell him," Greg called back. "And thanks!"

As the rain swept down again Henry climbed back into the cab and started on the drive round to their own little island, thanking the ghost of his great grandfather who had insisted on living above the sea bed.

Inside the house the log fire had been burning in its ancient home since late September, so unkind had the climate become. Even the family's dogs, George and his young pup, dozed fitfully, half wanting to be out and doing and half glad to be indoors in safety and comfort. Their mood of boredom, tinged with the canine anxiety which comes with high winds, was shared by Stephen who at the age of almost fourteen had thought himself impervious to the weather's moods. True, daily on the way to school recently his legs and feet had been soaked, and it was only the presence of the classroom fire and a towel kept at school which had made it anything like comfortable. He was used to that. He was not used to having to dry himself out day after dismal day.

He had always been an active, open air type, loving to help his father around the little farm which provided their food and enough to trade with others in the area to buy the things they couldn't produce. It was an unusual existence for the times, but two previous generations had already opted for a way of earning a living which had been seen by most as abnormal for educated men. His father had known no other way of life at first hand, and certainly none that had attracted him so much. So Henry had taken on the ways which had been part of his upbringing.

Stephen's temperament followed his father's. He had a good circle of friends at school, amongst them Mary and Greg. They had all talked casually about the merits and drawbacks of their parents' lives; some couldn't understand what Stephen and the Beales saw in having apparently so little variety to their life, and so little entertainment in the 1950s sense of the word. Some envied Stephen and others commiserated with him because his father was always present. He couldn't understand their attitude, and wondered what kind of people they had as parents. Many of his contemporaries couldn't appreciate the arguments he brought up to counter theirs. They had been able to understand that life was different if your mother had died two years previously, but pointed out that there were two others in the circle whose fathers had been killed in the war. This, they said, was nearly the same thing.

For Stephen, naturally more active than most, working with his father was a fact of life, a life he loved, a life which was as natural to him as breathing. His brother Peter, by then 18, had been different. He had found farm work spiritually stifling. Friendships with older school friends in Kingsbridge had started keeping him away at weekends, then led to his missing mornings at school. Eventually there had been a showdown with his father one traumatic afternoon (in Stephen's absence). School had been skipped again, and Peter had insisted that he should leave education and get a job. He had lived with a friend in Kingsbridge for a time, then found a job in Torquay where he now lived.

Although Henry had been desperately disappointed, he had really no option but to agree. Living in a small house alongside a bear with such a sore head would have been intolerable. He would not stand in his elder son's way.

It meant that more of the work on the farm fell to Stephen, who rose to the challenge and thrived on it. Father and son had a rare emotional and work rapport, a source of immense comfort to each. Stephen took that for granted, having known no other. It was all the more surprising to him when some of his less lucky school friends offered sympathy when they learnt that he was apparently required to do so much work on the farm. They couldn't understand that he didn't see it as work.

Because of the weather only just eight Jerseys and half a dozen pigs were still being kept near the house. As 'house animals', they had chickens and geese, the first for eggs and the second as burglar alarms and occasionally for food. The remainder had been boarded out to neighbours' farms on higher ground.

At last the many little jobs around the farm were done. They had milked the wet, steaming cows, had found that all the hens had sensibly kept in their coops which made gathering the eggs much easier and more pleasant. The two dogs who had been following them around all the time were soaked and looked miserable. Used to the routine of drying dogs before they 'dried' you, Henry and

Stephen had trained them both to sit on the doormat whilst towels were fetched. Father and son each took a dog and dried them vigorously. They were encouraged to shake dry afterwards, and only then allowed in.

The fire in the living-room beckoned the dogs. Few words were spoken until father and son had changed into dry clothes once again and were preparing a meal.

"Dad, do you really think that Beales' will be flooded? I mean, it's never happened before, and they do have a high bank between their place and the stream."

"With this weather, anything could happen. It's not been seen before in my lifetime, nor is there anything in Dad's old diaries. I know that because I thought I'd read through to see if there were any suggestions – you know, things we could do to stave off the worst of it, or any pointers from his experience. But there's nothing. Nothing like this, anyway."

"So what do we do? Just wait? Or do we watch for problems?"

"There's a limit to what we can do, Stephen. You can see precious little through the rain until you're right on top of the bank, and there's more of them over at Beales' to keep watch. I've told John to get all his family into their Land Rover and drive like a bat out of hell up here at the first sign of even more serious flooding, and that's all we can do apart from getting to the phone quickly if it rings. They've already loaded bedding and spare clothes into the wagon and the trailer. If it happens, we'll put them somewhere – you might find Mary and Greg on your floor in the morning!"

"You'd wake me, surely, if they did come?"

"Do you know how difficult it is to wake you once you're asleep, Steve? Remember that thunderstorm you slept through last summer?"

Stephen looked sheepish. "Er...I remember you telling me about it afterwards."

"Well, that storm echoed round the valley for two solid hours, and there were cracks right overhead fit to wake the dead. In fact, at one point I went into your room to check you were still breathing, and found you sleeping like a lamb. So if you think I'm going to be able to wake you, think again!"

"You will try though?"

"All right. In fact if they do get here I might need you to help. You can take on Mr and Mrs Beale and I'll comfort Mary and Greg."

"What! Me? Why that way round?"

"Because they'll be too upset to be of much use to their children, and won't want to show it in front of you. I'll be able to sort out the other two."

"All right, if you think so."

"We'll see how it works out. I'm leaving the fire made up and I'll try and come down in the night to make sure it's kept going well. The same with the Aga. If you do wake up by some miracle, could you do the same? And we'll keep the water going on the Aga, too.

"Right now I'm going to phone them to see what the situation is. Switch the radio on, will you, and we'll catch the news."

Stephen crossed to the large valve set which gave its usual loud pop as he switched it on. There was always a delay whilst it warmed up and before he could tune in. He heard "Oh!" from his father's concerned voice by the telephone in the hall.

"What's the matter, dad?" he called.

"Dead as a dodo. The wires must have come down in the wind. Hm... what to do now... I'd better chance my arm and have a look at the situation. Radio on?"

The chimes of Big Ben gave the answer, followed by the news reader telling the rest of the country once again how the south west was being battered by fierce storms for yet another night, but that the depression in the Atlantic which was causing the problem should be the last of the succession which had made the region's life so miserable. The weather, he told the nation, should begin to improve some time over the following day.

"Doesn't help us tonight. Why can't..." Henry was interrupted by the radio.

*"Concern is growing over the condition of two reservoirs in South Devon. These are old, and are due to be demolished as soon as there are replacements for them high on Dartmoor. Over the War years they have been kept artificially low to relieve pressure on the old retaining walls which have recently been showing signs of weakness.*

*"One result of the exceptionally high rainfall has been that the water levels in these reservoirs has been rising faster than it can be released. The level of water in them is now abnormally high, and the Water Board report that it is impossible for any remedial action to be taken to keep it from rising further. There is a high possibility of damage if the pressure of water on the dams grows much greater.*

*"Officials are standing by to alert owners of all properties which could be affected. Police and the army will be brought in if the situation worsens."*

12

*"In Parliament today the Leader…"*

# 2 - Tragedy

Henry motioned to Stephen to switch off. In the silence that followed he could see his father thinking hard. They knew one of the reservoirs particularly well. Flear reservoir was a large Y-shaped stretch of water just north east of Kingsbridge, occupying the valleys of two rivers and a third they flowed into, roughly between Buckland and East Allington. If it burst, its water would pour down the remainder of the valley and into the old bed of the estuary, probably raising the flood levels enough to drown all the settlements which had been established since the estuary had been drained. If the other reservoir suffered the same fate, the consequences wouldn't bear thinking about.

"That changes things. It's no good, Steve. I'll have to get them here now. If the water in the channels doesn't get them those bloody reservoirs will. I'd never live with myself if we just stood by and they got drowned. They might not even have heard the news anyway."

"I'll come with you."

"No. I need you here, and I certainly need all the room in the truck to bring back as much as possible for them. What you need to do is make sure there is hot water on the Aga, and that both it and the fire in here are made up. Dig out a load more towels, too. Put them by the fire to get warm - don't set the place alight, though. Change the sheets on my bed – the Beales can have that and I'll sleep by the fire. You'd better make enough space in your room for Mary and Greg. We can't stand on ceremony – the place is too small to give the girl her own room. She'll have to muck in with you and her brother. Keep the dogs in." He was struggling back into his wet waterproofs as he spoke. "If you think of anything else that'll help five wet people, then do it. I'll be back as soon as I can get them ready."

He turned and opened the inner door. Stephen grabbed the dogs as they tried to push past him.

"And Steve..." Henry stopped, suddenly unsure why he was about to say what was on his lips.

"Yes, Dad?"

"Nothing, except... I'm proud of you, that's all. Don't let us down."

And with that he was out of the house, the wind slamming the outer door behind him.

Left to himself, Stephen wondered what to tackle first. The towels... that was it. They could be warming whilst he arranged everything else. He went to the old fashioned chest of drawers in the hall and found the family's entire stock of towels, some of which he hadn't seen since his mother died. He wondered what his father would think about his using them, but decided that he should do what was necessary and stop being sentimental.

Assembling the wooden clothes horses in front of the fire he started to hang towels on them. Memories receded to the times, a long time ago it seemed, when at the age of seven he would use these same two horses, safely draped with blankets around the sides and on top; a private lair where he would sit and read for hours, emerging eventually, blinking and confused, to find half a morning gone and a meal ready. Grinning at the remembrance, comforted by it, he completed his task, then carefully made up the fire.

For company he decided to turn on the radio again, and chose the Light Programme where sometimes they played modern music, much to his delight and his father's disgust. It was their one real bone of contention. He could hear a band playing as he added fuel to the Aga in the kitchen, and filled the two kettles and as many saucepans as he could fit onto its ample boiling and warming surfaces.

Up in his father's room he stripped off the bed and then remembered that he should have taken the fresh linen from the drawer when he had removed the towels. His journey back downstairs to the hall brought him within earshot of the radio again. He was suddenly aware that the music had stopped and an announcer's voice was talking with a note of official urgency.

*"... so all those within this area are urged to evacuate their homes and attain high ground immediately. Officials in towns and villages nearby have been alerted. Halls and schools are being prepared to accept all those who will be displaced by the emergency. It is still hoped that disaster may be averted but officials are now concerned to ensure local inhabitants are made aware of the possible dangers.*

*"To repeat, this is a police message for all those in the low lying areas between the South Devon towns of Salcombe and Kingsbridge. A warning of inundation has been made by the Home Office in view of the worsening condition of the Flear reservoir. All those within the area should evacuate to high ground immediately and seek shelter at the nearest village or town. We will bring you further news as it develops. That is the end of the police warning."*

Stephen listened aghast, suddenly more than anxious about his friends, not to mention his father. He wondered what would happen to him if... no. He wouldn't think of that. Far better to carry on with the preparations his father wanted him to make. Dad wouldn't have gone out if there was any real danger to their home, would he?

His brain still in a whirl, he retrieved the bedclothes from where they had dropped when he heard the announcement start and headed upstairs again. After readying his father's room he went into his own and looked at the familiar area in a new light. His bed was a large single which covered most of the floor and left precious little spare. Small it may have been, but his own, comfortable space it still was. His lifestyle needed little floor area for play – the rest of the house provided that. Besides, most of his time when not at school was spent around the farm doing work which was really all the play he wanted. Time spent in his room was for reading or sleeping: he was almost always too physically tired, although spiritually fulfilled, to play energetically as most others at school seemed to.

Now he was wondering how he could find more space in the room so the three of them could share it. When his brother had lived at home they had shared the bed, as for years the family had not had enough money to buy two smaller replacements. Indeed, the room was not big enough to accommodate them even if they had. It was a matter of habit to him, and sharing was fairly common even in the 1950s. Over the years people had done so as a matter of course and necessity. It was not something that had ever come up at school, of course, but Mary and Greg knew as they were frequent visitors.

Stephen wondered whether the three of them could share, but was aware that his friends had separate rooms at their farm and such closeness was foreign to them. He shrugged. There's room for one more on the floor, he thought. He'd get enough sheets and blankets from downstairs to make up another bed. Two could share and one could sleep on the floor. They would decide who later.

A dull rumble made him look towards the window. He had been unaware of any lightning, but was hopeful of seeing the next flash. Although he stared out into the streaming night for almost two minutes he saw nothing but the slanting rain and the trees bowing before the gale force, southerly wind.

Downstairs again, he thought to check on the towels around the fire and the water on the Aga. All seemed to be in order, although the dogs were restless and just staring at the north facing window. Stephen attributed this to the thunder, and he wondered what else he could do to make things ready. A cup of tea. That was it. He'd make a big pot, so they could all have plenty once the six of them were together. He checked the time. It was just over two hours since his father had left the house, and about an hour since he had heard the police warning. Surely this was enough time for the Beales to make themselves ready and to reach the safety of their island?

After a worrying few moments of indecision, Stephen came to the conclusion that he could afford to go to one of the island's many vantage points to see if there was any sign of their truck returning. He went once again to the lobby where his boots and waterproofs hung and busied himself in forcing warm feet into cold, wet wellingtons and arms into an oilskin which was so wet it might just as well have been inside out.

Fending off the dogs who wanted to keep him company, he opened the door and was aware of a distant rumbling noise which was growing louder as the moments passed.

Suddenly scared of what he might see, and helped by the southerly wind, he ran down the track which led to the north of the island from where the noise was coming. At the brow of the hill, just before the road headed down westward and then north toward Beales' Farm, the trees came to an end. He stopped there, gasping. The valley bottom was dark. He was expecting that. But with a sickness in the pit of his stomach he realised that there was no twinkle of lights in the distance where the Beales' home was.

As he had run to his vantage point the noise had been growing louder. With a shock he understood what it was. Before he had a chance to react – though by that time there was nothing he could have done except ensure his own safety – there came the roar of a hard-pressed engine. With a feeling of almost numbing relief he recognised it as his father's truck, which was towing a trailer. As it reached the brow of the hill where he stood the lights picked him out and his father stopped with a shriek from the brakes.

"I've got a load of their furniture and stuff," he shouted at his son as if he was actually expecting to see him standing there like a captain at the wheel of a storm-tossed ship. "Help me dump it and then I'll... what the hell's that?"

"Dad... it's... it's the water from the reservoirs... I'm sure of it. It's coming!"

Henry's face went white. Wrenching open the cab door he jumped down and looked back over the valley.

Coming towards the island, suddenly visible even in the near darkness, a wall of angry rwater was sweeping down the valley inundating everything in its path. Borne with it and in its wake, heavy spars, planks and a wide variety of other heavy flotsam could be seen. As it swept down and over the Beales' land it had spread out so that some of the force had dissipated. But just before Loft Island the shores of the old estuary narrowed and a second small island stood in the middle of the channel, concentrating the water into two rips.

It was at the southern end of the western rip that the Beales' farm stood.

Stephen heard his father, in a tone he had never used before, mutter: "Oh, God, no. Their light's gone. But I've got to... but..."

Henry turned away, his hands over his face. Stephen watched him, disbelievingly. First his friends' home gone, then his father seemed to be crying. Then his brain caught up with events and his mouth dropped open. "No!" he whispered. "Not... surely not... Dad?"

Suddenly aware, his father turned to him and the two figures clung together, weeping, as the rain and wind swept around them, and the killing flood lapped at the skirts of their own island of safety. As if out of respect the engine of the truck had stalled, and the return of the uninterrupted sounds of the storm caused them to disengage and look at each other.

They continued watching in horror, hoping against hope for a sign of life in the flood, but seeing only raging water coursing towards the sea. Stephen shivered. His father, now grimly fully aware of their loss, was at once concerned. "Come on. There's nothing more we can do. No point in catching our death..." He broke off, bitterly. He turned away toward the truck. Stephen still gazed into the darkness, motionless. "Stephen! Come on home."

His son was still numb with shock as if the full realisation of his friends' fate had still to sink in. His father pulled at him.

About to turn away, Stephen stiffened. "Dad, wait. I think I heard something."

"What?" Perhaps before this night Henry would have told him not to be silly and imagine things. His attitude, their attitude to each other, were being subtly tested by the events. Instead he turned back and said again "What? What did you hear?"

"Don't know. Wait."

They peered out into the blackness once again, trying to filter out the noises of the weather. After a moment: "There!" exclaimed Stephen. "Did you hear that?"

"No. You've got better hearing. What was it?"

"It was a call... I think. Dad, could it be...?"

"We've got to find out. Come on. With me. Go quietly. We can't afford to miss it, whatever it was."

With ears pinned they started off down the slope toward the new water level. As they dropped into the lee of the hill the force and noise of the wind abated. The relief was almost tangible. With their sense of hearing in effect restored, they heard the call when next it came, weakly, from their left and toward the water. "Over there!" shouted Stephen. Henry had heard as well, and was already pushing his way through the soaking undergrowth.

Right at the water's edge, surrounded by a jumble of dunnage and almost indistinguishable from it, was what appeared to be a bundle of rags; a bundle which nevertheless moved and called weakly. "Help! Please! Where am I?"

Hearing the voice, Stephen stumbled and almost fell.

Mary. Alive.

His father crossed to her in two bounds, and crouched at her side. "All right, Mary. You're safe now. It's Henry Loft and Stephen. We'll soon have you warm and dry."

"Mum? Dad?"

Henry thought quickly. "You're the first we've found. We'll get you safe and then come back for the others. Are you hurt?"

"No. Cold."

"Steve... Oh God, I don't like to ask you this, but can you look for the others while I take Mary back and put her in front of the fire? It'll be quicker that way and I'll be back sooner with the truck."

"All right. I'll go this way," said Stephen, pointing right. "What do I do if I find - anyone?"

"Keep them warm and out of the wind and water. Wait there with them. I'll sound the horn at the top when I'm back. When you hear it, come running if you can. If you go the other way put a cross of stones in the middle of the road so I know. All right?"

"OK."

For the second time that evening his father gripped Stephen's shoulder. "Be careful," was all he could say.

Henry lifted Mary into his arms as if she was a sack of feathers and started off up the hill towards the truck. He didn't look back. He couldn't trust himself not to run back to his son and get him, too, into the dry safety of their home. The water streaming down his face was not only rain.

He nearly missed his own farmyard gate on the way back. The house was in darkness. Henry realised that the overhead lines must be down.

Once they were indoors, Mary seemed to respond better. Henry put her on her feet and found she could stand. He was glad the house was so familiar to her, as were the dogs who, puzzled, pushed round them to welcome them, wondering why they were not involved as well.

"Are you hurting anywhere?" he asked Mary again.

"No, I was just so cold in the water. Please, Mr Loft, find Mum and Dad and Greg. The water took us all at the same time. They were with me at the start, but we drifted..."

Henry interrupted her. "So long as you're OK, Mary, that's all I need to know. There'll be time for talk later. Let me get some candles, so we can see what's happening. Sit in there." He pointed to the living room. "Take off your wet clothes and get yourself into towels in front of the fire. "

He bustled off to find their emergency supplies of candles, all ready in jam jars so they were safe. He brought in the hurricane lamp that they usually used around the farm buildings, so there was enough light in the room.

"I asked Steve to heat water, so there should be a kettle boiling in the kitchen. If you feel OK make some tea for us, will you? Don't forget there'll be six, but get yourself warm and dry first. We'll be some time."

"OK Mr Loft, and..." she gulped. "...Thank you."

Henry nodded to her, trying to look happier than he felt. He thought it was nothing short of a miracle that she had survived being taken off her feet by what amounted to a young tidal wave and deposited none too gently in a patch of scrub some half a mile further on. As to her parents and brother - well, he didn't hold out much hope, but if anyone could find them as quickly as himself it was Stephen.

The thought suddenly came to him. *I've just asked my thirteen year old son to look for what could easily be dead bodies! Oh God. What have I done?* He rushed from the house, leaving Mary bemused, and almost wondering what she had done to make him angry, but she knew he was anxious about Stephen as well as her own family. She had no idea of the real reason.

He found Stephen at last. He was with Greg, who was lying on what was now the beach, on his stomach. Stephen was kneeling at his head, alternately pushing his friend's back and lifting the arms which he had carefully placed under his sideways facing head. For the third time that night Henry realised what a son he had. Some time ago the school had put on a course in artificial respiration. It had caused much laughter and ribaldry at the time, as the three friends had reported afterwards, but he could see that it had sunk in. He ran over to his son.

"The Beales are over there," said Stephen wearily. "The backs of their heads have been crushed. I don't know if Greg's alive or not."

"Where are they?" asked his father shortly.

"Behind the next hedge, over there." He nodded to his right. "Dad, can you take over, please? I don't know if I'm doing this right."

"Keep going just for a moment. I'm going to look for the other two."

"But Dad, I told you they were dead." His voice shook, and Henry realised he was at last near breaking point.

He knelt down beside him. "You really are doing it right. Better than I could because I'd put too much pressure on and break his back. Just two more minutes, please, Steve?"

His son looked at him, resignedly. "All right, but... hurry back?"

"Don't worry."

He was up and running in a second, battling against the wind which was starting to reach this side of the island again. He reached the next clearing and saw the two bodies immediately, even though they were surrounded by a scattering of debris that the flood must have collected in its first hectic rush from the reservoir. Looking at the size of some of the baulks of timber he once again wondered how it was that the two children's bodies were apparently undamaged. Not so their parents'. One look at them told him that whatever had hit them must have done so with such force that not only were their skulls crushed from behind, but that their limbs must have taken

20

a battering as well. Nobody could live with injuries that serious. Appalled, he turned hastily away, remembered his son and the work he was doing and rushed back.

Stephen had stopped, and was just kneeling there,

"All right, Steve, I'm back. And you're right, I'm afraid, as I knew you would be. Let me take over now, eh?"

"I think he's dead, too, Dad."

"What?"

"He made a noise while you were gone, so I stopped. I thought he was breathing, so I turned him over. His eyes were open and he was looking at me. He knew who I was. He said 'Stephen, look after them for me,' and then stopped breathing again and his eyes stayed open. I yelled for you, but you didn't come, so I turned him over and there was another noise. I turned him back again and all down his stomach there was blood. Oh, Dad..." And he buried his face in his father's shoulder.

As the forecaster had predicted, the rain was now falling in almost a solid sheet. Neither of the grief-stricken figures had a spot of dry skin. To have waited there any longer would have been to court a further disaster.

"Steve?" Henry said, gently; "Steve, we've got to get indoors."

"We must... you know... do something for them." Stephen was trying to gather himself, although the blow of what he had experienced was crushing him. To have seen one of his close friends die, and to realise the devastation this and the loss of her parents would have on Mary, was too much to bear. Still, a small corner of his psyche was lit by common sense, and he gradually became aware that life must go on; that at least Mary had been salvaged from the wreck of the night.

"I know, son. But unless we get warm and dry soon we'll be in no fit state to do anything for anyone. So come on, now."

"Can't we cover them up, at least?"

"I suppose we must. It seems the right thing... I'll come back with something from the house."

"I want to be here too."

"You've done enough for one night. Home, now, and look after Mary."

"They're my friends too, Dad."

"I know, I know. First things first, OK?"

They turned away at last, leaving the ruined bodies of Greg and his parents to be cleansed by the torrent of rain. At the top of the hill the wind hit them again and nearly blew them backwards. Opening the truck doors was no mean feat but the relief once inside was indescribable. Henry pulled the starter, half expecting the engine to be soaked and not to start. To his surprise it did, and in silence he drove to the house.

"We've got no electricity, by the way, just to add to our problems. Steve, stay in the kitchen, out of the way while I tell her, will you? If I need you, I'll call."

Stephen nodded, relieved that the responsibility had been lifted from him. As he came into the warmth tiredness overcame him despite his grief and he felt himself swaying. Grim determination drove him into the kitchen, where he found both the kettles were boiling hard. Fearful lest they should boil dry, he managed to revive himself enough to use the contents of one of them to heat the teapot, and removed the other completely. He had just made the tea when his father reappeared. Suddenly scared, he looked up.

"No, she's all right." said Henry, reading his expression. "She's just so spark out I can't wake her. It's probably for the best. She may face it better in the morning."

Stephen nodded, and nearly fell over. "Tea's in the pot, Dad. I don't know if I can keep awake any longer."

"All right, Steve. You've done well tonight. I mean that. There are adults who couldn't have gone through what you've done and kept a level head. Go to bed. I'll sort Mary out – I'll bring her up in a minute."

Steve staggered off to his room, too tired to argue. He was dimly aware that he should be doing something but his brain had given up. He collapsed in the hallway, too exhausted to climb the stairs, and never felt his father lift him, walk up the stairs with him and put him to bed as if he were a child.

Henry returned to the living-room, and sat for a few minutes taking stock of all that had happened that night. He looked at the sleeping girl on the sofa and smiled at her peaceful expression. Always pretty, Mary looked positively angelic asleep, and he was hating the thought of what he would have to tell her in the morning. He wondered what would be best to do for her tonight. If he left her here the fire would go out and she would be cold, even if he wrapped her in bedclothes. She should sleep in a bed. His? He could sleep downstairs. But then he thought of all he had to do in the morning, and how he needed a good night's sleep himself. Would it matter if she and Stephen shared? Who would get up first, and what would they think?

He remembered back to the journey to Beales that afternoon, after he had collected them from the bus. He thought how readily she chose to sit on Stephen's lap rather than her brother's... Greg! Oh hell, what a terrible waste of a young life.

Would Mary think it out of place to share her friend's bed for a night? Would anything untoward happen? No, not with last night's horror in her mind still. And she was only just turned twelve, and even if his son was a year older nothing could happen.

Very gently he scooped her up and carried her up to Stephen's bedroom. As he turned back the coverings, Stephen stirred, probably awakened by disturbing memories.

"Dad?"

"You've got a visitor, if you don't mind. Look after her, would you? She'll wake after you in the morning anyway, I should think. Get up without waking her, won't you? Goodnight."

Stephen mumbled something as his father went back downstairs. Drowsily he stared at Mary. A look of tenderness and sorrow came over him, and he reached out to touch her face, very gently.

He slept.

Henry returned to the kitchen and took a pull at his tea, wondering again how matters would resolve themselves in the morning. That sent his mind back to this evening's grim work, and his half promise to Stephen that they would cover up the three Beales. With a sigh of resignation he donned his waterproofs yet again and set off down to the water's edge, this time on foot so as not to risk waking up his charges with the noise of the pick-up's engine. His charges! The thought hit him. He was no longer a farmer with a son who helped him, but the father of two children. Wasn't he? His mind worked on, wondering what effect the presence of a girl of his son's age would have on Stephen. Or on him. The thought that Mary was not really his responsibility never crossed his mind.

# 3 - Help

To Henry's surprise it was Stephen who woke him in the morning, well before his alarm clock. It was still dark. The electricity was still off. He heard his son go downstairs to the kitchen to make up the Aga and brew a pot of tea. Quietly he joined him there.

"Dad, you agreed we should go back and cover them up."

"Yes, Steve. I know. You were in no state to go out, so I went."

"Oh. Sorry."

"Hmm. I reckon you did quite enough last night anyway, as I said then. Aren't you tired still?"

"Yes, but I thought there'd be so much that needed doing today I'd better get up."

"You're right, but one of the important things is to make sure you get enough sleep, otherwise you won't be fit for anything. Are you feeling OK? No sore throat or sniffles from being so cold for so long? You really should go back to bed and have your sleep out."

"Dad, I'm fine. Anyway, there's the farm to see to and... well, we've got to contact the authorities, haven't we?"

"Yes, but most important, we've got to make sure we're here when Mary wakes up, although I should imagine she'll sleep on this morning, farmer's daughter or no. If you're certain you're fit and ready, we'll start on the milking and make sure everything else is as well as it can be. I don't know what the water level's going to be like now." The house was surrounded by trees, so it wasn't possible to tell from the windows. "I imagine that they'll have got rid of most of it when the tide was low enough. It may be some time before anyone gets here, though, and I'm sure the phone's still dead. There's one positive thing, though."

"What's that?"

"It's stopped raining."

Stephen listened. Rain had become so much a fact of life for him over the previous months that he'd given up his usual habit of checking the weather as a waste of time. This morning he'd left his curtains closed for fear of waking Mary.

He was not prepared for the thick mist that enveloped them as they left. They squelched their way to the shippon. Fortunately it had been built on far too big a scale for the part of the herd the island farm had ever supported. Old Grandfather Loft had been ambitious of buying even more land, but had never quite managed it. The big building did mean that enough of the herd could be comfortably accommodated in winter with space to spare whilst the remainder boarded out on neighbours' land.

They completed all the jobs of habit, then Henry left Stephen to finish the milking, a job he knew his son enjoyed. Stephen was wondering how soon it would be before the water retreated enough to enable a drying out process to begin. Neither father nor son had been anywhere yet apart from the immediate area of the house and farmyard. When he had finished milking, he filled the tank over their cooler and set it running, which fortunately it did by force of gravity. He thought he would take himself off to see the state of their meadows.

As he drew nearer the brow of the hill his nose wrinkled. He could smell the sea. At first he thought that the wind was still strong enough to blow its influence all the way from the sea wall by Salcombe, but soon realised that with the rain's departure the wind had dropped. Anyway, wind and mist together would have been unusual.

He climbed down toward the south of the island, having deliberately avoided the north which held unpleasant memories for him, as well as something more tangible. As he did so the salt smell grew stronger. He was soon passing trees and bushes which showed signs of having been soaked and torn by fast water, and eventually was surprised to reach the water itself.

The sea smell was strong. He put a hand into the edge and tasted it.
Salt.

He ran back to the farm in record time, to find nobody in the kitchen or living room. Once again anxious he bounded up the stairs to find his father sitting on his bed with Mary in his arms, her head pushed against his shoulder. His noisy entrance made his father look up, and his face told him that Mary had learnt just now about the death of her parents and brother.

She looked up too. To his surprise there were no tears in her eyes.

"You tried to save him." She paused. "Thank you."

He said, suddenly touched by her serenity: "Mary..."

But the shock was once again too much for him and he could feel the tears starting. He did the best thing he could by crossing the room and flinging his arms around them both. Tears fell free, not just from him but now from Mary as well.

For ages, it seemed, they sat like that. At length Henry eased himself free and looked at them.

"Stay together," he said.

"It was worse for Greg," she said at last. "He must have been hurting a lot."

He shook his head. "He didn't sound as though he was. Did Dad tell you that he started breathing just before he... died? He said 'Stephen, look after them for me.' It was almost a normal voice. I don't think that whatever happened to him was hurting."

She nodded. Then "What am I going to do?" she asked quietly.

"Greg asked us to look after you. That's what we're going to do."

"You mean, I'm going to live here?"

"Unless you don't want to."

"Are you're sure your father wants that too?"

"I told him what Greg said. He will."

"Can we go downstairs and make sure?"

"Yes. Come on"

"OK …. oh. I'm only wearing …. What?"

"Looks like one of my thick shirts."

"Oh."

"Your clothes are probably still wet." He made no move to go. She threw caution to the winds, pulled the shirt firmly down and swung her legs off the bed. He turned and led her down to the kitchen.

"Mr Loft, can I talk to you for a minute, please?"

Henry turned and looked at them. He saw a pretty girl, with tousled brown hair and dark eyes, still a child but nevertheless with an aura of capability around her. His son, physically the sturdier thanks to his extra year or so and the constant work around the farm, was also really still just a child. Then he remembered what Stephen had accomplished the previous day, how his unquestioning, willing part in running the farm had made him seem more like a partner than a young son. He recognised how that young son had grown up so much in just the two years since Edith had died. Growing up was not just about the count of days, after all, but about what you packed into them, and how you reacted to it.

"Of course, Mary."

She turned to Stephen. "Sorry, but I need to say this on my own. Please? I'll tell you afterwards, I promise."

Stephen looked astonished, then almost offended. He turned without a word, and went up the stairs, slowly, grimly.

Henry watched, concerned. Then, gently: "What is it, Mary?"

"Mr Loft, how long can I stay here, please?"

Henry's mouth dropped. He suddenly understood. Stephen must have told her she could stay here, he thought, and was obviously expecting her to live here. Well, that's what he was expecting, too, wasn't it?

He crossed to her and put his arms on her shoulders. "Mary, what has that son of mine been saying to you? Did he tell you what Greg said? Because if he did, he was right to do so. Even without Greg's words I'd have asked you if you would like to live here, but with that still ringing in Stephen's and my ears I want even more to ask you.

"But what do you think about the idea? We've not as much room here as you had so it'd be a bit of a crush unless we can rearrange things. You may not like the idea, but you and Stephen were in the same bed last night.

You were both spark out, so I didn't have an option. But it's not an ideal solution – if it is one at all, even for the time being until we can afford two single beds.

"Well, that's where we stand. What do you think?"

She paused before responding.

"I'd like that very much, Mr Loft. I promise I won't be a nuisance. And don't forget - there's furniture at our farm…" She trailed off.

"I know, my dear. But we'll take one step at a time, shall we? Can we get Steve in now and ask his opinions? He and I are used to acting as one in everything to do with the farm, so I wouldn't want him to think he's being left out now. OK?"

He crossed to the door and opened it. Stephen was nowhere to be seen. Henry called for him. Slow footsteps on the stairs told of his approach, but his face when he appeared told Henry that everything was not right. He glanced at Mary without a smile and spoke to his father.

"We always talked about everything together."

Once again Henry understood.

"We did and we still will. Look, you told Mary that we expected and wanted; that is that she should stay here, especially after Greg…" He swallowed. "She doesn't know – or she didn't until I told her – that we work as one and that to a very large extent what you say to people goes for me too. She wasn't sure that I'd agree to her living here. It's obviously more than important to her. She wanted to be certain I was going to welcome her as well, that I wasn't just going to go along with you for the time being and then change my mind. So she felt she had to speak to me alone, so neither of us would be embarrassed, and so that she could get an answer from each horse's mouth.

"Don't be hard on her. She needs to be certain we both want her here. I've said that I do, that I agree with you, unreservedly. So now we're all three of the same mind. Mary wants to live here, and we both want her to live here. So we're back to normal now. Agreed?"

Stephen looked relieved. "Agreed," he said. "And now I can say what I was going to when Mary came down? I've been down to the water and…"

"What d'you mean, down to the water?" Henry interrupted. "It's dropped by now, surely?"

"No, dad. That's what I'm telling you. It's still there and," he paused for effect, "it's salt."

There was a silence as the news sank in. Henry understood quickly. Mary didn't grasp its meaning at all.

"Why should it be salt?" she asked.

"Because the sea's come up this far, somehow," said Henry slowly. "What's gone on overnight that we don't know about yet? When's the first radio news? Oh, damn …" He looked around at the candles.

"Dad, it's going to be ages before anyone gets here," said Stephen, a note of alarm in his voice. "There's… um... things we've got to do." He was thinking about the morbid flotsam on their north beach. "Is there any way we can get anywhere – say when the tide goes out?'

"Possibly," said Henry, his mind racing. "I think we'd better go and look at the road a bit later to see if the surface is still all right to drive on. If the banks are still there, that is; if they haven't been swept away by the force of the first flood when the dam burst. You don't know about the tides, I suppose? Living this far from the sea I never keep up with them."

"No. Some of the others at school do, those that live in Salcombe. But we've never needed them here."

"Where are Mum and Dad, and Greg?" asked Mary quietly. "I think we should... I mean... " She stopped.

"Do the right thing for them, you mean? We covered them last night. It seemed the right thing to do. It wasn't a job for you and Stephen - no, Steve, don't argue. I appreciated your offer of help but it had to be my responsibility. In fact, I'm not sure what has to happen next is really mine either. The authorities need to be told, and there's a limit to what we can do until they have been. I'm not sure I wouldn't get into trouble even if I just moved them up here."

A movement outside, visible in the strengthening light of day, caught their eyes. The dogs were startled too, and started barking furiously.

"All right, lads, all right. That's enough," called Henry, and they subsided, still grumbling. There was a knock at the door.

To their surprise, their visitors were in uniform, one that Henry didn't recognise at first but which was familiar enough to Mary and Stephen as they were often seen near the school in Kingsbridge. The Civil Defence had found their farm, and the two men standing at the door were obviously pleased to find what seemed to be near normality.

"You're still here, then, and not washed away," said the first, jovially. "That's a relief, when you see what's happened elsewhere. There's not a lot left of your neighbour's farm up the road. Completely washed away, it was. Gone. Foundations are under water now, of course. And there's not a sign that anything was there. But..."

There was a strangled sob, and Mary bolted out of the room. Stephen looked angrily at the Civil Defence man and followed her.

"Oo-er. Were they friends of yours? Sorry, didn't know. Can't know everything, can we Arthur?"

His opposite number was looking downright uncomfortable, and said in a quiet voice "It'd be surprising if they weren't friends, Bert, seeing as their farms are adjoining and they both have youngsters. Sorry, sir, if we've

28

caused an upset."

"You don't know the half of it. Really, please, use a bit of tact. I appreciate your coming, but you've got to realise that we've had one hell of a night of it. She is from Beales farm, that girl; the Beales' daughter. It's her home you've just told her about. We had to pull her out of the water last night."

"Cor, blast," said Bert, in a quieter voice. "I'd not have said anything if I'd known. Sorry. I should have thought ahead. I was so relieved to find you still here and safe that my tongue just ran away. I'd better go and see the girl. Do you know where her parents are?"

"Dead," said Henry, shortly. "On our north hill. So's her brother."

There was a silence.

"Wheee... I think I just put my foot in it in a big way," said Bert. His ebullience had deflated over the previous few moments, and he was looking sorry for himself.

"Poor lass. Can I go and talk to her, please? I need to set matters right."

"Let my lad be with her for a while, eh? He's feeling a bit protective this morning, I think. Hardly surprising, really. They've known each other since they were born."

"Yes, but..." started Bert doubtfully. "I mean, no offence, but they're only children. Shouldn't there be an adult there to try and comfort her?"

Henry bristled. "Look here, 'Bert'. My son tried to revive her brother last night with artificial respiration after he was washed ashore with what looks like a big hole in his stomach. He revived just long enough to ask Stephen to look after his sister and parents. What Greg didn't know was that my son had just found the Beales washed up nearby with their skulls smashed in.

"I realise you don't know either of those youngsters, but just trust me when I tell you that I do, will you? If I thought there should be an adult with them because Stephen couldn't cope do you think I'd still be here talking to you? I know you're here to help, and I appreciate that, but from now on please treat Stephen as someone with common sense and strength of mind and body, will you? And be a bit tactful with Mary. She's tough, being a farmer's daughter, but to lose parents and brother in one night is enough to upset an adult.

"For what it's worth, I shall be looking after her – sorry, *we* shall be looking after her – here from now on."

Arthur intervened, quietly, as before.

"Excuse me, sir, but we're from Kingsbridge and I don't know your name, just as we didn't know the name of the girl's family. We do need that, as you'll realise. But we do also want to know how we can help you all."

Henry looked at him, and read a sincere and capable gaze.

"My name is Loft. The other family, as you now know, are the Beales. And the most important things you can do for us is to arrange for the bodies to be dealt with and let us know why there's still water – salt water – at the bottom of the hill. Oh, and how did you get here in this mist anyway? By road?"

"No, Mr Loft, by boat, all the way from Salcombe. Having no power here… Oh, hallo." This was to Stephen and Mary who had returned to the kitchen.

"Look, Miss," broke in Bert. "I really am dreadfully sorry that I was such an unfeeling ass just now. Please, accept my apologies, even if you write me down as a tactless so-and-so. The last thing I wanted to do was to upset anyone. That's not what I joined the Civil Defence for; quite the opposite in fact. Please will you forgive me, or would you prefer me to go outside and leave Arthur to explain and to tell you what sort of help we can offer?"

Mary looked at him, surprised to see and hear how genuine he was. His eyes were serious, she thought: he was taking her seriously.

"That's all right," she said. "You weren't to know."

Stephen still looked thunderous.

Arthur carried on from where he stopped. "Having no power means that you've not heard the news. The sea wall's gone. The pressure of the storm from the sea was quite terrific last night, and although the wall was built as strongly as they knew how all those years ago, it was getting on a bit. I suppose because of the Great War, the recession and then this last war, it can't have got much maintenance. Anyway, it suffered a lot last night from the south, and then when the Flear Reservoir burst and all that water swept down the valley, that was the last straw. The deep estuary between Salcombe and the Bar must be littered with masonry and all sorts.

"All the artificial pounds in the middle are damaged, too. Their construction was only light, as you know. The reservoir water made short work of them. Possibly without all the water standing in the fields below Kingsbridge the story might have been different, but as it is there's not a lot left of the valley's defences down there. The sea is able to flow in and out as it must have done two centuries ago."

The Lofts and Mary looked at him aghast as the news sank in.

"What about all our pastures?" asked Henry quietly, his mind trying to find something positive from the wreckage.

"Probably useless, I'm afraid, Mr Loft. The salt will have ruined it already, I imagine; or if not it will within a week. There's no ready cure for a destroyed sea wall - not when it's gone that far.

"What about all our animals?" asked Mary, suddenly distraught. "There were cows on the lower hillsides where Dad arranged with farmers to get them out of the middle. There were sheep, too."

Arthur looked at Henry, enquiringly.

"You'd better let us know the worst," said the latter.

"Well, if they're above the valley floor, Mary, they should be OK. The sheep too."

"Yes, I know that, that's why they were put there. But who's going to milk the cows and feed them all?"

Henry butted in. "If they're on a farmer's land he'll make sure they're cared for. No farmer is going to stand by and let animals suffer, even with the problems all this will have brought them. Who were they left with?"

"I don't know his name. It was on the western side, just below Park Farm, I think."

"That'll be Peter Symes' land. He'll look after them. He's mainly arable there, and there won't be a lot he can do with all the water about. He'll be glad to have some beasts to care for, after all these years without. You know Mark and Jimmy Symes. You're at school with them. Anyway, you've no cause to be worrying about animals yet."

Mary looked relieved, as if she would have gone immediately over to the fields to gather her animals around her had the answer been any different.

"What we need to do," said the quiet Arthur, "is to make sure that you have enough food and fuel here for your animals and yourselves. We don't know when they'll get an electricity supply back to you, and certainly it'll be months, if not years, before anyone even thinks about repairing the sea wall, I should think. What you're going to need for the moment is a boat."

Both Henry and Stephen looked startled. "Why," asked Henry. "Is there no chance of using the road if we time it right?"

"None at all," Bert replied, in the sensible tone to which he had settled once his earlier indiscretions had passed. "The water level at low tide is about four feet, and at high tide must be about twelve or more. We don't know exactly yet, but that seems to be what the flood marks are telling us. Don't forget that your island rises from the bed of the old estuary, and the road was well below the top of it. It's even well below the low water line, we think." He glanced at Mary, to make sure she was not being upset.

Gradually Mary was coming to terms with the idea that her home was gone, swept away. Like many people of twelve, the emotional importance to her of losing her parents and brother were finely balanced against her own security and established routines. That sounds callous, selfish; yet it is a natural instinct which is probably borne of the prehistoric instincts of self-preservation. Although she couldn't put it into words, Mary was unhappy about the way she was thinking. She loved her parents and brother. It had been a happy, caring family and she was feeling the loss more keenly now, more than just an unspecified spiritual ache. Still other matters were coming to the forefront of her mind and now and again, for a few moments, the immediate memory of her loss would vanish. When she had time once again to think, to weigh her situation, then her bereavement became that much harder to bear. Yet in the long term - again as happens to us all - the repetition of these waves of loss would become less frequent, until all that would be left would be the wave-worn furrow in her memory.

"So just how," asked Henry, "are we meant to get around? I mean, where are we going to graze the animals? How do we sell milk and buy – well, everything else? How does he – how do they – get to school?"

Stephen suddenly remembered this was Friday, and he should be leaving for school. Despite their situation, he grinned to himself.

Arthur and Bert looked at each other. "We can take you to Salcombe or Kingsbridge," said Arthur quietly. "But there's no real answer except a boat, for what I imagine is going to be quite a long time."

Henry looked dismayed. "I can't afford to buy a boat! You tell me that I've just lost all my pasture and arable, except the little we've got on the island, and I'm expected to buy a boat? How can I? Anyway, only Salcombe people have boats, and they're going to need all theirs."

Arthur looked uncomfortable. "I know, I know," he said. "What we're here for is to try and help now, immediately. I can't say we have all the answers to your problems. They're best thrashed out with the Council offices in Salcombe. I mean, they must be about to develop some sort of emergency help for people like yourselves. Do you want us to take you in?"

Henry paused. "Sorry," he said. "I'm not getting at you, really. It's just that... well, you see the situation we're in. And – oh, no – look at the time! We haven't fed the pigs or chickens yet!"

Stephen made a quick decision. "Dad, you go with them into Salcombe and do whatever you have to. Mary and I will stay here and look after the animals, won't we, Mary?"

She nodded.

They followed Arthur and Bert down toward the northern end of the island. Henry managed to get some paces ahead with Arthur and voiced his other main concern about the bodies of Mary's brother and parents. They discussed, in low voices, what would be the best way of transporting them.

"Leave it to us," said Arthur. "The first stop for all of us in Salcombe needs to be the Police Station. We'll put the problem to them, and they can arrange for them to be fetched. I think it would be best if you were back here when they came, no matter how good that son of yours is with Mary, just to have an official presence, sort of thing. Also, I think we all need to think what is the best thing to do for Mary."

Henry looked at him. "That's easy," he said. "She's living with us."

"I know. I wasn't talking about that. She needs to be sure that she's a part of everything that's done for them, but not at too close quarters. We need to talk about it on the way."

The start of the road winding down the hill was in places on a fairly high bank, and provided an easier way of embarking and disembarking from the motor launch that their visitors were using. Very soon the adults were in the boat. Henry's instructions to Stephen about what to do for his charges were unnecessary really, but he still gave them, with his son joining in at the end of each sentence and even reminding his father that they had eggs to collect as well.

It was the one slightly lighter moment of the morning.

# 4 - Police

They watched the boat chug away until it rounded Halwell Point and turned to the south. This was the first time they'd been able to take in the scene properly. Where before there were slightly undulating green fields which offered pasture lush enough to delight any farmer, there was now an unbroken expanse of water. As far as they could see to the north, where the hills divided at the end of what had been the Beales' farmland, the land was completely covered.

"It's very pretty," said Mary quietly.

Stephen remembered the countless times that he and Greg, and Mary, had played over those fields, as well as around and in the farmhouse that was now demolished, drowned. He remembered suddenly the presence of his friend, and of Greg's and Mary's parents, in little clearings nearby. His eyes filled. As if a tap had been turned, tears fell down his face. There was no warning, no mounting grief, just a sudden awareness that he had lost a part of his life, too.

Mary was still watching the place where her home used to be. She suddenly turned and looked at Stephen, catching his change of mood as if by telepathy. Turning, she gently touched his arm, the tears starting to prick her own eyes. Stephen was mistily aware of her. He sat on the road, and Mary joined him.

"They were friends," was all he could say. Mary nodded, unable to speak. She found herself putting an arm round his back until it gripped his other shoulder. He did the same for her, and they sat in silence.

It was conscience which attacked him next, and he jumped up, dislodging her arm almost abruptly. "Come on," he said gruffly. "We've got animals to look after."

They found the pigs rooting around anxiously, and their reproachful looks made them both, the son and daughter of farming families, feel guilty. They don't realise what's happened, thought Stephen. Won't they be surprised when they find an inland sea where they used to roam around!

"I don't know how we're going to get rid of all that milk" said Stephen when they had at last finished the feeding. "There's no way we can transport it to the stand for collection - that's the other side of the water, and it's gone collection time anyway."

Mary suddenly said: "Steve, I think we've got a boat! Dad always says he's going to get it…" she paused …"*said* that he was going to get it back."

Stephen paused at the change of tense, stabbed by it. Then his eyes opened and he said quietly: "If we could find it, that would save a lot of our troubles. Where is it?"

She frowned. "I don't know. I think Dad had it before Greg was born, 'cos he always talked about it as if his sailing days were long ago. It must be in Salcombe somewhere. I don't know who's got it."

"How can we find out? Do any of your Dad's friends live in Salcombe?"

"Well, there's one or two... oh dear." She stopped suddenly. Stephen looked at her enquiringly. "It's just that, well, there'll have to be a funeral, won't there?"

"Yes, there will, I suppose. That'll be horrible."

There was a silence.

Tentatively Stephen asked "How do we find out, then?"

She shook her head, as if to dislodge the disagreeable thoughts. "One lives over a shop in Fore Street. I can't remember what it's called, but I think it's some sort of food shop. I've not been there for ages. I don't even know if I'd recognise it."

"Can we try, some time? It'll make all the difference."

"Yes. We must."

They continued with the farm's many jobs, jobs that had they realised it were providing the therapy of ordinariness. Fortunately the animal feed and bedding were still in good supply, and there was no immediate danger of running out, but both of them realised that transporting it in bulk would be a difficult business. They would need to use greater quantities, too, as their pasture was almost all gone.

In Salcombe, the arrival of a boat from the flooded areas was still a novelty. Two centuries previously, when the sea had extended as far inland as Kingsbridge, Salcombe had been a busy port. Their destination, just as it had been for visiting seagoing crews, was the old Hard in the town centre. It was nearest the Police Station. Henry's heart sank as he saw the crowd of people taking in their surroundings and exclaiming over what must have been one of the first arrivals by boat from the north in living memory.

Willing hands held the launch as she came alongside, almost too willing perhaps. The painter was grabbed by a small boy who proceeded to pull hard on it, which threatened to drag them all toward the stone slope and damage the launch. Shouts stopped him, Bert regained control and skilfully moored the vessel. They had agreed on the voyage that nothing should be said until they reached the Police. Hardly surprisingly, bystanders found the three very evasive about their point of embarkation and about the night's events. Arthur eventually took control and said in a louder voice than Henry had heard him use for the whole morning: "Please ask no more questions. We are in duty bound to report to the Police first and foremost, and after that they may be prepared to give information." At that the crowd gave them some peace, and they made their way to Fore Street and up the hill to the Police Station.

The small office was in turmoil. There was a queue - if a press of people five deep at the enquiry counter could be so titled - and only one policeman on duty, the Sergeant. Fortunately he was one of the solid, unflappable types, and was ensuring that the urgent cases were dealt with first. He noticed the Civil Defence uniforms and looked enquiringly at Bert and Arthur. Bert nodded and gestured toward the station's inner rooms.

"Quiet, everybody, *if* you please," called the Sergeant, and the level of hubbub dropped. "Come round into the office, please chaps, Mark can take over 'ere."

At this there was a chorus of groans. "*Thank* you," called the hard pressed Sergeant again. "I told you that we've got to deal first with matters in the order of priority. These gentlemen are priority."

They entered the office. Sergeant Franks introduced them to his Inspector, seconded to the station to help with the crisis. The pleasantries complete, Henry told his story, as concisely as possible, and ended by saying: "My main concerns are, of course, the bodies of my friends, which I regard as a priority, and how we are to survive from now on with no pasture for the foreseeable future. Oh, and also the loan of a boat is going to be a necessity. We can do nothing without."

"It strikes me," said the Inspector, "that the best we can do for you is to bring you to one of the reception centres we've set up for people who've lost their homes. At least that'll bring the girl out of the way so we can deal with the bodies of her family, and find a home or something to take her on. It'll be easier to find somewhere for you and your son to live, too."

Henry looked at him, horrified. "My family has owned that island for two hundred years," he said hotly. "We're not giving it up. No, we'll be living on it and being self-sufficient in future as we have in the past. I'm not living anywhere else, and Stephen won't want to, either. As for Mary, I already told you that she's living with us; her brother's dying words asked us to look after her. She's asked us if she can, and both Stephen and I want her to. So there's no question about it. All three of us are staying put. All we want is a boat and somewhere to graze our animals. Surely that's not out of the question?"

"I'd feel happier if you were all here, so we can make sure you're being looked after." said the Inspector, as if that was the end of the matter. He turned to his Sergeant. "Make arrangements, will you, Franks. Send out...."

"Just a minute, just a minute," Henry interrupted angrily. "You haven't listened to a thing I've said, have you? We. Are. Staying. Put. At home. Not moving anywhere. I'll make arrangements to find replacement grazing with another farmer, if it's too difficult for you. But I do need your help with transport. But I repeat, we are not moving to Salcombe, or Kingsbridge, or anywhere else. That's final."

"Oh come on, Mr Loft, be reasonable. Think of your son, and Mary, come to that. I mean, I'm sure the authorities won't let her stay on with you."

"And why not?" asked Henry.

"Because you're a single man. You don't get single men adopting girls."

"If Stephen had been a girl I'd not have let her go. What's the difference? Anyway, as I've told you already, Mary wants to stay with us and we want her to. I'll see the appropriate authorities about making the situation official. Now, are you going to help us with a boat, or do I go to the Council with *all* my difficulties?"

The Inspector looked at him stonily. "If you're ignoring my advice, what gives you the idea that I should help you, eh? Do you think I can conjure up a boat from thin air?"

It was Henry's turn to look furious, but before he could say anything Sergeant Franks cleared his throat noisily.

"Er, sir, and Mr Loft, if you'll excuse my butting in, there's one thing we need to arrange quickly, and that's the removal of the bodies. Whether we like it or not there's two children on their own on the island, and if I remember rightly from what you said, sir, the bodies are just covered over with tarpaulins, aren't they?"

"Yes." Henry's thoughts went once again to Mary. "We've got to get them moved. How do we do that, Sergeant?"

The Inspector ignored Henry's attempt to cut him out of the conversation. "We'll get the undertakers to come back with us in the boat. I'll go, Franks, and I'll make arrangements to bring back the children with me, even if Mr Loft wants to stay there afterwards."

Henry stood up, his face now white with anger. "You will do no such thing. I can't stop the Police from coming onto my land because there are three bodies there. But as soon as you've moved them and satisfied yourselves that everything is above board I want you off. If I find you talking to my son or to Mary and trying to persuade them to leave the island against their will, I will get my solicitor to put in such a complaint against you that your feet won't touch the floor. What's your name?" This last was barked in his best army Sergeant Major's voice. The Inspector visibly jumped.

"Moffat, sir, Inspector George Moffat." And his jaw clamped shut as if he regretted saying anything.

"Well, Moffat," continued Henry in a tone of voice that his son would have found difficult to recognise, "I mean what I say. You will not take my son away from me, nor will you persuade or force me to leave my home. Any effort on your part to take Mary Beale away from where she wants to be will also be the subject of a complaint against you. I shall go now to my Solicitor and give him the details of what has happened and what has been said here and how exceptionally unhelpful I have found your attitude. You, Sergeant Franks, are welcome to Lofts' at any time, as usual, and I should suggest to you that you summarise the events of the last ten minutes here in your notebook. You may well need an aide memoire when the complaints come before your Inspector's superiors."

He paused. "Now then, Moffat, before I go to my solicitor, are you going to exonerate yourself a little by helping to find me the loan of a boat?"

Inspector Moffat had recovered some of his composure. He said coldly, "We are a Police force, sir, not a boatyard."

Henry looked at him contemptuously, then turned and left the office. In the outer area of the station he found a silent group of people watching the door, and he looked at them, puzzled. "We 'eared you, sir," said one of them. "You gev' 'im what for, you did!"

Another was a tough looking, middle aged man with a twinkle in his eye. "Iffen you needs a boat, sir, ask in the Shipwrights. Bound to be summun in there'll be able to help."

"Thanks. Thanks very much," said Henry. "Good to know someone's on our side."

"Ar, you'll find a lot who is, sir. Take no notice of hirm; comes from Kingsbridge, he do"

Henry almost smiled. The door behind him had opened again and out stepped Arthur, just in time to hear the last remark. "And so do I, Ron, as you well know. And haven't I been buying you drinks this last twenty years?"

"Ah, yes," replied Ron, "but you're adopted Salcombe, you are!"

"I'll have a go in the Shipwrights for you if you like," volunteered Arthur to Henry. "Franks and Bert are trying to calm Moffat down a bit, and tell him about you. I know he's not from these parts - not really even from Kingsbridge - but he should have more tact and more sense than that. They'll do their bit, and probably tell him you don't act Army Instructor all the time!"

"He really got my goat. He didn't listen, then he tried to railroad me into giving up my family, not to mention the farm and all that I've worked for all these years. The man's inhuman. I spent six hideous years fighting to avoid types like that being in power, and here is one as a bloody Police Inspector …. Oh, sorry, Madam." This to a woman waiting in the queue to get at the counter. "I mean what I say about a solicitor, you know. If I've upset him that much he's just the sort to try and make life impossible. Who's seeing to the undertakers, by the way?"

"You'll have to leave that to the Police, Mr Loft …"

"Henry, please."

"Henry... they'll make all the arrangements. But you do have one upper hand."

"What?"

"The Civil Defence is the only organisation with the authority to enter the flooded area at the moment, unless the army have been given it whilst we've been away."

"So the Police are dependent on you for transport to the island?"

"Yes, as is everyone else."

"That makes me feel a lot better. Look, how about you doing what you can in the Shipwrights for me while I see the solicitor, then we can go and talk to someone in the Council, if you're prepared to, that is."

"When we set out this morning we were told to help anyone on the islands or the few farms with houses on the valley floor. Well, we know what happened to them - all of them got out except the Beales. And you're above the water line, so it's our duty to help you. So we're all yours."

Henry thanked him, and went to see his solicitor, who was relieved to see his client safe and well, sad to hear about the Beales, and incensed when Henry told him about the Inspector's attitude. He made notes, and the two talked for a time about Henry's options.

"Maintaining an income would seem to be a concern," said old Mr Merryweather, who had been in business helping at least two generations of Salcombe's population. "You have always said that your needs are few, but remember – that younger son of yours is reaching an age when he will want to spread his wings, and children of that age do not come cheaply. And now you intend to take on another one….well, you need to ensure there is as much income as before, if not more.

"Also, my advice to you would be to consider adopting the young girl if you are serious about offering her a home. If this policeman has a grudge against you it might not be difficult for the authorities to be persuaded that she is best served by more conventional treatment, as they would see it. You have scant room at your house, I believe. That would also be a factor. No, to be sure, arrange to start the adoption procedures. We can help you with that, of course. But," and his eyes twinkled, "you must confer with the young lady first. Yes, always consult the ladies." He smiled gently at Henry.

"You talk very good sense, Mr Merryweather, as always, and thank you. I suppose you can't magic a boat out of somewhere with your legal mind?"

"Alas, Mr Loft, I cannot. If I possessed one I might even lend it to you on a permanent basis, or until the waters were tamed again, but I do not and therefore cannot."

"Well, it was worth a try. Shall we leave it, then, that you will arrange the papers and contacts for me for Mary, and make a note of what I've told you about Inspector Moffat, and see what my rights are about the land that

I've lost? I'll try and see you in about a week or ten days, if that's all right."

Mr Merryweather bowed. Henry recognised the old man's signal that the interview was over, wished him farewell as if he, too, was still living in Victoria's reign, and was soon blinking in the sunshine again. He decided his next stop should be the council offices, so continued up Fore Street and into Cliff Road.

His enquiry to the hard-pressed Council official about what was to be done, met a stone wall. He was told that it was far too early to say, and hadn't the Police got everything under control yet anyway? Henry asked to see a Councillor, but was told there were none in the building as they were probably all at home, arranging the drying out of cellars and the mending of roofs. He asked them to let him know as soon as any decisions were made which would affect Loft Island or his vanished land, but the replies left him little hope of any real action at all, even by way of information. The fight was out of him now, following such a short night's sleep and the argument with the Police Inspector. He had no heart to bluster at the defenceless official.

Once back in Fore Street he visited the dairy shop to see if he could make arrangements for an alternative point for their daily milk collection. To his surprise he found them accommodating and helpful, and they had already thought of a suitable place. Making his way back to the Hard he was surprised to see, once again, a sizeable crowd of people gathered around two official cars drawn up nearby. He excused his way past them and headed for the boat, hoping that Arthur and Bert would have returned with some good news. They had, and with them was a police officer with a lot of scrambled egg on his uniform, and a tall, lugubrious looking man whom Henry vaguely recognised. As he approached, Arthur saw him and nudged the police officer, who swung round.

"Mr Loft? Good. I'm glad to meet you. You've had rather a night of it, I hear."

"You could say that. Have you come to help, or have you been talking to that Inspector of yours?"

"Both. Mr Loft, I am Superintendent Birch, and I'm based at Exeter. I've come down to see the damage at first hand and to judge how best we can co-ordinate everybody's efforts. I've been briefed about your particular circumstances, and am appalled at what you and your family have gone through. Firstly we need to arrange for the bodies to be brought here so that post mortems can take place and burials arranged. I gather from my Inspector that your own immediate problems are concerned with transport and the Beale girl, and we'll have to see what we can do about that. I'm just waiting for the doctor to arrive, and then he and Mr Mustchin here can set off in the Civil Defence boat."

"Superintendent, I appreciate your action. But I have only one problem, and that is transport. I need to borrow - or even hire - a boat until the floods subside. Mary Beale is *not* a problem, as I explained to your Inspector whatever-his-name-is. I have been asked by her, and by her brother before he died, to look after her and that is what I am going to do."

"I see. Well, so long as you're sure, and if the authorities approve, I'm sure that would be a weight off their shoulders."

Henry was so surprised at this reaction that he was momentarily at a loss for words. He became aware of the people around him who appeared fascinated by what was going on, looking, as they were, firstly at the scant remnants of the dam between Snapes and Scoble Points, and secondly trying to eavesdrop on the conversations around them to discover what was happening. He was pleased to see Arthur and Bert pushing their way through the crowd.

"Ah, Edgar," said Bert to the thin man with the Superintendent, "I've been looking for you in the Shipwrights. Mr Loft here is the farmer on Loft Island, and he's badly in need of a boat. At the moment he can't do anything at all as he's surrounded by water, and even when the tide's out what remains of the roads are going to be covered. What's the chances of you lending him one of your hire fleet until things sort themselves out a bit?"

Henry found himself the subject of scrutiny by the most piercing, knowing eyes he had ever seen. Feeling that Bert's request was rather much considering he'd never met the man before, he smiled, held out his hand and introduced himself.

"I know who you are," said the lugubrious one with the steely stare. As soon as he opened his mouth the spell of the eyes vanished, so homely was his voice. "We're just about to go to your island to recover your friends' bodies. Yes, I can spare you a motor launch until the season starts, but then I'll have to have her back. We're likely to get a few visitors more this year now they've got all this water to play on. You'll find your own fuel, of course?"

Henry assured him he would and asked where he could pick up the boat.

"Don't you worry. When we get back I'll go down to the yard and one of my people can bring her up for you."

"I don't want to cause you work," Henry started.

"You've been through enough, you and yours," said Edgar. "If we can't help each other out in times of trouble then it's a poor show. I'm sorting out the burial for the Beales, poor things, and it's glad I am that there are no more drowned last night in that lot. So if you like I'm getting something out of it."

"And that's something else," said Henry. "Who's going to pay for the funeral? There's only their daughter left, and she doesn't have access to any money - nor any property either. What there was is either under water or washed away."

"First things first. We've got to do the right thing for them that's dead and make sure the living are looked after. Money comes second. Why, if she has none then the government will have to pay. If they don't then it's down to the council or whoever it was let the dams burst. Why else did they start up this welfare state thing, anyway?"

Henry agreed with him wholeheartedly, and thanked him for being one of the few who had been really helpful that morning. "Apart from Arthur and Bert, of course," he added hurriedly.

Superintendent Birch called to them. With him was a short, bald man whom Henry recognised as one of the town's doctors, someone he had not had to consult since his wife's death. The Superintendent introduced everyone, and the group made its way to the civil defence boat watched by the curious crowd. With all six aboard the small launch was as fully loaded as she could be, and it was a cautious voyage up between the two Points where a swell from the still rough sea was making itself felt even two miles inland from the Bar.

# 5 - Boat

Stephen was secretly worried that his charge might take it into her head to visit the bodies of her brother and parents. He had been very worried indeed as they bade farewell to the boat, as they were then very close to where the bodies lay. Now, his main concern was to keep finding jobs for them both to do so that there would be no time to think about anything else. But even on a small farm jobs seem to be self-generating, so the two of them kept busy doing the little tasks for which time could never be found in the normal run of days. If Mary realised what he was trying to do she said nothing, although she was tiring after four hours when Stephen suddenly announced: "Come on. They'll be back soon, I hope. Let's get the kettle on."

"Shall I make some sandwiches?"

He realised with a shock that he was hungry. "Yes, please. I've no idea how many there'll be, so we'd better make lots. The bread's in the larder over there and so's the butter. You should find some lamb in there too, and probably other things to put in them. I'll get the kettles on. D'you think two'll be enough?"

"I suppose so. I don't know how many are coming either. But if they're moving … you know …" She tailed off into silence once again.

Stephen looked at her. She was just staring into space, her face blank. "Why me?" she said quietly. Then as the apparent selfishness of this struck her: "Why *them?*"

"God wanted them?"

Mary looked at him in some surprise. "*I* want them. God could have them later."

"Perhaps he knows best."

He could see she wasn't convinced but no other thoughts crossed his mind apart from a realisation of her inner turmoil, an emotion he had faced two years previously when his mother had died. He had felt himself to be lost, deprived, then; how much worse to have lost both parents, your brother and your home in one fell swoop. He couldn't think of anything more awful.

Nor could Mary. Two factors were keeping her from going to lie down somewhere and allow herself to break down completely. One was that she had been kept busy all morning by Stephen. The other was that what had happened to her was so big that she couldn't fully come to terms with it.

Without further comment she set herself to cutting bread and making sandwiches. Stephen watched her for a moment, then set to with kettles and teapot.

Half an hour later they heard Henry's arrival at the farm, together with

Arthur. Bert had elected to stay and help with the examination of the bodies and the preparations for moving them. Henry told the two in the kitchen what was happening.

"But I want to see them!" exclaimed Mary.

"You'll get a chance later when the authorities have satisfied themselves that what we say happened is true. It's got to be that way, even when it's as obvious as this. If they made exceptions for just one case where there hadn't been a doctor present when the person passed away then it could happen every time. And then really suspicious deaths might be missed."

"I want to go down now. They're my parents!"

Henry was so astonished at her reaction he wasn't quick enough to stop her slipping out of the door. He looked at Arthur.

"Now what do I do?" he asked.

"I'll go after her," said Stephen. "She needs someone with her."

"I know. We'd best all go. If you're sure you want to, Steve."

"I don't think I want to, but we've got to look after her."

They rejoined the footpath and hurried along it. As they reached the boats, which were once again moored at the start of the road leading down from the island, they heard voices off to the left, and standing just by the ring of undergrowth around the beach where the body of her brother lay, was Mary. She seemed to be tensing herself, whilst listening to the comments that the doctor and superintendent were making.

"It's difficult to say what caused an injury like that, exactly. It was obviously some sort of blunt pointed thing, and see by the edges of the wound there are splinters. Could it be a small tree or something?"

"No. That wouldn't leave splinters of wood. I know, how about a piece of fencing? He could have been washed at some speed onto that. I wonder if they had any chestnut paling around the farm."

Mary pushed her way through the bushes, before Henry and Stephen could reach her.

"Yes," she said. "We did."

The five men swung round as one. The split second before their reaction, seemed to her like fifteen minutes as though she was in a slow motion film. Calmly she took in the scene. Greg's body lay face up, hands by his side, quite naturally as though he were asleep. All that appeared wrong was that his skin colour was a grey white; were it not for this and what she had been told she would have believed him still alive.

In two bounds Bert was across to her. "You shouldn't be here," he said.

"Why not?" she asked, simply.

"Mary, he's dead."

"I know." This so matter of factly that he could say nothing. She crossed to her brother's body and knelt by it, watched by the representatives of officialdom and the Loft father and son who had joined them. Tenderly she stroked Greg's head, then her attention was drawn to the terrible wound which, although washed of blood by the rain, still was wide and deep enough to show the organs underneath. She sobbed suddenly, and turned her head. Stephen ran over to her, suddenly aware of the eighteen months between them and the responsibility he felt this gave him. He pulled her to her feet and held her against him, more to stop her seeing her brother's mortal wound than to comfort her. He pulled her away, to where Henry stood.

"Cover him up," the Superintendent said. "With reverence, please gentlemen."

He crossed to the Lofts and Mary. "We wanted to spare her this," he said, glaring at Henry.

"I'm sorry, I really am. I wanted to stop her coming down too, but she was determined. Perhaps it's for the best, though."

"How can it be! How can you say that?"

"She needed to be sure, in herself. I remember when my wife died. I couldn't believe what the doctors were saying to me, although they were telling me that she was dead and there was nothing I could do..." A pause. "No. There are some things you have to see for yourself before they become real."

He turned to Mary and Stephen. "Take her back, Steve. I can't imagine she wants to stay here now."

Stephen gently turned the weeping girl and pushed back through the bushes. They walked some way up the road, before Mary gave a shudder and pushed free of Stephen's arm.

"Let me be alone." She walked on, determinedly, then turned onto a small footpath which led around to the east of the island. Stephen watched her, wondering what to do. He felt he couldn't just leave her, but knew that there were times when solitude was necessary. She couldn't go anywhere or come to any harm on the island, after all. A sixth sense told him that he should still be nearby if needed, and he was about to start after her when Henry appeared. Stephen explained his dilemma.

Henry was glad to have them both out of the way of the examination of the bodies of the Beale parents which were so much more damaged than Greg's. "Can you follow her? But keep quiet so that she doesn't realise it? Keep her within earshot, but don't let her see or hear you. Can you do that?"

"Like stalking an animal? Yes, I should be able to, by now." Trying to get close to rabbits or badgers was a favourite pastime of theirs.

"I'll see you back at the house. Whatever you do, don't let her go right round the island and stumble across her parents before we've got them into the coffins and safely on board. I'll go and hurry them up."

He turned back, and Stephen started on his tracking exercise. There were fortunately few turnings from the little path Mary had taken, and he carefully followed it as quietly as he could. Every corner he came to he paused, and cautiously looked and listened for any sign of his quarry ahead. The path led to a high plateau overlooking what was now a narrow channel between the island and the mainland, and as he approached the more open ground his progress became even more cautious.

From the cover of a bush his caution was rewarded. Mary slowed, looked over her shoulder, and went slowly over to a rock which gave a vantage point over the water and up the estuary toward where her home had been. By now the tide had receded. Areas of muddied grass were showing near the island. She sat there for some time, sometimes just staring and sometimes holding her head in her hands. In tears, thought Stephen.

His own emotions were new to him. He had been badly affected the previous night when his friend had died more or less in his arms. He had had a shock, as had Mary, in seeing the state of his friend's body. Like most of us he had never witnessed before a fatal injury at close quarters. He had had to – had chosen to – care for Mary in her reaction to her triple tragedy. There had been few chances for his own grief and pain to surface.

Now, as he watched her, unable through her request to comfort her, yet torn by her sorrow and his own, he felt his eyes mist. The mental stress of the last eighteen hours welled up in him and he too sobbed. Unbidden, his voice gave him away. Mary looked round sharply.

"I told you I wanted to be alone!" she started, tearfully and angrily. "Why can't you... Where are you? What's the matter?"

He had turned his back so she wouldn't see, but had forgotten that the bushes still hid him from her. She crossed to where the muffled sounds were coming from, and found him, racked by sobs, head buried in his hands just as hers had been.

Moments later they were both sitting on the rock in a joint hug, with misting eyes watching the drowned pastures.

The bodies were examined, notes taken, opinions exchanged, certificates issued, coffins silently filled. Loading onto the boat was a tricky business and it was decided that only the Superintendent, Edgar Mustchin as the undertaker and Arthur as the better boatman should return to Salcombe. Bert, now completely subdued, the doctor and of course Henry, would stay on the island for the next trip. The three walked back to the house, conversation resuming only slowly.

"I don't know about you," said Henry at length, "but I'm ravenous."

None of them had stopped to eat since the early morning, and all agreed with him. It was a relief to remember that there was food prepared at the house. Henry fully expected to see his son and Mary there, and was worried to find they weren't. He was about to voice his concerns when they returned.

Mary, still pink eyed, crossed to Henry. "I'm sorry, Mr Loft. I shouldn't have done that, but I felt I had to. I think I feel better now. Excuse me." And she left the room. Henry looked at his son and was astonished to see that his eyes were also suspiciously pink. His mind raced.

"Bert, Dr Mays; take a plate of food each into the living room, please. We'll bring some tea in a minute."

"I'll make it, Henry," offered Bert.

"Thank you but no. I want to have a chat to Steve, and it'll give me a chance."

When they had gone Henry looked enquiringly at his son. "Well?"

"She's OK, Dad. She just needed to be on her own for a while and get it out of her system. She spent a long time just sitting, looking over the old pastures and where the house was, and – well – crying. But she's OK now."

"I could see that, and hear it too from what she said to me. But what about you?"

"Oh, I'm all right."

"Stephen, Stephen… Look at me." He gripped his son's shoulders and looked straight into his pink-rimmed eyes. "I know you quite well, you know. I have done for nearly fourteen years. I also know what you went through last night, as well as what you've been through just now. You've taken on more than I could have done at thirteen – or should want to at thirty-five. Since you came home from school yesterday you've done everything for the farm, for Greg, and now you've taken Mary's troubles on your shoulders, too. How about putting some of the burden onto mine, eh?"

Looking at his father, and seeing nothing but compassion and understanding, he felt his eyes fill again. Older as he felt he had become over the previous day he felt Henry's embrace comforting, whilst at the same time he wondered why that should be. He had grown up, hadn't he? He was old enough not to need that sort of baby treatment?

Oddly, part of his psyche didn't think so.

They rejoined the three in the living room once the tea was made and Stephen had regained his usual equilibrium. Mary was talking quietly to the doctor about her experiences of the previous evening. She seemed totally composed. The three adults were listening intently. As Stephen entered Bert glanced at him with a look of admiration. When Mary had reached the end of her story she looked at Henry, who smiled at her. "Mr Loft has asked me to live here, and I want to," she finished.

"That's right, and I'll tell any busybody from the police the same," said Henry emphatically.

After they had eaten, Stephen found that his head was nodding. He had been up even earlier than usual that morning, and the previous late night meant he had only achieved a few hours' sleep. Mary was better off, but not by much. Her night had been longer, but she had more to recover from.

"... and by the way, are either of you two gentlemen used to dealing with animals?" Henry was asking.

"I am," Bert was first to answer. "I was brought up on a farm."

Henry looked at the doctor. "Sorry," he grinned. "Not in my scope, I'm afraid."

"Well, for the last few hours, as well as last night before the excitement started, Stephen has been looking after the farm and the house. I think it's about time both he and Mary made up for some of the sleep they've lost. If you're happy to give us a hand, doctor, I can tell you how you can best help. If Bert's able to milk by hand, then we'll get it all done before the boat returns. You two, upstairs with you and get your heads down for a bit. I'll wake you when there's something new happening."

With the fire's soporific warmth on top of the tiredness that was by that time natural to them Henry's words were as effective as laudanum. Neither was in a fit state to argue. Henry swept the others out of the house with the dogs and peace returned. The two looked at each other.

"I can hardly keep my eyes open," Stephen admitted. "Do you mind if I sleep for a bit?"

"No. I was almost asleep by the end of tea, anyway."

They went to Stephen's room, and its owner flung himself on the bed. A moment's hesitation was all Mary took before lying down at his side with the matter-of-fact attitude of exhausted youth.

They didn't hear the knocking as Edgar returned to the house with Arthur. There was no response, so the two men went to listen outside where sounds of milking directed them to the dairy. The sight of a uniformed Civil Defence officer and a suited doctor respectively milking and pitchforking hay was something neither Arthur nor Edgar would ever forget.

"I've got your boat for you." Edgar knew how to behave in a dairy so as not to scare the cows off the milking. "She's a reasonable size – I expect you'll need to be carrying churns and hay bales and other cargoes, won't you?"

"That's wonderful. Thank you so very much. Once they've sorted the water out I'll get her back to you. You'd better let me pay monthly, if you wouldn't mind."

"I never said anything about paying. We won't be needing her until Easter, if then, or the end of May at the earliest. We'll take stock then, but

48

I'm sure they'll have done something by then to get the water back where it should be."

"Well, I'm even more obliged to you. I'll not try to pretend that money here is plentiful, and we really can't afford anything we've not budgeted for. So you're very kind."

Edgar shrugged off his thanks. "Drop me in some butter now and again. That'll do fine. Even without rationing some things bought in a shop don't taste like they used to."

Henry assured him it would be done.

When the milking was finished – both Bert and the doctor were enjoying themselves so much they stayed on to do it – they returned to the house. Henry called upstairs to fetch down Stephen and Mary. No-one appeared. Surprised, he went to Stephen's room and found the two of them fast asleep, fully clothed down to their shoes. They had heard nothing. Stephen was in his usual place, back to the window, on his side, curved in a gentle 5ft. 6in. crescent. Mary, shorter than him by some five inches, formed a parallel curve just touching him.

Not wanting to wake them, yet conscious that Stephen would be upset if he didn't see the boat now it had arrived, Henry said quietly, "The boat's here, Stephen, Mary. Come now if you want to see it."

There was a "hmm" from the depth of his son's dreams: Mary made no sound. Henry decided that sleep was the order of the day. They would be living with the boat for quite a few months, by the sound of it. He carefully left the room and, for a change, closed the door.

Henry returned to their new, convenient landing stage that until only a day ago – was it really only a day? – had been the road off their island. They spent some time examining the motor launch that Edgar was lending them, and the workings of its engine were explained.

"If there's anything I don't remember I'll get Stephen to come and ask," he joked. "I've no doubt he'll be tinkering with it and using it more than me."

"Good luck to him!" said Edgar. "But don't let him forget that the tide will be sweeping in and out of the estuary now. It won't stop just because he's not ready for it. In time you'll all get used to it, but be aware of its strength."

"How dangerous is it, then?"

"If you know what it can do, it's not. Before we lost the sea walls it was strong enough going up Batson, especially at springs. Now it's got a four mile estuary to fill and empty again. We don't know it's strength yet, but it'll doubtless rip through the narrow parts. And don't forget this island of yours creates a narrow on either side."

"I'd not thought of that," said Henry. "Perhaps I'd better stop them going out on their own."

"Well, that's up to you. But a lad with your son's spirit would feel cooped up by that, especially when he's been used to free movement. Better to teach him safety. Better still, when it's a reasonable day and slack tide, send them down to me. I'll see what we can do to make them sailors."

"I think I'd better come too. It's ages since I really was at home in a boat."

"That's settled, then. Bring us some milk, and butter, and anything else you want to get rid of, and we'll work out a rate of exchange. Anything over, I'll tell my family and neighbours about, and we'll get it sold for you."

Thanks and farewells were made and Edgar's boat took his helpers and the visitors away. Henry returned to the quiet house with the dogs who had been his constant shadows since his return from Salcombe. To avoid waking the two sleepers he spent a while tidying up the cowshed. No matter how well intentioned his helpers – and he was glad to have had them with him – he thrived on routine just as the cows did. No, he thought, not on routine itself, but everything left as it should be so any one of the family knew where to find it. As he worked, he felt himself becoming drowsier, until after about three-quarters of an hour he could continue no further but took himself off to the house. "Just forty winks," he thought, lying down on the sofa.

Mary woke to find the room dark. Breathing quietly by her side was Stephen. Both were fully clothed, lying just on top of the bed, but despite that she felt cold. Drowsy still, she tried to pull back the sheets and eiderdown to cover herself properly, but felt guilty about leaving Stephen outside in the cold. His back was hard against the wall as usual and he wouldn't be able to get under the covers from that side without moving the bed. Gently she tried to wake him, but he was too fast asleep.

She noticed that they were both still wearing shoes and decided she should do something about that. Her own were no problem, and she untied Stephen's easily enough, but when she tried to ease them off his feet he muttered something and pulled his knees up to his chest. That meant he was effectively taking up all the bed so she could neither free the bedclothes nor even lie back down again. Her desire for warmth and sleep, both of which were being denied to her, brought over a wave of emotion so strong that she sat heavily down on the bottom of the bed and gazed into the darkness, tears welling in her eyes. How could he be so selfish when all she wanted to do was get both of them warm and go to sleep? Her parents wouldn't have allowed this to happen. Not even her brother would be so unkind, but then she had never shared a room with her brother, far less a bed. She deserved to be able to sleep in peace.

A sob and a sniff broke the silence.

Downstairs the dogs heard the unaccustomed sound. They woke, aware of distress and a stranger in the house. Another sound of misery brought George to his feet. He stretched, yawned, and slowly padded upstairs. The closed door puzzled him, and he stood with his head on one side, listening. He could almost feel the waves of unhappiness coming from the room with the small sounds.

He scratched at the door. There was an intake of breath and "Who is it?" Mary quavered.

George whined quietly. Steps crossed the room and the door opened. He sat and looked up, head still on one side.

"George," whispered Mary, her mood lightened by the presence of another creature awake. "Did you hear me? I don't want to wake him."

The dog entered the room, looked at his master's son asleep, and at Mary. She sat back on the bed. George sat in front of her and put his head on her knee. She scratched him gently behind the ears, and his eyes closed in ecstasy. She shivered, and at once the dog was alert again. He whined, and immediately Stephen's eyes were open.

"What's up?" he said loudly. "What's happened this time?"

"Shhh. You'll wake your father!" exclaimed Mary. Stephen looked bewildered for a moment as his brain caught up with events. He focussed on Mary, then saw George.

"What's up?" he asked again, but quieter this time.

"I woke up, cold, and found I was dressed. I stood up, and you moved, and I can't get back in the bed."

"What's George doing here? Oh, I'm sorry."

"He came up when I moved. I think he felt sorry for me."

"OK George. Well done. Bed."

With a sorrowful backward glance George padded downstairs again. Stephen looked at Mary. "Sorry," he said again. "You should have woken me. I'm cold, too. You must be freezing."

"I am."

"Get into bed properly then. You'll soon get warm. I'm going to."

He started by removing his shoes, puzzling for a minute at the untied laces.

"I undid them. I thought I could get you under the covers, but not with shoes on. That was when you moved."

He smiled. "Thank you."

He was still too tired and bemused to worry about undressing in company, and his lack of concern soon stilled her own natural reticence. In silence they each undressed: in innocence they climbed into the bed; in company they slept until morning.

# 6 – Milk and Town

Dawn and the stirring of the dogs woke Henry, although sooner or later the pain in his back would have done so. He cursed his stupidity in not going to bed properly, and winced as he tried to swing his legs over the side of the sofa from his uncomfortable, semi-recumbent position. At last he managed it, and stumbled into the kitchen to fill the kettle. At length the sound of his movements woke the two upstairs, for the first time more or less simultaneously.

Each had the sort of character which is at its best in the early morning. Both Mary and Stephen woke even-tempered, so it was natural that a smile was the first thing that crossed each face.

"Dad's up."

"I know. I can hear him."

"Do you want the bathroom first?"

"I'd better. I'm on the outside."

"OK."

While she was gone he lay back again, thinking drowsily. Poor kid. She'd just lost everything, and now all she had was half a bed. He half smiled to himself. If his other friends at school knew he had just spent two nights in bed with a girl… But then Mary was only a kid, after all. And a friend. She didn't count. At least, not that way. Perhaps, after all, he'd be better off saying nothing about it. They'd probably laugh. And anyway it wouldn't be fair on her. But would she tell anyone? He'd better ask her. For a kid she was good company though, and it was nice to have someone warm beside him. How would she think? What did she think of him anyway? She didn't really have much chance to avoid his company even if she wanted to. Perhaps it was because of his dad saying she could stay that rshe had said she wanted to, after all. Perhaps she was just grateful to his dad and to himself for trying to save her brother. Perhaps…

"Oh blast!" he said out loud.

In the bathroom Mary was doing things automatically, the way she'd always done them. She wondered at herself that she was accepting everything that was happening to her and around her almost without question. Surely she should be prostate with grief or something, having lost her home, her parents and her brother just over a day ago? The idea suddenly stabbed her again, and she paused in the middle of brushing her teeth so that the involuntary tremor running through her made her cough on the toothpaste. This jogged her mind like a record jumping a groove, and she laughed at herself, although very quietly.

Why were they being so nice to her? Would they go on being nice and letting her stay there or would they get tired of her and make her go away?

What happened if there was one of those misunderstandings that sometimes happen between parents and children? Would they still want her then? She couldn't help but start feeling small and lost. She must be careful, that's all, and never show if she was unhappy with what they said. They'd been kind so far. Anyway, come to think of it, she'd known them both for ages. But she'd not known Mr Loft as a sort of father. But then, he was good with Steve, wasn't he? Steve seemed to regard him as an equal, somehow. And as for Steve himself... well. From being a good school and real life friend he was suddenly a sort of brother. Oh, Greg! Oh damn! She mustn't think that way or they'd think she was a sour-puss like her great-aunt was. She tried to make herself look cheerful, pulled the plug and washed the basin round.

In the bedroom she found Stephen asleep again. Feeling self-righteous she twitched back the bedclothes and was suddenly aware he had nothing on except his underpants. Like that he looked as if he were her own age, not a year older and nearly half a foot taller. All worries about how he was going to treat her in the time ahead evaporated, and as he stirred again she said in a conversational tone "Come on, lazybones. Get up. It's milking time!"

For a second he looked annoyed then embarrassed, then laughed at her sheepishly. "Come on yourself! I'll be out of the bathroom and dressed before you've finished combing your hair."

He swung himself across the bed and grabbed her arm to pull himself up, pulling her off her balance so that they both collapsed back onto the bed, roaring with laughter. The remaining fears she had imagined in the bathroom vanished with the sound: surely with Stephen on her side his father would want her to stay.

He wriggled out from under her, eyes bright with laughter, hair like a haystack and clothing awry. She grinned back. "And put something on before you see your father!"

He looked down at himself. "Oops. Well, you can't talk!" He hitched up his pants and marched out to the bathroom trying to muster his dignity. She pulled down Henry's shirt which was still serving her as a nightie.

She did beat him downstairs, but not by much. Finding two mugs of tea on the table, with an empty one standing on the wooden draining board, she picked up one, found it wasn't sugared and tasted the other, only to find that the same. Oh dear. Where was the sugar?

"In the larder, silly." She'd not heard him arrive, but Stephen had watched and put two and two together. She found it, and added two spoonfuls to her tea. She pushed the jar toward Stephen who answered by taking a gulp from his mug. "Never touch the stuff. Spoils the tea."

Demurely she replaced it in the larder, wondering why she hadn't noticed the previous night.

They joined Henry in the milking shed, and found him already hard at work. "I've organised a late collection until they get rid of the water," he explained. "So it should give us enough time to ferry it over to the stand even if we start as late as this."

They made short work of it, the three of them, and at last, hindered by the dogs, loaded the five heavy churns into the truck to avoid having to carry them down to the boat. The cows were let out into their much abbreviated grazing, and Henry wondered, not for the first time, how long it would be until he had to reduce the herd's size, or find temporary grazing elsewhere. The weather had completely changed from the long period of unrest, and was now almost spring-like, as if in apology. The novelty of loading the motor launch, which neither Mary nor Stephen had seen, fascinated them, although the loading process caused them some headaches. They managed eventually, with no spillage. Stephen watched enthralled as his father found the fuel tap, then the bakelite switch which was the boat's idea of an ignition key, and fitted the starting handle to its spindle. He carefully turned it until he felt the resistance of the piston in its cylinder, then swung hard, as he had been shown. To the surprise of all of them the engine sputtered into life as though impatient to be away. The dogs backed away, growling, but the apparent unconcern of the humans led them to approach again, gingerly. They needed some persuasion to climb on board, and stayed as far away as possible from the engine.

The short journey across from the island to the road-head at Lincombe and their temporary milk stand was a new experience for each of them. Once again the expanse of water surprised Henry – it was high tide – but for his son and Mary it was a completely new angle on life.

Mary's view was ambivalent. Like the others she was intrigued by the incongruity of the strangeness in such a familiar area. The hills she had seen every day of her life seemed lower and more distant, and the sight of them mirrored in the ruffled water made her feel odd. It crossed her mind that away to the north was the site of a house from which she, her parents and her brother had been ripped by the water, the same water that now stood so calm and gentle in the early spring sunshine. She shuddered, and looked toward the south.

"Are you cold, Mary?" Henry was aware of the cool southerly breeze which now had no hedges or other impediment on its way up the valley.

She shook her head. "No, I'm fine. Just thinking."

He looked at her quizzically, and the boat immediately veered away from the line he was following. He corrected it, but not before Stephen had glanced anxiously at him.

They made the shore, just where one of the little streams feeding the estuary had been bridged, and one of the roads onto the valley bottom now led down into the water instead. This provided a hard landing, where they could struggle to lift their load from the boat. Fortunately this was near their milk stand, and they had only to wheel the heavy churns on their rim a short distance to it.

"I don't know what the chap's going to say when he gets here and finds he's got to lift them onto his lorry," said Henry. "They're inclined not to be the most helpful of people at times."

"Surely he'll realise, Dad. You could always tell him we're going to build a slope up to it, so it won't be more than a few days he'll have to lift."

"I don't even know if one man can lift a churn that high. I'd better stay here and help him, I think. But what d'you mean about a slope? Who's going to build that?

"I'll have a go, if Mary will help and you lift the timbers for us."

"The idea's an excellent one, Steve, and it's certainly a job for all of us. It's too heavy for you two, and too heavy for me alone. It's got to be as solid as the main stand. I don't even know if I've got the skill to do it."

"Well, ask Edgar then. He's a boatbuilder, so he must be able to help us with wood."

"Edgar's done enough for us – oh  by the way, he wants us to visit him in Salcombe to learn more about how to use the boat. I was thinking we could get down later. But you're right, we should get this done. If the man doesn't collect the milk that's a fair chunk of income down the drain."

"There should be something from our cattle too," Mary told him.

He looked at her. "Yes… yes there should. But I don't know how to persuade anyone to pay it to you."

There was a pause. They scanned the road for signs of the milk lorry.

"What time did he say he was coming?" asked Mary.

"Nine o'clock. He was getting one of them to divert on his way to Kingsbridge."

There was another silence, decorated by birdsong, the sighing of the breeze in the hedges, and the lapping of the water at its newly discovered banks.

At length they heard the sound of a lorry rumbling its way cautiously down the hill from Salcombe and jumped to their feet in hope. It was indeed their milk lorry. It pulled up with a squawk from the brakes which set Mary's teeth on edge, but to the relief of all of them two men jumped down from it. The dogs sniffed at them with wagging tails and were petted.

"Hallo hallo!" said the first. "You'll be the party I'm awaiting, then."

Henry smiled his welcome. "And I'm glad to see you - both. We were getting worried about getting the churns onto the wagon - we can't lift them onto the stand."

"What, no power? Well, Ted, we'll have to see what we can do, won't we?" And he beckoned his mate over. Before Henry had a chance to offer to help they had grasped the sides of the first churn and lifted it waist high. Ted bent his knees to bring his shoulder under it, straightened up with the driver steadying it, and slid it onto the lorry's flatbed. It was all done so easily and quickly that the onlookers gasped in amazement. The driver turned again and looked at them, amused.

"We don' just look at them and hope, you know," he said. "They don't jump up themselves, no matter what."

Henry laughed. "It looked so easy. But one of you won't be able to manage on his own, surely?"

"No," said Ted in a surprisingly squeaky voice that brought a half smile to Mary's lips. "But then Fred takes me back home to Kingsbridge after work every day, so he won't be on his own. And we do shift them for our bread and butter, you know."

"Of course," said Henry, even more relieved. "So that means we don't have to wait for you so I can help the lift."

"No, we reckon you've got your work cut out as it is with this little lot coming to visit twice a day." He pointed at the water. "What you going to do when the tide's out?"

"We hadn't got that far yet. It's been enough of a struggle to get everything done as it is. But you're right; the tide won't be this high every day."

"It'll be about 50 minutes later tomorrow," chipped in a voice. Stephen had been remembering geography lessons.

"Quite right, boy. And as we're half way between springs and neaps now, it's close on the hour at the moment. So tomorrow..."

"......It'll be coming in at this time, and we'll have to land further down the road."

"Ar," nodded the driver approvingly. "But you don' leave they ol' churns where you land - they'll get drowned else. In our yard we've got a liddle ol' trolley. Tomorrow we'll leave her under the stand, look, then the next day you'll be able to get her down to the boat, load on the churns, and pull up to rthe stand again. Leave them on, and it'll be an easier lift for us."

"That's wonderful," said Henry. "Thank you very much indeed. Are you sure that'll be all right with your yard manager?"

"I asked him just now, look, and he says it's fine."

"You mean you'd thought about us before you left and asked if you could borrow it?"

"No, I mean just now. I am the yard manager." He grinned, and Ted roared with laughter at Henry's expression.

After a good-natured farewell punctuated with thanks from Henry, Mary and Stephen they watched the milk lorry wind its way up the hill up toward the so-called 'main' road.

"I'm glad that's all arranged," said Henry. "That was a real worry to me for the future. At least that's one small bit of income that we won't lose, even for the time being."

"Are we going to be all right, Dad? Will money really be tighter?"

"We've got enough in the bank for a while to act as a cushion. I'm ashamed to say because of the war years when the supply ministry persuaded us to produce more, the income increased to a disgraceful amount. We put it aside for ... Huh!" He paused. "You know the saying? A rainy day!"

His two charges looked at him blankly for a moment before two pennies dropped simultaneously, and despite all the previous days' heartache they laughed.

The launch needed quite a bit of strength to refloat it as the tide had retreated. It was all they could do to drag her down the rocky beach, and then only by removing enough of the loose stones from behind her as she encountered them. Once again George and Ben were reluctant to jump in, but once they were afloat they decided they didn't want to be left behind and each half ran, half swam out to them. Hurriedly Henry started the engine and manoeuvred close to the road as it disappeared into the water. The dogs swam round them, walked ashore and jumped in without further ado, soaking all three with their vigorous shaking.

"They don't do that at home," said Stephen.

"Your mother and I trained George not to, and Ben soon got the message," his father replied. "This obviously doesn't count as being home."

"I wish it did," said Mary. "I'm soaked!"

"We'll have to train them better than that," Henry agreed. "And we'll have to make sure we manage the boat better than that ourselves too. We can't go through that palaver every day."

"How about going down to Edgar's now?" suggested Stephen. "We need to be shown how to manage her. She's a lot bigger than the little rowing boat Greg and I take out. Oh..."

Mary looked at him sharply. Another stab of misery.

"Yes," Henry said gently. "She is. And we could all do with lessons. We'll go down now, and I'll see if there's any news yet from the Council, although I doubt it."

They turned the boat toward Salcombe. As they rounded Tosnos point they suddenly found themselves in the middle of a flotilla of small boats, powered variously by oars, sail and motors, all milling around as if they were maritime ants. It was difficult to keep clear of so many. Alone of the three on the launch Mary had some idea of how they should behave as she had read quite a lot of Arthur Ransome's books, and after a couple of unpleasant encounters she quickly told Henry, as he appeared to have no idea, that 'steam gives away to sail'. He was grateful to her, and with warnings like "The boat with the red sail on your left has just turned suddenly and is coming your way," from Stephen and "Watch out for the one with the white sail – she's just tacking" from Mary, he zigzagged his way past the fleet. They passed through the remains of the first of the two dam walls which had kept the sea artificially from the valleys to the north. As they approached the second they were confronted by a further barrage of dinghies and what appeared to be half of Salcombe's fishing fleet. Stephen noticed in one that passed quite close a man with a large camera who was doing his best to keep immobile on the boat as she ploughed her way upstream. He realised that these were probably pressmen coming to report on the events of the last few days. Wisely he said nothing, hoping that three people in yet another boat would be lost in the melee. They passed the second of the two retaining walls by Scoble Point, and emerged into the choppy area of water between Southpool Creek and Salcombe's waterfront.

Once again there appeared to be a large crowd of people on the main public Hard, where even more of the fishing fleet was waiting. It seemed that the whole world was trying to become waterborne so as to marvel at all the changes.

They carefully avoided the crowded areas of water and headed for the boatyard owned by Edgar's family. Henry was careful now to attract no attention by steering the boat badly, and went so slowly at one point that the tide setting out of Batson Creek was taking them back toward the main channel. He increased the engine speed and gingerly nosed the boat toward the steps by the yard. Once there, Stephen clambered over a moored dinghy, the painter in his hands. There were steps set into the boatyard's retaining wall which, because of the drop of the tide, was some six feet above water level. He climbed them - fortunately the rope was long - and looked round.

Noises of the rhythmic beats of a hammer came from the large shed some twenty feet away from the dockside where he stood. He could also hear the regular swish of a plane as sliver after sliver of wood was trimmed from a boat's timber. The south west wind brought the mingled smell of fresh wood, of tar, and of paint to his nose, and he paused, entranced. There was a fishing boat half in, half out of the water on the slipway to his left, and lobster pots from it lay in untidy piles. A motor dinghy like theirs lay chocked up in front of the old, black-tarred shed, a gaping hole in her bows. Stephen winced, and wondered how it had happened. So entranced was he by this different world that he was startled by his father calling from below: "Steve! Wake up! Is there anyone there?"

He reluctantly dragged himself from his reverie and looked around. Apart from the sounds of industry in the shed there was no sign of life. He thought of the boat below and looked round for a way of mooring her. One of the series of rings set near the edge of the wall seemed obvious, so he looped the rope through it and wondered what to do next. Well, a boat wouldn't pull more than a cow, would it? He'd use the draw hitch they used on the farm. Once secured he looked over and called out: "Come on up. There's no one around, but someone's in the shed."

Henry switched off the launch's engine, told the dogs to stay there and with Mary clambered up to join Stephen.

"We'd better have a look in the workshops and see if Edgar's around," said Henry.

They crossed to the shed, where two men were working on a small sailing dinghy, a trim little craft of the local design which, although obviously quite old in years, was well cared for despite the two new planks which had just been worked into her hull. In another corner stood a nearly complete launch like theirs, with planking being nailed into place. It was this work that Stephen had heard from outside, and the noise of planing was being made by a man working on her transom. Henry waited for a gap in the work and asked quietly if Edgar was around. The man nailing planks, having a row of nails in his mouth ready for applying to the next bit of plank, nodded in the direction of the office and mumbled "'Ee's o'er 'ere I er o'ice" before removing a nailr from his lips and starting it with the hammer in one easy movement. Mary was fascinated, and could have watched him for hours, but they made their way to the 'o'ice' and Henry knocked on the door.

Edgar was pleased to see them, not just because they had decided to take his advice, but because it rescued him from the paperwork which he detested. They made their way back to the boat. Edgar looked at Stephen's knot and said "Hmm. Farmyard stuff, but it'll hold OK."

"What should I do, please?" asked Stephen.

"We usually just tie a half hitch round the rope, here. But if you've got wind or a tide rip you'd need a strong knot like a round turn and two half hitches. Look..."

So they had their first lesson in boat handling. Mary and Stephen, being both practical people and used to learning, picked up the few knots and bends Edgar showed them quite quickly; Henry took a bit longer. "You've got to keep practising, day after day, until they're second nature," Edgar told them. "You know when they're second nature when they tie themselves in the dark, in winter, with a force eight blowing and snow on the ground. Oh, and with one hand. No, I'm not joking. There'll be a time when you wished you could. Right. Now let's get on the water and we'll talk tides as we go."

"Are we allowed to steer?" asked Mary.

"You bet. It's to make sure that you and Stephen are safe on the water that I'm so keen to teach you. Almost all Salcombe children are watermen from birth, it seems. They learn to swim before they can walk, and can sail a boat not long after. We've got a few years of instinct to make up for."

They were all except Edgar in the launch by this time. He untied Stephen's knot and unhurriedly walked over the dinghy to join them, using the movement of his body to push the prow out into the current. Henry was alarmed at this, and was about to comment when their teacher casually flicked on the ignition and swung the starting handle. The engine fired immediately as it always had so far. He stood at the tiller, pipe in his mouth, steering them in a lazy circle until they were facing the main estuary and the crowds of boats. The dogs knew him, so apart from a welcome as the boat drifted away from the wall there was no fuss.

"Right," he said. "Who's first?"

One by one he made them steer the boat by heading directly for a particular mark, so they could gauge the strength of the current and the wind on their progress through the water. They learnt the rule of the road at sea, and he told them of a little booklet they could buy to act as a reference in case they forgot. He took them down from Salcombe, past the ferry and the Marine Hotel right down past Small's Cove and Mill Bay on the east side, then headed toward North Sands so they could see at close quarters the rocks which partially cross the estuary mouth.

"Unless you really have to," he said, "Don't go outside those rocks. It's more or less open sea outside, and unless you're prepared for it and really up with the weather it can be dicey in a small boat. But North and South Sands are all right usually - they're sheltered. The real problem is the Bar, which you can't see at this tide or in this wind. But given a gale from the south the sea breaks over it and makes it impossible to get into the estuary. Whatever happens don't go outside that. You're not equipped, and it'd take a long time before anybody realised you were in trouble if your engine gave up or you ran out of fuel."

"I'll second that," said Henry. "I'm not venturing outside in anything short of a liner, and you two aren't to, either."

There were no arguments. Both of them were slightly in awe of the jagged black rocks which rose to the surface and which had appeared, from the north, to block the channel to the sea. The idea of a similar, submerged range of rocks under the surface, making the passage dangerous in heavy weather, was definitely scary. Edgar gave them some of the names of the rocks and bays around Start Point and Bolt Head, and told them the tale of the Herzogin Cecilie, the four-masted, steel barque which after braving the weather of the Bay of Biscay, The Falklands seas, and Cape Horn, ran onto Bolt Tail in a mist eighteen years before. She'd been towed off Bolt Tail's rocks to a shallower beach in Starehole Bay where they hoped to salvage her, but instead her back was broken, and she sank into the sand over the years. Now she was lost from sight except at the lowest of spring tides.

"1936 that was," said Edgar. "And the chap who took off the Captain - he was last, off, of course, still tells how the man paused before jumping onto his fishing boat, and with a look on his face like death, looked round at his condemned ship and just said quietly 'Oh, my God.'"

It silenced their questions for a while, and he took them northward again, back toward his Yard. Henry remembered their problem of the morning, when the dropping tide had grounded them and asked how to avoid it. He could foresee the same happening when the boat was moored on the island.

"Ah, you want running moorings," replied Edgar. "I'll give you a good mudweight with a block on it. Rig a rope through that straight to the shore and through a mooring ring there, then out to a buoy. Tie it to the buoy, then down to the weight again. If the weight's in deep water so the dinghy's always afloat, you can pull on the rope once you're on land and she'll be taken out to deep water. Pull the other way and she comes back to the water's edge. Simple, really!"

"That's just what we need on the island," said Stephen, "but how about when we're on the ordinary shore?"

"Look in that cupboard under the bows."

Stephen did so, and found a large, green painted weight.

"That's your mudweight for shallow water. Works better than the anchor, sometimes, and by putting the anchor out at one end of the boat and the weight at the other you can make her lie the way round you want her to. Keep an eye open, though, 'cos a sideways pull on an anchor won't hold for long. If you're very careful you can rig the two as a running mooring, but there are lots of anchors lost that way, so be careful. And by the way, remember that an anchor rope or chain has to be attached to something at *both* ends."

They looked at him, puzzled, then one by one understood what he was telling them, and laughed.

"Yeah, you can laugh, but the number of people who just chuck out their anchor and watch chain and rope follow it into the water is nobody's business."

# 7 - Statements

The remainder of the journey back to Edgar's yard was spent partly in conversation and partly in learning as they were told the names of the coves and landmarks, and what to look out for, both in foul weather and in strong tidal conditions. They took turns at the helm and were gently criticised or warmly commended by their tutor as he saw fit. At the end, as they passed the town's main Hard again, he pronounced them much improved. "Although you can't hope to take on thirty five years of experience in half a day." They assured him they wouldn't be complacent.

As they neared the yard they spotted a sleek, black car waiting at the end of the cul-de-sac by the side entrance. "Hmm," said Edgar, "Looks official."

"Is anything the matter?" asked Henry.

"Nothing that I know about, but since the war there's been a lot of nosey parkering going on in the name of officialdom, and I don't like it. I wonder what this lot wants."

They moored and left the two dogs to look after the boat. In the shed they found a slightly sheepish foreman who pointed toward the office and said "Sorry, Boss. We told 'un you weren't yere, but they did'n tak' no for an answer."

"OK Pete," Edgar told him. I'll go and see what they want."

He turned to the others to wish them good luck, but as he did so his office door opened. The Police Inspector whom Henry had met two days previously stood in the doorway, and behind him they could see a smaller man, dressed in an old fashioned suit that seemed out of place in a boatyard.

"We saw you all return," said Inspector Moffat, "and actually it's Mr Loft I need to speak to."

"I see," said Edgar. "And I suppose you want to carry on using my office, do you?"

"Needs must, Mr Mustchin, needs must. I'm sure you don't mind, for a moment or two."

"What's wrong with our own police who we know, Inspector? Don't you trust them?"

"It's not a question of trust, Mr Mustchin. I have been seconded to Salcombe in the immediate aftermath of the crisis to take charge. That is what I am doing. Now, may we speak to Mr Loft, please?"

Edgar and Henry exchanged glances. Henry was swiftly making up his mind whether to involve Stephen and Mary, and in the end decided that there was unlikely to be anything Moffat could say that would upset them. After all, the man had made police inspector; he couldn't be completely brainless. He beckoned to Mary and Stephen and they all trooped into the little office. Henry couldn't resist asking for Edgar's permission to come in before crossing the threshold.

"I don't think we need the children, thank you Mr Loft."

Henry immediately bristled. "My son is involved with me - we have always been a genuine team. Mary is now a part of that team too. We are a family. Anything you want to say to me is their business too."

"Mr Loft, why do you always jump down my throat? I'm only trying to be reasonable."

"You didn't get off to a very good start with me yesterday where reasonableness is concerned. It's hardly surprising that I should be wary. Further, you are once again treating us – my family and me – as if we were items to be disposed of as you feel appropriate. That is not acceptable to me, as it wasn't the other day, and I hope neither Stephen nor Mary will allow themselves to be bullied by you either. Certainly if they feel that out of politeness there is a limit to what they can say to indicate they cannot accept your attitude then I shall have no compunction about being forthright on their behalf."

Stephen was taken aback to hear his father talking like this to a policeman, when he had always been brought up to regard the police as being there to help and to be trusted. Mary was in something of the same mind.

Inspector Moffat was about to rejoin battle when the smaller man coughed gently. "If I may interject, lady and gentlemen; I see no useful purpose in antagonism, when all we need to do is to exchange information. You may realise, Mr Loft, that you are, under the present circumstances, a difficult… um … *family* to correspond with in that you live now on an island; hence our visit here. My apologies to Mr Mustchin for our intrusion onto his premises. I needed to meet up with you informally, and as soon as it was possible. My name is John Fraser. I am the Coroner, you see, and it is my duty to ensure that the events of the other night are made public, are examined, and any action is taken that is appropriate."

He paused for breath. Inspector Moffat's eyes gleamed with triumph. Before he had a chance to speak Henry said quietly: "Yes, of course, sir. I quite understand, and please don't assume that I am naturally abrasive. I will do everything I can to ensure we all comply with the law."

"Thank you, Mr Loft. Now, I don't object to these children being here so long as they are not upset by the questions I want to ask, but I leave that in your and their capable hands." He looked at them and smiled. "In fact, I think I need to speak to you – Mary Beale, I believe? – to discover the course of the events which led up to your being found on Loft Island. Are you happy to answer some questions?"

She looked startled, then nodded.

"Can you tell me what happened immediately before the water came?"

Neither Henry nor Stephen had asked her as direct a question as that, and Mary was taken off her guard. She realised as soon as Mr Fraser had identified himself that he was going to ask questions which would rake up the shallowly buried memories of two nights previously. She gulped nervously, and Henry shot her a glance. "You don't have to give an answer now, Mary, unless you think you can. I don't want you to get upset. You say what you think you can."

Mary nodded. There was a pause. She remembered afterwards that the sound of planing had resumed outside where Pete and the others had resumed their jobs. The sound soothed her, regular as it was. She thought back to the night of chaos, the last night she had spent with her brother and parents as the water rose around their farmstead and they had all fought to save the animals.

"Mr Loft collected the hens when we got back from school, but the pigs were being a nuisance," she remembered. "He'd gone off with them and Dad was..." she faltered.

"All right, Mary," said Henry quietly. "Take your time."

"...Dad was trying to get the pigs together but they were just running around. Greg and I helped..." she swallowed hard, and continued with fight and determination in her voice. "...helped round them up again and got them to go in. When we'd done that Greg and I went inside 'cos Mum was getting all sorts of stuff ready for when we went, but Dad asked her and Greg to help load the crates of pigs onto the trailer. So they went out. Then they came back and started getting a lot of furniture and glasses and plates and some food, and loaded that too. When they came back again they told us to go and change out of uniform and pack that in cases, and pack a lot of other stuff as well – enough for a week, Mum said. Greg helped me. Then we took the cases downstairs and had a cup of tea."

She paused. Stephen looked at her admiringly. He couldn't know that every event of the night was etched on her memory; would remain there until worn away by years of life.

Inspector Moffat cleared his throat and looked at his watch, actions noted by Henry but fortunately missed by Mary. The Coroner looked at him, holding his eyes for a moment, then turned back to Mary. "That's very clear indeed, Mary. It helps me to understand how you were all doing everything you could to save your animals, your belongings and, of course, yourselves, just as you should have done. Can you tell me what happened next?"

"Yes. We'd just sat down when the lights went out. Dad and Mum told Greg and me to sit still and they went to find our candles. They lit them, and we sat in the lounge, then Mum made some sandwiches. When we'd finished them, Dad and Mum went outside to look at the water again and saw it was a lot higher, then we saw headlights coming towards us and…"

"Mary, Mary, sorry to interrupt, but were you outside by that time too?"

"Yes. Mum and Dad had come in again and told us to get ready and get into the Land Rover 'cos it wouldn't be safe to stay there much longer, so we got our cases and went outside. When we got there we saw the headlights, and it was Mr Loft. He took a lot of furniture that was on the ground floor of the house into the lorry, and our cases, and he said he'd pull the trailer back to the Island. When he'd gone Dad said we could get a few more things into the Land Rover now, before we followed him, and so we got that big sideboard of Gran's and some chairs and things but when Dad tried to move off the wheels just slipped on the mud and got deeper and deeper in. He and Mum and Greg went to get some sacks and things to put under the wheels and I was just going to find a spade when we heard a funny noise, like a thunder storm but more rumbly. I remember that. Then a bit later when we were standing by the Land Rover we heard this rushing, rumbling sound with crashes in it."

She stopped short. This time there was absolute silence in the room. The boat builders were by then at the opposite end of the shed, sitting round the stove, drinking tea. Unseen by anyone, Stephen's hand found Mary's, and squeezed it gently. She looked at him sharply, then managed to smile weakly before looking away, out of the window at the calm weather and sunshine outside. How different it was from *that* night. She could hardly believe what was still in her mind's eye. The numbing sight of a wall of water breaking over their house. The physical shock like an earthquake as it struck the building. The crushing weight of water, lessened by her standing nearer the house than the others, but catching them with a force of tons. The shock of the coldness and the pain as she was borne away with the flood as it continued relentlessly down the valley. How she screamed for her mother. How she was sure she was going to die. How she was sure that they would all die and see each other in Heaven…

… How she came to, lying on a shore and finding herself alive. The calling; the sound of someone approaching; the debilitating relief as she found it was Henry and Stephen.

Her voice quavered to a halt. She was out of words, completely. Her mind, taken back to that night, was almost as exhausted as it had been then. She sat in silence, staring blankly in front of her, wondering why her left hand was warm, then looking at it to find someone gripping it. Stephen. He changed his hand on hers and put his arm round her shoulders, whispering so only she could hear: "It's all right. It's all over now."

Then he wondered at himself, Stephen the non-demonstrative. Living without a mother for two years, and working on the farm almost all his spare time, had meant that he was very far from any apron strings. He knew nothing of his father's late night visits to his room to check on his sleep and his well being, or of the look of love in his eyes as he watched his young son asleep. Here he was, his arm round a girl as if he was his own elder brother back from a night in Salcombe with his fiancée. He checked himself only for a moment before realising yet again how the events the girl had suffered, both that night and remembering it just now, must have upset her.

And was it 'all over now'? Hardly. Her parents were still dead. She still had no brother. True, his Dad was now her Dad, but really could never be one, just as he couldn't really be her brother. But he'd have a good try to be in Greg's place. He found himself sharing the sense of loss she felt so strongly, perhaps for the first time. He had reacted to the shock of the deaths, naturally, but it suddenly hit him that he would never enjoy the casual but meaningful companionship of his friend again.

He tried to weigh his reactions and feelings against those at the time his mother had died. It felt very similar, yet not the same; a deeper loss in some ways, yet not so deep in others. He felt guilty about that - surely his mother's death should mean far, far more? He shook his head impatiently and returned his attention to his surroundings. His father had taken up the tale and was describing his mad drive over almost submerged roads which seemed to be flooding more by the minute.

The Coroner interrupted him. "Thank you, Mr Loft, but I think that can wait until the Inquest. I really wanted to save Mary the pain of having to stand in front of a room full of people in order to recount what happened. I'm going to have to ask you to do so, of course, and to give us full details of your discovery of the bodies."

"You realise, sir, that it was my son who actually found them?"

Again a glance passed between the Coroner and the Inspector. Stephen thought he could detect a momentary expression of fury cross the Coroner's face.

"It had been hinted at, but I was assured that it was actually you who found them,"

Henry, too, had not missed the suppressed anger. "That's strange, sir, because I told the Inspector here very clearly indeed that Stephen had found them and had rendered first aid to Greg Beale, which was temporarily effective."

By now the Coroner was looking decidedly furious. " I see," he barked. "This means, I'm afraid, that I shall have to ask Stephen to attend the Inquest as a material witness, young though he is." His voice softened. "Are you ready for that, young man? Can you get events clear in your mind so as to be able to give us as good an account as Mary?"

It was really the last thing Stephen wanted to do and his mind balked at the thought. But it was necessary; it would somehow support his lost friend and the parents. What choice did he have?

"Yes sir. I'll make sure of it."

"Right. Good. I will get a message to you once the date and time of the inquest are final. Once you know, please can you both be there with fifteen minutes to spare and one of us will explain procedure to you.

"Mr Mustchin, thank you so much for the use of your office and I apologise for the intrusion. We will leave you in peace. Inspector Moffat, I think we need to talk." He rose and swept out of the office, the Inspector following meekly behind. Edgar looked at Henry, but he only had time for Mary who was still sitting with Stephen on the edge of a table. He crossed to her and hugged her.

"That was really unfair on you, Mary, but it did save you the need to go through it in Court which would have been a nerve-racking experience. I'm sorry it was necessary, and as sorry that we had no warning of it. But you did marvellously well, and were clear and concise - just what the Coroner wanted. Really well done, and I'm proud of you."

Stephen looked pleased. Mary said nothing. Henry glanced at her, surprised. Her face was expressionless, like a windowless house.

"What's the matter?" he asked, drawing her to one side. "Was that too much for you?"

She seemed to come to, with some difficulty, and looked at Henry stupidly for a moment. Then her eyes filled, and she bolted out of the boatshed. Henry looked at his son who returned his stare uncomprehendingly. Then as one they hurried out of the shed and looked round the yard outside. She was nowhere to be found. Henry headed over to the water's edge and checked their boat. Just as he did so they heard a car start up outside – the Coroner's, thought Henry – and start off. But only for a second, then there was a screech of brakes.

Once again father and son looked at each other, this time aghast. As one they ran to the gate into the lane in time to see the Inspector, who had been driving, open his door and hurry forward. They rushed to join him, just as the Coroner emerged from the car's passenger door. The three of them collided in the narrow roadway. As they disentangled themselves and faced the front of the vehicle they saw Mary being helped to her feet by Inspector Moffat who also looked ashen.

"She ran straight in front of me. I thought I'd run her over." Even *his* voice was shaking.

Henry put his arms around the distraught, tearful Mary. "Come with me," he said. "I can see there's something happened." He looked round. The door of the nearby newsagent's shop was open, and he thought that would be a refuge for them. The shopkeeper was already on her way out, and took the hint from Henry's beseeching glance.

"Come you in, and sit down, my dear. We'll have a dish o'tea." She led the way in behind the counter and pointed out two chairs by the fire in her front room. "Let her sit there. I'll show your boy in and he can brew the tea. Now then...."

She clattered out again to her counter where Stephen had been joined by Inspector Mofatt and the Coroner. "You go through the room she's in, look, and make tea," she said to Stephen. Then to the two men: "There's no need for you two to go through. Let her recover. You've done enough damage, young George Moffat, running her over like that. And none of your lip or I'll be telling your Mum how you nearly run over a little girl who's no older than you was when she first brought you down to see her old Nanny's shop."

The Inspector's mouth dropped open comically. The Coroner looked at him, this time with open contempt on his face.

"A word, please. Outside. We shall return shortly, or we may need to visit you at Loft Island if the family needs to leave. We still have some words to exchange, I imagine. I certainly have, and I think Inspector Moffat will, too." And he swept the embarrassed policeman out of the shop.

In the inner room there was a moment's silence. Then "Phew!" from Stephen.

"Yes," said the shopkeeper, "phew indeed. I think that George'll be getting his fortune told shortly. I'm beginning to feel quite sorry for him. He was a good little babby, but when he got older – why, he'd have his nose into everybody's business. I fair went off him then, I can tell you."

"Are you really his Granny?" asked Stephen.

"Lor' bless you no. His old Mum, she wanted to work, see, so they took me on to do for him as Nanny. Nice couple they are, you'd like them. But him? Well, I dunno what went wrong. I blame that fancy school they sent him to. Gave him ideas above his station. Anyway, young man, you go and brew some tea for us all. It's straight through to the kitchen, and don't interrupt those two on the way. Look around, you'll find everything."

Stephen went obediently through the back room, where Mary was still sobbing into his father's shoulder. He was happy that Henry had relieved him from the responsibility of looking after her for a while – he felt that he couldn't cope with emotion so deep. His father's intervention meant that now he didn't have to. He found the makings for tea easily enough, and put the kettle on the gas, realising inconsequentially how lucky they were at his home not to rely on gas or electricity for cooking. Since the flood they had made do with candles and lanterns for lighting; but for cooking, coal or wood had always been there. He wondered whether they needed any coal yet. He heard the door close as the shopkeeper returned to her counter.

A few gentle words from the room next door brought him back to the present, and he wondered what was wrong with Mary. He heard a tearful voice speak up.

"I'm all right. Please…" A pause. "It just hit me – I remember what else happened that night. I don't know how I forgot." Another pause, and a sniff. Stephen listened, on tenterhooks.

"When the first wave came over, I was by the house and I could see the others by the garden shed where we keep sacks and things. Just as the noise started Mum and Dad went inside and Greg was just by the door. He smiled at me…" She paused again, and buried her face in Henry's lapel while her shoulders shook helplessly. Stephen looked impatiently at the kettle, hoping it wouldn't boil and interrupt Mary's telling of the story. She recovered again, and looked at Henry with her eyes streaming.

"The shed fell down on top of them. I heard them scream. Then a bit of it hit Greg in the tummy and he doubled up and was washed away…"

Henry looked at her aghast. Hearing the final instalment of the story brought Stephen to the kitchen door, gaping stupidly, and he was as unsurprised to see tears welling in his father's eyes as he was to feel them start in his own. Instinct took over from his relief at having his father there to give support, and he crossed to the sofa where they were sitting and joined in the comforting embrace to support Mary.

The kettle boiled, but none of them heard it.

The sound brought in the shopkeeper, who looked at the scene, shook her head wonderingly and crossed to the kitchen. It was the suddenness of the whistle stopping that separated the three, and they looked at each other, each with red eyes, each incapable of steady speech. There was the noise of a teapot being filled and emptied, of tea being spooned, of water pouring. Then silence.

"Steve?" Henry's voice sounded strange. "Tea?"

He looked at his father, and nodded, starting slowly to the door. Looking up, he saw such a look of compassion on the old lady's face that he couldn't help but smile gently to her. They retreated into the kitchen.

"Are you all right, boy? You all look to have taken on a turn."

Stephen sniffed and cleared his throat, and nodded. "We've just heard something else that happened the night of the flood. It happened to Mary, and she's only just remembered it."

"It'll be the shock made her," she said, nodding. "Happened a lot in the first war. Lad here came home from hospital, wounded, he was, but recovering. Then one day he stood a bit close to the Lifeboat maroon. Made a lot of 'em jump, like always, but him, he dived for cover like he were still in the trenches. Trouble was, he dived off the Hard and they had to fish him out. Stark staring mad, he was for a bit, then gradually the truth came out."

She paused, her eyes distant. "Got better, eventually. Wouldn't ever talk about the war; he'd always walk out the room if the subject came up."

She paused again. "Ended up marrying me. Got killed in the last lot, coming back from Plymouth one night."

Her own eyes misted over, and the two of them stared at the wall for a while.

"Well, there you are," she said sharply, as if pulling herself together. "He wasn't the only one, and I wasn't the only one who lost somebody. We were happy, and that's more than can be said for some." She busied herself with the tea, and soon a steaming cupful was pushed into Stephen's hands. They took a cup each to Mary and Henry, who seemed to have regained some composure, although Mary was still visibly shaken.

"I know who you are," said the shopkeeper unexpectedly, when they had all sat down. "But you don't know me. I'm Mary Whittaker, and this is my shop. I've heard tales about you I can't hardly believe, but I dessay they're part true. I'm not going to pry, but if you want something I can help you with, then I will, and be glad to do it. But right now, you're to stay here as long as you want and welcome. But I'm going to have to serve behind my counter – the kids'll think I've gone soft, else!"

And she hoisted herself from her perch and went out.

Stephen looked enquiringly at Mary and his father, who cleared his throat. "I think the worst has just come out, Mary, hasn't it?"

Mary nodded, still unable to speak properly, her normally attractive face disfigured by tears.

Henry spoke softly, smoothing her hair: "Now it has, you really can start to think straight again, and some of those dreams will go away. Oh, Steve doesn't know, he sleeps through anything. But I heard you muttering and turning last night, and once you called out... Oh well. You've nothing to fear now. No more hidden experiences. Peace."

Mary looked at him, wonderingly, then reached up and kissed him.

# 8 - Arrangements

They bid their farewells to Mary Whittaker, who exhorted each of them to take care of the others and to stand no nonsense from anyone. "And if you ever need someone to talk to, or somewhere to stay, I'd be glad to see you," she said as they made ready to walk back to the boatyard.

By that time none of the boatbuilders was there, as it was past five o'clock. Edgar was still in his office, and greeted them with relief.

"I saw old Mary take over," he said. "She's a good'un. Trust her and you'll come to no harm. Lucky she was there, though, to sort out that Inspector."

"I think the Coroner would have done if she hadn't," Henry replied. "In fact I think he probably has. The man as good as lied to him to avoid having Steve speak the truth at an inquest. It's plain he doesn't believe that someone younger than him can be responsible for important things like trying to save a life."

Edgar shot Stephen a penetrating glance. "I'd heard as much," he said, "but I didn't want to pry. If you did that, young man, you've done better than most who are four times your age. Deserves a medal, that does."

"It didn't work, though, Mr Mustchin. Greg still died."

"I know, lad. But you know that you did everything possible for him, and nobody could have done more. Simple as that. He'd be saying thank you to you now, if he could – and for all we know, perhaps he is. He'd certainly not be blaming you for doing your best, especially when your best is everybody else's best as well."

Stephen looked his thanks. Once again he couldn't trust himself to speak. He could feel Mary's eyes looking at him strangely. Abruptly he swallowed, muttered something about readying the boat, and turned toward the boatyard steps. Mary thanked Edgar quietly and followed him. The two men looked at each other.

"Look after them, Henry. I think you've got two grand youngsters there."

Henry smiled back. "I'm beginning to think you're right."

The voyage back to the island was a quiet one. The tide was by this time low, so they dragged the anchor way up the 'beach', covered as it was by soggy, withering grass which made all three of them think once again of its previous, green lushness. And there they left the boat, although, as Henry said, they'd have to return to rig running moorings for her after milking.

They were all glad to be back on their own territory, especially the dogs who had been left in the boat for longer than anyone intended. They were puzzled by the change in routine, as well as by the presence of water all around their island; water that made them sneeze if they tried to drink it.

With relief they followed the three around as they fed hens, milked the few cows and did the other farmyard jobs, perhaps wondering why they were no longer being asked to help drive the cows in from the low pastures. Strange things, these humans!

Rigging the running moorings proved simpler than they all expected in one way, but physically much harder work. The tide was at its lowest, and whilst this showed them the lowest point of the water, it meant that they had to haul the heavy mudweight out to it, on the slippery, dying grass. The rope was looped through the pulley that Edgar had thoughtfully fitted to the lump of lead for that very purpose, and one end taken to the boat. Mary took the other end to the island and then stopped, wondering what to do with it next. She shouted to Henry and Stephen. "Now what do I do?"

They looked at her, then Henry realised. Edgar was so used to using a mooring ring for the landward end of the system that he hadn't mentioned any alternatives.

"Oh," said Henry.

"Is there anything else in the boat, Dad?"

"Have a look, will you? I'll go and have a look up there."

He climbed back onto their old road and joined Mary just above the high water mark, wondering what to do. Get a mooring ring from the Yard and cement it in somewhere? From the boat came a yell: "What about a simple post, Dad?"

"Yes. You're right. That's the easiest way. I'll go and get something. In the meantime, get the anchor, will you? Dig it in up here and make fast for the moment. It'll not go anywhere then."

"*She* won't."

"What?"

"A boat is female."

"Oh yes. All right."

They fixed the post between them, with no further difficulty. Mary was feeling rather ignored by this time – there is a limit to the number of people who can be usefully employed hammering in a post. And the other two had worked together for such a long time that they seemed to ignore her. She once again began to think of what she would be doing if she were at home, and before long the tears were once again rolling down her cheeks.

Neither of the others noticed. To hold a post steady needs full concentration, as does aiming a heavy sledgehammer, especially when to miss means injuring your son. Mary took herself off, out of sight, feeling very small, and not a little aggrieved at being out of the team. She felt lonely again, and the thought that this wasn't really her family came once more to the forefront of her mind.

She remembered back to the afternoon's events. Her returned memories flashed into her brain, as vividly as if she was still there with the water crashing in on them all. She felt sick, dropped firstly to her knees then slowly sank to the ground as the misery overwhelmed her.

What it was that turned the corner for her she could never describe. Perhaps it was all the support and easy acceptance that Henry and Stephen had offered and freely given. Perhaps it was the way Henry had argued with the Police Inspector so vehemently on her behalf. Could it be that, with Henry, she felt safe; as safe as she had with her own father? She had always liked him, and what he had done and said since that night had made her feel very close to him. He certainly seemed to like her, in a fatherly way.

And Stephen! He was a friend, yes. He had been ever since they started at the same school. No, before. She couldn't remember a time when he hadn't been around. But suddenly, to have almost saved her brother's life, to have reported his last words to his father – who had believed him unquestioningly, something else that spoke volumes for Henry – and to have shown how much he cared for her in so many little ways... She suddenly felt a rush of something like love for this boy who seemed so amazingly self-assured for somebody only eighteen months older than herself. Would she ever be like that? She couldn't imagine herself reacting like that. She needed to rely on parents... no, on Henry. And on Stephen.

She was aware that her name was being called. Stephen, she thought; it's a child's voice. There was an urgency in it that she couldn't understand; was it irritation? Or was it alarm? Or was it downright anger? No: she'd never heard Stephen sound angry, and Henry only twice, when he was talking to Bert and later to the Inspector.

She listened again, and heard Stephen calling her. She recognised it this time, as worry. She sat up and called back. He must have been nearby – she hadn't actually gone very far from the road, just into a thicket – because he appeared almost immediately.

"Are you all right? We've been worried for you. You just vanished. When we'd finished knocking in the mooring post we looked for you, but you'd gone."

She looked at him. He seemed genuinely concerned, just as he had the morning after the storm. Good old, *dependable* Steve.

"I've just been thinking, that's all. I'm sorry if I've worried you. I just needed some time to myself. And you and Mr Loft didn't really need me back there, did you?"

He looked slightly ashamed, she thought.

"Dad said we'd rather gone off like a bull at a gate. We ignored you, he said, and just got on with it. Sorry. I didn't mean to leave you out."

She nodded.

"Come on, let's find Dad."

They tracked Henry down by the crashing in the undergrowth on the opposite side of the island. Stephen waited for a pause and for Henry to shout Mary's name. Then he shouted back that she was found and safe.

When he joined them, Henry was covered with scratches and had brambles sticking to him everywhere. It didn't seem to bother him, though, for his first words were "Are you all right?"

They both assured him that she was, and she explained the reasons for her departure once again. Henry understood, and he put his arm round her shoulders. She winced as one of the stray brambles on his jacket stuck in her arm.

Later, as they were eating, Henry voiced a problem that had been bothering him since Mary's arrival.

"We've got to do something about a room of your own, Mary. When there was no time to think about it, it was just about acceptable that you share with Stephen, but we've got to do something about it for you. Trouble is, I don't know what. The house isn't big enough to make a room upstairs for you, although we could down here. The kitchen could be adapted, but it'd mean quite a bit of work..." He paused, thinking onward.

Stephen chipped in. "But Dad, I don't mind her being with me. I used to share with Peter when he was here. I'm used to it."

He couldn't understand what was in his father's look. Amusement? Concern? I-know-better? Not quite. A mixture of them, perhaps, but something else besides.

"Don't grow up before your age." He didn't understand that, either. "Mary doesn't want to share with you. She's a girl, and she's used to a room of her own. No. We've got to do something for her." He paused again.

"But Mr Loft..." piped up Mary.

"And that's another thing, Mary. It's a mouthful for you to keep on calling me 'Mr Loft.' It's not the done thing for you to call me Henry, I suppose, although I can't for the life of me think why, but we've got to think of something else. It's just too unfriendly, otherwise." He paused again.

"But *Henry*..." she said, grasping the nettle, having been presented with it. Henry looked at her, startled, and then laughed a full, sincere laugh.

"And why not?" he said, noticing the approving grin on his son's face. "We're in this together now, so why not? Perhaps in a few years all children will be calling their parents by their Christian names. It might make some of them stop being so scared of them. Who knows? And what are you 'But Henry'-ing me for, pray?"

"I don't mind sharing with Stephen, either. I think I'd like to, at least for the moment."

He looked at her, perplexed. How could he explain to her? What would

74

happen when his son started becoming a man, if he hadn't already? What would happen when she started becoming a woman? No, it was out of the question. But still he could see no quick solution to the problem. Something had to happen, though, before the authorities came to visit to gauge his suitability as an adoptive parent. If they saw or even heard that a boy and a girl of their ages were sharing a bed they would probably faint and take Mary away immediately. And Stephen, too. Besides which it was wrong. Wasn't it? Was it? After all, nothing could happen at that age. Stephen wasn't mature enough and, so far as he could tell, had no interest in Mary apart from as a friend. What was true for the elder was certainly true for the younger. No. Nothing could happen. But nobody must know, and they must make her a room as soon as possible.

"All right," he said at last. "We've got to make a room for you, Mary, and we'll have to do it soon before we get any authorities visiting us. Until then, as far as the outside world is concerned I'm sleeping down here and you're in my room."

She looked worried. "But... *Henry*... I don't want to make you leave your room. I'd prefer to share Stephen's."

"For the time being, you shall. I'm just saying what we must lead everybody else to think. If some people hear that you two are sharing not just a room but a bed they will be most concerned."

"Why, Dad? Why would they worry? I shared for years."

"That was with your brother. Mary's a girl."

"You used to sleep with Mum... Oh."

"Yes. Oh. That's what I mean. We'll let it go for the moment, but as soon as we can we'll make space."

Mary still looked puzzled.

"There's another problem we need to think about, although it's linked. I never told you what nearly happened at Salcombe yesterday, did I?" And he outlined the argument with the Inspector.

"... although you must have guessed something like that happened because of the man's attitude earlier. Anyway, I talked to old Merryweather – you know, the Solicitor – and told him what had happened. One of his comments made me think about the farm, although I'd have got round to it eventually I suppose. We've got to have more grazing for the cattle than we have now, even in the short term. There's about two weeks worth here at this time of year, but until the water disappears and the meadows sweeten again the cattle have got to be somewhere else. That'll be a big commitment of time and money. They'll need looking after, milked, grazed, and brought in during the winter, and so on. How do we operate a dairy – how do we *get* to a dairy – from here?"

There was a long pause.

"Perhaps he's right," he continued. "Perhaps we should leave, and find a smallholding on land."

There was immediate pandemonium from his two charges. "We can't leave here!" "Oh, no. We mustn't." "There's something we can do!" "It's lovely here!" "I want to stay and farm here for ever!"

"I know, I know. It'd be like giving up, wouldn't it? And neither the Lofts nor the Beales are scared of a fight, so together there's no way. I hope. But the welfare of the animals comes first – we're farmers, not a factory."

Another pause. Then "There's something else," said Mary. The others looked at her. "All our herd is over with Mark and Jimmy's parents at Park Farm."

"I'd forgotten about them. How many are there?"

"We've got twenty five cows."

Henry gave a whistle. "I knew your Dad was increasing his herd, but I never realised there were that many now. He must have spent a small fortune on them! You don't know what agreement he'd come to with Peter Symes, do you?"

Mary shook her head. "No, Dad never said. He thought it would only be for a few days. I know Mark and Jimmy had to clear out their old shippon, 'cos they grumbled about it at school until they saw I was listening."

"Hmm. Sounds as if he's doing the job properly then. I wonder."

"You think he might take them on permanently, Dad?"

"Yes. And if he's agreed to look after so many, it wouldn't make all that much difference if he took on ours as well. They're all Jerseys, and from just as good backgrounds. Oh, there's too much work for his lot to take them all on for more than a short time, without help anyway. But if we could come to an arrangement it might work. You see, he would hire someone to look after the lot, and charge us so much per beast for their care and lodging, then pay us what he gets for the milk. Hmmm… He might just do it. You said he was quite looking forward to getting into animals again, didn't you?"

She nodded again. "Dad said he'd only given up 'cos the Ministry told him to concentrate on arable during the war. He's got a dairy still, that's why he could take ours so easily."

"I don't know about easily. Taking so many on all at once is not an easy task. And there's feed to consider."

"Oh, Dad gave him a lot of ours, enough for a fortnight."

"Good old John, thinking forward as usual…" But this was too much for Mary, and with a gulp she hurried from the room again. Footsteps could be heard mounting the stairs to Stephen's room. He looked at his father enquiringly.

"No, let her sort herself out. Give her five minutes or so, then one of us can go up. I know it's early days, but until the funeral, particularly, she'll be weepy. Poor little kid. She's full young to be losing her family."

Stephen said nothing, but thought back two years to when the bottom had fallen out of his own world. His father, knowing him, and still feeling the pain himself, also sat in silence, staring at the wall and at one of the other chairs in the room.

Time passed. At length, footsteps were heard again and Mary came back into the room. "Sorry," she said. "I'm better now."

Henry beckoned to her; she crossed to him and didn't resist when he turned her round and sat her on his knee. "You have a good deal of sorrowing to do, Mary. Nobody will be ashamed of you or think it anything but entirely natural when you show your feelings. It'd be unnatural if you didn't."

She said nothing, but settled back against his jacket.

"Have you decided what to do about the rest of the animals?" she asked.

Stephen thought back to earlier that evening, of how she was almost left out of the work on the moorings. "No," he said swiftly, before Henry could speak, "we've been waiting for you."

Again she said nothing., but Henry felt a little movement which perhaps spoke of a wriggle of contentment.

Henry broke the silence. "What the solicitor said to make me think of all this concerned our income. We live simply, compared with most people. Apart from food and clothes our wants are few. Our heating has been mainly by wood, so is much of the cooking. We don't use much electricity – when there is any," and he pointed to the candle glowing in its jar. "But we do need an income, and if anything we'll need to increase it. Wood won't be so easy to get now there's a stretch of water to carry it over. Lord knows when – or how – they'll get electricity or telephone back to us. If it isn't until the water goes then we could be in for a long gap. We've got your hens and pigs, Mary, and I really think we'll have to look at increasing on smaller animals like that."

Stephen wasn't so sure about being a chicken farmer or a pig farmer. They didn't seem as important as cows, or even a flock of sheep.

"Sheep!" he said suddenly. "If we can take on pigs, how 'bout more sheep?"

"What do they eat?" asked his father quietly.

"Grass. Oh."

"Yes. Nice idea, but what's true for cows is as true for sheep. You need quite a number to make it viable, too, so they're just as good at keeping grass short as cows, in the long run. Better, in fact, because they graze closer."

"Goats? Not turkeys, please. Horses? No, grass again. Pet rabbits? Oh, no; please not! Hey, if not cows, then how about a couple of prime Jersey bulls? I know how much we have to pay for A.I., and if others can get money that way, how about us?"

"That's not so silly," said his father. "Use them for A.I. until they're too old, then sell them at market – mind you, I doubt if anyone would want beef that's been on the hoof that long. If it were that easy everybody would do it."

"But with the smaller animals it'd help," pleaded Stephen.

"Trouble is, we'd have to buy them young, and it'd take quite a few years for them to prove themselves and become sought after – if they ever did. Ideally we should be looking at buying a really good mature animal now, and then bidding for some of his young as they came along. But you're talking money to do that, lots of it."

"All ours were heifers," added Mary.

Henry's mind raced ahead. Think of a couple of Jersey bulls, or more, separately penned on an island out of harm's way. Then think of a herd of Jerseys, owned by the same family, which could be serviced by the bulls when necessary. The continuation at little cost of a milking herd, with a beef herd thrown in, and money from Artificial Insemination. It sounded good. And they could cope with it, with care. Two bulls were easier to deal with than eight cows and a few sheep.

"You know, the finances could work out, if we could afford them in the first place."

As they sat staring into the flames, thinking about what other possibilities there were, gradually Mary, and then Stephen dozed off. It had been another tiring day, with even more fresh air and more new things to learn than usual. They were still suffering the reaction from the night of the storm. Henry felt himself nodding, too, roused himself and jumped up. The movement woke the dogs, who woke the other two, who looked at Henry drowsily.

"I'm just going to look round, as usual," he said. "You two go on up. I'll see you in the morning."

They followed his instructions, aware now how tired they were. Stephen's return from brushing his teeth found Mary already in bed. He had to disturb her to get to his side, and was surprised to see that, like him, she was wearing pyjamas. Henry had found her a pair of his old ones. She had wondered what Stephen's reaction would be, ready to be annoyed if he teased her, but was almost disappointed when he didn't.

They settled down to sleep. When Henry knocked softly on the door about half an hour later there was no sound. He put his head around the door, as he had done with Stephen so many times before, and smiled to see the double crescent in the bed.

78

# 9 – Church, Susan, Peter

Mary was first up in the morning. She had an ulterior motive.

She made the tea, and then wondered if she had started things off too early. It *was* Sunday. She was pleased to hear Henry's feet on the stairs, and to hear him humming as he approached. He smiled when he saw her.

"That's a nice thought, Mary. Thank you. Are you sure you've had enough sleep, though? That son... Stephen didn't push you out of the bed, I hope."

He thought he had stopped himself in time from referring to Stephen as his son. But the fact that he *had* stopped himself gave Mary a pang of separateness. Fortunately she understood that Henry couldn't alter the speech habits of thirteen years so quickly, and let the slip pass.

"*Henry,*" she started. It still made him smile to hear his name come from unusual and unaccustomed lips. "May we go to church this morning, please?"

"I don't see why not," he said. "We used to go regularly before my wife died. Yes, it's a good idea. You go and give Stephen a shout, and I'll start the milking."

"Can't I do the milking with you, and leave Stephen asleep?"

He smiled at her. "Get one over on him? Yes, of course you can. Come on."

When Stephen woke some three quarters of an hour later he was surprised to see nobody by his side, pleased to find the tea made, mortified to find it only tepid and ashamed to find himself alone in the house. He rushed back upstairs and flung on his clothes, splashed some water around his face and rushed down to the shippon, where he found milking in full progress. Mary smiled at him sweetly when he appeared, tousle headed.

"Hallo, Stephen," she said innocently.

"Why didn't you wake me?" he blustered back.

"I was going to bring you a nice cup of tea, but we decided to do the milking instead."

"Hallo, old son. Sleep OK? Can you feed the pigs this morning, as Mary's beaten you to it in here?"

He nodded, grumpily, Mary thought, and went outside again. A few minutes later, though, she heard him whistling as he clanked his way down to feed their augmented families of pigs. Some of them were her parents' animals! Oh, no, she thought as tears welled up in her eyes. Not again. She stopped thinking, and leant her forehead heavily against the cow's flank. She looked round reproachfully and blew a gale of hay-scented breath into Mary's ear. Mary milked on, automatically, and soon the rhythmic movements, as familiar to her as breathing, calmed her pain again. She was all the more determined to go to church, though.

They reconvened in the kitchen. Mary had gone to help Stephen with the chickens, and had found him to be back in good humour. When church was mentioned, he rolled his eyes to the ceiling, a sign noticed by Mary.

"I'd like to go," she said quietly, and immediately he was apologetic and understanding.

"Come on, you lot," said Henry. "We can't go smelling like a farmyard, or looking like hayricks either, Stephen. Change, the pair of you."

Mary looked at him, her eyes suddenly filling again, her mouth open.

"What's up?"

"I've got no other clothes!"

"Oh, crumbs! I never thought! Oh." He thought.

"I've got some quite new shirts, Dad. You could use one of them. They're white, but the collar's soft, so it'll look like a blouse, perhaps."

"I need a skirt, though."

Henry was thinking through the few remaining items of his wife's clothing which even after two years he couldn't bring himself to destroy. There were items there which meant so much to him, because of when she had worn them, or just because they were too new. Was there anything there? Could he bear to see them worn by someone else – even a child?

He pulled himself together. Needs dictated. He motioned to her to follow him; Stephen tagged along too. In his bedroom he went to a drawer and opened it with some difficulty.

"Most of these will be far too big for you, Mary, but I seem to remember a pleated skirt…"

It was a light fawn colour, with large pleats, so that when they had pinned it the extra pleats were hidden almost unnoticeably. They – actually Mary, who was better at it – pinned it up to a reasonable level and pressed it with the iron. It looked a bit full, but the disguise was good enough. Mary went to their room to change, closing the door on Stephen, much to his chagrin. When she came down again both of them had to admit that the simple colours suited her.

"I know, we can ask Mrs Whittaker if she'd alter it for me on Monday."

Henry was about to tell her it had been his wife's when he bit back the words. Why shouldn't Mary wear it? It was doing no good in the bottom of a never-opened chest of drawers. Stephen knew the skirt's origin, but clothes don't have the associations for youth as they do for adults.

Their running moorings worked perfectly, their boat coming straight to what they were already regarding and calling 'The Hard'. This time the dogs were left on guard.

As they climbed the hill toward Salcombe's church they began to be aware of people glancing at them. Others heading in the same direction obviously knew who they were. It was with some relief that they recognised Mrs Whittaker as they overtook her, and fell in with her for the rest of the climb, and sat with her in church.

The service was a surprising comfort for each of them in their own way. For Mary, having been brought up as a churchgoer, it was the comfort of familiarity, of continuation, and of following her nascent beliefs. For Stephen it was a harkening back to the days when his mother had been alive, when the family of four had all attended fairly regularly. It was the same for Henry, too, though his beliefs had been tarnished by age and the misfortune of his wife's death.

It was the sermon that made them each sit up. The vicar had been at the church only six months – Henry remembered the fuss of his arrival – and was a young man fresh from the army via Theological College. He had a happy knack of putting over his message in simple language which was nevertheless effective. No wonder the church was so full.

He spoke of the end of the hurricane's tail, for that was the cause of the appalling weather which had resulted in such a disaster that had robbed the area and its families of lives and land. For those concerned the tragedy was the greater since if the structures which gave way had been stronger, there would have been more time to escape, or inundation would have been avoided. Did the Victorian engineers in the area skimp on their work? If so it was unusual, but time would tell. In the meantime there was work to be done to help those who had been bereaved, displaced, or had their mode of life altered. "We have more than one representative from families in one or other of these difficulties with us today. I welcome them, as does the community at large. I have been here only a short time, yet I have been impressed by the generosity of spirit that this community possesses and, more importantly, shares with others.

"You who need help have only to ask, and if help is possible it will be given. That includes help from the church, of course, and particularly from me. We will be starting a fund to alleviate some of the suffering for those families in greatest need. That will hardly help their mental anguish, of course, but will assist with the material needs. I encourage everyone here to contribute to it and I hope you will entrust the PCC and me with its use."

The burning question, he continued, was what would happen next. "Believe it or not, this can be largely up to us as local people – if you will excuse my counting myself amongst you in this way. Certainly the source of the water in the hills must be stopped. But consider this: This estuary was dammed by landowners in Victorian times who wanted to increase their holdings. In those days a powerful group could do almost anything against the wishes of local people if they were strong enough. We – you – are now in the situation where we can decide whether or not we want the dam and its other works reinstated."

At this there was a murmuring around the church. He let it continue for a few seconds. "I do not recommend one course or another. But we need to decide what is for the best. One thing particularly has changed since it was all built. Since the war people are starting to look for leisure pursuits, for holiday destinations. True, they come here already and we largely welcome them, but we are primarily a farming and a fishing community. If the estuary remained we could still be that, but we could also become much more of a holiday resort, and people on holiday spend money."

"Now I have either stirred up a hornet's nest, or I have given you food for thought. So I will give you an assurance: that I have only the wellbeing of the people of this area at heart.

And with that he ended, leaving a most untypical buzz in the church while he regained his seat.

After the service, they stopped in the porch, along with quite a number of others who had been less than happy about the sermon's sentiments. As the vicar appeared there was a chorus of calls along the lines of "'yere, we want to talk to you…!"

And there the poor man stood, for about five minutes, trying to achieve enough of a breathing space so that he could string together a sentence without getting interrupted. At length he was forced to beckon to them all to follow him out into the churchyard, where he resorted almost to parade ground tactics. The surprise of such a voice coming from such a mild mannered man was enough to stun them all.

"I stand by what I said. If you remember I said that this whole community will help those of you who are deprived of land by the return of the water, *if it is allowed to remain*. I do not recommend that course; neither do I recommend that we should go for the return of the dam above all other considerations. We need to consider, to weigh up all the advantages and disadvantages to both options, and to any other choices which may become obvious.

"I can assure you of this. *Whatever* you, and the rest of the people of this area finally decide, I will stand beside you. I will also ensure that as much weight as I can muster is given to the need for those who have been disadvantaged by the catastrophe to obtain compensation, and as generous a compensation as possible. My reason for raising all this so early, when wounds are still fresh, is simple. The dam may be reinstated, or it may not. Until a final decision is made none of your insurances will pay out. Think of that."

"Which side are you really on, Vicar?" asked Henry.

"As I said in my sermon, I'm not on any side, except what is best for the people in this area. You were pointed out to me as one of those who have had a desperately hard time of it so far. And God knows that Mary has too. I know now that you are both part of self-reliant families, but if ever you do need moral support – or, insofar as I can give it, practical support – then you must come and see me without delay. But about your concerns, I would say that on the one hand you should look for a long term solution to your absence of land, and I will help you find a contact if I can. On the other hand you all, on an island, could stand to take advantage of the visitor trade if anybody can."

As is the nature of groups of aggrieved people there were more comments from those who needed to have his standpoint explained again and again. Eventually he was allowed to get away, but the knot of people still stood there discussing matters. Henry had believed what the vicar had said, and did his best to calm the fears of some of the older residents who had lost land.

He succeeded in part, and as his own attempts earlier in the week to talk to council members had failed, he wondered if the vicar, being on the spot, could make the necessary contacts and hurry discussions along. Would today be a good day to talk to him? He thought, particularly in view of the man's thoughts about speed, that it would. It occurred to him that he might also sound him out about the Inspector's attitude about Mary.

As they walked back round towards the porch, they were approached by a pleasant looking woman who had been waiting patiently for the group to disperse. She smiled shyly, and introduced herself as Miss Merryweather. "I'm the daughter of the Solicitor in Fore Street and I have the little café just opposite. I knew your parents, Mary, and I'm desperately sorry to hear what happened. If you need somewhere to live, or if there's anything else I can do, please tell me. You'd be more than welcome. I'd feel it was returning some of the kindnesses that your parents have done for me in the past."

"Thank you, Miss Merryweather. It's nice of you, but I've got a home. I'm living with Stephen and Henry."

She appeared a little taken aback. "That's nice for you, my dear, and I'm so glad they've been nice to you. But are you sure it's right for you to be staying with a single man and his son, with all due respects to you all. People might talk. You'd be better off living in the town, surely?"

Henry could see his son starting to bristle. "Miss Merryweather, thank you for your concern, but Mary has accepted our offer after a promise we made to her brother as he was dying. As for people talking, I am happy to be judged by my reputation. I certainly have every wish to ensure Mary's situation is secure, and so after discussing it with her and with Stephen I will be seeking to adopt her. In fact your father is already starting the process off for me."

"I see. In which case I beg your pardon. I had no idea of the background to the matter. I didn't mean to cause offence to you, Mr... um..."

"Loft."

"Mr Loft. I am glad that Mary has such good friends. And I wish you all a speedy resolution to your problems. I should warn you, though, that Mary's great-aunt is an acquaintance of mine, and she telephoned me last night, asking for news. Unaware of what you've just told me, I told her what had happened. She's most concerned, as you would expect, and I am afraid she's unlikely to leave matters there. In fact she said she would be contacting my father tomorrow to engage him to discover your whereabouts, Mary. At least I could not tell her that, as this is the first I knew about where you were."

"There shouldn't be a problem, surely, Miss Merryweather? When she speaks to your father she will understand, and her mind will be put at rest."

"You don't know her, Mr Loft. She is very much of the old school, and a very *particular* lady as well. I now understand the situation, and I can tell you are, in my father's terminology, an *honourable* man, now I've met you. She is likely to be extremely single minded, and will insist on what she sees as her rights."

"What about *my* rights!" Mary burst out. "She visited us last year – I'd never seen her before – and I *hated* her. I won't go and live with her. I *won't.*"

Her face crumpled at this latest blow, and she turned away, back into the church. Stephen followed.

"Shouldn't you go after her too, Mr Loft? Your son might upset her more."

Henry wondered why he couldn't bring himself to be angry. Surely this woman's attitude matched Inspector Franks'? Something held him back.

"Miss Merryweather, Stephen found her after she'd nearly drowned. He then found her brother and tried to save his life: he died in my son's arms. The last thing he asked was that Stephen should look after his sister and his parents. We lost the parents, my neighbours and good friends; but their daughter was spared. In view of this, she's precious to us both. Stephen lost his mother two years back, and the experience aged him beyond his years. He knows from bitter experience what to say and what not to say."

She turned and looked after the two young figures as they disappeared into the church. Then, quietly: "I think I underestimated him, as well as you. I had no idea of the details. I'm so sorry. How can I apologise enough?"

"What you can do for us, if you will, is to make sure the correct version of the news gets to as many people in town as possible. We may need public opinion on our side if this great-aunt makes too many waves and my adoption case goes to court. Will you do that for us, for *her*? And should you hear of anyone who wants to rent out some grazing, could you tell me that, too?"

"I certainly shall, Mr Loft. And I shall ask my father to do the same, although I imagine you have already done so."

"I have. But please feel free to do so as well. Ah, here they come. Mary looks happier."

She did indeed. "I've told the vicar. He's going to help make sure I stay with you. So that's all right. He wants to see you."

"We'd better go. Goodbye, Miss Merryweather, and thank you for any help you can give us."

She was just turning away when she stopped short. "Just a minute, I forgot to say what I was going to start off with! Oh, what a memory! Mary, your father, a long time ago, asked me to look after a little dinghy for him. I asked a friend of mine to use it now and again to keep it in trim, and he has. It's upturned on trestles at the back of the café, and it strikes me that you might all need it now."

Mary's face lit up. "I didn't know who had it! They'd said there was one in Salcombe that belonged to us, but we don't know where. Oh, thank you. Can we see it, please? When can we take it?"

"Later, Mary," Henry laughed at her enthusiasm. "We've a vicar to see first. If it's all right with Miss Merryweather we'll go down after that and have a look."

"I shall look forward to it. I can't promise to launch it for you, but between the four of us we should be able to do so."

They thanked her and entered the church again.

If anything their clergyman was even more indignant than Mary that there should be a prospect that she should not be allowed to live in a suitable home where she wanted to be. If common sense powered by goodwill was allowed to run the country, he said, there would be no doubt at all that she should live on Loft Island.

"I've had a little experience with the adoption people," he said. "Unless there are very good reasons against it they will always favour a relative taking responsibility. What we have to do is to get as many reasons against as we can, and put them to your solicitor. And to the local Council, too. They have a say, for some reason. In fact, it often seems to me that the only person who isn't asked is the person or people most affected."

"But that's not fair!" Mary almost wailed. "Do you mean that whatever I want, nobody will listen?"

"Not quite, Mary," the vicar continued. "True, it could be that bad if nobody asks the right questions or if you imagine that everybody knows in advance what you want. But the judges aren't necessarily as sensible as you or Mr Loft or Stephen, and can only take notice of what they have in front of them. Unfortunately, the word of an adult in court outweighs that of a minor, even when it's that minor's happiness or even wellbeing at stake. Wrong, I know: but we must deal with the law as it stands, not as we would like it."

"Therefore we need to get as many people as possible who know us to say that Mary would be better off in a happy, caring home where she's loved and wanted and welcome, and not stuck with an elderly relative in Harrogate."

"That's where she lives, is it? Well, that's another point. She would have to change schools to live there, so we'll need to get her present teacher to say something too."

"I'd better make a list of all these and more," said Henry. "Reverend, thank you. Please, if anything else occurs to you can you make a note? I think we've got a lot of visiting to do, and a lot of persuading as well to make sure people are prepared to stand up in court. You two can do your bit in thinking of others who will be on our side."

"Don't forget that as well as those *on* your side to make a list of any others who would be against you. There are some even locally who are like your great-aunt, Mary, who think that a father and son family is not 'suitable' for a girl's upbringing. And don't attack me! I'm not one of them. Just gather intelligence – that means knowing who are your enemies, then you can find ways of countering them. I'll be doing the same for you."

They thanked him. Henry told him that he would return in a day or two and compare notes. "I also want to talk to you about the subject of your sermon again, when I – when we've had a chance to think about it," he added.

They visited Miss Merryweather's café. Because of the visitors who were in the town to see the results of the flooding they found her open, despite it being Sunday. "I got back from church," she explained shamefacedly, "and there was this crowd of people looking in the window. I asked them what the matter was and they said they were trying to find when I opened. Well, I can't afford to turn down business nowadays, can I? And they did look hungry."

They laughed.

"Your boat's out the back. It's the only one there. Have a look, and if you think you can get her to the water, then do. Or if you'd rather, wait 'til tomorrow when my friend comes. He'll get her in for you." It was surprising how much more talkative she was once on her own territory. At her invitation they trooped through her kitchen and out of the back door.

There, upturned on two trestles, was a dinghy. Her hull was planked – Edgar told them later she was clinker built, and based on the Salcombe lugger, a design developed by the local boatyards and suited to estuary and shallow sea work. She appeared to be newly varnished inside and out; her mast gleamed as if it were still wet. The ropes on her looked the worse for wear, and of sails there was no sign. But by appearance she was a trim a little vessel that ever longed to be in water.

Henry looked at her and saw a safe little craft, difficult to capsize, well tended from stem to stern, something which spoke for her general condition, he thought. Mary and Stephen saw a summer ahead full of learning to sail, of endless fun, and exploring their new maritime world.

"Wow."

A small word shared, but enough to express a heartful of emotion.

"Dad, when can we sail her?" Henry was so surprised that he was speechless for a moment. Stephen looked at Mary, too, but she was much too engrossed in the sight of her boat to realise what she had said.

Henry cleared his throat noisily, and swallowed. "Neither of you has sailed before, have you? Nor have I. We need to know what we're doing first. It's all right to get blown in the same direction as the wind, but what happens when it blows somewhere you don't want to go? We need to talk to Edgar. And some of those ropes look as if they could do with renewing before she goes too far."

"But surely we could take her back to the island, Dad?" It was Stephen this time.

"I can tow you, I suppose, but we'll have to bring her back to Edgar's tomorrow, if there's time. Can we launch her, though?"

"Yes, Henry, look." Henry was not surprised at the return of his Christian name. He looked in the direction she was pointing. Part of the fence at the side of the little back garden was removable, and gave access to a lane which led past the backs of other shops and houses, and came out by the Hard at the bottom of Union Street.

"OK," he said. "Let's go and see Miss Merryweather. She may agree to our taking it now."

"Her."

"Pardon?"

"Her. Taking her now. A boat is female."

"So she is. Come on, then."

Miss Merryweather was foundering under the weight of customers. A practical and efficient lady, she had been coping with the rush well, until a party of eight had asked for little short of a full breakfast each, and were reluctant to take no for an answer when she explained that she hadn't any bacon or sausages left. Feeling sorry for her, Henry nodded towards the sink that was already piled high with dirty dishes. He washed up in his usual quick way, born of his dislike of the job and the need, on a farm, to get on with something more productive. The others found drying-up cloths and set to, managing to keep pace with him. They were well on the way when Miss Merryweather bustled back to try and find an alternative for the eight, and gasped with delight when she saw what was happening.

"Oh that *is* nice of you," she said, and meant it.

"The least we could do," replied Henry. "Have they decided what they want, yet?"

"Yes. Two teas, two coffees, three fruit juices and a hot water!"

"What? No quail in aspic? No passion fruit cocktail? Oh dear!"

She laughed, and it seemed as though years had dropped from her face. Henry wondered how old she was. Stephen suddenly warmed to her. Mary thought that she wasn't such a dry old stick after all. "It's amazing how people think that the word 'café' translates as 'anything, at any time'" she said, and smiled again. Like a cloudy day, thought Henry, when the sun makes an unexpected appearance. He found himself laughing, really laughing, for the first time in three days or probably more: there hadn't been much to laugh at during the storms as the community watched the waters rise. And it wasn't that much of a joke, was it? 'I'm not falling am I? At my age?' His thoughts were perhaps unworthy of his dead wife, and he shut himself off abruptly.

"I suppose you've no staff on duty at this time of year?" he asked.

"No. I have one girl full time in summer, and someone else part time when I need the help," she explained. "It's only our being the nation's talking point at the moment that's brought the crowds, as I said. At this time of day during the week I'd normally get four fishermen in, and think myself lucky. Here, I'd better do these drinks, or they'll walk out." She busied herself with tea and coffee and hot water, taking some of the newly dried cups and saucers off their growing pile.

Some twenty minutes later they were done, the growing pile of dirty crockery conquered, the café emptying. With relief Henry emptied the sink, and Mary and Stephen hung their teatowels to dry.

With Miss Merryweather now able to talk they asked if they might take the dinghy back with them.

"Why yes, if you're sure you can launch her. You've seen the access to the Hard – it's a long carry but three usually do it. Here, I'll give you a hand. They'll be all right out there. We'll get her half way and I'll pop back."

Even with no mast, centreboard or fittings she was quite heavy. Turning her off the trestles was no mean feat, but they managed somehow without damaging the varnish or themselves. They stood her on her keel and Stephen held her steady while Miss Merryweather saw to her customers. With Stephen at the bow, Mary and Miss Merryweather amidships and

Henry struggling on his own at the stern they lugged her along the narrow lane. Half way they stopped, changed sides and rested, then continued. They stopped abruptly again as a call came from behind them: "Do you want a hand?"

Henry gave a start.

"Peter!"

They nearly dropped the boat. Poor Miss Merryweather was so startled that she did actually drop her side. Had the dinghy not been so strongly built she might have been damaged.

"*Peter*!" said Henry again. "I didn't know you were coming down!" It was indeed his elder son, a broad, stocky 19 year old with the same engaging grin on his face that both Henry and Stephen were often wearing.

"Of course you didn't, Dad, the phone's down. How could I tell you? This is the first chance I've had to get away from work to see you – the man said that he didn't care if my family was drowned, if I went to check I'd be out of a job. I figured if you were drowned there's not a lot I could do, and if you weren't then two days wouldn't make a difference. I'm going to go for a new job as soon as I can. But who's this?"

"Miss Merryweather, who owns the café, and…"

"Yes, I know Miss Merryweather, she's fed me many times in the past. How are you? It's good to see you again. But who's the attractive young lady who was almost left holding the boat?"

Stephen spoke up, as if in protection. "This is Mary Beale. You remember? From just north of us? She lost both her parents and her brother in the flood."

Peter was as talkative, normally, as his father and brother were inclined to taciturnity. This time he was rendered wordless, but just looked at Mary, horrified, who blushed and looked as if she were near to tears. Peter suddenly pushed past his brother and father, stooped to Mary, lifted her off her feet and hugged her as though trying to persuade himself she was still alive. He spent a long time holding her like this, looking straight out over the water, seeing nothing except a sundrenched farmyard with two ten-year-olds and an eight-year-old playing amongst the hay.

# 10 - Dinghy

With Peter's help, once he had been told the story of the dinghy, she was soon in the water. They returned to the café with Miss Merryweather who found the sails after a considerable search. "My friend never sailed her," she explained. "He would borrow space in one of the boatyards when he thought she needed attention, and then row her round to it."

They thanked her for keeping her so long and so well and assured her that they would be asking Edgar for his help before sailing her. Henry told her she must visit them on the island before the main season started and she became busy.

Leaving Mary and Stephen in charge of 'their' dinghy, Henry took Peter to Island Creek where he had moored the launch. Although not a waterman, Peter was impressed by the effective simplicity of the running moorings, and was glad when his unaccustomed entry into a floating vessel was over. They took her round to join the others, only to find the dinghy moored to a ring and nobody there. Before Henry had a chance to be worried, a masthead appeared at the end of the lane from the café, nearly impaling two of the visiting sightseers. Mary appeared soon after, apologised to them, and continued walking forward. Stephen carried the other end of the mast along with the gaff which he shouted to his father to collect.

They stowed the spars in the boat as best they could. Mary and Stephen elected to be towed in the dinghy and to keep all secure. Peter and his father were in the launch. Having had to tow many reluctant trailers from muddy fields in his time, Henry was aware that he mustn't snatch at the towrope but take the strain gently. One or two fishermen were watching and nodded approvingly as the launch headed slowly away, the dinghy easing after her.

Peter had never seen the remains of the dam at close quarters, and was amazed that there should have been such a force of water to be able to sweep away so apparently solid a structure. Broken masonry was evident at the side of the narrow channel as well as inside the area which had formed the lakes containing the rivers' water until the next low tide.

"So where have all the rest of the walls gone?" he asked.

"Nobody really knows, apart from the fact it was all swept down toward the sea," answered Henry. "How far it reached isn't known, and probably won't be for some time. They don't even know if they're going to rebuild, yet." And he relayed what the vicar had said that morning, particularly what he had said about the future, and holidaymakers.

When they arrived home Peter watched as they pulled the launch back to permanently deep water using the running moorings. They had decided to leave the dinghy beached, and between the four of them carried her up to level ground.

Peter had had time to think. "What you told me about the Vicar's sermon – it's a thought, you know, Dad. If there are going to be a lot of tourists coming here you may be able to cash in on them. After all, you live on the only proper island in the estuary, somewhere romantic, with a farm. There are lots of city kids who have never seen the sea, never even seen a cow. To them, milk comes from a bottle and eggs from a box."

Henry looked at him as if he were crazy. "How's that going to help us? They come onto the island, they look round, they go away. More trouble than it's worth."

"Not if you charge them when they land, and sell them food and things. What about souvenirs?"

"If you think I'm going to welcome a lot of strangers on to my farm just to be able to get money from them, think again. I think Torquay's got at your mind, son."

"Dad…" Stephen hesitated. His father looked at him sharply.

"Dad…it's *our* farm. Mine and now Mary's, as well as yours."

"Yes, I know that, but really, would you want it ruined by lots of trippers? What about our privacy? What about the disturbance to the animals?"

"But how are we going to cope if we've got no grazing?"

There was silence.

It took some time for Henry's mood to lift – in fact he was inclined to be ashamed at himself for reacting. His elder son's presence was unsettling to him in some way. Perhaps he still hadn't really forgiven him for leaving to go to Torquay, or maybe he was subconsciously jealous that Peter had achieved independence, and now he was hearing about the continuing happiness of a relationship. It seemed unfair so soon after his happiness had ended in the death of his wife. Or it may have been that he was feeling disloyal to his wife's memory by the surprise of having been attracted to Miss Merryweather.

Stephen had been torn between seeing his brother and staying with the dinghy. Mary hardly knew Peter and was more interested in her boat, so hesitated there. Stephen noticed, and felt he shouldn't leave her. "We're going to look at her properly," he announced. "See you later."

"Rather Mary than me, eh Steve? Don't blame you!" His brother taunted. Suddenly glad they wouldn't be with Peter to be talked to like that, Stephen turned away. How his brother had changed on the eighteen months' absence. He never used to talk to treat him that way. When they had been at the farm together, even when Peter had been late home or latterly just away, the five years in age between them hadn't made them strangers. Sharing a small house meant that intimacy had been at a maximum and privacy at a minimum, so from an early age he had been dimly aware of his brother's increasing physical maturity, something which had been far more obvious than his mental development. Shouldn't he feel the same about him now that he was eighteen as he had at sixteen when he had left home? He felt a sharp pang of regret that yet something else had changed, had gone for good.

Mary was watching him gaze after his father and brother, a lost look in his eyes. "Don't you want to go with them?"

He shook his head impatiently. "They're just going to talk. I'd rather be looking after the boat."

They looked her over properly, examining her inside and out. There were big metal tanks under each thwart and another under the small fore-deck, neither of which they had really noticed before.

"I think they're just sealed," said Stephen. "You know, so that they'll help keep her afloat if she's full of water."

"Why should she get full of water?"

"If she capsizes."

"But she's wooden. She'll float anyway."

"Suppose so. But perhaps not high enough. Anyway, they'd not put them there without a reason. Can we put the mast in? Why has it got those wires coming down from it?"

"I looked at some other boats at Edgar's. They go onto those rings just by the sides, and this one goes right to the front."

"The bow."

"Yes. I suppose it's so it doesn't snap with the weight of the sail."

"Let's put it in."

Since neither of them was tall, they had a considerable struggle with the heavy mast. Whilst it was horizontal there was no problem, but once they approached the vertical, the squared-off bottom of it would always swing away from the hole in the centre thwart which was its upper seating. Stephen stopped in exasperation. "Can't we tie the bottom so it doesn't swing?" he asked the world at large.

He thought, then hit on a plan. They lifted the mast until the base was adjacent to its seating. A rope was tied around the square section, as close to the end as possible, led through the thwart and secured to a convenient cleat nearby. This time, it couldn't go anywhere; they pushed it carefully vertical, then carefully lifted it into position so the base slid neatly into its seating. The rope untied, they secured the stays as Mary had seen, and stood back.

"She looks more like a sailing boat now," said Mary.

Just that simple action had given her the right proportions. She had life. Encouraged, they found the sail bag and, as it was another calm day, got the two sails out and spread them over the grass. Kept in Miss

Merryweather's house they had stayed dry and were in good condition. Comparing the fixings on the smaller sail – the jib – with what was available on the hull they soon discovered how it was fastened.

"But we're stupid," said Stephen. "We've forgotten to rig the ropes which hoist them. Look, one goes through that hole there with the pulley in it, and the other, the sail in front, must hang from that pulley there. We'll have to take the mast down again."

"Can't we just see how the big one goes and think about that afterwards?" Mary wasn't keen on struggling again with the mast just yet. She wanted to get tidy in her mind the idea of how it all went together before starting to deal with the practical details.

They did their best. They realised that the long edge of the sail must be away from the mast, so the opposite side fitted on to it by the loops of rope, each with five wooden thimbles threaded between knots on it, to act as runners as the sail was raised or lowered. They were held to the sail with small shackles. But the two would-be riggers were stuck for a long time on the sail's top and bottom. Both seemed to have laces which they assumed secured it to the two spars.

"But why one at the top and another at the bottom?" Mary asked, voicing Stephen's thoughts.

"Perhaps one of them is pulled up there somehow."

"Would that work?"

"Don't know. I suppose it must. Let's take it that it is. And the bottom must lace onto the boom. Which is which, anyway? And what are these other laces for, either side of the sail at the bottom? I can't see that they do anything."

They sat looking at the parts of boat they had spread over the grass.

"Let's compare the two wooden bits," said Mary, and pulled the gaff and the boom together. "There's a ridge worn here, just over half way along this one. Does a rope get tied round it?"

"Could be. It could be the one that pulls it up the mast. What is there on the other one?"

"This one's got a sort of round bit at the end. Like a crutch."

"Does it fit round the mast?" asked Stephen excitedly.

They dragged it over and tried it. It did.

"That's the boom," he exclaimed delightedly. "It's got to be that shape so it swings round. So the bottom of the sail laces onto that, and the top onto the other bit. Let's do it!"

They laced the sail onto the boom, using the bottom-most laces, then fixed the gaff to its head. Once again they sat back and looked at it.

"Well, I think that'll work."

"It looks right. But we need the rope up the mast and down again, one for each sail, before we hoist them."

"I know, but at least we know how the sails go on."

"How do we control the sails?

"What?"

"Well, the small one's got a rope either side so I suppose you hold each one to stop it blowing away. But what about the big one?"

"Hmm," said Stephen. "You've got a point."

And so they found the block and tackle which, after a lot of trial and error, they decided needed to be connected to the boom, near its end, and to the traveller, a block which ran on an iron bar above the tiller. The second block and tackle they stowed away as a spare.

"I can't wait to take her on the water and see how she works."

"How about getting the mast down again and threading the ropes through the pulleys?"

"Come on then."

They loosened the stays again. Stephen tried lifting out the mast but was having great difficulty in budging it when an alarmed "Oy!" came from the path. They looked round. It was Henry and Peter.

"What are you doing?" asked the former. "You can't sail until you've had lessons. I thought we'd agreed that."

"I'm only finding out how to rig her, Dad, I'm not sailing her."

"It's a bit pointless, Stephen. You've probably done it wrong and Edgar'll have to start again."

Stephen looked at his father, dismayed. He had never put him down like that before. Usually he would get nothing but encouragement in finding his own way around something. And it suddenly hurt to be treated like a child in front of Mary. And his brother.

"Dad, we've thought it all through, and this is the way she's rigged. I'm sure of it. We'll ask Edgar, and if we're wrong I'll take the blame." He said this in as even a tone as he could manage.

Peter's look of surprise was enough for him, especially when it turned to a half-smile. "I think you've met your match there, Dad," he said. "It sounds like you've just talked yourself into a bet."

Henry was still annoyed, but unlike his son he couldn't turn the feeling away. "I don't want the boat ruined before they've even sailed her."

This was too much for Mary, who could see Stephen suddenly being treated like a small boy. "It's my boat," she said hotly. "I decided we should rig her, and if it's wrong then I'll put it right. With Stephen's help." And she glared defiantly at Henry, who almost glared back at the younger two as he asked himself why he was feeling so antagonistic suddenly.

They seemed to hold the pose, so to speak, for some moments, as Henry's thought processes eased from their destructive course. He shook his head impatiently.

"I'm sorry, you two. That was unreasonable of me. I don't know what's the matter. There's so much I've got to think about, and so much we need to do to make sure we can still live on the island. Peter thinks I'm mad, and that we should sell up – as if anyone would buy it – and go and work in town or in Torquay, near him. It all sounded so reasonable that I was tempted, until I realised that I'm not alone, I can't talk just for me, and that once we sold this place, if we could, it would be the end for you… You *two*… as well."

"Dad, I'm not leaving here. It's ours. It's home. Yours and mine, and now Mary's."

"And not mine any more, Steve?" asked Peter.

"If you wanted to come back, then yes, somehow we'd make room. But you don't… Do you?" Stephen had a vision of Peter coming back and sharing his room again as they had for so many years. His subconscious mind was sending a strong message that he found Mary's presence at night to be something sweet, and calming, and somehow right in an unknown way. It was something that he had just accepted. Peter's presence had always been a matter of fact, at times a nuisance, but something you had to accept like having to wear a school cap. Then common sense took over. He would hardly sleep with his brother at his age now. His subconscious floated the idea that one day he and Mary…. He dismissed the notion as not applying to him.

"No. It's too quiet for me here, I like Life around me. And besides, if the land that's left can't support you three, it's not going to support me as well, is it?"

They stood in silence looking over the estuary. Mary realised she was once more looking at where her home used to be, shuddered, and turned away. Peter looked at her, realisation dawning. He was about to go to her but stopped himself and looked at Stephen, who was already turning to put his arm round her shoulders. They walked away.

"He's good with her, Dad."

"Hmm? Oh yes. Very good. It's surprising where he's suddenly got all this sense of responsibility from, and the ability to care. I think he's put on about two years in the last few days."

"He was always a steady chap, you know, even when he was younger. But Mum dying really steadied him even more, before his time."

"I know I can't do anything else, because I need his help on the farm, but do you think he needs more time to himself, really? It seems to me sometimes that his life is so different from other kids of his age."

"It is. Very. And for most boys I'd probably say that you weren't really being fair. But he's always loved this place, and helping to work the farm;

far more than I ever did."

"Do you think he'll choose to leave, too?"

Peter thought, then shrugged his shoulders. "He might, as he gets older, but I don't think so. He's got that obstinate streak in him that says 'Lofts' Farm, before everything.' Well, perhaps not before you, and not before Mary, now; but before most entertainments that kids usually want – that I wanted."

Henry smiled ruefully at this, remembering the late night arguments, conducted in whispers to avoid waking Stephen, who proved himself unwakeable, and the bad feeling and the bitterness of the final departure; followed by the growing, glad awareness that his younger son was the real enthusiast for their land, how comforting that had been, and how comforting – indispensable – that enthusiasm still was.

Peter's bus and train connections were delicately balanced as it was a Sunday, so he had to leave quite early. Missing the bus from Salcombe could be corrected by taxi, at a price, or by a phone call to his next door neighbour in Torquay to get a message to Dot, his girlfriend. Getting to work on time the next day would be a problem, though. If he missed the train at Kingsbridge, on the other hand, he would be stuck there overnight. "Unless," said Stephen, who had returned by that time, "you hitch a lift on a boat back down here."

"That's not very likely, is it, twit?" said his brother.

As they walked back slowly to their harbour, Peter dropped behind his father and Mary, touching Stephen's arm to delay him.

"Steve, I know it's difficult for me now to come here without annoying him. He's never really forgiven me, you know. I'm sorry if I made him a bit sour, I'm sure he's not like that all the time."

"No, he's not. And I don't think it's you, I think he's just worried about money, and the idea of opening the island up to strangers is something he doesn't like. I don't know that I do."

"Well, whatever you decide, there's one thing." He paused.

"What."

"Dad told me the full story of the storm, and what you did, and he's obviously bursting with pride for you. The funny thing is..."

This time there was no interruption within the pause.

"...so am I."

Stephen suddenly started liking his brother again.

They reached the bus terminus at Island Quay in plenty of time, and both Henry and Stephen were by this time being so friendly to Peter that he was wishing he'd agreed to stay the night. But work was calling, and his girlfriend, and he had been unsure of his welcome anyway. As the driver and conductor walked over to start their journey he turned to Stephen.

"I know you're going to anyway, but look after Mary. She's a great girl, and she deserves to have a great boy to look after her. And look after Dad for me, will you? He might not know it, but I still…" he gulped "…love him, you know."

He went quickly to sit on the upper deck where they couldn't see his face. As the bus pulled away he reappeared, looked at them and waved frantically.

"Perhaps he's not so bad after all," said Henry.

They chugged back to the island as the light failed – it was still March, after all.

"Damn," said Henry, quietly. "We've got no lights."

"It's light enough. We can see."

"Yes, Mary, but we're meant to show them, so people can see us," he explained. "If there's a big boat coming in, her look out won't notice something as small as us, even in this light, and they might run into us. Not that I think that's very likely at this time of year."

They arrived home safely: the dogs were glad to be back on dry land. They still were unused to the continuous noise of the engine so near to them.

By the time they had milked the cows and fed the other animals it was distinctly dark, and after such a full day they were all tired.

"Monday tomorrow," said Henry. "School."

"Dad! How can we?" "Henry…not yet, please!"

"I suppose I'd better go in myself to tell them what's happened. It wouldn't be fair on you two to expect you to start as if nothing had happened. They've probably got most of the news – I certainly hope so, because the alternative might be that they think you're…" He trailed off, not wanting to voice the word 'dead'. Mary did it for him.

"You don't need to be polite, Henry, I'm really quite used to the idea."

He shot her a smile. "Sorry. I didn't mean to be coy. It's just that I don't want to cause you any unnecessary grief. Yes. It could be that they've heard nothing about all this and have no way of discovering what's happened to you."

"When do you think we'll have to go back, Dad?"

"It depends when the inquest is, and the funerals." This time he was deliberately frank to see what Mary's reaction would be.

"Hmm," she said, calmly. "That's a thought."

Henry was amazed. His memory of Stephen's reaction to his mother's death had faded. At the time it was the news of the cancer that had caused him most anguish; the decline and the death were milestones on the path of the inevitable. After so much suffering he was almost glad when the death occurred, although guilty and disgusted with himself for thinking that way.

It didn't stop him missing her, and it didn't stop him loving and honouring her memory. It was in no small way that his love of her caused his fierce love of the land they owned, particularly the island, because each was a part of him.

Nor was Mary, in her turn, reacting in the way that Henry thought might be 'normal'. The blow was pressing down on her, yet with the resilience of childhood she was able to withstand its weight on an hour by hour basis. The triggers which sent the waves of tearful despair, of the undefined emotion that is bereavement, were complex. There could be talk of death, of parents, even specifically of the death of her parents. She would be sad, but could cope. Talk of one of the small, personal happenings – something as simple as how the barn door on their drowned house always squeaked in a wind – would bring down the curtains of emotion onto a suddenly darkened mind.

They unwound from the day's events in front of the living room fire, as peaceful a domestic scene as you could wish for, giving the lie to the traumas of the day. In time the chorus of yawns from around him persuaded Henry to order them upstairs, and they went with little grumbling. Stephen was beginning to find that going to bed was not just the necessity it had been all his life. There seemed to be a spark about it suddenly: not something to speak of or even to think about, but the difference between plain boiled potatoes and potatoes boiled with salt in the water. He had no idea why, or even that it was happening. It was just a part of the day that appealed to him more than previously.

Mary, the first in bed, watched his broadening back as he sat on the bed to take off his slippers. Her subconscious mind was weighing him against her brother; if she had to lose a brother, was there a proper substitute here? Yes, there was, and a bit more besides, somehow. It was interesting to find out so much new about someone she thought she knew so well. How the back, turned to her now, seemed so much more triangular than the ordinary thin boy's back she thought she knew from playing in the summer sun, or watching as her friend and his friend, her brother, had taken their marks at swimming contests at school. Why had she missed being impressed before?

He swivelled round on the bed to lie flat, and caught her looking at him.

"What's up?"

"Nothing."

"Oh. I thought I'd done something wrong."

"No."

"Good. Tired?"

"Yes. I'm going to sleep well tonight."

"So'm I. Soon. Good night."

"Good night... Stephen."

He shot her a glance as if to ask why she was suddenly using his name, but saw no untoward expression on her face. He settled his head on the pillow and closed his eyes, allowing the waves of tiredness to wash over him.

There was a rustle, and a kiss landed on his forehead.

Surprised, he looked up. Mary's face was so close he could feel her breath. He looked straight into her eyes, his eyebrows raised in surprise.

She came closer and kissed him there again.

"Thank you," she whispered. He said nothing. He didn't trust himself. Why did he feel choked up, as if it was still the night of the storm and he'd just saved her life again? Why did he want to throw his arms around her neck and bawl into her shoulders with the pain and loss of his friend and her parents ?

But the last he knew he was smiling weakly and closing his eyes again. They slept.

# 11 – Mr Merryweather

They were just leaving the next morning after the milk had cooled and was in churns, when they saw a dinghy approaching their makeshift Hard. A hail over the water announced Arthur.

"Can I come ashore?" he asked politely as they disembarked again, seeing he was coming to speak to them. They made room for him, and Mary caught the painter he threw to her.

"I've official news," he started. "They've fixed the date for the inquest and I've been sent up to tell you."

"This could decide our movements for the next day or so," Henry commented.

"Well, yes; it's on Wednesday, at 10 o'clock so you've not got a long wait. They want you all, really, but the Coroner is going to take Mary's evidence as given to him in the presence of the Police, apparently. I dare say you know more about that than I do, though."

He smiled. Henry told him about the interview of Saturday. He nodded. "That'll be it, then. And may I say, Mary, I think you're lucky. No Court appearance is pleasant, and Coroners' Courts are usually less so. But they'll need your two menfolk to speak, so wish them good luck."

To be classed with his father in that pleased Stephen greatly, except that he was still dreading the appearance.

"The other thing is that they're releasing the... er... bodies..." he flashed a glance to Mary who looked down at the ground "today, and the funerals can go ahead. I think Edgar will want to talk to you about that. And he says there's no cause to worry about cost. That'll be sorted later. And your Solicitor wants to talk to you urgently, and to Mary. Apparently it's to do with the Beales' insurance."

This was unexpected. They were all anticipating the inquest and inevitably the funerals, but nothing else. A glimmer of light started glowing at the back of Henry's mind. He wondered if their fusty but intelligent, helpful old Solicitor had found something which could help his new charge.

"And is there anything you need doing?" finished Arthur. "I see I've missed the milking, but if you want a hand with churn carrying, I'm here."

They took him up on his offer, and were almost expecting him to know their two friends on the milk lorry when it came, so small a community it seemed to be. Almost all the people they had recently met for the first time had spared them the time of day, had offered help, and seemed to know everyone else around them. As one of them put it: "It's only they incomers from Plymouth and Exeter what's uppity. All us old'ns looks after each other, see?"

As they waved the lorry off down the road Henry thought of something.

"We'll have to go to Salcombe now, to see these people and see what we need to do. But there's something else you could do for us, Arthur, in a semi-official capacity, the next time you're in Kingsbridge."

"If I can, I will, unofficially or not. Ask away."

"You could go to their school and tell them that Stephen and Mary are OK and that we'll be in contact as soon as possible, and they'll be back there soon, too."

Arthur laughed. "Do you really think they don't know? What you went through has gone back and forth across the valley – sorry – the Estuary – and has got so embellished on the way that the truth is hardly recognisable. The school will be full of it, like all the other schools around. It's a way for them to make geography more interesting. I know young Mark and Jimmy from Park Farm have given the true version of it more times than they can remember, and once the inquest is over everybody else will know it as well. But I'll certainly go in there, officially, and tell them what you told me. And if I don't get a cheer from them all for you I'll be surprised."

They went their separate ways: Arthur towards Kingsbridge and the others to Salcombe with the sailing dinghy in tow.

"Where first, dad?"

"Just wondering the same myself. I suppose we'd better find the Coroner, or his office. Maybe the Police are the best starting point. At least they'll know where to find him. Then what? Edgar? But I suppose Mr Merryweather is on the way, and it may be he has some information we should learn first. You know, in a way it's a good thing we've got so few animals to see to. I couldn't take all this time away from the farm otherwise."

That silenced them both. They each were conscious of a hole in their lives, the hole left by the animals which were being cared for by other people on their behalf.

Their docking at the main Hard was far less traumatic than that first morning. All the sightseers and Press had gone by now. After all, there was little to see from Salcombe itself except for the abutments of the ruined sea wall. All the parts that were interesting, the flooded areas, were tucked out of sight around Snapes Point, and there were precious few vantage points near the water which were easily accessible to anyone not in the know. True, the grass up at Snapes, on the top, had become very worn very quickly, with the cars that the gentlemen of the press seemed to possess in abundance, but the average inquisitive visitor had to make do with the few hire boats and the goodwill of the locals to take them round.

They found nobody at the Police Station except old, friendly Sergeant Franks. Henry was relieved not to find Inspector Moffat there; more so to hear he had returned to Kingsbridge, but less so to hear that he'd be back for the inquest.

"Which is Wednesday, as you know by now. Arthur's seen you? Yes, I thought so. It's really nothing to worry about, you each have to answer questions as they're put to you. From what's public knowledge already there's going to be nothing nasty to worry about – apart from your dreadful loss, Miss, that is; and I'm right sorry it happened to you, I'll say that. But you've got some real friends with these two, you're lucky."

Mary smiled shakily at him.

"The thing is, you need to be at the Council Office at 10 o'clock, a quarter to, preferably. Can you make that? I know you've got milking."

"Yes, we've arrangements in hand for that, so with a slightly earlier start we'll be all right, thanks."

"That's all right, then; not that I could have done anything about it 'cos you'd still have had to be there. But don't worry. I hear the Coroner's seen you and talked to Mary, so you know him. He'll keep it as informal as he can."

"Thank you," said Henry. "That's a great help, and we'll see you there too, no doubt?"

"Yes. I have to give my account of what happened the following day. There's nothing I could have done that night, obviously, so that part of it will be yours."

"Hmm. Right," said Henry. "But look; when the Coroner and that Moffat had gone, Mary told us more. It was that memory which had led to your sudden need to be alone, Mary, wasn't it? So we need to add more to what the Coroner noted down. Can you take it, or do we need to see the Coroner?"

He had to look in a book to find out what was acceptable, but finally nodded.

"I can take it, if you're happy to tell me, Miss."

So Mary, in a small voice, and very slowly, dictated what she remembered. It was a little easier than when sitting with Henry and Stephen in Mrs Whittaker's sitting room, especially as she had to speak at the speed that the Sergeant could write. After she had finished he looked at her.

"You've been through a lot, girl. Phew. I'll get this typed up and we'll talk to the Coroner about it. He'll have read it by Wednesday."

"Thanks," said Henry, holding Mary's hand again. "And about what happens next, have you heard anything? Has the Council decided what's going to happen?"

"No, I'm afraid not. I think the whole thing's too big for Salcombe on its own. It's going to be a problem for the County Council at least. In fact it may even go to Parliament. Imagine that! Little Salcombe being talked about by Winston Churchill! They'll have to search to find us on the map.

They probably can't even pronounce it properly."

Apart from Mary, who was still recovering, they all laughed at the idea. Henry realised that it didn't help them greatly, though. The longer it took to decide how and when the system was going to be rebuilt, the longer it would take to finalise any insurance payments that may be due. And they needed money, and soon. It was fixed in his mind that even if the salt water was finally banished, it would take year upon year for the land to sweeten again. Too long for their money to last out. His expression of seriousness caught the Sergeant's eye, and he looked at Henry enquiringly.

"No, it's nothing," said Henry. "More correctly, it's nothing you or the Police can help with. I'm just concerned about the uncertainty of it all. We don't know whether to look for ways of making use of the water while it's here, or wait and see if anyone's going to compensate us, or just wait. And there's the electricity to think of, too. The Board isn't going to relay the line until they know whether they've got to lay it under water or on poles. The same with the phone, but I'm not so concerned about that. We'd only just got it laid on, after all. I just wish someone, somewhere, would make a decision so that we could decide which way to go."

"Strikes me it's going to take a while if the County's involved, and if it does go to London then you're probably looking at years before a decision's made. Then there's the planning, contracting and building stages.... Well, if it's completely back to normal this side of five years I reckon it'll be a miracle."

There was a silence as they all digested this. Both Stephen and Mary's thoughts were mixed. Mary didn't want to see the ruins of her old house again, and have to endure the sight of the sullied home of so much happiness, so many memories. Stephen thought that having the water there permanently was scope for a lot of fun, for sailing, swimming, mudlarking, but he was also very aware of the farm and the need for it to continue.

Then Henry let out a low whistle. "And I said the Police couldn't help! You've set the scene for us. I can't argue with anything you've said and I think you're right, it *will* take ages to get it back to normal, and even then the land will be foul for years. We're going to have to think hard about this."

"Try talking to the Vicar, Dad. You know he was interested in it."

"I think we need a family conference, the three of us and him. And with anyone else we can think of who could give information or help. I wonder if old Merryweather would get involved for us? Hmm, that's a thought...."

He trailed off into silence.

"For what it's worth, Mr Loft, although I shouldn't voice an opinion and this isn't official, I think you're wise to start making things happen, because otherwise they won't. There's a lot of people who'd just sit down, wringing their hands and wondering who is going to help them. The answer is, of course, nobody."

"You sound as if you have a recent case in mind."

"Oh, I do. If you knew the number of people who come here complaining about trees having been blown down in their garden, or who is going to clean up their flooded cellar, or something else like that, you'd be surprised. And they really look at you old-fashioned when you say that it's not Police business and they should ask the professionals. I confess there have been one or two I've told about your plight, to let them know there's those in real trouble."

"And does that quieten them down?"

"Most certainly. They deflate like pricked balloons."

They all laughed at that. Even Mary.

From the Police Station they made their way to the Solicitor's office where they were all received by that gentleman with equal grave courtesy. After the preliminaries, Mr Merryweather paused.

"It is indeed gratifying that you were able to respond so rapidly to my invitation here, for I have several separate matters to bring to your notice. I fear this will not be a quick matter, and normally I would suggest that those who would prefer not to be detained in a dry, dusty solicitor's office should seek amusement outside. In this case, I feel that I know the character of you two by repute, and know that you would wish to be here to take in all I have to impart, and to take part in the decisions you have to make as a family."

He paused for breath. Stephen and Mary looked at each other, smiled faintly and nodded to him.

"Firstly, I have progressed as far as possible the desires for Mr Loft to adopt Miss Beale. We have hit a snag – three snags – almost immediately. Firstly the rule is that there must be a period of time allowed for the adopters to acquaint themselves with the adoptee, and vice versa. I believe we could circumvent that by the fact that you three have known each other for a considerable period."

"Ever since Mary was born," Henry put in.

"Quite. The second snag is that you, Mr Loft, are a widower. The court is extremely reluctant to allow a man on his own to adopt a girl. You understand that my opinion, or specific cases, do not count in this. Come the hearing, I can and shall, with your permission, speak up for you, as will half the population of Salcombe."

"But is that what the law says?" asked Henry.

"The law leaves it to the adoption hearing to act in the best interests of the child. Most courts – in fact almost all courts – take that not to include being adopted by a single man."

"Is there nothing we can do to sway them?"

"Very little. And all that can be done you are doing and I shall continue to act on it on your behalf."

"What have I been doing? I've not done anything."

Mr Merryweather looked at him, and his face softened visibly.

"What you have done, my friend, is to be a damn good father to this young man, a damn good friend to this young lady and her family, and a fair, steady and level-headed man in Salcombe."

This was so unlike the normal Mr Merryweather that Henry, who would have been embarrassed into silence by such a soliloquy, was shocked as well and his jaw dropped comically. His son, who knew it all to be true, said loudly "Bravo! Well said, sir!"

Mary just beamed at the solicitor, despite the bad news he had started with.

Henry cleared his throat. "I say," he said. "That was a bit fulsome, wasn't it?"

"Maybe. But it's also true. Until recently you were known only to individuals in the town. Since your name was made more public by these tragic circumstances people have been talking about you, and everybody says the same."

"Well, they're very kind. I'm sure I don't really deserve it."

"The people are always right, Mr Loft. Ask any government at election time. Now, I mentioned three snags. The third is likely, I fear, to be the most pernicious. It concerns your great aunt, Miss Beale. I'm told, by my daughter – I understand that you encountered her recently – that the lady is due to visit the area soon with the intention of claiming her right to take over responsibility for you. She sees it as her duty to offer you a home with her as she believes she is your only surviving relative. I understand she has been told about the current situation and misunderstands it, as she insists it is unsuitable. She is most insistent that Miss Beale be given over to her keeping. The unhappy part of it is that the law is on her side. A relative is seen as the best person to provide a home under these circumstances."

By this time Mary's face had grown thunderous. "I'm *not* going to live with her. I want to stay here. They can't make me go! I *won't*. I *won't*. I hate her." She looked mutinous. Mr Merryweather was taken aback by this outburst, but thought back to his own daughter's childhood. She had never had to face the extraordinary tragedies of this girl, yet at stages in her life there had been times when she had issued an outburst like this. Part of growing up, he supposed, yet in his daughter's day it would have been straight back to the nursery if she had done so.

He shook his head. Mary misunderstood him.

"What do you mean, no? It's *my* life, not hers. I won't go. If they make me they'll have to kidnap me. If they do, I'll run away. I *won't* go."

"Miss Beale, I was not denying you, nor was I trying to. Your wishes are abundantly clear and rest assured I shall tell everyone who has an interest exactly that. However, you must also do the same, and can I suggest to you most strongly that to lose your temper in that way with other people would not be in your best interests. Others see you, and hear you, and judge. If they see a little girl lose her temper they will judge her to be one, and be more ready to do what they think is best. If they see composure and hear a steady, reasoned argument they will again judge that what they see and hear is sense, and jump to your aid. By all means tell as many as possible that you have no affinity with your great aunt, that you have met her but once and didn't enjoy her company, that your school and all your friends are here, and finally, that if you are taken away by force it will be absolutely against your will and what everybody else agrees is in your best interest. Then they will listen. But talk of running away and what people see as wilful misbehaviour will really do you no service at all."

This was as near as the solicitor ever came to telling anybody off, and the fact was not lost on any of them. He waited for it to sink in, then continued.

"In fact, I believe that running away from your great aunt would be dangerous, as you would have no money with which to travel and would have to do so illegally. I could not condone that, and I am sure that in happier times your parents would not have wished it, and that Mr Loft wouldn't wish it now. Besides, if you were intercepted by the Police you would merely be returned to your great aunt."

Mary still looked mutinous. "But Mr Merryweather, how else can I get back here if I don't run away?"

"You would have to leave it to the law and to me. I would do everything I could to persuade the right people. You would have to be content with that."

She said nothing further, but the unhappy, mutinous look hung on her face.

"In this context, I must tell you that the lady has contacted me this morning to – ahh – engage my Firm to discover your whereabouts. I have told her that I am not in a position to take on the case owing to pressure of work from local people following the catastrophe. I like to believe that she understands, but in fact I don't think she did, since she snorted in a most unladylike way and I believe would have put the telephone receiver down. She wished to discover if there was another solicitor in Salcombe and I had to tell her about Mr Smith. He and I have little to do with each other apart from on business, yet I telephoned him and told him of the situation. He was noncommittal, yet I think he might take your part too, especially as he is indeed overburdened by cases at the moment."

"So you think he might turn her down as well?" asked Henry.

"There is a possibility. However, it is a fact that she needs only talk to the Police, since they are the arbiters of the law. And as we have discussed, she has superficially the greater right in law to your company." He bowed to Mary, who failed completely to respond.

"I think we have taken that subject as far as we can today. We can only now spread information around the town and fight our corner wherever we may. The next subject is linked to it, however. It is unlikely that Miss Beale knows it, since I confess to having forgotten, but many years ago I acted for her parents. I have of course researched the case."

This time Mary's ears had pricked up and she was all agog. "They came to me shortly before the birth of their son to arrange for an insurance policy to cover him in the event of the death of one of them. Naturally I complied with their wishes. Two years later they visited again to make similar arrangements for their second child whose birth was imminent. At that time I checked with them that they had each made a will to ensure their property was distributed properly, and after some persuasion each filed a simple document with me to cover matters."

This time there was silence in the room.

"I have these documents here. I have not yet opened them, since it is not my business to do so without the authority of the respective author, or the authority of a member of the family or the executor after the author's death. I take it that you would now wish me to open them?"

This was to Mary, who nodded breathlessly, her eyes by this time brimming, yet not with any sound of weeping.

Each will was read. The solicitor cut through the verbal red tape for them in a way that was as incisive as his normal speech bordered on the verbose. Essentially, all the family's property and money was to be passed to the surviving spouse or divided equally between the two children, or given to the surviving child. There was a proviso that if the recipients were still minors, all property was to be left in trust, with any income being made available to the guardian at the behest of the executor. Mr Merryweather's firm was appointed executor.

"This means that there would be some sort of income from leasing the property if you were not going to live in it, and an amount from interest accruing at the bank. There is also the matter of the insurance policies. I have not yet rediscovered the extent of the cover, but will do so now if it is your wish."

Mary nodded again. The solicitor opened another dossier.

The amount was not a fortune. It would be enough to help with the expense of board and lodging and school expenses and clothing if administered well. To Mary it sounded like a fortune, though, and she was very excited – until she remember the reason why the money was coming to her.

"Hmm, there's something here," Mr Merryweather continued. The policy they took out first, for your brother. It will also pay out on the death of either parent. Hmm, now….let's see….yes. It will only pay out if the beneficiary succeeds the insured. What that means is that if Greg had died before his parents it would not pay out. As he died afterwards, it must. But then he left no will. So his estate is shared amongst his surviving relatives. Which means you, Miss Beale, and your great aunt. Hmm…. I wonder if we can do anything about that."

"Oh, let her have the money, please; I just don't want her to have *me!*" Mary was emphatic about that, and the solicitor was pleased to see that the look of mulish obstinacy on her face had been replaced by the light of battle.

"I think we'll leave that subject for the moment, particularly as there is nothing we can actually do apart from supplying the information to all the insurance companies concerned. In this respect, however, Mr Loft, may I suggest that you correspond with your own insurers so that they have the basic information about your losses as at the moment. This will mean that they have a formal contact from you on which to start their claim file. If you prefer, of course, I will act for you. So far as Miss Beale's property is concerned, the insurance claim may well be more complex since I have no knowledge of the company her parents chose all those years ago…."

"The Abbey," Mary interrupted.

He looked at her sharply over his glasses until her eyes dropped to her lap.

"Miss Beale, you are the most mentally alive girl of – what, twelve? – that it has ever been my privilege to meet. Apart from my daughter, that is. You put me to shame. The most obvious thing to do was to ask you, yet I failed to do so. I apologise: it will not happen again. The Abbey. Naturally I shall make enquiries with them for their policy numbers. Can you remember any other insurances they may have mentioned?"

Mary shook her head, once again tongue tied.

"Then that is an excellent start. Do not expect results on that score soon. There are too many uncertainties still for an insurance company to make up its mind swiftly, but with my firm on the case and, more importantly, actively on your side, there are a number of avenues which may be explored which the average gentleman of the public may omit to consider."

Both Mary and Stephen were trying to unravel the old man's Dickensian way of speaking. Much of the knitting of his phraseology went over their heads before they had a chance to unravel the wool, yet the sense of what he was doing, how hard he was prepared to work for them because he admired them, came through strongly. Mary had forgiven him the part of his remarks about her great aunt because she could tell he would be in the forefront of the attack against the idea. Stephen was aware that they had an ally who, for all his verbosity, had a sharp brain and a thorough grasp of their problems. More, his very solidity and age spoke of an ability to cope and a well of experience from which he could draw time and time again.

"The next matter is conjectural. There is a swell of opinion in the area that the water should be allowed, nay encouraged, to stay where it is. That is that the whole valley should revert to being a large estuary *in perpetua*. There are advantages to this for the community as a whole, but considerable disadvantages for you and all those whose land extends onto the valley floor."

"We had the beginnings of a discussion about it with the Vicar," Henry broke in. "He is of the opinion that it would be better for the community as a whole. He thinks it will attract visitors in large numbers who will spend lots of money. But I don't know…"

"None of us knows. I must not publicly have an opinion, since I may well be asked to stand for one side or the other in the event of an enquiry. It would be unprofessional of me to venture an opinion. Indeed, privately, I can see advantages and disadvantages to both sides and have not the skill to weigh them each against the other. What I can and will do is to ensure that compensation for loss of use or loss of land is sought from the relevant authority or authorities. But here again, I cannot pretend that to be a short task or a simple one. We can move nowhere until the decision is made, anyway."

"Mr Merryweather, how do we go about influencing opinion? We're stuck on the island with no post, no phone and not even any electricity. We have no contact except when we come to town or someone calls on us."

"That is pertinent. I think I need to contact the Electricity Board and the phone company on your behalf and ask them what they intend to do in view of the likely delay. Once again, I have no knowledge of their time scale, but they should be aware that you rely upon electricity for farming, and that you have two young children in the house." He paused and his eyes twinkled at the subjects of his comments. "I see no need to tell them the advanced age of those children or their flexibility and ability to cope. No. Let youth work for you for a change. We should be able to get a cable relaid to you fairly quickly."

"That would be wonderful. But what we also need is some idea of how to plan for the long term. As you have said, nothing is going to happen quickly, but I have to take action quickly and I don't want to do something now which is going to leave us at a disadvantage when a decision is finally taken. I mean, do I sell off the milking herd? Do we sell some of the animals on the island? It's all so indefinite."

"I understand your predicament. Frankly I have no answers, apart from – what's the saying? – hedging your bets. If you can persuade whoever is looking after the herd to continue doing so for a long period, then do so. Similarly with the other animals. Perhaps someone could assume responsibility for them if you have inadequate grazing or facilities on the island. You need to look at each problem and decide on it, then see how your decision sits with whichever way the decision over the estuary goes. It won't be easy. As you do it, discuss the decisions with Mary. She has her head screwed on the right way. Oh, and with Stephen too." He looked over his glasses at Stephen to make sure he understood this to be teasing.

# 12 – Learning to sail

Each of them was silent after leaving the solicitor and walking round to the boatyard, each busy with thoughts about what they had heard.

It was quite surprising the number of people who bade them a good morning and asked after their welfare: even people they had never seen before. It seemed that all their friends had been spreading news of them, and their escapades had caught the imagination of the whole community. They were just about to pass Mary Whittaker's shop when she caught sight of them and rushed out to greet them. It took a long time to assure her they were all well, not cold, not hungry and not in any immediate need of a cup of tea. "But we'll come and see you when we've seen Edgar," promised Henry.

As they entered the boatyard and were seen by some of the shipwrights working on one of the fishing fleet which had been hauled up the slipway it was noticeable that one of the men made a beeline for the main shed. By the time they entered it, looking for Edgar, they saw a group of men hurriedly cover something with a large tarpaulin. It seemed so obviously for their benefit that Henry wondered what it was. Before he could ask or investigate the owner came from his office, all smiles, hand outstretched.

"Good to see you. I'm glad you could come. What I want is to talk to you, and I thought that while I do, my foreman could start talking sailing to Mary and Stephen. I heard her boat had come to light, and I hoped you'd come and see me before you tried to take off in her. Pete!"

One of the men who had been fiddling with the tarpaulin came over. "These are the two, Pete. Can you show them how to rig one of the yawls? They'll need to know about the theory of sailing too. See what you can do, will you? They're not thick, and they're not nervous, so they don't need mollycoddling."

It was all done so swiftly that they were out of the shed before they realised it. Henry was aware Edgar was trying to talk to him alone, and knew there must be a good reason for it.

"That could have been just what we were trying to avoid," he said when the two were out of earshot. "Under that tarp are three coffins, and the last thing I wanted was for Mary to see them. Look, I've had words with the Vicar, and he wanted to talk to you about arrangements for the service and so on. But well, I thought it'd be better if he just used his common sense and went ahead with whatever seemed best. I hope you don't mind, but I don't imagine you're an expert at these things, and I'm sure Mary's not, and they are her family. He's allocated a plot for them to be buried in, and I've spoken to the mason in the town. He can fall in with everything that's being done and do a memorial stone for all three. What we do need is some words to go on it, though, and that's where I thought you'd want Mary to come in."

"It sounds as if you've been very busy, Edgar, and I'm grateful to you. But I'm not sure if we can afford coffins and gravestones, or even a plot in the churchyard. It's all very expensive, you know."

"That's what I meant about the mason falling in with our plans. You see, the Vicar has been talking to a lot of people who were touched by the whole story. In any case the town needs a memorial to the land that's been lost, as well as the lives. Even if we do get the dams rebuilt, it won't be next week, and by the time it would be ready people may have forgotten the tragedy. We all want a memorial for a well loved family, and the land they farmed.

"You know he mentioned a fund? Well, it rather took off. So the cost of all that is covered. And so is that boat I lent you. It seems there's enough for that too, as well as money for others."

Henry felt astonished, initially, that there should be such feeling, but supposed it was not every day that the area suffered an inundation. On reflection he thought the others would be delighted that there should be such goodwill towards his old friends. Mary would be amazed when she discovered, he thought, but pleased; it should help her feel less alone in the world. He was also touched by the man's obvious sincerity.

"We'll let it ride until after the funerals, as usual," Edgar continued, "and then perhaps you could quietly ask Mary how she wants them remembered by everyone else, and then separately by her. That way the pain will have subsided a bit, she'll have had time to say goodbye, and the invisible line will have been drawn for her."

Henry said nothing to this, but realised what a thoughtful friend had been found for them – one of many – in their time of need. It was a shame that no higher-powered friend had come forward who could tell him when things would get back to normal.

After the pause whilst he digested all this, he looked at Edgar with a relieved smile.

"It looks as if you have it sewn up for us, Edgar. Thank you. How we're going to thank the people who donated I don't know. Do we know who they are?"

"No, and you won't, either. They all insisted it had to be done 'from the town', not from a group of individuals. So if you want to say anything, the local paper will be your only chance. You're newsworthy, so they'll print anything you say."

That set Henry's mind racing.

"D'you mean that? Anything?"

"Well, almost, I should think. Why?"

"I need to think. You see, there's all this rot about her great aunt taking Mary away because she thinks we're no good for her. She's her nearest relative, it seems, and she has the right. But Mary wants above all else to stay with us, and we want her to, as you know. In fact I want to adopt her. So I was wondering if I could somehow slip that into any chat I have with the reporters to see if I can get the public on my side."

"It's a thought. The only trouble is... well, once you tell the papers you never know how some of them react. I mean, what happens if the News of the World gets hold of it? Aren't they likely to stress the small girl, single man side of it? That would hurt you all if you saw it, and might even damage your case."

"They wouldn't do that!"

"Perhaps you don't read the gutter press. My son used to do a Sunday paper round and sometimes he'd bring back one of the really juicy ones. The trouble is, everybody likes scandal that's there for the reading. You think that if it's in the paper and available to everybody the subjects deserve all they get. And then you start reading between the lines and asking yourself 'What if it was me? What if I'd made a mistake and that was me in that photo or with those headlines above me?' And then suddenly it's not so titillating after all. It's sad, then it's intrusive, then it's disgusting, then you start blaming the newspaper for the whole thing."

Henry looked at him in astonishment at so long a speech.

"Sorry," said Edgar with a rueful smile. "It's a bit of a crusade of mine. But I mean it. And worse than you getting hurt I'd hate it to be Mary. Or Stephen"

"You're right, Edgar, I suppose. I must say I don't think that sort of press would be interested in a little story like us, but it wouldn't be fair on them to take the chance. It's a shame, though, for they could really sway people's opinions."

"I know, I know. But your best course of action to reach as many people as possible will be to get your friendly vicar on your side, get him to put it into sermons and notices and ask if he's prepared to seek support from the surrounding vicars and parishes. Between here and Kingsbridge, if you cover all those from east coast to west, there are a lot, and if you go north from there, well!"

"I'll do that. He seemed eager to help."

"I'm sure he was... hang on; they're coming back."

"Dad, I think you ought to come and look at this, too. Oh, sorry; am I interrupting?"

His father smiled. "No, Steve. We'd just finished. Yes, I'll come down."

But Stephen made no move, but looked from his father to Edgar.

"It's about the funerals, isn't it?"

The two men glanced at each other. "Yes," said Henry quietly. "It is."

"We know. They were the coffins, weren't they?" He nodded at the tarpaulin covered items.

"Yes, son," said Edgar. "They are. We wanted to keep them from Mary before she has to see them at the funeral."

Stephen's brow wrinkled. "Oh," was all he said.

Quieter now, he followed the two down to the water's edge where Mary and Pete were standing, looking at the fully rigged yawl. Pete turned and grinned.

"They got her right anyhow!" he said. "'Nother few hours and they'd have worked out the sails an' all. 'Nother week and they'd be teachin' us!"

Henry smiled back. "I'm glad they're so intelligent."

"No, choose how, they work so well together they're better together than me an' the missus. I were taught to rig a boat by my dad, and he by his, but these two have taught theirselves. Naturals, I call 'em."

Stephen was wearing a wide grin. He had forgotten about coffins.

Before he had time to protest, Henry was bundled into the boat by his two charges and Pete, and they were given their first sailing lesson. He had taken a look at her existing running rigging and judged that it was good enough for the fairly light wind of that day, but would need to be renewed for maximum reliability.

The wind was south westerly, although the town on its hill caused eddies which made its direction difficult to judge. Pete steered across Batson Creek, and as they reached the centre of the channel the wind became a little stronger. He motioned Mary to take the tiller.

"Keep her so m'dear. Steer straight. See how the wind takes the sails, pushes them to starb'd, then spills out aft? That's what pushes you along. Like this you want the sheet just so; any more out and the luff starts to flap....look....see?" He let the rope out that he was holding, and it ran through the blocks allowing the boom to swing further out under the force of the wind. The part of the sail nearest the mast started flapping slightly.

"That tells you to haul in the sheet."

"Pardon me," said Mary, "but is the sheet the rope you're holding?"

"Why yes," he said as if she'd been sailing all her life. "And that's the luff, by the mast there. And if I haul in further..." He did so. The boat slowed, and heeled over more. "... She don't like it, see, and she goes over a bit and you don't go so fast. Your job is to keep her close enough hauled to stop the luff flapping, but not too close that you make her want to capsize. 'Cos that's what she'd do in a decent wind. Not in this little breath. Here, you take her properly. Oh, hang on, we'll go about first or we'll be running aground on Snapes. Let's have the tiller. Ready about!"

The others looked at him. He caught their expressions. "Oh yes. Just mind the boom as it swings over, and you, Mary, change sides as I do. You sir, when I push the tiller over, release that rope, the one held in those jaws, and when she's settled down again pull in on the one the other side. But stay sat 'midships. Lee ho!"

It wasn't the best tack in the world. There was some little confusion as the boat swung round, but no cracked heads. Stephen and Henry between them sorted out the jib sheets which they had been introduced to just five seconds previously, and soon they were heading on a short leg straight across the creek. Pete explained, this time in words of one syllable, what he was doing, why he had to cross at that angle. He had hardly finished when they had to change course again to continue in their original direction down the creek, otherwise they would have sailed into the bank. Once safely on course he handed over to Mary, who gingerly took over both sheet and the tiller this time.

Fortunately she was used by now to steering their borrowed motor boat, so the feel of the tiller was no surprise apart from its lack of vibration. The pull on the sheet was manageable, and she couldn't resist the temptation to pull it in, then release it to see what happened.

"That's it, gal. Try her out. Get the feel of her."

So Mary steered as straight as she knew how straight up the creek, adjusting first the steering, then the sail, until she had an idea of what would happen.

"Now then. I want you to go about. Feel where the wind's coming from? No, not on your finger, on your cheek. That's it, from the port quarter. You've got to head up into it....NOT YET!"

Mary swung the dinghy back onto her course.

"When I say so, swing her up into it and past where its blowing from, then straighten up on the new course. The sail'll swing over like it did when we went about with me earlier, and you just let it go out the other side. As it swings over, you change sides. And *mind* your *head*."

Mary nodded.

"OK. Ready about....Lee ho!"

All in all it was a good effort. Mary found that there were lots of things to do at once, but she managed. Stephen took the lead from what Pete had told his father earlier and altered the jib correctly, as their tutor noticed with approval.

"Not bad. Now, you're going to have to do it again in a minute. We'll hit the mud, else. Don't forget, say 'ready about', then when we're ready it's 'lee ho'. Then turn into the wind, change sides and away on your new course. Got that? It's all yours, but do it soon."

"Ready about," called Mary's clear voice, then "Lee ho!"

"That's it," said Pete when they had settled down again. "If you can do that every time there'll be no trouble. Don't push the tiller so hard round though, if you bring her round gentler she'll be far happier. She's female, and you've always got to treat them gentle."

Henry looked at him sharply.

"Now then. You've steered further round this time, 'cos the creek bends to the south a bit. Can you feel where the wind's blowing?"

"It's coming from nearer the front of the boat."

"The bow," said Stephen reproachfully.

"Right. And see what's happening to the luff of the sail?"

Mary looked at the billowing part of the mainsail.

"It's flapping. Should I pull in the sheet?"

"Try it."

She pulled in slowly until the flapping stopped. "Is that it?" she asked.

"That's it. Any more and she won't go so fast. Any less and she'll flap again and not go so fast."

Mary was enjoying herself. If this was all there was to sailing, she wondered, why had she never done it before? This brought one of those flashes from the past which quite filled her mind. How Greg would have loved this! Wouldn't her parents have been proud that she had learnt to sail before him? And slowly the tears started to roll down her cheeks, and the boat swung slowly off course, heading for the bank.

Pete looked at her sharply. "Yere…don't take on so. Steer to port or she'll gybe." Mary looked at him, blindly. "Steer to *port*…to the left. Come on gal."

Just before the wind caught the leech of the sail in a gybe Mary recovered enough to do as she had been told. The boat settled down. Mary thrust the sheet and tiller into Pete's waiting hands and made her way forward. Stephen put his arm round her.

"You were doing so well! What went wrong?"

"I just thought how much Greg would have loved this. And he never had the chance! Oh Stephen. Why? Why him?"

She buried her face in his shoulder and wept. Pete said nothing but looked straight forward. Henry was concerned for his charge's welfare but realised his son was the best medicine for her at the moment.

Over Mary's head Stephen looked at his father and raised his eyebrows. Henry nodded back. Neither knew what the other meant in so many words, but the contact was comforting to each.

Pete was looking worried. "I've got to go about and turn back," he said. "Keep your heads down. Ready about…lee ho."

Skilfully he manoeuvred the boat round until she was heading back towards the town. Henry adjusted the jib, as before. As they continued on the long reach Mary recovered some of her composure and lifted her head from Stephen's shoulder She took in their surroundings, then looked at Henry who smiled at her gently. It was his turn to lift his eyebrows. She smiled shakily back. "Sorry," she mouthed.

He shook his head, and gave that quiet smile again. Beside her, Stephen moved his head. "All right?" he asked.

She nodded, then looked at Pete. "I'm sorry," she repeated.

"I reckon you deserve a few tears, gal. I'd be pretty het up myself if I'd been through all that. So don't worry 'bout me. Anyway, you were doing all right. We'll make a sailor out of you, but now it's your mate's turn."

Stephen needed no second invitation, and carefully made his way up to the stern. Over the next five minutes he went through the same training as Mary. Some of their manoeuvres were not strictly necessary in returning them to the boatyard, but Pete wanted to give him as much practice as he could. He fared as well, only getting flustered once when there was a sudden eddy in the wind as they sailed past the Town Creek. As they approached the yard Pete took over again and talked to them about approaching land or another boat, and suggested that until they'd had a lot of practice it'd be better to head up to the wind and drop the anchor before lowering and stowing sail, then rowing ashore.

"Is that what you're going to do?" asked Mary.

"Lor' bless you no," exclaimed Pete, and told them to keep out of the way of the boom. He headed straight for the wall before the steps. As he kept a straight course a crash seemed inevitable, but at the last moment he turned into the wind, the boom centralised, and the dinghy slid in toward the steps in the shelter the wall provided. Stephen hardly needed to fend off at all, and jumped ashore with the painter.

Ashore they thanked Pete for his patience and help, and thanked Edgar for giving him the time to teach them.

"You'll need another four or so goes before you're really safe to take her out alone, and then only in quite calm conditions," he told them. "Don't forget nobody's really got the hang of the tides yet so there's no good advice to follow."

Henry looked at him as if this didn't make sense.

"We've not had water flowing in and out past Snapes for the last two hundred year. I wasn't around then and I don't know anyone else we could ask!"

They all laughed, enlightened.

"What do we do about renewing the rigging?" asked Mary.

"Ah. Well, if you're prepared to do the work, I reckon we could help. Can you work out how to do it?"

"I'll try."

"I'll help," chipped in Stephen.

"I meant, *we'll* try."

"In that case I've got some good hemp here, just about enough for a little craft like her."

"I'm afraid we're going to have to decline that for the moment, Edgar. We've got to sort out our finances first. I'm not saying we won't be able to in a couple of days, but I've got to do my sums and talk to the bank manager before we can spend money on anything but food and petrol. Sorry, Mary. But I don't want us to go broke."

"But Dad, if we have good rigging it'll save on petrol in the boat."

"Whoa, whoa...who said anything about money? This was salvage from a boat we rescued from the rocks last year. The owner told us to keep everything 'cos he'd gone off the idea of sailing any more. So it strikes me since you've come *on* to the idea of sailing, it's a good exchange. Agreed? And if they were to sail her and the rigging failed and you got hurt, I'd never forgive myself."

"Well, if you're sure, Edgar..."

"'Course I'm sure. But look, you can tie landsmen's knots but I bet you've not done any splicing or whatnot. You'd better take some old ends, and a book, and...CHARLIE!......Charlie's old marlinspike that's so thin it's no good for anything except small stuff. Chas, I've got a good home for your old spike, If you've a mind to let it go. These two need a hand opening the lay of their new rope as they rig her."

"Ar."

In later life, if ever she needed to imagine an ancient mariner, Mary would always think of Charlie from Edgar's boatyard. A face so weathered and lined that it looked like a walnut, pierced by the lightest blue eyes she had ever seen, accentuated by a nose as red at the tip as a cherry, and a pair of lips whose corners were permanently upturned in a smile: the whole framed by snowy white hair which flowed around rather than sat on the contours of his head.

"Ar," he grunted again. "I reckon you two deserves her. Bin with me long time she 'as, gone round the world a coupler times an all. But yere's me getting fat as I get old, and she's got thin so she's not much use either. So mebbe if I use me new fat spike, I'll get thin and go back a-sailin'."

Edgar laughed. "I'm not having that, Chas. You're too much use here!"

"Don' you listen. Talk the hind leg off a donkey, that 'un. You have me old spike and good luck. But look after her, eh? She's a part of me."

Mary stretched out her hand to his, but instead of taking the old spike she held the hand, leant forward and kissed the gnarled face. "We'll look after it," she said softly. "Thank you."

They could see the old man was touched, for he said nothing but just smiled, so sadly that they wondered what was the matter.

118

"Had a gal like you," he said. "Married a townee from Exeter. Never see her now, or her young 'uns."

Mary looked at him, astonished. "How old is she?" she asked.

"'Bout forty. Her daughter's your age though."

"We'll come and see you," she said, unable to think of anything that would console the old man. "Won't we, Steve?"

"Yes. It'd be nice to." Secretly he thought they'd have so much to do that the last thing they'd want was to go and talk to an old man. But Mary had decided for them, and he thought it was only fair they should try.

As they were about to leave the yard Mary remembered the tarpaulin covered items in the corner.

"Are these the coffins? Mum's, and Dad's and Greg's?"

Edgar looked at Henry. He looked worried, but gave no other clue as to his thoughts.

"Yes," said Edgar quietly. "They are."

"I want a look, please."

He stared strangely at her for a moment. Then briskly, as if it was a boat ready for launching, he pulled away the covering. The two full size and one smaller tastefully plain coffins gleamed back at their spectators.

There was silence.

"Are they in there?" whispered Mary.

Edgar shook his head. "Not yet. We'll be taking them up to the undertakers directly."

"How are they carried?"

"There's six men to each. Two each side at the front, two in the middle and two at the back."

"Even for Greg?"

There was silence for a long time. Then in a choked voice: "Even for Greg."

"Especially for Greg," added Henry's voice, quietly.

Mary turned to him. "Can you be one of them? For Mum or Dad?"

Now it was the turn of Henry's eyes to fill, for his voice to choke up. Tears running down his face, he swept Mary into his arms as if she had been a lost lamb.

"Yes...for you, yes." They were silent, each of them, once again nursing grief, of thoughts of happier times and complete families.

"Can I?" Stephen's offer cut in on them, quiet as it was.

The two men looked at him. "If you're prepared to," said Henry, "and if Mary agrees."

"Yes."

"Can we get others from their school?" asked Edgar.

"Can we? Please?" asked Mary, grasping at the idea as if it had been her own.

Henry said nothing, not knowing what the reaction would be.

"I'll phone the school," said Edgar, glad to have something else to occupy his mind. "Come into the office."

While he phoned, Mary thought. "Will they be buried in the churchyard?" she asked at last.

"Yes," said Henry. "The town wants to honour them too. They were well liked in Salcombe, you know."

Mary's face was a study. She was proud to hear that, yet sorrowing that it should take their death for anyone to say so. She couldn't have put it in words, though, even for herself.

Henry, too, was thinking ahead. "We'll leave the marking of the graves until later, " he said, forestalling what he thought might be her next question.

"Why?" she asked.

"It'll give you time to think what best to put on them."

"But that's simple. Mum, Dad and Greg. Or, I suppose, Gregory. Although he always hates that. No: Greg."

"But how will people know who they are?"

"*I* shall."

"Yes. But although you're the major person in this, there are other people who feel their loss. Me for one, and Stephen for another. Don't you think people who only knew them as nice people will want to know more about them and why they're there? And what happens if, when you come back in fifty years time and there's a tree growing there, and long grass, and there's lots of stones saying 'Mum' and 'Dad', I wonder if you'll remember which ones are yours?"

She was silent, unconvinced. He went on in a quiet tone.

"Please, Mary, let other people in, too. We all loved them, you know."

Now it was her turn to weep once more, and she turned to Henry for support.

On the phone Edgar had managed to summon the headmistress from teaching a class, so important had her Secretary regarded the phone call and the request. "She wants to talk to you," he told Henry.

Despite his emotion Henry was glad to talk to her as it was one of the many things he felt he had needed to do. He explained their situation and that Mary would be living at their house from now on. "…I hope," he added.

"Is there some doubt then?" asked the phone.

"Her great aunt has a notion that I'm unsuitable, and that she would be a better person to take over her upbringing."

"Arrant nonsense," went the phone, "and you can tell her so from me."

"I shall, believe me. And thank you for being on our side. In fact I intend to adopt her officially, and she wants that too."

"By far the best option," said the distant voice. "If you want my presence at any hearing you must let me know. You give them my love, and tell them that the whole school cheered when they heard they were still alive, and went completely silent when we told them about her parents and brother. If you knew the little comments and questions we keep getting and overhearing here, your heart would be warmed. It's taught the staff a thing or two about children, believe me. Gone are the days of the little china dolls expected to sit in the corner and be seen but not heard. But can any of us do anything practical to help?"

"Apart from arrange a power supply and phone to the Island? Well yes, you can, and that's why Edgar originally phoned you."

"Edgar?"

"Yes. Edgar Mustchin, the owner of one of the boatyards in Salcombe. It's his phone we're using."

"Ah, that Edgar. Good. How can we help?"

"We don't know when the funeral's going to be yet, so this may not be possible, or you may not even agree to it."

"Tell me what you need."

"Mary's asked me to be one of the pall bearers, and Stephen has asked if he can be one, too. Edgar has suggested that some of Mary's friends might be asked to be bearers for Greg."

There was silence for such a long time on the phone that Henry wondered if the line had gone dead.

"Hallo? Hallo?"

"I'll phone you back," she said in a strange voice, and the line did go dead. Henry looked at Edgar in surprise.

"She cut me off."

"Well, phone her back. You're welcome."

"No, I mean she said she'd phone back, and then just put down the phone. She's always been so level headed when I've spoken to her."

"What's happening?" asked Stephen.

"She'll phone back. I don't know what's happening, yet."

They waited, and after about five minutes the phone rang.

"I'm so sorry, Mr Loft. I had this mental picture of six children carrying a seventh's coffin into church and it just made me cry. I'm so sorry to cut you off like that. Yes, I think it's a really wonderful idea: very sad, of course, and that's what made me break down, but really wonderful. I'll ask some of their friends – Greg's mainly, if I can – and get their parents' consent. If it's a school day there won't be a problem with their being available of course, but I can't speak for the weekends. I can't imagine any objections though, can you? How can I tell you when I've done all that?"

"You could use Edgar's phone, if he doesn't mind. We'll be down here most days until things get back to normal. I'll ask him."

Before he could say anything Edgar was nodding. "I'll take messages for you. You can use the phone when you need it."

"That's fine, Miss Armitage. Please phone here. Edgar has agreed to take messages for us."

"Right, I shall start work immediately. Can I do anything else?"

"Not really, I don't think, unless you know any way of persuading the adoption authorities to see sense."

"If anything occurs to me I'll certainly let you know."

Farewells over, they broke the connection.

"Well," said Edgar peaceably, "things are coming together."

Mary, now more or less recovered, nodded. So did Henry.

"I think we'd better head back to the Island," he said. "We need a bit of peace to collect our thoughts. Well, I do, and I'm pretty sure there are things we want to talk about."

"I'm sure. Don't forget, if you need anything or to use the phone, or to talk, or sailing lessons, we're all here."

"Edgar, you're so very kind. Thank you so much for all you're doing."

He shook his head and smiled. Henry led the way out of the office. As Mary and Stephen turned to go they found strong arms around their shoulders.

"Some people are worth it," whispered Edgar.

# 13 – Sailing lessons

Nothing much was said on the voyage back to the Island. Indeed, conversations would have been difficult since Henry was alone in the motor boat and Mary and Stephen in the dinghy at the end of a tow rope.

Mary had noticed that Stephen had been very quiet most of the morning except when actually doing something. She kept glancing at him to see why. He seemed normal enough, but there was something missing. She didn't like to say anything in case he was annoyed with her: she wanted no argument, or he might refuse to carry the coffin. She suddenly realised that the thought of her brother in a coffin, carried by her best friends and other friends from school, was no longer immediately upsetting. She was somehow filled with pride that he and they would want to do that for him, and for her. She felt tearful again, but it was a different kind of emotion. Buoyed up by this gratitude that her friends would react in such a way she looked, bright eyed, at Stephen again. He caught the glance, his face lit up, and the first smile she had noticed on it for an hour appeared on it. That was enough. He was all right. She returned the smile and said nothing. Nor did he.

Not until they had moored the launch and done their best with the dinghy with the promise that they'd fix running moorings for her later was the silence broken.

"I'm for a cup of tea and something to eat," said Henry. "It'll be ready in about half an hour. I need to think for a bit and I'm better left in peace for the moment if you don't mind. Can you go for a walk, and come back in half an hour? Then we must get on with the milking."

They had all been through so much that morning that they were each quite happy to be at a loose end for a while. Henry made tracks for the house, and Mary looked at Stephen.

"Do you want to be alone for a while too?"

"No. Why?"

"You've been so quiet this morning, I wondered what was wrong."

"It just feels so…wrong."

"What does."

"Everything. Not being able to nip up the lane to see Greg, and then discussing his funeral as if it was someone you hardly knew. And now I've offered to carry his…his…"

He turned away, abruptly, shoulders bowed. Mary was at a loss. She couldn't deal with this. She was the one who had lost everything, not him. Or had he? She supposed, after all, he had. But did a best friend match up to a brother? Oh well, he'd offered her a shoulder to cry on many times over the last few days. Perhaps it was her turn now. It was a bit disturbing to see one of her towers of strength in tears, though.

She walked round him to face him and just put her arms round him. It stopped him from turning away so she shouldn't see him crying. Turning away had been his first inclination. She said nothing, but just held him while he cried himself to a standstill.

And tears were running down her face too.

When he felt a bit better he put his arm around her and silently they walked. Neither could describe the route they took, but the wind in their faces and the movement of their limbs and the old, familiar sights of the island reassured their subconscious minds that not everything had changed, that spring was upon them, and they should be happier than they felt. The hints of the subconscious usually, eventually, take precedence over the demands of the immediate, and after a while their hearts lightened. Speech returned, not in great quantity, but enough for each to reassure the other that they felt better. If Mary noticed that Stephen's hand had sought hers as they walked she made no comment, but each drew comfort from the contact.

They found themselves at the farmhouse, and if Henry noticed still-reddened eyes he also noticed no lingering unhappiness. Gradually normality returned: they ate, cleared away, and went to the waiting farm jobs.

"I was going to ask each of you something earlier, when there was so little being said between you."

"Oh really? What was that, Dad?"

"I was going to ask if you were still friends."

There was a shocked silence.

"But she's *family*, Dad!"

"I know. But even in families people fall out. I didn't ask the question because I could see the answer as you walked up to the door."

"Dad, Mary and I have known each other for *years*. We know we couldn't fall out."

"And do you think the same way, Mary? But I suppose now isn't a fair time to ask you, with him sat there in front of you."

"I'd still say the same, Henry. I still like him."

"I'm glad about that. Because you're going through a lot of heartache, and that's something which puts a lot of strain on a friendship sometimes. Keep going through all this, and perhaps one day I'll see you meeting at the foot of the chancel steps."

They both looked puzzled.

"Married," he explained.

They both laughed.

They spent time in casual chat, all secretly glad to be at ease and defer any unpleasant decisions and new plans. The evening drew on, though, and it was by the light of the lanterns that Henry broached the awkward subjects.

"Stephen, I think you and I will need to go back to the Yard at some point for a bit of a practice for the funeral. Sorry, Mary, but it had to be said. What we don't want is either of us, or anybody else, making a mistake. We'll try to work it in with some sailing practice too, and why don't we go and see Miss Merryweather?"

Mary's face had dropped as he started speaking of graver matters. Now she was silent. Unseen by his father, Stephen's hand dropped to hers.

"Would you mind that, Mary? It's just that I don't want to upset you more than necessary."

"No, I want to watch what happens. That way I'll be part of it, too."

"But I suppose we need to practise. I've never carried....I've never done anything like this before. We'll probably be all over the place to start with."

"Will the coffins be full?"

"Oh no," said Henry quickly. "They'll use different ones."

"I still want to watch."

Henry looked at Stephen, but he was watching Mary, trying to read her thought processes. There was a strained silence.

"Well, if you're positive you want to be there, I'm not going to try to stop you. Others might, and if they persuade you then I shan't be sorry, but knowing you they probably won't. At least we'll get you some sailing practice out of the day, if you've a mind for it after all that."

Mary was about to speak when the two dogs simultaneously woke, growling and looking intently toward the door. They were listening for something, heads on one side, and starting to bristle. There was the faintest of noises outside, and immediately they fairly let rip with their ferocious sounding barking. There was a knock at the door.

"OK lads, OK! That's enough! Thank you!" Henry managed to quieten them to growling. "Stay!"

He went to the door and found Edgar there, to his surprise, for it was fully dark by now and a trip to an Island with no electric lights was not an easy matter, as Edgar pointed out.

"I knew it would be a bit difficult finding my way," he said, "but I wasn't expecting the amount of wildlife you've got around here. It's like nature study at school, by ear! Then it's all peaceful as you get near the house, until your burglar alarms start going." He scratched one of the burglar alarms behind the ears.

They gave him a tremendous welcome. Stephen went to put the kettle on again. While it boiled he explained the reason for the call.

"It's that headmistress of yours, Miss Armitage. She phoned just as I was leaving saying she'd asked Greg's and Stephen's classmates if any would like to volunteer. Everyone in the class put his hand up."

He paused for this to sink in. "She said she wasn't surprised. You two are a popular pair of friends. She had to whittle down the number, so she set them all an exercise to write down why they wanted to do it, the girls as well. She said that when, an hour ago, she sat down to read them she was weeping before she knew it. It seems she's learning a lot about the people in her charge."

He paused again to check their reaction. Seeing nothing but bright eyes and rapt expressions he continued. "Those who gave the best reasons were still too many, so out of them she's chosen those who are Stephen's height and who are physically strongest. 'We don't have to worry about Stephen in that respect of course,' she said."

Stephen gave a half smile in the semi-darkness.

"So we've got five capable volunteers and Stephen making the sixth, and two reserves in case of illness or lack of parental permission. The important thing is that Miss Armitage has sent messages home with them all to ask parents to give their consent and to contact her immediately by message or phone to the school. All the volunteers are sure they'll be allowed to, so she called me to ask if we can arrange a practice tomorrow once we have the final permissions."

The three looked at each other. "We've just been talking about that," said Stephen. "I've never done anything like it before, so we were going to come down to your yard tomorrow and ask if we could try."

"I know. That's because I mentioned it to Henry. So I can phone Miss Armitage first thing in the morning and find out if and when they're coming, and we can make final arrangements."

"Thanks again, Edgar, for all you're doing. That will be more than helpful. We'll get down to you as soon as we can, with dinghy in tow, so that if there's time perhaps you or Pete could shout directions at them again. It's good to keep them busy."

Edgar grinned suddenly. "I'll keep them busy. I'm not needed in the yard tomorrow, so I can grab a few hours with my friends. I'll take you all out once the school's come and gone, or before if they'll be late."

The kettle boiled. Mary went to make the tea.

"What's Mary going to be doing while you're practising?" asked Edgar when she was out of sight.

"She wants to watch. I've – we've – tried to persuade her not to but she insists."

"I think we let her. She can always walk away tomorrow and cry in private. Come the funeral itself she won't be able to. But she'll be in good company then, because everybody will be affected."

126

"I hope you're right, Edgar. I know you seem to have been right about most things up to now, but I wouldn't want her to be mentally scarred."

"She's young, she's intelligent. Most youngsters are far more resilient than we imagine – look at the London kids some of the farms round here had during the war who learnt one day that their home had been bombed and everyone in it killed. Parents, elder brothers and sisters, the lot. Gone. Give the kids a month to recover and they've bounced back to laughter. No, they get over it quicker than we do, Henry. And it's not as if she wasn't going to see them when the actual funeral takes place."

"I'm not sure I'm going to be able to bounce back," said a low voice from the shadows of the room. "And I'd be surprised if Mary does either. She's lost all she had. *Everything.* How can you really recover from that?"

The two adults had all but forgotten Stephen was in the room. Henry turned sharply to his son.

"It's hard, Steve. Devilish hard. I went through it when your mother died, don't forget, and……"

"No Dad, you didn't. Not as much. You had me, and you had the farm. You didn't lose *everything.* Mary didn't even have any clothes to change into."

There was a pause.

"He's right, Henry. And for the last few days she's been busily working, playing and occasionally crying alongside you two, not sitting around moping. She's kept herself occupied like a strong minded adult would, and we've all forgotten just what she's lost. She probably doesn't realise it herself yet, because she's got nobody else's tragedies in her memory to contrast her own against. It'll be years before she does, and then the immediate sting of grief will have more or less gone out of it."

"I think the funeral will see her crying all the way through, and she's going to need you then more than ever. And you, Steve."

"Will I be able to sit by you at the funeral?"

"I don't know. I think you should, for her sake. And for your own. You're entitled to grieve as well, you know."

"I'll have too much to do carrying the coffin to cry."

"Steve….funerals are about grief. They're the occasions in everyone's life when men cry as well as women, so you'll be joining a lot of us when your emotions get the better of you. Don't fight it. Let the tears run then. Show what you thought of them and be proud of it. Not only that, but it'll make you feel better too."

Stephen looked at his father, imagining ahead, thinking; and his eyes grew shinier as he thought, and he shook…. He jumped to his feet and rushed upstairs.

Edgar and Henry looked at each other. "Should you go to him?" asked

Edgar.

"No. I know him, and I know the feeling. He's better sorting himself out. Perhaps Mary could help, but I'm not going to suggest it in case I'm wrong."

They sat in thoughtful silence until Mary brought in the teapot, whereupon Henry went to fetch the tray of cups which he found neatly laid out, with a plate of bread and butter, jam, plates, all of which she'd been quietly assembling as they were talking. They laid the table, and all was ready as Stephen quietly rejoined them. Neither of the men said anything, to his relief. Mary looked at him, and he smiled at her a little weakly. In the gloom she couldn't see the suspicious redness of his eyes.

They chatted idly for another half an hour, when Stephen stifled a yawn.

"Bed, I think, for you two. We've got to be up and doing tomorrow."

"Dad, Edgar's our guest too. It wouldn't be polite for us to go and leave him."

"It's all right, Steve. I'm just off anyway. Like you, I've got an early start in the morning. We have to make the best of the daylight, you know. The war's been over for years, but we don't see the need to spend good money on electric light when there's real light available free." He rose. "Good night, Henry. Good night, Steve and Mary, and thank you for the tea. It was very welcome."

They gave him their goodnights, and watched the light of his torch vanish behind the trees. Back in the living room Stephen gave a snort of laughter. "I suddenly thought," he said. "What if you'd invited him upstairs to tuck me in bed like you used to with Auntie Marje when I was young? He wouldn't have known what to say! Just like she didn't that time Peter was in bed before me and she came up, and found him half naked on top of the bed! I won't ever forget her face!"

"I don't think you need worry about my asking relatives to kiss you goodnight any more, young man, let alone friends. There's something about you that says you wouldn't exactly welcome it. Mary might, though; perhaps I should have asked Edgar to tuck her into bed."

"No thank you," said Mary promptly. "Edgar's nice and kind, but I don't want anyone kissing me goodnight except Stephen – oh, and you of course." She smiled at Henry, hoping he hadn't noticed. He had, but was ignoring it. Stephen was blushing furiously.

"Good night, Dad," he said, terminating the conversation swiftly, and turned for the door. Mary half turned, thought better of it and turned back to Henry.

"Good night," she whispered as she put her arms round his neck and kissed him. He smiled as he kissed her, and ruffled her hair as she turned away again.

"Sleep well."

Upstairs she found Stephen sitting on the bed staring into space.

"What did you say that for?" he asked as she entered the room.

"Why shouldn't I?"

"It makes it all sound....soppy."

"I'm not soppy!"

"I didn't say you were. I mean, fancy telling Dad that I kiss you goodnight."

"I didn't."

"More or less, you did."

"Well you do."

"When?"

"That first night. And probably since, too."

"Well I won't any more."

"Why not?"

"Because they'll think it's soppy."

"Who will?"

"Everybody."

"But nobody's watching."

"Dad knows."

"That's different. He's not going to tell anyone."

"He might."

"What? And spread it about that we're sharing a bed?"

The logic to this was inescapable. Stephen fell silent, and started taking off his shirt.

"Stephen?"

The voice was quieter, not argumentative. He looked at her.

"Sorry. I won't say anything again. Will you kiss me goodnight later. Please?"

"All right," he said a little ungraciously.

She was getting so used to sharing the room with him now. Getting undressed was not as embarrassing as it had been. As it was she was in her underwear before she realised, and made a rush for the bathroom. He grinned to himself, knowing her thoughts, but secretly glad he could get into bed without her watching.

She returned a few minutes later, to his astonishment still just in briefs, and snatched her pyjamas from where they lay on the floor from the morning. He grinned again as she swept from the room.

Eventually they were still, and the light was out. As quietly as he could he raised himself on his elbow and leant across to plant a gentle kiss on her cheek. She turned as he lay down again, leant forward in her turn and kissed his nose.

As the launch chugged her way toward the town, towing the dinghy, they were once again silent. There was too much on their minds for conversation. They berthed at the boatyard without incident and went straight to the office where they hoped Edgar would have news.

"None at the moment," he said, "but they've not been in school long. She'll call when she's ready. Come on. Let's get you sailing."

He put them through their paces again, just as Pete had done. But instead of taking them down toward Batson, where the wind was inclined to be quirky, he headed out into the main estuary and down towards the rocks that partly blocked the channel. They had only been close to the shore here on infrequent visits, apart from their training trip with the launch. With no motor chugging away, at the mercy of the wind and weather, it seemed a very wide, exposed stretch of water, with far more of a chop to it than Batson Creek or the estuary from Salcombe to Loft Island. On the west there were no real landing places between the gardens by the ferry steps and North Sands, discounting the Yacht Club and the Marine Hotel, as the valley sides were so steep. That in itself made it the more inhospitable. In the middle of the channel, with water for a long distance either side and the black rocks guarding the mouth of the estuary like teeth, it seemed a bleak place to be for the inexperienced or the motorless. Mary and Stephen were affected by the wildness and Henry was worried in case something untoward happened. Edgar was concerned that his charges should get as much from the experience as possible by way of sailing ability, sailing experience and respect for the sea. He also wanted to do all he could to take their minds off events that might be unfolding back at the boatyard.

So he put them through their paces, covering and recovering all they had learnt with Pete. Mary and Stephen picked it up quickly, being used to learning, and were soon tacking neatly, automatically. The swirl in the water as the dinghy went about grew less and less ruffled as they got to know how she handled.

Until, that is, Henry took over. "She's not a tractor, Henry," Edgar exclaimed as the tiller went over too suddenly again, leaving a boiling in the water behind them that spoke of wasted speed.

"It's just that there's so much to think about," Henry complained, laughing at himself. "I think I'd better leave it to these two."

"Come on, Dad," said Mary. "You can't let us do something you don't know how to do yourself."

He looked at her, face softening at being called Dad by her. The dinghy headed away from the wind.

"Look out!" said Edgar. "Any more and she'll gybe!"

"Which way?" asked Henry.

"Toward the wind….quick!"

Henry made the correction with another patch of troubled water. Nothing was said.

"What's a gybe?" asked Stephen.

"Haven't you been reading that book? You know by now that you can switch the boat round so the wind blows in the other side. You've been doing it all morning. Well if you're running before the wind like we shall be when we turn, the wind's obviously aft. So it's all right so long as you steer in a straight line to keep it there. What happens if you turn a bit too far so the wind's on the same side as the sail?"

They thought for a moment.

"It could catch the edge of the sail, and blow it over." Mary came up with the answer.

"Quite right. And the stronger the wind, the more force the boom will have when it comes over. So what could happen?"

"It'd bash your head in," said Stephen tactlessly. Mary was thinking sailing, fortunately, and didn't notice. Henry looked sharply at her.

"Yes," continued Edgar. "And it might even snap the mast. So we pull the boom in before we alter course, and let it out on the other side. I'll show you in a minute, then you can practise all the way up to Salcombe again."

Under his careful directions they turned, with Stephen on the helm. He altered course until the wind was directly behind them: Stephen could feel it on the back of his neck. If it altered, or he altered course, he could feel it on one of his cheeks.

"Henry, can you pull the jib across so it fills out on the other side? That's what we call 'goose winged'," he explained as the little sail, which had been flapping uselessly in the shelter of the mainsail, filled out happily on the other side of the forestay. "There's only one other thing we need to do to get the best out of her, and that's pull up the centreboard. See how to do it, Mary?"

She obediently hauled on the rope which raised the metal plate into its casing in the middle of the boat.

Like this, with a fully aware helmsman, two sails working, and a reduced drag, they fairly shot up the estuary. It was most exhilarating. All too soon, Edgar told Stephen he had to alter course to the east to avoid Biddlehead. "Remember what I said. Haul in the sheet until the sail's flapping a little, then alter course *slightly*, and it'll go over. When it does, *keep the course*, let the sail out and she'll be OK again."

He gulped nervously, thinking about cracked heads.

"Gybing!" called Edgar.

Stephen hauled in the sheet, watching the edge of the sail. So keen was he that the boat altered course without his noticing. The next thing he knew was the boom starting to swing over. He shouted, and ducked.

"Gybe-oh!" sang out Edgar.

Stephen looked up cautiously. The boom was opposite where it had been, and the edge was flapping dangerously. Making sure he was steering a straight course, he carefully let out the sheet until the boom was once again nearly at right angles to the boat. He let out the breath which seemed to have been in his lungs for ages, and looked round. What was wrong? Oh yes.

"Dad, pull over the jib, please."

Edgar laughed. "That's right, son. Twice. Firstly look after your ship. Secondly, never let on there's anything wrong that's your fault. I see she took you a bit by surprise there. You've got to make sure you hold course, or at least she steers where you decide, not where she wants to go. It worked out all right, but only because you'd pulled in the sheet before you started. And when you do gybe, shout like I did so we all know what's happening.

"Right. Now gybe the other way when we've passed the point.

This time it went better, Stephen kept to a straight line until he was ready, then eased the tiller over. The subtle change enabled him to pull the boom over the rest of the way and to let it out to port again in a beautifully controlled way. His father followed suit with the jib, and they received a round of applause from Mary and Edgar.

"That's good," said the latter. "Now change places with Mary, and let her try."

"Er...do you think I'd better have another go?" asked Stephen, nodding ahead to the rapidly approaching sand of Mill Bay.

"Blast yes!" said Edgar. "And quick about it!"

And he was. Quick and efficient. With only a few yards to spare they gybed, then had to haul the mainsail in to reach north west to avoid the slipway that jutted out from the north of the bay. But something was wrong. Although they were sailing at a good rate through the water they were also heading sideways onto the woodwork, heeling over rather too much as they did so.

"Mary! The centreboard! Quick!" called Edgar. And Mary, remembering what he had said earlier needed no better or closer example of the centreboard's purpose in life. She let it down hastily, and immediately their boat stopped slipping sideways, righted herself, and cleared the bay.

"Whew!" said Stephen. "You have to have your wits about you when you're near the shore, don't you?"

"You certainly do. The only good thing about it is that the nearer you are to it, the shallower the water is for you when you have to abandon a ship that's damaged," Edgar said grimly. "That was really my fault, and a

132

simple error too. Just goes to show that there must only be one helmsman at a time. What he or she says, goes. Now then, Mary, you switch with Stephen, when he's ready, and we'll bring the wind aft again so you can practise."

Carefully they swapped. Mary, who had been watching what was happening to her boat, had learnt well, and as soon as she was certain they were all settled, brought the dinghy round and let out the sheet as she did so.

"Centreboard up!" she commanded, and Stephen set to with a will. "Jib out to port!" and this time it was Henry's turn.

She had very obviously learnt from the mistakes of the others, and really kept her wits about her as they dog-legged north eastwards up the Estuary. Her last gybe brought them directly in line for Batson Creek, and they reached across the channel easily. As they neared the boatyard, Edgar gave her directions on how to make the approach. "Reach past the steps, then haul her close in. Beat up to about six feet from the wall, and head up straight into the wind. She'll make it under the way she's got."

Mary looked at him despairingly. "I didn't understand. Can you say that again?"

He repeated the first sentence, then stopped as he saw the look of bewilderment return to her face.

"Oh!" he laughed. "I'll try English, shall I? Sail as you are until you're just past the steps. Haul in the mainsail then, and turn toward the wall. When you're a couple of yards away head into the wind and let her drift in. Sorry. You were sailing so well I forgot you weren't up with quick use of the normal terms yet."

She did well up to the point of heading up to the wind so as to take the wind off the sails. The flapping sail so near her unnerved her, and she steered away from the steps. As they neared the wall Edgar hung on to a chain, and ordered the lowering of the sail. Mary and Stephen gathered it in as best they could as Henry lowered the halyards. It was not an elegant manoeuvre, but had the desired effect. Edgar pulled them along the wall to the steps, with the jib trying to sweep him into the water. Henry saw what was happening and pulled it from him, then found the halyard and lowered it carefully. Edgar leapt ashore with the painter, and the others tidied the boat. He helped them stow the sails, and they trooped up the steps to the office.

There seemed to be a crowd of people in the shed. And suddenly there was a whoop, and Mary and Stephen found themselves surrounded by friends, their friends from school, whom they hadn't seen for a week. But once the initial joy of seeing them both safe and well was over, there was a sudden silence. Stephen knew why immediately, for he was as much at a loss for anything to say that would heal their pain as they were to express their feelings about Mary's family. But she was unconscious of the pause.

"We've been learning to sail. Look! That's my boat. Well, it's ours now, of course and it needs some work done on the rigging. But isn't she great? She's the best thing that's happened to me. To us."

They all peered over the quay. The little dinghy lay quiet, empty of people yet full of promise, full of adventure, full of potential fun. She also provided an immediate opportunity for them all to realise that life, for Mary, was going on. She was dealing with the greatest loss in her life in her own way. It was apparent that she wanted no solemn faces and quietness, just a continuation of the old camaraderie. They were all still a little cautious with her, though, not really knowing exactly what reactions to expect, what to say, what to avoid.

She was congratulated on the discovery but said that it was sheer chance and that she couldn't have got this far without Stephen and Henry.

"Henry?" said someone.

"Stephen's dad, Mr Loft," she explained.

"Do you call him Henry?"

"Yes, except when I forget and call him Dad."

There was no response to that.

# 14 - Rehearsal

Mary watched whilst Edgar and Miss Armitage organised Stephen and five of the other seven into pairs of equal height. It had been arranged that the coffins would be carried from the nearby Church House, where it had been agreed they could rest the night, into the church for the service. That meant a shorter, flatter journey than would have been necessary if they were to be taken up the hill all the way from the undertakers' premises. Edgar had opened them, and loaded them up with timber and stones to be about the correct weights, and when the lids were replaced the six boys were spaced evenly round the smallest one. Two of the boatyard workers lifted it so that it was at shoulder height, and each pair of boys shuffled their shoulders underneath it from left and right.

"Link each other's arms underneath," ordered Edgar, "then support the edge of the wood with the other hand."

There was a moment of confusion whilst twelve anxious hands fumbled for opposing arms, then the links were made and everyone felt much more secure. In a way the human contact helped too, and each of them realised that if this was only a rehearsal, in the actual thing it would be even more of a comfort. The right and left arms came up to the woodwork to steady it, and found brass handles there to hold.

It all felt as solid as a rock, and between the six of them not at all heavy.

"Good. Now, when you start walking you must all start on the outside foot. If you don't, you'll rock from side to side, and we don't want that. You, in the front, on the left: what's your name?"

"Will, Sir."

"You give the orders, Will, on my command. I'll be walking in front. Now, can you go from where you are up to the door? You start them, Will, I suggest by saying 'ready….go' in three syllables as if it was one, two, three. OK? When you're ready, then."

Will looked round as best he could. "No, no lad," cried Edgar. "You keep looking ahead. You know they're all there. If they weren't you'd be dropping it. You're a team, and the team is there when the leader wants them. The leader at the moment is Will. Go on, Will."

The reluctant leader cleared his throat. "rea…dy…go," he intoned, and took a step forward.

"You're meant to take the time from what he says," said Edgar when they'd sorted out the mess. "It's meant to be 'rea…dy…go'…*step*. Take your time from what he says. Think of a music lesson, where the conductor counts you in. you know, sort of '2…3…4…'"

This time they got it right, and moved nearly as one man to the door, there to receive congratulations from all concerned.

"Ok lads, that was well done. Do it like that on the day and you'll do us all proud. Now then, you need to be able to turn corners, and to turn round. You're facing the door. Will can start you off. This time he says 'turn…round…rea…dy…go'. Now, the front men have to turn left and the back men right. The middle ones have to shuffle round as best they can. Just keep hold, and go where it's obvious that you should."

Now they had the feel of it they managed well, and had soon turned 180 degrees in their own length. Another round of applause. "Last movement, boys," called Edgar. "A straight line from where you are to the door to our quay, then turn right and follow the wall round to the door to your left. Then bring it back here. Don't forget that if you turn right, the people on the right move slower. So what happens to the people on the left?"

"They move faster," someone called.

"They do indeed. We'll do this part, then you can have a rest."

Carefully they shuffled round the corners, nearly upsetting the coffin on occasions when people missed their footing. What had seemed so light a load to start with, easily managed, was starting to weigh down on them. They were glad when they had circuited the boatyard and come to a halt. Two of Edgar's staff took the ends of the coffin and laid it on the two trestles which had supported it originally. They stood away from it, rubbing their shoulders and swinging their arms about to stop the ache.

When they had rested Edgar got the same crew again, this time changing sides. He walked them up and down, round turns to the right, turns to the left and all-round turns. Then he got them to lift the coffin from its trestles, and to replace it there. "There'll always be trestles," he told them. "The only time there won't be is when we come to the graveyard and lower it into the ground. And that'll be a job for my men. You'll just put it onto the trestles nearby and walk to the graveside."

She didn't cry, or react, but Mary felt as if she'd just been hit in the stomach. That was all so final. The idea of watching as the bodies of her family were finally taken into the earth…. 'dust to dust, ashes to ashes'… She made no sound: nobody noticed: nobody came to comfort her. But tears rolled down her cheeks unbidden, all the same.

Altogether they made a good job of it. Then the sombre youngsters went outside, and like canaries being taken into the sun, as soon as they were in the open they started talking. Mary followed them more slowly, unconscious of the redness of her eyes and the stains on her cheeks. She stood on the outside of the noisy group, watching, and slowly but surely the normality of their chatter infected her and she started to laugh at some of the normal, everyday, schoolday, things that were being laughed about. Laughter is a tonic for the illness of solemnity.

Soon Stephen noticed her. More, he noticed her red-rimmed eyes and

136

the marks on her cheeks. He crossed to her and marched her round the corner of the building, out of sight of the revellers.

"I'm sorry," he said. "I was so caught up with them that I never noticed you weren't there. It was a bit um....overwhelming, wasn't it? Are you all right?"

She nodded.

"You've been crying, I know, and I'm sorry I wasn't there to...well...to be there. Are you really all right?"

"Yes. It's good to see them and hear them laughing again. I feel all right now. I was a bit – you know – in there when Edgar talked about lowering the coffins into the ground..." She deliberately said the words again, to see what effect they had on her. She felt the same kick in the stomach, but less, and no tears this time. But Stephen noticed the pause, and put his arm round her.

After a while she carefully disengaged herself. "Not in front of them, Steve."

Funny, he thought, how after all these years of calling me Stephen she's just now starting to call me by the shortened name my father uses for me. And then not all the time. Only when we're alone, and something's just between us. And why didn't she want to be seen with my arm round her? It's only to offer support.

They found their friends down at the water's edge looking enviously at the dinghy. "Can you sail her?" "How does she go?" "What's sailing like?" "Have you been out alone in her?" The questions were coming thick and fast. Stephen left the explaining to Mary, and as her quiet voice took over they, too, were hushed.

"We've not been out on our own yet 'cos we're only just learning how to sail. But Edgar's taken us down to the rocks and across to Mill Cove, and up nearly as far as Batson. He's teaching us, you know."

"But how does sailing work? How can you go the other way?"

"What?"

"The other way. You know, the way the wind isn't blowing."

"It's simple. You tack."

"What?"

"Tack. You go first with the wind on your port quarter and the sail out to starboard, then turn against the wind and sail with the sail out to port and the wind on your starboard beam."

"What?"

She did her best to explain, this time without the nautical terms. At the end of it the questioner still wasn't sure, so she gave up. They wandered back to the building, and found Henry at full steam ahead as a coffin bearer. It dampened their mood again. When Edgar was happy he asked two of the first team of boys to stand out, whilst the two spares were put through their paces. Satisfied eventually, he turned to Miss Armitage with a smile.

"If they ever want to do it for a living, let me know. The only thing we've got to do now is have lunch and then it's up to the church for a rehearsal."

Lunch! It had been a long morning: farm jobs, sailing, meeting old friends, practising undertaking... they had hardly stopped. It had never occurred to Henry to take anything with them, and now he found himself with eleven hungry mouths to feed: eight boys, one girl, Miss Armitage and himself. The headmistress had not thought to try and provide lunch either. Most of her pupils brought packed lunches to school, but in the excitement they had all been left there.

Henry had a brainwave. Miss Merryweather's café. Like one of his own dogs he rounded up his flock and they walked round the waterfront, past the Customs Quay, past the Fortescue Arms and into Fore Street. They found her café empty, with its owner sitting reading the paper. When she saw Henry in the lead her face lit up, then altered comically into astonishment as more and more boys seemed to come from nowhere. When at last she saw Miss Armitage her astonishment was complete, and she sat down heavily on a chair.

"Hallo, Miss," she gasped.

"Hallo Susan. It's good to see you again."

I've been left that school these eighteen years, thought Miss Merryweather, and she still remembers my Christian name as if it had been yesterday I left. And she doesn't seem surprised to see me.

Miss Armitage smiled at her. "I'm cheating, my dear. I tried to think of all the people I might meet in the course of our sad duty today, and as I was looking through the old address lists I came on your name, and remembered it with pleasure. I enjoyed your time at the school, and I hope you did too. You've only changed a little, you know, although you're taller than you were at fourteen. But you look happy, and that's the main thing."

"Miss Armitage... and so many people! What on earth brings you to Salcombe?"

Henry butted in to explain, and Miss Merryweather was once again speechless.

"But right now we have to feed the five thousand, and where better than to do it but here? Would you like me to help you in the kitchen whilst my extended family keeps Miss Armitage in order? Or would you like me to stay here like a good little boy?"

She looked at him for a second, then at last he was treated to that smile again, that looked like sunshine after a rainy week.

"Come and help me, if you will, please."

And whilst the boys and Mary talked amongst themselves as if nothing untoward was happening, involving their Headmistress in the chatter from time to time, the two of them worked in the kitchen. And if Miss Armitage's ears caught occasional peals of laughter from the two preparing food, she was glad, and told no one.

The afternoon turned out to be a time consuming and rather boring affair. The new Vicar and the older Undertaker each had his own views on how things should be done, and as each was being excruciatingly polite to the other, progress was not good. On more than one occasion Henry had to slip some words in, to try and break a courteously expressed deadlock, and after an hour he had had enough.

"Vicar, Edgar, I think I'd like to talk to you both, alone, please."

The antagonists looked at each other in surprise, but meekly followed him out of the church. Out of earshot he looked at them square in the eye.

"Gentlemen… look, you're both so concerned about doing it right, And being wonderfully polite to each other, that I'm sorry to say this. But we're getting nowhere fast. Now my family and I owe each of you a very great deal for what you've done for us so far, and I don't want to appear rude to you and risk making you feel that I'm an ingrate. That's not the case. But each of you trying to persuade the other to do things his own way is confusing all of us, boring the kids, and distressing Mary. All she wants to do is get it over with. I want to get her back to the Island so she and Stephen can get a good night's sleep to set them up for another difficult day tomorrow. I'm sorry but there has to be progress, and I would so much appreciate your co-operation with each other more than what's going on at the moment."

He paused, whilst the two looked at each other. "Please?"

There was a guffaw of laughter as Edgar realised what had really been happening. He had always had difficulty reconciling himself to the new man's ways, and previously had managed to persuade him that the old ways were the best. But there was no precedent for what had to happen this time, and he had now been forced to realise it. He offered his hand to the Vicar, who took it with a smile.

"We've both been treading our own paths in trying to get it all to run without a hitch along the path that we each think is best, haven't we? Trouble is, the paths have been parallel, but that's about it. Shall we try the middle way?

"Gladly," said the Vicar. "I'll try – if *we* try – to think what's best for Mary, for Henry here and for the people of the town: and if I try not to bring untried ideas in, and you try not to insist on the past, then we should come up with something that will be acceptable. It's got to be simple. The ceremony has its own solemnity without our trying to increase it. And we should be giving thanks for lives, not wallowing in ceremony, anyway.

Edgar smiled again, conscious that the ice between them had been broken for the first time in a year.

The form of the ceremony they decided was simple, basic, uncomplicated by anything but respect. Three parties of bearers would bring in the laden coffins from the nearby church house: mother first carried by Edgar's staff, followed by the son supported by his young bearers, and guarded in the rear by the father who would be borne by Henry with other well known local men. The service would follow the traditional pattern, with little out of the ordinary until the address. "You'll have to leave that to me," said the Vicar. "But I promise it won't be full of self-pity for the family or the town."

They'd all then be taken to the churchyard where temporary wooden crosses would be placed at the head of each, and the burial performed.

At the first mention of a reception afterwards Mary put her foot down.

"No. I'm not going to anything like that. They had one when my aunt died and it was horrible. All I wanted was to think about her and remember her, not talk about everything else but her."

"We've got to do something, Mary, to thank all the people who have come and supported us."

"Yes, but not then. Not for me. I'd want to sail away with Stephen and think."

"It's your day, Mary. If Stephen agrees, and if Edgar thinks you're safe with the dinghy by then, then it's up to you."

She turned to him. "What about it, Stephen? Will you do that?"

He agreed readily, glad to get out of what he thought would be a stuffy affair.

The rehearsals over, they walked back to the boatyard. As it was late, the Kingsbridge contingent had to leave straight away. Mary had a private word with Henry, who had a private word with Edgar, who looked at the weather, and the tide, and nodded. Mary said nothing, but grabbed Stephen's arm and, followed like sheep by their friends, marched him down to the quayside. She turned to face the others.

"We'll see you in a day or so, I expect," she said in her most formal tones. Then, as she remembered what they had all just been doing for her and for her family, she reverted to the real Mary. "And thanks for...oh, everything."

She turned and marched Stephen down the steps so quickly that he hardly had a chance to wave his farewells. She boarded their dinghy and hissed at him. "Help me get her underway. Henry says we can sail back to the Island."

He looked at her, suddenly comprehending, and grinned at her in his slow way. They set about raising the sails, her on the main and him on the jib. Remembering all they had learnt she carefully held the boat into the wind until all was ready. Stephen cast off and gave them a hefty push away from the slimy wall. Mary hauled in the sheet, Stephen saw to the jib sheets and they were away. A cheer rang out from the boatyard, where their friends had been watching with envy and admiration, seeing their sure movements and the ease with which they had set off. If only they knew the butterflies in Mary's stomach as she had made ready. Stephen had been worried too, but just as he was conscious of being crew he was aware that Mary was skipper, with the main responsibility. But the watchers from the boatyard sensed the exultation in the dinghy as her skipper and crew made such a neat departure.

They were very careful on that trip. Neither of them took their attention away from the sails, from the wind direction, from the boats around them, for a moment. Each checked on the other: few faults were found. There was a moment or two of fluster as they gybed from Batson Creek around Snapes toward the north and home. The turn was so gradual that they couldn't decide the right moment to bring the mainsail across and eventually the wind decided for them: but no heads were in the way and the rigging held. No damage was done. Once sailing normally again they breathed a sigh of relief.

"That was close."

"Yes. We need to improve on that."

"We've only done it a few times though."

"True. But I don't want to see the boom knock you into the water."

He'd been about to say something about it smashing her skull, but thought ahead, and didn't.

"We'd better look at the rigging when we get back."

"Yes. It's about time we used that knots book."

She had a look at the stays, and how they were held to the gunwale. That seemed simple enough: just loop after loop of thin cord, wound round and secured with turns round the loops. The sheet in her hand was different, though, as it was finished off with a whipping. Although she had seen it before she hadn't the faintest idea how to start it. She'd learn. They'd learn. The book would help, and if not there were Edgar and Charlie and Pete.

As they neared their landing point they made a fair effort at stowing the mainsail on the move. Beaching under the jib alone wasn't so easy, as it had very little pulling power, but they made it before the tide swept them past the roadway. They hauled the dinghy up as far as they could and looked at her critically.

"How about the mast and the rigging on that first?" asked Stephen. "If the main halyards were to go that would bring the boom down on us. And if the stays gave way I don't know what'd happen."

So while Mary wrestled with the hitches of the mainstays Stephen went to fetch the cordage they'd been given. By the time he returned Mary was fuming at the knots, her fingers sore.

"We've got new stuff to replace them," said Stephen. "Let's just cut them. They're wet, that's why you can't undo them."

"What's the difference," Mary snapped.

"It shrinks when it's wet."

She made no comment, but calmed down as he beat the problem into submission with the knife. They were about to unship the mast when the sound of an engine announced Henry's arrival, and after they had helped him with the moorings he helped them lift and lower the heavy mast. Then it was milking time, then time for a meal, and then it was getting dark.

"Oh damn," said Mary as they were finally finished with eating. The others looked at her.

"We've left the dinghy in bits. We won't be able to sail tomorrow."

"I'd forgotten," exclaimed Stephen. "Blast."

"I don't think you'll have much time for sailing tomorrow anyway. We're expected at the Coroner's court, if you remember. I think that's going to take the morning at least. And any free time afterwards we can spend on the rigging. It's not a five-minute job, you know."

"That's why we wanted to do it in bits," said Mary, "so we can sail the boat in between."

"Well, tomorrow afternoon will give you enough time to do a couple of your 'bits' and if the weather's good, some time for sailing afterwards."

"Did we leave anything down there, Mary?" asked Stephen?

"Don't think so. Why?"

"Just wondered, 'cos I can't remember bringing anything back here."

"It doesn't really matter, does it?" asked Henry.

"No, not unless the book's there as well. I don't remember bringing that back either."

"Well if it isn't here, you'd better go and fetch it, then, especially if the marlinespike's there too. We don't want to lose that for Charlie."

She had forgotten that, and looked enquiringly at Stephen. He nodded, and they rose as one to go out. Henry sat, content to let them correct their own mistake. The dogs, inactive now for most of the day since most of the animals that provided their work had been moved to the mainland, decided to walk with them.

The evening air was cool and fresh, a hint of spring still about it. They walked slowly, looking around for signs of anything amiss with the farm and its stock, although the dogs were experienced enough to know if anything was wrong. Once past the buildings Stephen expected to be able to walk faster, but Mary was still dragging her feet. He looked round.

"Stephen, are you worried about tomorrow?"

"No. Why should I be?"

"The inquest."

He halted. "I'd forgotten about that."

A silence.

"Well, are you?"

"I don't know," he answered slowly. "I know well enough what happened, and I can tell them that. But it depends what questions they ask, I suppose."

"But what about standing up in front of a lot of strangers? I'd die if it was me."

"Oh. I'd thought of that. It's really no worse than standing up and reading the lesson at assembly."

That hadn't occurred to her, and she let it sink in.

"But then you've got the words in front of you. You've only got to read them."

"But it's better. If the words are mine I don't have to worry about reading them."

The logic to that was shaky, but she accepted it.

# 15 - Inquest

They all rose early the next morning. Stephen hadn't slept well, felt tired and was monosyllabic: despite his assurances to Mary he had been dreading having to speak in front of a courtroom full of adult strangers. The nearer the day approached the more difficulty he had in putting the prospect out of his mind. It was a rather careless son who made mistakes with the milking, muttered curses under his breath, snapped at Mary for her one mistake, and was silent with his father. Henry was himself quiet, so he seemed not to notice. He too was dreading the experience, and was worried for Stephen, too.

At the breakfast table there was none of the usual conversation or teasing, and Mary eventually guessed why. She wondered whether to broach the subject, but instead told her menfolk that she would wash up. This stirred Henry, who buttonholed her at the sink.

"I'll do it with you, Mary. There's no need to do it alone."

"It's really all right," she said quietly so that only he could hear. "Do you and Stephen want to talk about later?"

He looked at her in surprise. "Do you think we should? He seems a bit off sorts this morning. I'd have thought he was better left alone."

"Well… I'm not sure, but I think he's worried."

"What about?"

"Having to stand and talk."

He said nothing for a moment.

"Would it surprise you to learn that I'm worried too?"

From her look he gathered that it would. "Well, I am. And if I am, Stephen almost certainly is. Perhaps you're right. A woman's intuition, eh? Thank you, Mary."

"I'll wash up."

"We'll help when we've had a chat."

She nodded. Henry went to find his son who was nowhere to be seen downstairs. So he climbed up to the bedroom. Stephen was stretched out on the bed, fully clothed, staring at the wall.

For the first time in his son's life, Henry didn't know what to say. Before, most of what his son had faced consisted of either a child's business for which a father can give pointers, or emergencies which they would deal with together as a team. Here was a problem that each of them faced, but he instinctively knew that Stephen's worries were anxieties of entering the unknown, where he would be facing senior officialdom on his own and where he would have to rely solely on his own wits to get him through the ordeal. He wondered how to approach it.

His weight on the bed made his son jump and look round. For a fleeting moment Henry thought he saw a look of fear in the boy's eyes, but a frown quickly replaced that.

"Dad, I was miles away."

"Yes, so was I, all through milking and breakfast, trying to think about how to say what I have to. And do you know, I was so engrossed in my own problems that I completely forgot that you have the same ones."

"Do I?"

"Well, don't you?"

"I don't know. I'm just not looking forward to it, that's all."

"Me neither. But we're the only ones who can tie up this bit of Salcombe's history."

"History? What d'you mean?"

"I mean that when someone comes to write about what happened in March 1954, they'll look at the records of all that went through the newspapers and the courts, and they'll read all about a father and a son who lived on an island. They'll read how the son saved the life of a girl who became his sister – or at least his closest friend, perhaps – and how he did everything he could to save the life of his best friend who was beyond help. They'll read about how he discovered the bodies of the parents, and perhaps, some fifty years on, they'll come to realise just what a special young man this was. One who wasn't scared of near-hurricane winds, or torrential rains, or the onslaught of flood water, or discomfort, or being on his own, but just dealt with each problem as it presented itself. They'll think that they must breed them strong of body and mind in Devon: and they wouldn't be wrong. With any of it.

"Who knows, they might even give some credit to the young man's father for being right once or twice!"

Stephen's mouth was open, and his eyes suspiciously bright. But he said nothing, and lay back down again, looking up at the ceiling, blinking. Henry rose to his feet.

"I'll give you a yell before we go, OK?"

Stephen nodded. He listened to the footsteps on the stairs. Him? Important? In a history book? Really? It sounded impossible. And brave? Him? Well, if his father said so, perhaps. But he didn't feel it. Not now. Actually, not then either. But if he could face what his father seemed to think was real danger and not turn aside, surely to face a crowd of people was easy? Part of him felt better, and able to look the world in the eye and have it turn aside when he said boo! loudly enough as he would to a bullying goose. He did his best to ignore the part that was telling him that he still had to talk from memory to a crowd of strangers.

The yell that he was still dreading came all too soon. Unwillingly he swung his legs off the bed and stood. He felt less certain once out of the sanctuary of his bed, but told himself not to be stupid. Think of history, and what he had done that night. That was it. Compared with that a courtroom would be comfortable! He grinned as he remembered the cold wetness, standing in the torrential rain and howling wind, listening. The grin soon changed as the night's grim findings returned to his mind. No: there was no help for it. He had to go. He'd brazen it out for the Beales, and especially for Greg. And for Mary, too, of course.

He found her downstairs, and gave her a welcoming smile, as if nothing was wrong. He received one in return, which made him feel better. At least Mary didn't have to go through it. The thought occurred to him that if he didn't put up a good show she might have to. That made him more determined, and not for the first time in his life, protective towards her.

They left the disappointed dogs on the island once more and made their journey to the milk stand. It was an incongruous sight, a man, a boy and a girl, handling heavy milk churns from a boat whilst dressed in their best clothes. For Henry had insisted they do so to show respect. He was in his hated suit, Mary was in a cut down dress of his dead wife's, and Stephen, much to his disgust, was in his short-trousered school uniform. He swore to himself that he would make Henry buy him a pair of long trousers for school after this. More and more of his friends turned up in them, and he had himself worn long-legged cord trousers or heavy duty jeans around the farm through most of this year. He felt, at the moment, like a schoolboy again, not like someone who was destined for the history books.

The milk dropped off, they chugged their way to Edgar's yard, where Henry had arranged they should start, and where they knew the boat would be safe. They enjoyed the usual warm welcome, and set off toward the Court House.

He had been fine on the boat, both between the island and the milk stand and from there to Edgar's. But as soon as they started their walk to the town centre Stephen felt his heart start to beat faster, his throat to constrict, and a sick feeling start to appear in his stomach, He looked up at his father, but could deduce no nerves or concern: he was looking straight ahead, walking with long strides, his face set… No. He couldn't be worried. He looked too normal for that. As for himself, he felt really awful, worse than he had felt when he had to wait outside the headmistress's office when he had done something really silly at school for the first time, when he was eight. The remembrance comforted him a little. 'Well,' he thought, 'actually talking can't make me feel any worse, and I'll be talking my way into the history books.'

They arrived in the centre of the town with about half an hour to spare. Henry realised that if they went to the Court House first they would only have to wait, and that would make both him and Stephen even more nervous. He wondered what to do. Miss Merryweather's café! Of course. He shepherded them both along Fore Street and they were about to go in when Stephen realised what was happening.

"Dad, can't we just walk, please? I really don't want to eat or drink anything at the moment." I don't want to sit doing nothing either, he added silently to himself.

So they walked along the narrow street, past the newsagents, past the dairy, past the gents' outfitters....

The Outfitters... Stephen checked his speed. The window display was showing off country tweed jackets, riding breeches, casual shirts, smart shirts, smart trousers....and a sign in the corner said "School Outfitters."

"Dad..."

"Hallo?"

"When this is over, can we afford a pair of long trousers for me, for school, do you think? Please?"

The silence which greeted this request made him wonder if he had asked for too much, or if he had somehow annoyed his father beyond words. He looked round to see a look of astonishment and concern on Henry's face.

"D'you know, I'm so used to seeing you go off to school in shorts these last I-don't-know-how-many years, that it never struck me that you needed anything different. Steve, I'm so sorry. You should have said something earlier. You're quite right, and what is more it'd be nice for you if we got you them now, don't you think?"

His son was speechless as Henry grasped his arm and, with Mary in tow, marched him into the shop.

The speed at which the next fifteen minutes passed left him breathless.

"Good morning... sorry, we're in rather a hurry... my son has to give evidence at the Inquest any minute now, and as he's the hero of the piece we've got to get him looking the part, and he can't in short trousers. Can you fit him out, quickly, with a pair of long ones, and send me the bill, d'you think? Loft's the name, of Loft Island."

Stephen had never realised before just how good that address sounded.

The tailor looked him up and down, slowly, in contrast to his father's impatience.

"I reckon we can, sir, young sir... Now, you're about a 26 waist, I reckon, young sir, and inside leg... well, we'd better make that about 28. I'll check, if I may, young sir..." And he mumbled his way behind the counter to pick up a measuring tape. Stephen wondered what he meant by 'inside leg'. He was a little apprehensive of what the shopkeeper had in mind. But Henry wasn't batting an eyelid, and Mary was there too. Oh well. The man was returning.

"Right now, young sir, waist first, just to be certain..." the arms searched round his waist, pushing their way in through the layers of jacket and jumper. Then round to the front again where he read off the measurement with pleasure. "Ah yes, just as I thought…26 inches. Now, young sir, can you just make sure your shorts are as high up your legs as they'll go? There, just so. Now, if you'll excuse me…" And the long metal end of the tape poked into Stephen's shorts under the leg where thigh met bottom. He gasped. Mary giggled, and was looked at sharply by Henry.

But the tailor took no notice. Holding the tape in its rather delicate place he swiftly found a place just below Stephen's sock-clad ankle which seemed to satisfy him. He took both ends away and looked at the lower one. "Hmmm… 29 inches. Taller than I thought, young sir. Now, how much growing are you planning on doing in the next two years?" He looked at Stephen with a twinkle in his eye. Now that the embarrassing moment was over Stephen was quite relieved, but still didn't know what to answer. How did he know? But the tailor didn't seem to expect a response.

"Now then sir, young sir, we can offer you an elasticated waist which, of course, grows with you. But I think that's really a bit young for you. The adult styles are a little more expensive, but we have some pairs which give a good amount of adjustment, and the shorter styles are provided with extra material in the turn-up so as to enable the length to be let out. Of course, we'll be delighted to adjust them for you as time proceeds. Now if you'll excuse me one moment, I'll bring some for you to see."

And he bustled off. Henry looked at his watch. "We'll have to hurry," he said.

Of the three pairs that were shown them, they immediately discarded the elasticated waist pair, which is what the tailor intended. Between the two remaining there was little choice, apart from one being flannel and the other worsted. Stephen thought back to school and to the class above him where everyone was in long trousers. Most of them – the boys he thought of as the strong ones – wore worsted. Most of his own form seemed to favour flannel. He cogitated, then plumped for the worsted.

"Very good, young sir. The quality is very good, although worsted is not quite so *robust* as flannel."

"I'll go with his choice," said Henry quietly.

"Very good, sir. Would young sir care to try them on?"

Stephen looked round wildly. Surely he didn't have to change in full view of everyone? But the tailor was still talking. "The changing room is this way, young sir."

Henry called after him as he walked away with the tailor. "If they fit, keep them on. We've not got much time."

Stephen could be quick when he wanted to. It took him a few moments to realise that, although his school shorts came off over his shoes, the long

148

trousers wouldn't fit back over them. But he hurriedly made corrections, and was soon looking at himself in the long mirror.

His home had few mirrors. Certainly the only one of any size was in his father's bedroom where his mother had felt a need for it. He was used to seeing himself in partial reflections as he was passing shop windows, and then largely ignored what he saw as being just him, a young schoolboy scurrying to school. At home he'd only half noticed himself in working clothes or when dressed for play. Work clothes were roomy as opposed to smart, whilst anything else was just to keep the bits covered that needed covering. He'd not recently been able to take stock of himself properly, and certainly not whilst dressed smartly.

At first he was startled. The figure that stared thoughtfully back at him from the glass looked taller, more imposing, than he thought was right. He moved back, and studied what he saw. A serious face, with healthy, lightly weathered skin, pieced by two light green-blue eyes, the birthright of the Loft family. For some reason the whole face seemed older than he remembered; surely the nose was more pronounced? But it was the rest of him that really made him pause. For what had only recently been obviously a boy had started to become, since his mother's death, taller, slimmer, slightly more angular. The new trousers, being of a more modern, slimmer cut, had made the difference, perhaps.

He pulled himself together and grinned with something approaching pleasure. Not too bad! He suddenly felt ready to face the world, and stepped with bounce and confidence from the changing room.

"How do they fit, young sir? Let me see… Ah, *yes*. Sir is lucky to have such a … er… *normally proportioned* figure. They seem admirable. Are they comfortable?"

Stephen hadn't really considered this. They weren't digging in to him anywhere, so he assumed they must be. To cover his confusion he said: "Oh, er yes, thank you sir, very comfortable. Very good."

By this time they were walking toward Henry and Mary. Stephen thought they would say something about how much older he looked, but both were used to seeing him in long trousers and needed no large mirror to do so. They saw he looked smart, and the trousers seemed to fit well, and he looked very happy for the first time in the day, so that was enough.

"OK Steve? They look good on you," was all his father said. Mary just beamed at him. Oh well. Perhaps it was as well they made no fuss. He still felt good, though.

"If that is acceptable to sir…?"

"Oh yes, quite, thank you. Look we really have to rush now. Can you give me the bill, and I'll sign it, and you can send it to me or I'll return after the Inquest and collect it."

"Very well, sir. If you could return later to sign it that would be most acceptable. Er, there is one thing…"

Henry looked at him impatiently.

"If you'll excuse my saying so, if young sir sits down at the moment there might be a little discomfort… er… if I may?" And to Stephen's surprise the man whipped a pair of scissors from his top pocket and knelt behind him. He felt a hand enter his hip pocket, and his eyebrows went up in shock. There was some fumbling, then the tailor rose to his feet, a card label in his hand with threads dangling from it. "I felt it wise to remove this before you left, for fear it may… er… cause you some embarrassment."

Stephen, still red from the man's fumbling behind him, grinned ruefully. "Thanks," he managed.

"My pleasure, young sir, madam, sir, and thank you so much for your custom; I'm obliged to you and… er… good luck."

He bowed them out of the shop. Stephen was still self-conscious as he came into the public gaze once again, but as nobody passing spared his trousers a second glance he assumed all was well, that the trousers looked all right, and there were no more labels about his person. Strangely he was now more at rest than he had been, although aware that the Inquest was only five minutes away.

"We must hurry," urged Henry, and the three almost broke into a trot until the steep hill up to the offices slowed them. At the top they met with Mr Merryweather, and the look of relief on his face as they appeared was a picture. Swiftly, for him, he took them inside, stressed that they should answer only the questions put to them, that they should call the Coroner 'sir', that they should relax, that they weren't on trial so there was nothing at all to fear, and that if they couldn't remember something they were not to guess.

"Apart from that, just do as you are asked, be your normal selves, and remember that, although an Inquest is a function of the law it is somewhat less formal than a criminal case. Particularly, this one seeks to record what happened, not to apportion blame. The facts, the basic facts, are known."

He ushered them in to the impressive courtroom and showed them to seats near the front. There were other people sitting there already, and Stephen wondered who they were. He was about to ask the solicitor when a sharp voice called out.

"All rise!"

They did, and he was relieved to see the friendly Coroner who had spoken for so long to Mary. The first job was to swear in the jury, and Stephen was so interested a spectator that he forgot his nerves until, at last, the Coroner started his preamble. He wondered how long it would be until he had to stand up and speak, and what sort of questions he would be asked.

150

Once the introduction was over, with, for the first time, the cold mention of the death of his best friend and Greg's parents, he glanced at Mary. She was looking down at her hands, her face expressionless. The Coroner was starting again.

"Members of the Jury, this is a singular occurrence, not only because of the supposed causes of these deaths, but because, woven into the story are the experiences of two children. One was nearly a victim herself, and the other was the boy who, if you decide his testimony to be the truth, saved her life. Because the former is only just twelve years of age I have taken it upon myself to speak to her in front of friendly witnesses and a representative of the Police, and will put her story to you myself in preference to putting her through the ordeal of having to face questions on the witness stand. The latter is a boy of thirteen years, and to avoid increasing his anxiety I would propose to hear of his experiences first. Although this means that the course of events will be heard out of order, I am sure you will have no difficulty in identifying where exactly his experiences fit into the scheme of things." He bowed to the jury. They remained impassive.

"Call the first witness."

"Call Stephen Henry Loft," said a voice.

Stephen's skin tingled, and he felt his limbs go numb and his mind empty. He stood, feeling ungainly and awkward; suddenly older than his years, yet unable to rise to meet the requirements of such an age. Bereft of the knowledge of where to go he looked wildly at the front of the courtroom. A voice spoke by his right ear, and he jumped.

"Follow me, please," and then, once out of everyone else's earshot: "... and don't *worry*, son. I have to do this every day. There's nothing to worry about. We're all on your side."

He followed the usher to the front of the court, to an enclosed box at the top of two steps. Once there the usher turned to him and said very quietly: "Watch me; ignore everyone else for a minute, and speak up." Then louder: "Take the Bible in your left hand and raise your right. Repeat after me: 'I, Stephen Henry Loft...'"

This was old ground to Stephen. He loved radio plays, and had heard many courtroom scenes being staged. He had never dreamt of being in one.

"... so Help me, God," he finished, his voice now clear, full of the confidence of having known the first part of what was required of him. The usher winked at him and grinned, and sat down in front of the witness box facing the Coroner, who spoke directly to him for the first time.

"Are you Stephen Henry Loft, of Loft Island, Salcombe, in the County of Devonshire?"

"Yes, sir."

"Good, Stephen. Now we can get down to business. You will have been told that neither you nor anyone else is on trial here, so you have nothing to fear from me or anyone else in this Inquest. All we have to do is to present to the Jury the facts of what happened on the night in question, what led up to them, and what happened afterwards. The Jury then has to decide the technical cause of death, and that's it. So please, think of us as friends, if you can, people who have a job to do with which you can help, and we shall all be very happy. You included, I hope.

"Please will you tell the Jury where you were during the day of Thursday March 26th, 1954."

Stephen thought. "At school during the day, sir."

"And when did you return home?"

"At 4.15, when the bus leaves."

"You returned on the bus, did you?"

"Yes, sir: as far as Blanksmill, then we were taken home in Dad's truck."

"So that is normal?"

"No, normally we cycle from Blanksmill."

"You were not expecting to do so that day?"

"We were. Our cycles were at the back of the village shop as usual, but the bus was late because of the weather and Dad had already been at the shop to take us and them back home."

"And who are the 'we' that you are referring to?"

"Mary, Greg and me, sir."

"Is that Mary and Greg Beale?"

"Yes, sir."

"So you are in the truck by this time. Can you describe the journey, please?"

"Well, it was raining hard, and the water was flooding everything. We saw the ford was nearly up to the top of the bridge arch, and when we got out onto the valley floor it was nearly at the top of the riverbanks. I think it was as we were dropping off Mary and Greg at their house that we saw it come over the top in one place and start to spill over the fields. Then we – Dad and me – went home."

"So at that time although there was considerable flooding, there was no obvious danger so far as you could see?"

"No, sir. If there had been we would have taken all the Beales to our house, just as we'd said we would do if it got really bad."

"So you had offered them emergency accommodation, had you?"

"Yes sir. We were their friends…" He swallowed hard as a rush of grief overtook him. It passed, under the pressure of the event, and he shook his head to clear it.

The coroner's voice returned, now gentler, quieter. "I'm sorry, Stephen. It's a desperately sad thing, but we have to know exactly what happened. Are you all right to continue?"

"Yes sir." The moment had passed: his mind returned to the matter in hand.

"So if there had been any danger to them, what would you have done?"

"What my father asked me to do."

"And what would that have been?"

"I don't know, sir. But we took their pigs and chickens back with us to look after, and later Dad went back to get furniture and stuff, so I should think he'd have asked me to help with that."

"Quite so. What I'm trying to establish, Stephen, was that had there been an obvious and immediate danger to life, there was a means of escape open to them at that point."

"Yes, sir: we'd have rushed them back to our farm, with as much of their property as we could."

"Like the good neighbours that you undoubtedly were. Quite. But as it was, you and your father returned home with some of their livestock. Where was the rest?"

"I think Mr Beale had taken it to another farm nearby – yes, to Symes' farm where some of ours are being kept."

"He had already arranged this?"

"Yes sir. Like us he was worried that the heavier animals would get bogged down if the low fields got flooded."

"So we have the majority of their livestock already safe, the smaller animals now on your farm, and the humans with a ready escape route if anything untoward happened. So can you now describe what happened when you arrived home, please?"

Stephen thought back to that dismal evening, to the farm work and to the sanctuary of their warm, dry home. He slowly told of the growing alarm he'd felt after listening to the radio broadcast, and told how Henry had immediately taken the truck to get the Beales' furniture and tell them about the danger if they didn't already know. He told them, hesitating as he remembered the little details, trying to get them into the right order, omitting nothing. For now he was remembering for himself, not for the jury or the Coroner or for the history books, but for himself. He was reliving that night as if doing so would make it turn out differently, or at least take some of the horror away from his memory. As he told of the shock of the second radio broadcast, giving the warning to the area, he faltered, and swallowed hard.

"Stephen, I'm going to stop you there, just for a moment. And really just to let you draw breath and so I can tell you that if you need a break from talking, you only have to ask. And to say that I wish all witnesses I have to hear had as good and retentive memory as you. I think I was right to ask you to give your account first: you're setting the scene better than anyone else could. Would you like a drink of water?"

"Thank you, sir, I would."

The Coroner nodded to the usher, who scurried off, to reappear after a few moments with a jug of water and a glass. He poured it out for Stephen, who took it gratefully and drank deeply, suddenly feeling thirsty and tired. The drink revived him. He set the glass down and looked again at the Coroner.

"You were telling us about the public bulletin on the radio, Stephen. Can I ask if you remember what time that was?"

Stephen thought. Something told him he should know, but it took him a few seconds to realise the obvious. "It was after the evening news, sir, and there was a rock band playing. I should think it was about half past nine, or a quarter to ten."

"Very good. So you heard this, and then what did you do?"

He continued with the unfolding of his small actions to try and prepare for visitors, and then found himself at a loss when trying to describe the noise he had heard. "It was a sort of rumble, sir, but deep, as if it came from…um….the ground. It scared me a bit. But I knew Dad would be back soon, so I started to make the tea."

"And about what time was this?"

"About five minutes after the bulletin, sir."

"I see. And then what happened?"

"I'd done everything I could think of to prepare by this time, and I was getting a bit worried about Dad. So I thought if I left everything safe I could go and see if there was any sign of him." He described how he had gone to put on his still-wet waterproofs, and if the Coroner noticed him shiver as he spoke of them he made no comment.

"Once I was outside it was difficult to stand. The wind seemed to be blowing hard around the buildings, but it was only when I was away from the trees it really got bad. It was blowing me along, though." He gulped, realising he was starting to speak very fast. He made himself talk slower. "When I got to where I could see up the valley, there were no lights on."

He paused, thinking there should be a reaction to the comment. None came.

"I mean, I should have been able to see the lights in Beales' farmhouse. But there was nothing there. It was pitch black. Then I heard two things, the sound of water rushing and things breaking under its weight, and the noise of our truck coming back."

This time the relief in his voice was tangible. The Coroner looked at him

154

and interrupted. "Hold it there a moment, please Stephen. Let our recorder catch up with you. Have another glass of water."

He obeyed. When all was ready again he described how he had told his father about the lights, and in a hushed voice described the shock and the fear of what it had meant to them, and the fear as the water threatened to engulf them too. He was going to add that he had never seen his father in tears before, but decided against it. This time there was no sound to fill the pause he left.

"We just stood there, for a time, wondering if there was any hope…" He suddenly remembered Mary and turned to look at her. She was staring straight ahead, face white, bottom lip held in her teeth. His father's arm was around her. He caught his father's eye and looked meaningfully toward her. Henry made to escort her from the room, but she shook herself and looked at him, shaking her head. Seeing this, Stephen didn't know what to do. What he had to say next was bound to cause Mary grief.

"I heard a noise," he said simply. "Dad heard it too, the second time. We went down to the water and searched a bit, and there was Mary. Dad took her back to the house while I looked for Greg and Mr and Mrs Beale."

"One moment. Didn't you want to go back with Mary to the house to get dry?" It was obvious he didn't approve of a thirteen year old being left behind to look for dead bodies.

"Mary was too heavy for me to carry. And someone had to carry on looking for them. They might have been needing help."

The Coroner just nodded.

"I went on searching around, and then I suddenly found Mr and Mrs Beale. Their heads… er… they were obviously dead, so I had to leave them. A bit further round I came across Greg. He was still alive. But I found he wasn't breathing."

There was another silence, and this time Stephen felt his heartbeat race as a vision of his friend's dying face swam across his mind. The Coroner waited patiently, knowing that at this point he must neither prompt nor protect. His witness focussed on him again. "He died in my arms."

"How did you know that, Stephen?" the voice was so gentle that he responded immediately.

"As I was doing the Holger Neilson on him…"

"Sorry, what is that?"

"It's artificial respiration, where you…"

"Ah yes, I know what you mean now. Sorry, please go on."

"I'd found him lying on his front, but he wasn't breathing, so I knew I'd got to try and make him start again. So I did this Holger Neilson on him like we'd been taught in school. Dad came back and I told him about the others, and he went to check while I carried on. While he was away for those few minutes Greg made a noise, so I thought he was all right. I turned him over and his eyes were open"

He couldn't think of the moment without remembering the exact details of the last look his friend gave him. He couldn't put it into words, could find nothing to tell of the look on the face of a child who knew he had only seconds to live.

There was a longer pause. Then, almost under his breath he said:

"He said to me: 'Stephen, look after them for me.' Then he stopped breathing again, but his eyes stayed open."

This time there was no doubt about it. The tears were coursing down his face. He clung onto the edge of the witness box as if on a ship in a heavy sea and stared at the floor. The silence in court room was absolute.

A full minute passed. In the silence he felt his grief well up within him, and subside because he knew it must. He was in no hurry to continue. This was his moment, no one else's. If he said nothing, nothing would be said. He sensed it, and it was true.

When he was good and ready his red-rimmed but determined eyes looked straight at the Coroner, who looked back at him gravely. The man raised his eyebrows and dipped his head, asking mutely if he was able to continue. Stephen nodded wordlessly and cleared his throat. Tension in the room released as he did so.

The voice when he continued started off very shakily, but grew in strength as composure returned.

"It was then that I noticed that there was blood coming from his stomach somewhere. He must have been bleeding for some time. But I never saw it before then, I know." A thought hit him for the first time. "Do you think if I'd found that first, he would have survived?" The voice rose in panic at the thought. Could he actually have been responsible for Greg's death, instead of nearly saving his life?

"Stephen…think. If you had found and dealt with that, he would have died anyway because he wasn't breathing. You did right. And maybe when we get to the medical evidence you will find out more about it. But now, please could you tell me what happened next?"

He was a little pacified by this, but not completely convinced. His voice still had a worried edge to it as he went on.

"Soon after, Dad came back and I told him what had happened. We decided the best thing would be to go back to the house and look after Mary. She was alive and unharmed, after all. Dad would go back and cover the bodies up. So we did. Mary was asleep, so we put her in a bed, and I nearly collapsed afterwards. I don't remember anything else happening until the next morning."

He stopped there, wondering how to continue. Surely other people would tell the story from now on.

"Very good, Stephen, and thank you. One last question: are you sure that Greg's words were exactly as you describe? That he said, 'Stephen, look after them for me?' If they are not the exact words you need not worry: you have given evidence extremely well under difficult circumstances. To try to recall so much accurately is not easy. But if you are unsure of what he said, please say so: on the other hand if you are sure he said something different which you now remember you must say now what it was."

Stephen didn't pause. "No, sir, he said my name, and then said 'look after them for me.'"

"Thank you. I will say again that you have done well. And not just to stand there and tell us what happened but to have taken such an active part in the rescue operations of that night. I conduct these unhappy affairs in big cities, and very occasionally I have had to hear evidence from people of your age or a little older. Never before have I come across someone so positive and articulate as you. Well done. You may stand down."

The usher stirred and came round to open the door. As in a dream Stephen followed him through the murmuring people back to the seat next to his father.

Immediately he felt an arm round his shoulders, an arm that was hugging him so tightly it hurt. Neither its owner nor he said anything. Neither was capable of speech.

# 16 –Inquest continued (1)

The Coroner next called for an official from the Water Board, much to everybody's surprise. It transpired that they were responsible for the two dams which had burst. There was an angry rumble of conversation when this was heard, and the Clerk of the Court had to call for silence.

Water levels had been monitored over the period of heavy rain, but it had not been until the Thursday night that the danger became acute. The streams and rivers feeding the reservoirs had increased their flow dramatically during the day, and towards evening it started to become obvious that there was going to be no respite. Even had it stopped raining then, the water on the hills would have kept feeding the streams for at least two more days. On the other hand, all the outlets for the water had been opened, but water was still entering the reservoirs faster than it could escape.

Neither of the two supervisors, who were also called as witnesses, knew of any problem with the structural strength of the retaining walls. The official had never been told of any incipient problem. The local men seemed to think that any faults would have been told to them by the officials at the Board: the Board's representative was just as convinced that any problems should have been discovered by each reservoir's supervisor. Needless to say, nothing at all was done. It was only in the twenty-four hours before the disaster that one of the local men noticed 'undue movement' in one of the immense blocks halfway down the dam's retaining wall, and called in his supervisor as a matter of urgency. This started the train of events which led to a close examination of the structures, and more and more senior people were called in. It was not until late on the Thursday evening that the most senior engineers decided there was nothing to be done except evacuate the area in danger.

If the Beales had been indoors with the wireless on instead of worrying about saving their stock from rain-caused floods, they would still be alive. If Henry had insisted that they leave the furniture and just escape with him, they would still be alive. If…

All these thoughts and more were going through Henry's mind as he listened. Being a realist, he was convinced that if he had heard the wireless warning he would have done more to insist that they must all come with him immediately. But then, the Beales, although great friends and neighbours, had an obstinate streak, and he was far from convinced they would have attached as much urgency to the message – or his persuasion – as he would. If he had waited for more information over the airwaves… but then it would have still been too late and he would have been washed away as well. Leaving both Stephen and Mary… He shuddered. Stephen was aware of him and looked anxiously up at him.

At the end of the Water Board officials' evidence both Henry and Stephen thought there would be some comment from the Coroner, but none came. Stephen wanted to shout at him for allowing such crass stupidity to go unchecked, but naturally said nothing. There were rumbles of disgruntled conversation from the public gallery, though, and once again the Clerk had to step in.

"Call Henry Herbert Loft."

Although he had been expecting it, Henry gave a start as his name was called. He rose and all but tripped over Stephen's legs as he struggled to be ushered down to the witness box. Stephen whispered 'good luck!' to him as he passed: he was, after all, an old hand at the game now. He looked across to Mary whose face was still expressionless, and slipped into the seat next to her where his father had been sitting. Not for the first time his hand sought hers and held it. She looked sharply at him, and managed a shaky smile.

As Stephen had been before him, Henry was sworn in and was first asked to give his account of the evening. It was all old news to Mary and Stephen by now, and differed from Stephen's account only where Henry had made his journeys to the Blanksmill post office to collect his son and their friends, and later to go to Beales' Farm to persuade them to evacuate. He gave an account of the rising water level that was a little more detailed than Stephen's but just as accurate, and spoke of his great concern when he had heard the first news item.

"It sounded dangerous enough to start getting their things together, and for them to prepare to come over to us," he continued. "I can't help feeling that if it had been worded more strongly or if the official warning had been given before the news instead of ages afterwards, I'd have been able to persuade the Beales that they had to come immediately and collect their possessions later. But as it was all I knew was there was a possibility of danger later, and that nobody had used the word 'urgent' anywhere. But as it was the water level was rising fast with the water coming over the tops of the banks, and I was desperate to drop off their furniture and carpets and bedding, and get back to them. There was certainly enough time for that, even with the water levels.

"So I set off for the Island as fast as the truck would go without getting swamped, and the first thing I knew about the dams was when I saw Stephen at the top of the hill..."

"I must interrupt, Mr Loft. Which hill?"

"The hill up from the low levels onto the island, sir."

"Ah yes. So what happened there?"

"I stopped and told him to help me get the trailer unhitched from the truck so I could go back in a hurry to get them. I don't know what it was, but as I was driving I had had this feeling that something was about to happen – something that was going to make it essential I got back there as soon as I possibly could. But when I got down from the truck I could hear a… a noise…"

In his turn he too stopped, his throat constricted, as the full horror of that moment hit him once again. He had been so busy since that he had never really paused to think how close to death he had been himself.

Stephen watched him, agonised that his father, his strong willed, strong minded father, could be taken to the edge of tears by the events, and once more felt the secure world slip beneath him as he saw and shared in the man's grief. He wished he was somewhere else, or at least with Henry so he could comfort him by his presence. By his side Mary gave a whimper and pulled her hand away. In his emotion he had been squeezing it hard….too hard.

Henry recovered. In a rather tight voice he continued. Stephen released Mary's hand and said 'sorry' to her under his breath.

"We looked out over the north of the estuary. A wall of water was coming straight for the island. We could do nothing. It seemed touch and go whether it would get to us. The first surge was carrying tree trunks, railway sleepers, all sorts and sizes of pieces of wood. If it had been another six foot higher we'd have gone with it too. If I had returned ten seconds later I'd have gone with it."

He stopped again, bringing his emotions under control. The silence was again absolute. Both Stephen and Mary were staring straight ahead, imagining the unimaginable. What if… ? But he was speaking again.

"When the first surge was done we looked out toward the Beales' farm. I knew that it couldn't survive a hit like that, and of course there was nothing there to see. But Steve and I just looked and looked for ages, hoping that something would show. And we were about to turn away when Stephen stopped me when he heard a noise. We searched, and the rest you've heard from him."

"We have indeed, Mr Loft, and you have given a very succinct account. But I do need to hear from your own mouth the events of the next half an hour or so. Please take your time, but if you would prefer a break now please say so."

"No sir, I'll continue, thank you." Henry wanted to get this over with as quickly as possible. "We searched for the cause of the sound and found Mary, alive by some miracle, but soaked to the skin."

He paused as the door to the Court opened and someone swept noisily in, heels clacking on the stone floor. Henry stood looking at the Coroner: everyone else craned their heads round to look at the newcomer.

160

An elderly woman stood there, scanning the faces before her. She made no attempt to sit, and the pause in the proceedings grew longer.

"Madam! Will you please be seated so that we may continue?" The Coroner was genuinely astounded at the interruption.

"I'm searching for my great-niece, whom I understand may be here."

"Madam! This is a court of law. You will be seated *now*, or I shall have you ejected from the court.

Stephen was aware that Mary's hand had sought and found his. "It's *her*!" she whispered in an agonised tone. He suddenly understood. This was none other than the relative who was threatening to take Mary away. He looked for her again but, cowed by the Coroner's tone and words she had moved into the public area and was hidden amongst the faces there.

"Please proceed, Mr Loft. I apologise for the interruption and hope you have not been too much put off your stroke. You were saying that you had found Mary Beale, alive."

"Yes, alive, but wet through. So much against my better judgement I had to ask Stephen to continue a search for the rest of the family."

"Why against your better judgement?"

"Because I realised even then that they might not be as lucky as Mary. Because I had no idea what other horrors might have been washed down by the flood. I knew that Stephen couldn't carry Mary to the house on his own, but I also knew that, if there was anyone injured, they had to be found quickly."

"I understand. A dilemma indeed. Please continue."

"I carried Mary back to the house and told her to take off her wet things and dry off. Then, as she could stand and had recovered a bit, asked her to make some tea for us all when she felt up to it. I put her in a chair in front of the fire and rushed back to Steve.

"When I got there he was doing resuscitation on Greg. He said he'd found the parents, dead, but I had to make sure. I knew that he knew what he was doing, and I'd probably break the boy's ribs if I took over, so he carried on while I went to look at them."

He paused again, then continued quietly.

"When I saw them, I could see what he meant. There is no way anybody could survive injuries like those. Death must have been instantaneous."

Another long, silence, as if in requiem for the family. Stephen saw that tears were coursing silently down Mary's face, and his arm encircled her shoulder, drawing her to him. She buried her face in his shoulder, silently sobbing.

"So I rushed back to Steve and Greg. Steve was just kneeling at his side, and he told me what he told the court earlier, that Greg had died in his arms, after regaining consciousness for the moment when he told Stephen to look after his family."

"Thank you Mr Loft. I appreciate this is desperately hard for you, as well as for your son. But can you be sure of Greg's last words as reported to you by Stephen at the time, please?"

Henry hesitated for the first time. He couldn't quite remember what his son had said. He knew the result was that he'd asked him to look after 'them', but what the actual words that Stephen reported he couldn't remember.

"I... I can't be sure now exactly what Stephen said. I know it was along the lines of 'look after them', but exactly what... It just meant to me that a dying boy had put on us the charge of looking after his sister and parents. And with that, even if they were only strangers, I would consider myself bound. The Beales were our best friends – as Mary still is. Naturally both Stephen and I are going to honour Greg's dying wish as given to Stephen. Stephen had promised, and I did afterwards. And that is what Mary herself wants, too. It appears there is a distant elderly relative who may have some other ideas, but I stress that is not what Mary wants, and neither do we."

"Thank you, Mr Loft. I must warn you that your last comments are not part of this inquest and will not be recorded, no matter how vehemently your wishes are held. We are here only to establish the causes of the deaths, not the disposition of the living. The Jury will therefore disregard your comments about Miss Beale's future as not material to the case, except insofar as they help to establish your good character should they feel that such establishment be necessary.

"Returning to the night in question, can you describe what you did next?"

"Yes, sir. I was concerned for Stephen as he was wet through, cold and naturally shocked and depressed. So I ordered him back to the house to dry off and get warm. He was concerned about the... bodies... but I told him I would cover them once he was in and safe. And that's what I did. I got out some of the farm tarpaulins and laid one over the parents' bodies and the other one over Greg's, and weighed both down with some of the lumps of wood, and branches, and things that had been cast up onto the grass. Then I went back and got myself dry, and collapsed into bed."

"Mr Loft, thank you. You and your son have been through a lot, and I am aware that today is a further burden on your nerves. So it is for your new foster-daughter, Mary Beale. I call her so although it is unofficial as yet, but nobody could doubt the love that you and your son feel for her, or that you are well placed to offer her the home of her choosing. But the decision there is not mine to make, as you are aware.

"We shall break now for lunch, shall we say an hour? Until two o'clock then."

"All rise!" called the Clerk, and the Coroner swept out.

"Whew," said Henry as they emerged from the building. "I didn't enjoy that at all."

"Nor did I," his son replied, still slightly weak from the suppressed emotion of the morning. Mary said nothing. Henry noticed.

"Are you all right, Mary? It must be horrible for you, listening to it all being brought up again."

She nodded wordlessly, still looking straight ahead.

"Mary! Mary Beale! I have found you at last. Are you all right, child? I can't imagine what made them bring you here – this is no place for a small girl. Thank goodness I'm here now and you can come home with me. You need never think of the horrid memories of this place again."

The voice came from behind them. This was what Mary had been dreading. She had wanted to warn Henry about her great-aunt's appearance but had not had the opportunity. Nor had Stephen, for it had been driven from his mind by his father's performance whilst giving his evidence.

They both swung round to face the onslaught. Mary continued looking straight ahead.

"Good afternoon, Madam," said Henry in his most formal tones, quickly regaining his composure from the morning's stress. "I gather you are Mary's great-aunt?"

"I am indeed, young man. And it seems that I am just in time to save my young relative from further unpleasantness in that ridiculous courtroom."

"Miss…er…? I'm sorry, but although Mary has naturally mentioned you I have no knowledge of your surname. Strange, my family have been friends and neighbours of the Beales for as long as I've been alive, but we've never actually met you."

"That's as maybe. The fact is that I am here now, just in time to present sanctuary to my great-niece at the time she needs it."

"I see. Well, Miss…er… I have to tell you that Mary's presence is needed in the Inquest. Her own testimony is to be read out this afternoon and she needs to be there to ensure that it contains what she said, no more, no less. The Coroner is insistent on that. So I'm afraid that you will be unable to remove her. Indeed, she wishes to be there, no matter how distressing things are. It is the death of her parents and brother they are considering, after all."

"A court is not a suitable place for a young girl. The Coroner must realise that, and he will understand completely when I tell him that I have taken her away."

At this Mary swung round to face her too. Her eyes blazing, she stuttered: "Y-Y-you are not taking me anywhere, 'cos I won't go. I have to know about how Greg and Mummy and Daddy died, and I'm going to find out. I have to be there. And Henry understands that, and so does Stephen. I'm not going."

She pulled hard at Stephen's arm, unbalancing him so that he stumbled after her, down the hill toward Fore Street. Henry was left facing his adversary.

"Are you going to do nothing to stop him? Stop him taking my great-niece away?"

"From what I saw it was more your great-niece dragging my son away. But I'm glad to say that the law is on Mary's side. She *is* needed in the inquest this afternoon. Removing her would be contempt of court, or some such thing. And concerning your offer to her of a home, I have to tell you that her brother's request as he lay dying in my son's arms was that he should look after her. Even if I didn't know her at all, and don't forget that I've been their friend ever since I can remember, I'd regard the request of that dying boy as my bond. And Mary's wishes are that she should live with us, near her parents' land and in the area where she is known, where she goes to school and where her friends are."

This was digested for few moments. Then:

"And just who are you?"

"I think it would be best under the circumstances that you identify yourself. We have never met, I don't know you and you could be anybody."

This was obviously the wrong thing to say.

"Impertinence! Young man, my name is Marriatt, Ethel Marriatt. My sister was Mrs Beale's mother. That makes me Mary's great-aunt, in case you were unaware. And who might you be?"

"My name is Henry Loft. Of Loft Island. I farm the land that adjoins – that adjoined – the Beales'. I've been a friend of the Beales since I was born, as has my son Stephen. It was he who rescued Mary, having heard her cries with ears sharper than mine. He did everything he could to save her brother. Didn't you hear what I said in there?"

"Yes, yes; I heard. But of course that's rubbish. No boy that young can save someone's life."

Henry looked at her, seething inside with fury.

"Madam," he barked, after a short but potent silence. His voice had regained the sergeant-major tones he had last used on the unpleasant Inspector Moffat. It was as foreign to himself, hearing it emerge from his own mouth after all these years of peace, as it was to those who heard it who thought they knew him.

"Madam. I went through the hell of that night. I know what I saw. I know what my son had to do, what he did. Were it not for his insistence that he had heard something I would have insisted that he should return to

164

the house to get dry. That would have left Mary to die from cold. It would have meant that nobody could have given Greg some comfort in his last moments. Do not presume to tell me that what Stephen and I did that night was rubbish. Do not disbelieve my son when an entire Court and the force of the law take what he said on oath as the truth. Not now, not ever. In future, kindly leave us alone. Good day."

As she was uphill from him, turning his back naturally took him down toward Fore Street in Mary and Stephens' footsteps. With a brow like thunder he marched up Fore Street, seeing no-one and nothing.

But as he passed Miss Merryweather's café, two people who had only just recovered their own composure saw him. Stephen was in the middle of telling their friend what had happened when he saw a soldier-like figure march past and with a shock recognised his father behind the mask of fury. He shot a scared look at his companions, put both hands on Mary's shoulders to tell her, without words, to stay, then darted out into the street to follow. All the way up Fore Street marched the martinet, past the Shipwrights, past the ferry steps.

When at last Henry's ire had more or less evaporated he stopped in the middle of the road to gather the shreds of normal behaviour together. When he turned he saw a young man standing, looking at him as it were at a stranger, yet mirroring his own stance exactly.

In moments of unabated fury it is within the human condition to lose something. But the loss of that something, be it reason, self-control, the conditioning of politeness or something else for which there are no words, brings other realisations or sensitivities to the fore. So despite Henry's loss of composure on his route march up Salcombe's main road, he was eventually subconsciously aware of what he was doing, how it must appear, and actually what he looked like to an observer. It was at that point he realised that he had lost his temper more completely than ever before in his life, and wasn't proud of the fact. As he turned, at low ebb, he had a hand behind his back. The other came to cradle his brow as if to massage the brain within to its normal behaviour. And as he looked, it was as if he saw himself in a mirror. A slightly concave mirror.

The figure before him, with its mousy hair, blue-green eyes, worried look, wide mouth and shorter but slightly upturned nose, was him. Oh a younger version certainly, but him. But he started to notice the other influences: the slope of the forehead, the width of the nose, the wider cheeks. All the marks of his dead wife, whom he still missed.

Stephen.

Stephen, come to see that he was all right.

The last of the anger left his mind with the abruptness of the flood that had started it all, and was replaced by such a ferocity of love for his son and his new foster-daughter, strengthened as it was by a need to protect them, that he had not experienced up to that moment.

The rush of his father toward him didn't worry Stephen. But the strength of the arm around him nearly crushed the breath from him.

"Come on," said Henry. "I need a drink." And he almost frog-marched his son into the pub.

After a large Scotch and a ginger beer they both felt better.

They returned to the café.

# 17 – Inquest continued (2)

Miss Merryweather listened to the story of the morning with sympathy. When they came to recount the arrival of Mary's great-aunt she tossed her head.

"Typical."

They discussed the encounter outside the courtroom and he grew ever more agitated. When Stephen had described how he had followed his father to the Ferry and what transpired, Miss Merryweather was herself agitated.

"How could she?" she kept asking. "And after all you've done for the Beales. Oh really..."

"It's not her reaction to what we may have done for the Beales that angered me, Miss Merryweather, it's what Greg asked us to do, and what Mary wants. I just cannot understand what makes her tick. Why does she refuse to give any credibility to the report of Greg's last spoken words? Why is she so keen that Mary shouldn't be looked after by us? She must know even from what's been said so far that Mary would be far happier here. And that she wants to be here."

"Ah, but she belongs to a different generation and class, Mr Loft, although I shouldn't dare to say it. She is Victorian through and through, and believes that her view of how a young lady should be brought up is the only proper way for it to happen. You see, she never really approved of the marriage her sister made, nor of the marriage that the daughter made when she married someone she saw only as a Devon farmer. So now she believes that her great-niece can be snatched from the jaws of what she sees as the lower middle classes, she is determined that nothing will stand in her way."

There was a shocked silence. Then Henry stood up. "I think we'd better be going, Miss Merryweather. What do we owe you?" There was a taughtness in his voice which made her mouth gape open. Along, it may be said, with the mouths of Mary and Stephen.

"But surely you don't think that I hold with rubbish like that? How could I, being my father's daughter? I was always taught by my parents that people have the worth they demonstrate, and my experience since starting to think for myself has done nothing to change that. Rather, it has reinforced it. Besides, I try to be a Christian, and I believe that her view of things is actually completely against Christian teaching. Surely you can't believe, knowing me, that I could ever hold her opinion?"

She stood, gripping the table edge as if to lift it in the air to throw at anyone who dared to disbelieve her. There was a short, embarrassed pause.

Henry brushed his hand across his forehead, suddenly looking exhausted. He regained his chair and looked up at her.

"I'm sorry." A pause. "When I reacted I *thought* I knew you better than to believe what you were saying. I should have followed my true beliefs. I'm sorry."

Mary and Stephen looked from one to the other, trying to get the meanings behind the emotions. The flow of unhappiness between the adults was all that glimmered through the fog, and eventually with the uncomplicated, true perception of youth Mary said: "Whatever class she thinks she is, I want to stay here. Not with her. My friends are here. I hate it where she lives. And I want to be... home."

Miss Merryweather was with her in two steps. She sat on a chair in front of her so as to look directly into her eyes. "Yes, Mary. Your place is here, the more so because you want it to be. Although I have known your great-aunt for years it has been as a family acquaintance, not as a friend. And now she has actually caused you – all – so much misery she is even further from being a friend. She will receive no hospitality from me. I don't care how much my father taught me about being pleasant to people no matter what. In her case, so far as I am concerned, she has proved herself beyond the pale. I'm free to believe what I will; what did we fight the war for if not freedom?"

There was a whoop from Stephen, and a grin appeared on his face for the first time. "That's fighting talk, Susan! Good for you!"

"Stephen!" said his father. "I agree it's fighting talk, but there's no need to forget your manners."

Miss Merryweather looked at him, herself smiling. "I'm glad he broke the ice, Mr Loft. I think it's about time we started using each others' Christian names, don't you?"

He gave her a long look, and a sudden, glad smile stretched across his face. "Perhaps it is... perhaps it is... I'm sorry I was so rude just now, but it's been a horrible morning so far and I wasn't thinking straight. Will you forgive me?"

The café owner straightened. "There's nothing to forgive, even without an apology like that. I am and always have been on Mary's side, which means your side, ever since our first meeting outside the church."

Henry continued smiling at her, wishing he could do or say more. But Stephen had no such restraints. He just put his arms round her, and said simply: "Thank you, Susan," and kissed her on the cheek.

Once released, she caught Henry's look and held it. But he had not his son's lack of restraint.

Mercifully they failed to reconnect with Mary's troublesome relative on the return to the Inquest. No less a person than the coroner was anxiously waiting for them, the Clerk told them, and they were ushered in to his private chambers. He rose to greet them, and despite the formal clothes there was no shadow of formality on his voice. He ushered them into chairs.

"One thing the Law does require me to do," he started, "is to ensure that a statement which will be read out in court is signed, and witnessed, and that the giver of the statement acknowledges it to be theirs and that it is true. This affects you, Mary, and the first part we can do now.

"I have here...." and he produced an official looking sheaf of papers, "is what you said to me in Edgar's yard, and what you said in your statement to the Police. If you want to read it through, please do. You should, really, but I can assure you that it contains what you said, no more, no less. Or if you'd rather Mr Loft read it, that would be acceptable if you were to agree any changes. Afterwards I just need you to sign it, at the bottom of each page and at the end, and once right at the beginning."

Mary looked worriedly at Henry. "Would you like me to read it through?" he asked.

She nodded.

Henry found nothing that he could remember to be wrong, and a happier Mary carefully and slowly signed her name where she was shown. The Clerk was sent for, and he witnessed it.

"The only other thing we need from you, Mary, is that you should go into the witness box like Stephen did, but just answer 'yes' to the question I shall put to you. All I shall ask you is whether your name is Mary Beale, that you are resident at Loft Island, Salcombe, and that this is your statement. After that you may go back to your seat. It is very unlikely anyone will want to ask questions, and I shall do my best either to answer them by reference to this. But there is an outside chance that I have to recall you. If it does, just don't worry about it. No harm can come to you and I shall be as nice to you as I am now. All we are seeking, as I said to Stephen, is the truth of what happened. Is that all right?"

Mary gulped nervously. She hadn't been prepared for this.

Once they were in the court itself, she was so intent on searching out the exact path she must take from her seat to the witness box that she missed seeing her great-aunt reappear in the public seats. So did Stephen, who was concerned that Mary should remain in control of herself. Henry noticed, from the silence from the gallery which heralded the arrival of a stranger into the midst of the locals and the newspaper reporters. Without trying to show that he had seen her, he viewed the old lady's still thunderous expression with a sinking feeling in his gut.

Stephen rose with everyone else when told to do so. He had a weak feeling in his knees now, more so than when he knew he was to give his own evidence. They were told to sit. He sat.

The Coroner told the Inquest about Mary, about 'this amazingly brave girl'. "She was plucked from the storm, we have heard, by a boy just a few years her senior, whose actions place him in ability far above his actual years."

Despite his anxiety for Mary, Stephen blushed.

"I believe it would have been cruel beyond belief to ask Miss Mary Beale to stand up here, as her rescuer had to, to answer questions about the night of the disaster. Therefore I have taken the unofficial step, but one which I hope you will applaud, of taking her statement in less traumatic circumstances, but in the presence of witnesses. It was augmented by a further statement made officially to the Police. I propose therefore, to read these statements, having asked its author to certify that they are hers, and would ask the jury to accept it in lieu of the more normal spoken evidence.

"Would you please ask Miss Mary Beale to step into the witness box."

Stephen felt Mary's muscles tense under his hand as he released it from hers. She rose, and carefully followed the usher on the path she had examined for herself so minutely before. Stephen noticed her eyes were downcast all the way.

"Now, Mary, please just relax and just talk to me as we have before. Can you confirm that you are Mary Beale, now of Loft Island, Salcombe, in the County of South Devon?"

Stephen saw the familiar chin level itself, and the eyes look straight at the Coroner. He didn't see the faint smile as she acknowledged the official's gentle expression.

"Yes, sir; I am."

"Good. I am holding in front of you a file of papers. Do you recognise it?"

She looked carefully. "Could you open the cover, please, sir?"

The Coroner looked nonplussed, but did as he was asked.

"Yes, sir. Those are the statements I gave you and to Sergeant Franks and which have been checked, and I signed them."

He smiled delightedly at her. "Very good. Very good. Thank you. You may leave the witness box."

She did so, her confidence restored, and Stephen gave her a quick hug as she rejoined him.

Her account was read out. When the Coroner had finished there was a buzz of animated conversation around the public area, and indeed amongst the jurors. But there were no questions.

The rest of the evidence was from their Home Guard friends and from the doctor. As he was about to start speaking the Coroner motioned to him to stop.

"One minute, please. The evidence which is about to be given is of a medical nature, and is likely to contain graphical descriptions of the injuries which the deceased suffered. It is unsuitable, in my considerable experience, for those of a delicate disposition, for young people, or for those who were close to the victims. I therefore suggest that anyone in those categories should leave the court temporarily, or else be taken out. He looked meaningfully at Henry, who rose to the suggestion and ushered his charges out before they could protest.

"Dad…" "Henry…" Two indignant voices were raised as one but he shushed them.

"Two reasons. Firstly you both saw what Greg's injuries were and I see no reason why you should be forced to listen to a description of what you saw. And secondly Mary's great-aunt is in the gallery and I don't want her to be able to say once again that 'this is no place for children'. That's particularly so when the Coroner all but told me to take you out. So no arguments, please. We'll be told when the doctor's finished."

They both saw the sense in this, and waited outside the court, listening to the drone of the doctor's voice but being unable to distinguish any words. Suddenly there was a clatter on the stone stairs from the public gallery and Mary's great-aunt, white faced, a dainty handkerchief over her mouth, rushed down towards them, looking to neither left nor right, and vanished outside the building. The three looked at each other in surprise, and first Stephen, then Mary started into a fit of the giggles. Trying to keep any expression from his own face Henry told them to pull themselves together, but an event like that, in contrast with the strain and emotion of the day, had seized their imaginations. It took the reappearance of the usher to cause a very sudden collapse of their fit of laughter. The faces that re-entered the courtroom were more cheerful, yet still serious.

Next to give evidence were the various Police officers who had become involved. There were no surprises until Inspector Moffat entered the box. He had only just arrived at the courtroom. Stephen felt his father stiffen as the officer was called.

"On Friday 27 March 1954 I interviewed a Mr Henry Loft of Loft Island, Salcombe, South Devon. He had to report that three bodies had been washed ashore on his property. A survivor of the storm had also been washed ashore, unharmed, and he had given her shelter overnight. It transpired that the three bodies were those of Mr and Mrs John Beale of Beales' Farm, Salcombe, South Devon, and their son Gregory. The survivor was the daughter, Mary Beale of the same address. I made arrangements for the doctor to attend and for the bodies to be removed. I also tried to make arrangements for the surviving child to be taken into the care of the local authority, and for the Loft father and son to be accommodated in Salcombe as their farm now consisted of only a small island. Mr Loft declined, and refused to allow me to arrange for the survivor to be properly cared for. As she was not there I had no option but to ride with his desires for the time being. Later, I contacted him again and..."

"Just one moment, Inspector. Members of the Jury, as I said before the disposition and care of Mary Beale has nothing to do with this Inquest. You are therefore to ignore any comments about those matters. Inspector Moffat, you are not an expert in child care, I believe, and are not qualified to decide what is best for Mary Beale. Even if you were, this is not the time or place to do so. You will therefore restrict yourself to matters which involve the deaths and the subsequent actions of yourself and your officers."

Stephen watched the Inspector's face flush a bright red. Without realising, he gripped his father's arm with glee at the man's obvious anger and embarrassment. Serve him right for all the horrible things he had said!

It took the wind out of the Inspector's sails. He had lost his place completely in his story, and the Coroner had to question him to unearth the few other facts that he wanted. Eventually he left the witness box and walked out of the court, much to their relief.

Having heard from the few other interested parties, those who had seen the bodies and helped with their transport, the Coroner summed up the facts as presented. He instructed the jury about the options open to them – death by natural causes, death by misadventure, death caused by person or persons unknown – and they retired. There was subdued chatter in the courtroom for a short while. Stephen didn't know whether to try and persuade the others to go for a walk or whether they should stay. He was getting fidgety and could see that Mary was. But far sooner than they expected the jury returned, as did the Coroner, and they had to settle down again, this time very much on tenterhooks, although Henry was almost certain what the verdict was going to be. He wasn't wrong.

Death by misadventure.

Stephen and Mary heard this in some disbelief. Misadventure? What sort of adventure was it to be in your own home, when it all went horribly wrong? Surely, thought Mary, *somebody* must be to blame for it? What about the Water Board? If they had... But the Coroner was continuing.

"This incident and these deaths have been a great shock to this community. The inundation which still exists has also been a great shock to it. Perhaps we should be lucky, under the circumstances, that only three lives were lost. But three lives is three too many, and it is as well for the survivor from Beales' Farm that there was a highly able, trained neighbour at hand when her need was at hand. I refer of course to Stephen Loft, whose sense of responsibility, first aid ability and humanity have shone out from this Inquest like a beacon of hope for the future of this community. His efforts to save his young friend show a maturity far beyond his years and I hope that all his contemporaries take note of this and ready themselves to act similarly.

"The Jury has decided on its verdict, which has been recorded. It is not the part of an Inquest to comment further, and yet I feel this community would hope that others are never placed in anything like this situation. Therefore I express the hope that the various Water Boards around the country look to the events of this incident in order to ensure that the chain of responsibility for maintaining the basic soundness and suitability of the works for which they are responsible is maintained."

He rose. Everyone else rose. He left.

They encountered some reporters and photographers outside the Court House who wanted to talk to both Mary and Stephen. After hearing the sort of question that one particularly seedy individual was shouting at Mary, Henry's face set and he marched them both back down to Miss Merryweather's. She had seen their approach, pursued by the small gaggle of Press. She accepted them in, and ushered them straight into the kitchen, whose door she closed firmly. The first few of the Press were by this time inside the café, and saw her standing at the back, waiting courteously, her arms folded.

"We'd like to talk to the kid," said the first, walking up as if to brush her aside.

She moved not a muscle, just stood between the tables so they would have to push her out of the way to get to her kitchen.

"I have no goats here," she answered evenly. He looked nonplussed.

"No, I want to talk to the kid who's meant to have saved the girl."

"If you mean that you want to talk to the young man who has just had to give evidence in front of an Inquest, I'm afraid that he is exhausted and does not want to talk to anyone apart from his family and friends just now." She held her position. The man was trying to edge past her.

"No customers are permitted in my kitchen, if you *don't* mind. And you are not even customers." She looked at him squarely. Brought up by a solicitor, she could be very positive when she had to be, and now was one of those times.

"Oh dear," she said, "is that the time? I'm so sorry, but I shut at 4.00. Well it *has* been pleasant seeing you. Do call again when you're in town, but when I'm open would be nice. *Good*-bye."

She moved purposefully towards him. He had no option but to retreat, as did the others. She managed to shepherd them from the shop like that, locked the door and put up the 'closed' sign. The others, listening behind the kitchen door, heard her approaching footsteps and cheered as she appeared. Once there she received a kiss from Mary, a hug from Stephen; and then stood looking at Henry. He grinned sheepishly.

"You were wonderful," he said, and took her hand. For a moment Stephen thought he was going to kiss her, and readied himself to give a yelp of approval, but he thought a second time and just squeezed it gently. A look of disappointment seemed to pass across her face, but vanished under her sense of propriety. She smiled.

"What else could I do?" she asked. "You've all had an awful day, and the last thing you want is the London press hounding you, I should think. Anyway, did you say anything to that dreadful relative of yours, Mary? I looked out of the window during the afternoon and saw her striding back towards the Marine Hotel where she always stays. She looked really ill and upset."

Henry laughed grimly. "She was in court when the doctor gave his evidence, despite all of us being warned that it was inadvisable. I think she didn't like what she heard, just as none of us liked it on the night."

"No, indeed," she murmured thoughtfully. "I can understand that."

Stephen was silent, remembering those terrible wounds: heads crushed like eggshells and his own, young friend with a gaping hole in his belly. How many times had he exclaimed about such injuries, read about but never shown, in war comics. They were sanitised then, never drawn in all their appalling reality. Mary remembered seeing too: seeing the damage to her brother that she had been scared of seeing, yet which she had to see to make it real for her. And now there they were, the three of them, lying cold and dead in wooden boxes. Once more her eyes filled and she clung to Susan for comfort. Instinctively the protecting arms circled the shoulders.

There was a silence. Mary disengaged and looked up at another pair of kind, understanding eyes.

"Sorry."

"My dear, you have nothing to apologise about to me. But any time you need a hug, or a change from these two men, no matter how nice they are, you know where I am."

"Thank you."

"I mean it. But now..." she said, brightening up. "You're my guests, we can open the doors again, and have a cup of tea. And if those press men come anywhere near they'll have me to deal with."

# 18 - Funerals

Gradually their mood lightened. Susan Merryweather reopened the café and was soon busy serving a good crowd of people who had been at the Inquest and were now seeking refreshment. The others stayed more or less out of sight in the kitchen, cooking and washing up. Susan's frequent appearances, seeking jobs done or asking for help, took them out of themselves and by the time the last customers had gone they felt they had known her for years, rather than a few days. When all was done she flopped down into a chair and closed her eyes for a moment.

"That's one of the busiest afternoons I've had," she said. "What I'd have done without you I really don't know."

Henry looked at her with amusement – and something else – in his eyes. "The way you keep coming to our aid, I'm inclined to say the same about you!"

Her eyes opened. "Me? Surely not. That's twice you've helped me out when I really needed a second pair of hands, not to mention the other four hands, and I'm really grateful to you all."

"But Miss Merryweather...Susan..." Mary started. "you've been looking after the boat for so many years. You were a good friend to my parents. You've helped us today and...oh...everything." She ran out of words.

"Then let's just say that we've helped each other, shall we Mary? And for myself, I will continue to do so at any time you need help. But there is one thing I'd like."

"Name it," said Henry, "And if we can give it you shall have it."

"I've never been to Loft Island, and it's always fascinated me. And as it's now an island in the proper sense it's even more romantic. I'd love to visit you there."

This time the silence was momentary. "Come tomorrow. Come now!" said Stephen. "You can help with the milking!"

"Oh!" exclaimed his father. "The poor cows. Today's just made me lose all sense of time. We've got to go, Susan, and now. By all means come, although we'll be more hospitable tomorrow and we'll welcome you at any time you want. But now we must go. Oh my goodness."

Mary and Stephen shared his concern, although Mary thought privately that he sounded like the White Rabbit. She expected any moment to hear him say "Oh my beard and whiskers...."

They said their goodbyes and all but ran back to the boat. Soon they were chugging their way back to normal life and a small herd of anxious cows.

Later, when Mary had gone to bed and Henry and Stephen's

conversation was becoming more and more sporadic, Stephen remembered the troubles of Mary's great-aunt. "D'you think she's going to make trouble, Dad? I mean, you shut her up today, but will she try and get Mary again?"

"I'm afraid she's going to try, Steve. That's why she's here, there's little doubt. But how she thinks she's going to persuade us to give her up I can't begin to imagine. And I know she'll never make Mary go willingly with her."

"She won't make us give Mary up either, will she Dad?"

"She most certainly won't. But there's still one thing that worries me, and that's the sleeping arrangements. It's wrong, you and Mary sharing. And if anyone were to visit to check on our arrangements for her, they'd have forty fits if they knew. And as for the great-aunt; well, she'd have the police here accusing us of running a bawdy house."

"A *what*?"

"Oh... an establishment where people aren't too fussy about unmarried men and women sharing beds."

"Oh, a brothel. Well, Mary and I aren't men and women, we're too young for that. So it doesn't matter."

Henry looked at him, shocked. "Where did you pick up that term? School?"

"What, brothel? Yes, I suppose so. But surely nobody's going to think we're doing anything wrong up there?"

"Not everybody knows what sort of people you both are. Some people just like to see mischief wherever they can and spread the news around. It doesn't matter that the real explanation is entirely innocent, they won't *want* to believe it."

"So what are we going to do?"

"Well, I've been thinking. If we did try to form another room in the house it's bound to make one of the rooms far too small. There's certainly no more room upstairs anyway. Even our – my – bedroom isn't that big. And down here... well, the kitchen's about the right size, I don't think any of us would want this room any smaller, and that's it apart from the porch. We could extend that along the front of the building, as a kind of lean-to affair, but it'd probably be cold and leaky in winter. The alternative is to make another room in the corner of the cowshed, as near the house as possible."

"But who would sleep there?"

"Well, it shouldn't be Mary. It could be me, but then some busybody might say that there should be an adult in the house. It could be you, Steve, but I don't see why it should be if Mary has to sleep in the main house."

Privately Stephen didn't see why he should move out for her. He'd lived

176

in his little room since soon after he was born and didn't want to leave it. But all he said was: "Dad, how easy would it be to make another room out from the porch? Say, use the extended porch as the bedroom and use the rest of it as a porch? Then it wouldn't matter if it was cold or damp."

"Hmm. I suppose that makes sense. But who'd use it?"

"You, dad!"

He laughed, ruefully. "I suppose I asked for that. It would mean I'd finally move out of your mother's and my room…" He trailed off. There was an uncomfortable pause.

"Oh well, why not? You can't hang on to the past for ever. And it'll mean that you two are safe upstairs while I'm on guard. Nobody can have a problem with that. I'll get a bed for Mary, we can set to with cutting timber for the new porch, and I'll have to clear the present one out a bit and decorate it. I'll need you two to help. Will you do that?"

"Does that mean we don't have to go back to school?"

"It does not, Stephen! School's important, and you wouldn't have expected me to say anything else, would you?"

"I suppose not. But will it take long?"

"I don't know. We'll need to draw a plan first, to see how we're going to do it. But until it's finished and Mary has her own room, I'm sleeping down here if anybody asks. Mary has my room."

"But she won't want to move!"

"I think it would be best if she did. You don't want to lend her half your bed for ages."

"I do, Dad, it's… not a problem for me, at all."

Henry wondered if his son had been about to say 'it's nice'. Which indeed he had, but had stopped himself in time.

"Well, for the moment we tell everyone that you're in my room and I'm downstairs. In fact I'm not sure we shouldn't move anyway, just in case."

"Dad, nobody's going to know. We're all up in the mornings before anybody comes to call."

"True. That's one good thing. But I'll see. I'm certainly going to sleep in the bedroom tonight, and that's going to be very soon. And you're late, so get to bed. Goodnight."

"Goodnight, Dad. And… thanks."

The morning dawned rainy. It was nothing like the downpour which had led to the disaster, but enough to dampen spirits and make the diminished jobs around the farmyard uncomfortable once again. Breakfast was interrupted by the irrepressible Bert and the quiet Arthur, for whom they soon found cups of tea.

"How's it going, then? Still talking to each other?" asked Bert.

"I think so," Mary smiled at him, "Despite the weather."

"Well, it's better than it was *that* morning. But it's still uncomfortable, I agree. I shouldn't think you'll want to do much sailing today, will you? Which is a pity, because you'll be back at school soon."

"Not until after the funeral," said Stephen. "That's what Dad said, isn't it Dad?"

"That's right. But the funeral's going to be soon."

"Well…" Arthur started quietly. "That's actually why we're here. Since yesterday there's no reason why the service shouldn't go ahead. The message from the Vicar is that tomorrow would be a good day, if it's acceptable to you. At 11.00 in the morning."

"Well," said Henry eventually. "We knew it was coming."

The other two said nothing. Now the time was almost on them Mary found the tears once again very close. It was all so final, this prospect of putting bodies into the ground. No matter what people had said to her about her parents still being with her, as part of her, she knew that the solid, the comforting part of them was now dead. Gone. In boxes. About to be sealed in the ground for ever.

Henry found her outside, crying her eyes out into the shaggy coat of one of their dogs. He knew. He'd been through it. And he knew that the last thing he'd wanted was someone to try and stop him crying or even to discover him crying. He stood by the door and waited. And when at last the sobs subsided and she looked around to see if she was still alone she found and met his comforting, gentle eyes: eyes filled with the knowledge of what she had been going through. He joined her on the ground and put his arms round both child and dog. And Stephen, five minutes later, found them there. He too stood watching, trying hard to swallow and unable to see properly.

She looked up. "I know, I know. I'm silly to cry. I know all you've said to me. But…oh…" and the tears returned. At length Stephen could no longer keep up pretences either, and faced with the choice between a gasping flight to anywhere else to be alone and the comfort of his own father, friend and dog he was still young enough to choose the latter.

As people almost always do when they share unhappiness, they recovered with each of them feeling better. But not before their visitors had twice appeared at the door to see what was happening, and had twice returned to sit in silence inside.

The remainder of the morning, once their visitors had bid them farewell, was spent more or less in silence as they each tried not to upset the others. The result was that each of them *was* upset, or at best still unhappy, by the time the jobs around the farm and house were complete.

"Family conference," announced Henry at last. Mary wondered, just for an instant, whether that included her. She decided rightly that it did, and they sat round the kitchen table, with the dogs guarding the range as usual.

"This is pointless," he started, "this walking around with faces as long as… well, long. It does nobody any good. My friends, your family, would hate it. It does their memory no respect. Mary, how often were they silent and unhappy?"

"I can't remember them ever being very unhappy, unless Greg or I had been naughty."

"And have you and Stephen been naughty now? I can answer that. No. Very far from it. So they'd be willing us to continue as near normal as we can. So please, for my sake, and for your own, talk and act as normal. Why don't you go and work on the boat? You know you've got a lot to do."

They looked at him in surprise. But a spark had hit tinder in each of them and, with the prospect of something to do which wasn't the normal run of things, half smiles came to two faces. Despite the rain, they collected the ropes, knife and twine, and went down to their moorings. Because of the still-present preoccupation with events they were both quiet, both supportive and unusually polite with each other, and as a result a lot of the rigging was replaced with the minimum of time wasted. The knots and preparing the rope ends they left until they could bring down the book to help.

It was lunchtime before the rain stopped, but the day continued overcast and depressing. Henry joined them and all three carried on with their rigging. Henry wanted to make sure that the dinghy was sound; besides he too needed something to occupy his mind. Now that most of the land that used to occupy his time was under water, he found the day frustratingly long.

By the time it started raining again the dinghy was looking good, although Henry despaired that his efforts at touching up the varnish in the few places that needed it were getting wet.

That evening they all read books by lamplight. The rain continued.

By half-past eight, Stephen was so bored he elected to go to bed. It was Mary's bedtime too, and she looked at him in surprise. Since they had more or less settled down as a family he had resumed his normal bedtime of an hour later. He no longer assumed that his immediate presence was needed as comfort, but instead was conscious that she might need a little privacy. She, being twelve, was indeed starting to need it, but she felt that as it was Stephen who would have been with her she wouldn't have minded his presence at all.

They readied themselves, then read for a while. Stephen had finally found something to interest him. Mary was the first to doze off, and Henry's approach told Stephen at last that it was time for him to settle down too.

He awoke at about midnight to find that Mary's head was pressed close to his chest, and that an arm of hers had been draped over his shoulder. While still puzzling it out from his comatose state he realised that there were sobs racking her body, and it was this that had woken him. He put an arm over her, and the small, tear stained face lifted to look at him.

"Why me?" she asked. "Why *my* family?"

But he had no answer for her, unless hugging her was an answer in itself.

They woke late the next morning. Mary was first conscious of a feeling of general dread that she didn't understand until reality hit her, and she bit her lip to stop her immediate reaction which was to cry. She knew she had to be brave today. If she wasn't she was sure that she'd never stop crying at all. She looked at the wall. Stephen's wall. Her back was warm, which meant he was still in bed asleep. With her. it felt strange, still: but nice, companionable, comforting. He was nice, a good friend. She was lucky to have known someone for so long who was so nice.

She turned over. How ordinary he looked. Peaceful, asleep like this, and younger than when awake. She smiled faintly at him.

As if aware of her gaze, the eyes opened, and blinked. A yawn. A smile. "Wassertime?"

"Don't know. Looks late, though."

He looked up at the window where the sun was streaming in.

"Dad never woke us!

"It's the funeral."

"What?... Oh." He sounded deflated. "Yes, it is. How are you feeling?"

"OK, s'pose."

He nodded, and slid out of bed.

Funny, she thought, how gradually he was becoming more careless about appearing in – or more or less in – nightwear in front of her. She didn't mind. It was a compliment, really.

They found Henry once again nearly at the end of milking. He told them he wanted to get an early start but was happier, just today, on his own.

"Your time will come," he said as jovially as he could. "I'll get you to do it in the weekends when I lie in bed."

Their journey to the milk staithe was quiet, and of the lorry there was no sign. They returned to the island.

"How about getting to the town early?" asked Henry. "There'll be more to think about there, and we could keep Susan company for a while."

The idea appealed to Mary who was not looking forward to the passing of the few hours before they would otherwise have left the island. They all changed, and carefully made the voyage to the still quiet town. In the newsagent at the bottom of Fore Street they dawdled, waiting for Susan Merryweather to appear. When she did it was to a restrained but sincere greeting. She led them to the café and seemed to understand their feelings, because she put them to work, knowing the usual small crowd that would appear for their breakfasts. Mary was so busy keeping the kettle boiling and making tea that she didn't realise how much busier the little café was becoming. With a shock she heard Henry tell Susan that they'd have to be going soon. It was 9.30. They'd spent over an hour there, and she'd hardly realised.

At last they had to leave, and Mary was aware, all of a sudden, of the hush that fell over the crowded tables as they walked through. Susan spoke swiftly to one of the customers and handed him her keys. Henry stopped in surprise.

"What's happening?" he asked, as she donned a dark coat.

"I'm coming with you," she answered simply. "Did you think that I wouldn't?"

He just looked at her, then gently touched the hand that was still fastening her coat. The relief was overwhelming.

With even this lift to the spirit, it was with mounting apprehension that they climbed the hill toward the church and the vicarage. They found that Church House was open, and they hesitated outside. The Vicar joined them, and was his usual charming self. He took them to the Church and quickly accepted that Susan Merryweather would be in charge.

"You'll walk in front with Mary, then," he said. "I was going to have you next to me, but that's even better. Then we'll have Greg, then Mrs Beale then Mr Beale. Then as you come in, just look neither to right or left until you reach the front, and then turn in here." He showed the front pew."

"Will there be anybody there?" asked Mary.

"No. Nobody would be that insensitive. Besides, we've got the Verger who will make sure it's empty."

She nodded. They sat for some time in the little church, waiting, thinking. She had been brought up, not so much as a church-goer but certainly as a Christian, and at this stage she just wanted peace and quiet, to think of nothing in particular, but to try and look calmly at her churning emotions. She never saw the Verger signal to the Vicar, the Vicar beckon to Henry and Stephen, or that she was now alone with Susan.

Man and boy followed him to Church House where there was a small crowd waiting. Room was made for them to enter. As soon as they crossed the threshold Stephen felt there was something different, something quiet, dignified, sad, that he didn't understand. Henry knew: he had heard it before. A house where all the normal little noises are missing, where words are quiet, normal life is temporarily suspended, the outside world is muted, kept at bay. A house where the dead are being held in respect.

Stephen felt a shadow of his emotions of that night when the wind and water killed his best friend. A feeling of horror, of tragedy, of impotence to change anything despite the desperate need to do so. Numbed, he stood, waiting, in the hall.

And all of a sudden the remembrance of Greg's dream came to him. Had his friend really foreseen his own death? Surely not. That sort of prescience didn't exist outside fiction. Did it?

Poor old Greg.

Others were entering. He hardly recognised them. One touched his shoulder. He looked, and saw a school friend. He nodded a greeting, then again, and again. And all around there was silence, and he knew then that it was time for tears for them all, and without shame.

Mary's reverie in the church was gently interrupted by the Vicar. Pews were filling up, and it was time she went to the Church House and prepare herself to lead the procession. She looked fearfully around, thinking, almost, to see the ghosts of those who had died in the years before rise and show their allegiance to the newly dead, her family. They stopped outside the doors, and the three of them waited. They were joined, suddenly, by an elderly figure, dressed in black. With a shock Mary recognised her great-aunt. But before the old lady had a chance to speak the Vicar moved to her side, beckoning to a burly onlooker, who led her away towards the church.

A movement in the wide door of the house caught her eye: two boys, and the wooden end of a coffin. Neither of the boys was Stephen, and for a moment she thought he had betrayed her. Her eyes sought him out, and finally she found him, his face white and running with tears, struggling to hold up the centre of the box that contained his friend. Her jaw opened, and at that moment he looked straight at her.

His face was for her the end of any attempt at controlling her emotions. She broke from Susan's hand and crossed to him to hide her face in his jacket. The two cried together, one sobbing uncontrollably and the other just still, but with eyes streaming. Susan's hand round her shoulders eased her away from him, and, blindly, she let herself be guided at her side to the front of the procession.

With her gone, Stephen found he could come to terms with his job. So Mary missed seeing him, with their five friends from school, carry the coffin containing their dead classmate the short distance from the house to the church. Following them were the coffins of the adult Beales, with a white faced Henry helping to carry the body of his long term friend and colleague. Father and son were grim faced, both were looking anywhere to avoid the faces that surrounded and stared and wept.

Mary heard the footsteps approach the front of the church, but dared not turn or look. She was crying into her hands as it was. She knew that if she had actually looked at the coffins and their bearers she would have been completely unable to cope. It was not now the loss of her family that was causing her emotion but the knowledge of the solemnity of the occasion, that she was one of the main characters in it, and that what was happening was the final line under the lives of her loved ones. How could she face even more? They reached the reserved pew and turned into it.

She kept her eyes covered, unwilling to look even straight ahead. She heard shuffling, and words, and then felt Henry move to her side, his arm joining Susan's at her back. The words then meant nothing. Yet when, years later, she heard them again it felt as they were engraved on her mind and she knew them every one. At last she heard the prayers and invocations stop. There was a pause and the vicar continued in a more normal voice.

"I do not propose to make a long address. Those of you who were friends to the Beales can do the story of their lives more justice than any words of mine. I beg you all to do so, long and loud, for that is the greater memorial to them than any words in stone can ever be. And the greatest memorial still is the continuation of the life of Mary their daughter whom God has caused to be saved from death. Better, he has in his great mercy put her into the permanent care of her rescuers, her family's long time friends. And if there is to be any good coming from this unhappiness this is it: that she is with those whom she has chosen, and who have chosen her.

"This catastrophe, this monumental event which has altered the face of this area and the lives of so many is one which might have been foreseen. We must now ensure that we look with God's foresight on the works of man which affect our lives, and on those of God's own works which he designed us to control, to ensure that more lives are not taken, or unhappiness caused, by any omission or commission on our part. For if we fail in this we are not paying due respect to God or to the lives of those who were taken in the flood."

A pause, and she sensed a nearness in front of her. The same voice spoke quietly.

"This, Mary, is your day above all, to bid farewell to she who bore you, he who fathered you and he who was your life's companion. I say 'she bore', 'he fathered' and 'he was', yet the reality is that all those things are still true. Nothing can ever take away that, nor the love that they give you, nor the love that you give them. And do you hear the difference? The love *is*, not *was*. For nothing can change that either, especially now. That love will continue to your own life's end, undiminished until you yourself follow them to Heaven. Over the years the quality of the love will change; but like a fire changes its nature as it kindles, burns and lasts as glowing embers, its warmth never leaves. No, its warmth never leaves.

"If that warmth should ever be in danger of failing, if you should think that they have left your memory, then just talk to others, like your new family who are also their friends and who have a different kind of love for them. That will rekindle the glow so that once again you will feel the warmth of their presence."

Though the rain of her tears was still falling, his gentle, thoughtful words cleared a space between the clouds for her. She felt, at last, that there was something left from her old family to mix with the easy familiarity of the new. And his words of permanence gave her more stability than she had felt since that night when she had been offered a home with her old friends. If the vicar said it, what she had felt must be true, that Henry was deadly serious when he said she was a part of his family.

The service continued, but instead of returning to the total misery of before she was able to recognise familiar prayers, and even to join in, chokingly, with "Our Father, who art in Heaven…"

And the familiar blessing was comforting, too, so that when there was a general stir she felt able at last to look around her, and to see the faces of her companions also battered by emotion. She felt genuinely sorry for them, so distraught they looked. And then she saw the coffins, still standing in a line before the altar rail, two large and one only slightly smaller between them.

No, no… think of that love, that continuing love… Don't think of the empty, destroyed house, the familiar voices never to be heard again, the teasing of her brother, the special smells from the kitchen… she really must look up some of her mother's recipes and try them on Stephen and Henry. Ahh, but where were the books? Swept away by the water, never to be seen again?

The tears returned. But it was the first stage in that long, long process of healing, where the little things come to mind. The sudden thought of 'Oh, Mum'll like that, I must tell her', or 'I wonder if Greg managed to do that first time'. And the realisation that she could never again make that contact, never really find out. And the need to develop the strength of will to deal with it.

"Can you face going outside?" asked a strange voice at her side. Amidst the blurs of tears she recognised Henry, a Henry whose appearance shocked her. His normally ruddy, outdoor face was now white and seemed to have aged beyond measure. The eyes were as swollen from tears as her own. Nevertheless she nodded. This had to be seen through. She didn't really want to go anywhere. All she wanted was to stay at the front of the church, finish with her tears and then slip away. But that was not to be. The story of the day had to be followed to the end.

Henry followed his son from the pew, and Mary watched as they and the other bearers, including her and Stephen's white faced, tearstained friends, drifted back toward the three coffins at the foot of the sanctuary steps. She watched as, swayingly, the heavy, brass bound woodwork was lifted, carefully turned and borne past her. Ahh... past her. The last ever time she would be near to her mother... or was it her father... in this life, until she joined them in death.

At the thought she broke down completely, her knees gave way under her, and were it not for Susan's awareness she would have crumpled to the floor. She wished death would take her here, now, so she could join them. She thought of the loneliness, of how much she missed them, of the emptiness of her life now they were gone. But even in her extremity her sanity, her common sense forced itself back into her mind and she slowly recovered her equilibrium. Before too long, as though the event had never happened, she sat up, looked at Susan and nodded, rose, and stumbled into the aisle to follow the congregation to the churchyard.

Susan followed her quickly, arm over her shoulder protectively. They made their way into the fresh air which, although at first she hardly noticed she was outside, made Mary feel better. On the way down towards the new piles of earth her eyes looked out over Batson Creek to the green bulk of Snapes, and she knew that this was home, this is what her parents would have wanted, and that she must never leave here or she would be leaving them. And as for Greg... His spirit would always be here, sailing with them, laughing and running with Stephen and her as they went to school, played, or sat somewhere quietly contemplating.

No. Leaving was not an option. It would be betrayal.

As the group around the open graves made way for them she was able to look dispassionately at the things they had come to bury. She knew that the earth would hold them safe, that the people they had been were still with her in spirit, that just as she had vowed just then never to leave, they would not do so either. And Susan, checking her welfare carefully as the last ceremony progressed, saw that she was coping better than hoped or expected, and that the tears which she had expected to flow at this stage particularly were absent.

Not so with Stephen, though. Susan noticed with a rush of a different emotion that he had at last given in to the incredible strain of what he had been asked to do and to face, and had turned to his father to bury his face in his chest, nearly fourteen years old though he might be. And Henry was little better either. She wondered if she could...... And before she considered another moment she was almost dragging the astonished Mary over to her new family, so she could offer the comfort there that was so plainly needed. The Vicar paused in his carefully measured reading, but showed no surprise or annoyance at the interruption.

They watched the ceremony come to a close, huddled together as a group. Stephen was now the one sobbing uncontrollably, whilst Mary had herself come through her hiatus and could view the proceedings as it were from a distance. Earth was at last sprinkled on to the exposed woodwork in the joint grave, and even "Earth to earth, dust to dust..." could shock Mary no more.

The Service had done its job for her. It had brought her to the extremity, then had recovered her: the line had been drawn. For Henry and Stephen the opportunity had been squashed by the knowledge of the job they had to complete, and only when that was over could they come to the brink of their own horror.

The groups dispersed, leaving them there protected by the Vicar from the usual expressions of regret and sympathy that would have been unwelcome in the circumstances. He was aware of the unwavering presence of one old lady, and stood his ground between the four of them and her. As she moved forward he stepped in her way and spoke gently, firmly to her.

There was a discussion.

She was so insistent, Mary's great aunt, that he had to remind her at last that this was hallowed ground and that he held sway over it. He would not let her pass, for he had more than an idea she intended to be as tactless as she had previously. She glared at him, and stalked off.

When something like composure had set in to the group, Henry found that as well as the one arm circling his two charges, the other was around Susan. She was not in any way resisting the fact, nor did either of them either apologise to the other or move.

# 19 – Life, Susan, sailing, school

Evening found them, all of them, on the island.

How they had arrived there, Mary was almost uncertain. She remembered the departure from the churchyard, the looking back to the fresh graves, near which the sexton was hovering. Dimly she recollected being in the motor boat, being led along the path to the house, being sat in a chair, being given a cup of tea. But her eyes saw nothing in detail, she heard only dimly and gave mechanical answers.

The height of her emotions and the length of the morning had caused something approaching a mental and spiritual overload. Susan was uncertain what to do for her for the best. She should really go to bed, but it was not her position to say so. She made sure that the tea was drunk, that a sandwich was eaten. Then she looked questioningly at Henry. They made their way to the kitchen, alone. Stephen was just trying to settle his own still jangling emotions.

"Henry, she's had enough for one day. Can't she be put to bed?"

He looked at her. "Is that what's wrong? Is she just tired?"

"It's more than that. She's just had too much to take in for one day. The only thing to do would be to persuade her to rest, and I'm sure she'll sleep right through."

"I suppose it would be for the best," he mused. "Even if she doesn't, it might mean she'll be more alive later."

"May I take her up?"

"Yes. Er yes. I'd better show you where she can sleep." He thought hard. He couldn't allow even Susan to know that she was sharing a room and a bed with Stephen. He must go and make up his own bed for her.

"I need to make the bed," he announced. "It was stripped this morning and I've had no chance to do anything about it."

"Tell me when it's ready,"

He hurried through the living room, ignoring Stephen's enquiring glance. He followed his father upstairs.

"What's happening, dad?"

"I'm putting Mary in my bed for tonight. I don't think it's right that Susan should realise what's been happening up to now."

"She wouldn't mind."

"I don't know, and I don't want to find out the hard way, and certainly not today. So you can help, please, and pass me the bedclothes as I need them. Then Mary's going to have a rest, in bed, and with any luck she'll sleep until tomorrow."

"But dad, it's not three o'clock yet."

"I know. But she's not herself at all. Haven't you noticed?"

"But she'd be better in our bed. She's used to that."

"So she might. But Susan's going to help her up here, and I'm not having her realise you've been sharing."

There was no gainsaying him, so Stephen just helped where he could. The bed was made, and a fresh amount of bedding for Henry's later use was taken downstairs. Susan took this in and looked at Henry with a question in her eyes. He nodded. Quietly she crossed to Mary and sat beside her.

"Mary, I think we all need a rest, don't you? Shall I come upstairs with you?"

The eyes that looked back were vague, but the head nodded. Slowly she rose and allowed herself to be escorted up the stairs and into Henry's bedroom, where she lay on the bed with no encouragement needed.

"I think you kept command of yourself better than I could have done today, Mary," Susan whispered. "And control like that is tiring beyond belief. So rest now for a while, and come down when you want to. If you want to sleep for a bit, then why not? I shall, soon."

Mary looked at her and managed a shaky smile, then settled back more comfortably on the pillows and closed her eyes. Susan's hand ran gently through her hair a few times, and Mary could feel herself relaxing for the first time for hours. What if she did drop off for a while? It wouldn't matter, surely?

And without thinking about it, she fell asleep.

It was quite early, for him, that Stephen found himself wanting to go to bed. He had helped, as usual, with the farm's chores, what there was left of them, although he kept making silly mistakes. He tried giving chicken feed to their cows, who were not impressed, and for a long time stared at the udder of one of the cows, trying to think what to do next. But at last all was done. And he just said his good nights and stumbled upstairs, emotionally drained.

He tore off his clothes, as opposed to undressing, and just fell into bed. It felt strange, he thought, with no one else there, but sleep came before he could think anything more about it.

It was still dark when he sensed, rather than felt or saw, someone come to join him. Still more than half asleep he turned over and, without realising it, stretched out an arm to embrace the newcomer.

They slept.

He was surprised the next morning to find Mary with him as usual, and it took him some time to work out that she must have joined him during the night. Not that he minded: it seemed right for her to be there. He knew it was time he got up, and did so as carefully as he knew so as not to disturb her. But she had slept long, and the movements of bedclothes and mattress

188

were enough. She woke, to find him trying to climb over her at the precise moment that he was astride her sleeping form.

She yawned, saw him looking down at her. He did look silly, she thought, wearing nothing but underpants, one knee to her right and the other to her left. She giggled.

"You were meant to be asleep," he said.

"How could I with you leaping around the bed?"

"No, I mean you were meant to be asleep in Dad's bed."

"Too big. Too cold. Anyway, I sleep here. Don't I?"

"Yes....yes....I just wasn't expecting you to be here this morning, that's all."

There was a pause. They just looked at each other, smiling.

"Are you going to keep me prisoner here all day?" she said, at last.

"I could," he replied, as his grin widened.

"I could get you off in a moment."

"Yeah? You and whose army?"

"Who needs an army?" And she rolled over to try and dislodge him. It was probably just as well he was well balanced and aware, for he'd have landed on the floor with a thump if she'd been successful.

"Oh no you don't!" he said. "Girls who do that get tickled!"

And the next minute there were two people rolling on the bed, one still half in, one outside the bedclothes, tickling each other and laughing hysterically as they dug for each other's armpits and, in Mary's case, Stephen's feet. He couldn't reach hers. At length they collapsed back onto the bed, still laughing.

Henry heard the laughter from downstairs where he was making tea, and was pleased. No obvious emotional scars by the sound of it, he thought. Just good, honest play and laughter.

They made it downstairs soon after, still in good humour. But as Mary saw Henry she suddenly became serious.

"Good morning," she said, her face now straight.

"Hallo. Sleep all right?"

"Yes thanks."

"Good. Sounded like you did."

She looked at him, puzzled.

"The laughter, upstairs just now."

"Oh....yes....sorry."

"Sorry?! Sorry for laughing? Never be sorry for laughing, unless it's done at the wrong time or place."

"I thought it might be."

"Why?"

"Because of....yesterday."

"And today's today, and the last ever thing that my old friends would have wanted their daughter to do was to think she couldn't be happy when it was natural for her to be so. And what would Greg have said, seeing you suddenly get serious when you saw me? I'm a friend, aren't I, as well as everything else?"

He was almost winded by the speed she engaged him in a bear hug. The look on her face as she lifted her head to look at him was enough to say she understood, and that she knew that he did too.

It was a day without worries, almost light-hearted after the darkness of the previous week or so. Henry was very aware of the reasons for the lifting of the weight. He had been through it before, and although in the former case the situation was even more personal to him, he knew just how much relief there was in enduring that one day of public emotional hell, just so that the line was drawn, the spirit could be seen to be laid to rest, and the rest of life restarted. That didn't take away all the pain from losing a beloved family member by any stretch of the imagination, but the funeral formed a watershed and gave the chance for the living to rebuild.

In fact it was the first of many such days, and by the end of the week Henry felt it was time to mention school. To his surprise they were enthusiastic.

"It'll be good to see them again," said Mary.

He was surprised. "I thought school was everyone's least favourite activity. What's changed?"

"Everyone coming to the funeral. The way they were so nice, and..." she paused and looked at Stephen suspiciously bright eyed "... and the way they carried Greg."

He stood corrected.

That Sunday they went to church again. It seemed the right thing to do. Susan was there, and after the service she accepted an invitation to have lunch with them on the island.

"But no cooking for you," said Henry. "You must be sick of it, cooking all day in your café."

"Well, not to cook would be a nice change," she admitted. "But I enjoy doing it, really. I mean, I'd hardly have decided on a café to make a living if I didn't, would I?"

They laughed. "I always wondered why you did," said Henry. "I mean, if you wanted you could have your pick of a number of careers in Kingsbridge. Even in Salcombe there are offices which would have been a stepping stone to better things."

"You sound like my father," she said laughing. "According to him I'm the unfulfilled one of the family. But really, what more could I want than to do something that I enjoy, meet people whom I find fascinating, be a part

190

of the local community, and have lots of friends?"

"But don't you ever get bored?" asked Mary.

"Not at all, Mary. Well, I suppose there are times when it gets very quiet, or very busy indeed, and it's difficult to cope. But when it's quiet I can relax with a book, and when it's busy I just thank my lucky stars there's more money than usual coming in."

"Is it fun, then?"

"Well, apart from the washing up – as you all know well – yes. It's all the different people you meet that really makes it. You know, I get to know more about this town than most people do, even the local paper reporters. And I'm told so many confidences…" She paused. "D'you know, in some ways I'm almost a continuation of my father's business. People come to me for advice sometimes, and because I know a bit about Dad's work there are times I can at least give them a push in the right direction. But there are times when his expertise and, dare I say it, authority, are the best thing for them. And of course I recommend people to him and not to the opposition."

Mary thought.

"But why aren't you married?"

"*Mary*," said Henry. "That's hardly a tactful question."

"Sorry, Henry, but I don't see why."

Susan laughed. "It's all right. Most people I really know ask the same question in one way or another. I suppose the simple answer is that I've never found the right man. Once or twice I thought that I had, but then…" She trailed off. "Well, sometimes people let you down, that's all."

To Mary's surprise, Henry was looking straight at Susan's face, even after she'd finished. She didn't know what the look meant, but it was one she'd not seen before.

"You've done a good job on the dinghy," said Susan, as if to change the subject. "When do you think you'll get her finished?"

"Soon, I hope," said Stephen. "We've only got the centreboard to do now."

"Aren't you going back to school tomorrow? That won't leave you much time to work on her, will it?"

"That's true. We should be getting on with her now, I suppose. But there's lunch to cook, and…"

"Don't worry about lunch. If you two want to, you go and get on. I'm sure Henry and I can cook a meal together, can't we?"

Henry looked pleased, but said: "You know you're not here to cook. I wanted you to have a change, not work over a stove again."

"Cooking with someone else *is* a change, believe me. And one that's as good as a rest. Come on with you. You two go and spend an hour on the dinghy if you want, and we'll make a meal. If you're not back in an hour you'll go hungry. Ok?"

They grinned at each other. Stephen went to fetch the tin he'd been keeping the tools in, and collected the book and the remains of the rope from the lobby. They made their way down the island.

"Did you see how he looked at her?" asked Mary.

"Who?"

"Henry, at Susan."

"No?"

"I think he's soft on her."

"Who, Dad?"

"Yes."

"No...never. Well, I shouldn't think so. I mean, it's not that long since Mother died. Surely....?"

"How long is it? Some time ago, you said."

"I never thought.... Well! Mind you, if it's got to be anybody, I'd like it to be Susan."

"So would I."

He looked at her. He'd forgotten for a moment that she was now a part of the equation too. He smiled.

"Well, that's all right, then."

They worked on the dinghy, saying little; and what conversation there was consisted mainly of the practical communication needs of their work. When they had finished they stood back to look at her. In all honesty there was little visible difference. But golden rope where there had been grey and a sense of achievement in their hearts were the only rewards they needed.

"What are we going to do about it?" asked Stephen as they walked back.

"What?"

"Dad and Susan."

"What is there to do?"

"If we like the idea of them getting married, shouldn't we tell them?"

"I don't know. We don't know yet if they're thinking about getting married."

"True. But is it something we can find out?"

"I suppose we could try. Let's see what they say."

They found the objects of their inquisitiveness still busy with lunch when they returned, and obviously enjoying each other's company. Apart from a casual "Hallo, you two" from one and an "Everything all right?" from the other they were almost ignored. But the conversation between the two adults flowed like a clear stream.

They found themselves included more over the meal itself, yet the conversation steered more towards sailing and how the boat was and how school would be than to any budding relationships. Mary caught Stephen's eye from time to time and they both raised their eyebrows to each other in desperation.

"I'll wash up," said Mary, unexpectedly, when they had finished.

"I'll help," said Stephen.

In the kitchen Mary turned to him. "I was going to get Susan to help me so I could ask her. But you butted in."

"Dad wouldn't allow her to wash up after she'd cooked." said Stephen. "He has this rule: if you cook, you don't wash up."

"Oh. Yes. S'pose so."

But they never had a chance all afternoon either. At last Susan had to go, and to their surprise Henry asked Mary and Stephen to stay on the island. "Although there's nothing to stop you sailing, I suppose, if you'd like to. But please, don't be later than four o'clock. It's nearly dark then, and anyway I don't want you stranded by the tide, and I don't want to have to come and search for you in the dark."

They just looked at him. He'd never asked them not to go with him before. It was the clearest message they had that he and Susan might be more than social acquaintances. He had the grace to look uncomfortable. "Well, you don't want to be around me all the time, do you?" he asked, as if by explanation.

They enjoyed their sail, cold though the wind was. It was one of the first times they had been able to go north, up the estuary, and to see all that water stretching away from them where previously their cattle had grazed and their crops had grown was unsettling. Deliberately Stephen shied away from taking the dinghy over the top of the flooded farmhouse.

It intrigued them to see what differences the water had made to the hillsides. Parts that they used to walk on daily were now effectively cut off, whilst other areas which had been inaccessible without a long walk were now easily landed at and explored. One particular area seemed to draw Mary. It was the remains of the corner of a field. At the back were old woodlands, untouched for years because of the angle of the slope. Each side was bounded by thick hedges, and the woods had even crowded right up to them. Access had been by a track which had been built on the valley bottom but which now, of course, was well submerged. The trees which had ringed it still stood, their trunks marching up out of the water as the hillside rose. They encircled an area of water between the estuary and the shore, and the only entrance was a narrow passage between them. At low tide the water would leave even those trees high and dry, so adding even more privacy to the land. Not that it lacked any. The slope of the hill above saw to that.

"Can we land there?" she asked suddenly.

"Where?"

She pointed. All Stephen could see was a small entrance between submerged trees, and a patch of pasture, sloping, surrounded by woodland. But he made for it anyway, cautiously navigated his way through the entrance, and they moored.

She was out first, but just stood, looking. Slowly she turned round, and Stephen saw that her thoughts were miles away.

"It used to be ours," she said at last, as her gaze returned to Stephen.

"Still is, surely? I mean, just 'cos it's flooded it doesn't mean it becomes someone else's."

"P'raps. But it's lovely. And...." she added fiercely, "...I don't want to lose it. I want to live here."

"But aren't you going to live with us on the Island?"

"Oh yes. But I mean later. When I'm married."

He looked at her. A small part of his mind was telling him, almost against his will, that she'd always be with him, yet he knew she'd want to marry one day. An unspecified feeling of trouble settled on him. The small voice told him what to say, but he couldn't bring himself to.

There was silence for a long time.

"We could come here and camp," he said at last. She looked at him in unexpected delight.

"Now that *is* an idea," she said.

By the time they neared their Hard having made their way back to the island the conversation was in full flow again. Plans for what they'd do at camp, how far behind they'd be at school, what sort of welcome they'd get....all were discussed. Just before they stowed the sail Mary looked at him.

"Let's not say anything about our field to *anyone*. Not even Henry or Susan. They're going to have their secrets, let's have ours."

He thought. It went against the grain really, because he and his father shared everything. But he could see no harm in saying nothing. After all, the land was her family's, not his.

Henry was in a happy mood when they returned. But although he was as jovial as Stephen could ever remember, he refused to be drawn on the subject of Susan. Not her part in his future. At last he could stand dodging their leading questions no longer. Which was just as well, for they were running out of ways of asking them.

"Come on, you two. You've got school tomorrow. I've got to deliver you with the milk. In churns if necessary. The lorry will take you up to Blanksmill, and the bus will collect you from there."

They looked at him in surprise. "When did you arrange that, Dad?"

"At Susan's tonight. I'm sure there's nobody in the town she doesn't know. She got hold of the milk depot supervisor and he's agreed to the first

194

part of it. Then she got hold of old Stan – don't ask me how – to arrange the second part. He's thrilled you're due back, and said he'll do something special for you."

"What's he going to do?"

"He didn't say, so you'll have to wait. Now then, up you go, Mary. Then you can come down and talk for a while until it's time for Stephen to get ready."

This was their usual routine. It saved any embarrassment about conflicting use of the bathroom, and meant that each was well out of the way while the other was undressing.

"Dad...." said Stephen when Mary was upstairs.

"If it's about Susan, forget it. I know you were both trying to draw me out, to get me to say something about what's going on, but I'm not going to. So don't even try."

"But Dad...."

"Stephen, on this one I'm adamant. Now stop digging, or you'll get a blast from the hole or fall in it."

"All I wanted to say was…"

"STEPHEN!"

Henry got up and went into the kitchen. His son knew better than to follow him.

When Mary came down, looking very young in her pyjamas, she looked at him. He just shook his head.

"Shall I try?"

He shook it again. "He almost lost his temper with me when I tried. That's when he stomped off into the kitchen.

"Oh. Had I better go to bed?"

"Perhaps we both had."

"Come on then."

"Ok. I'll just shout goodnight to him."

He did so, then hurried away from the door before his father could realise what was happening.

Conversation in the bedroom was sporadic. Mary was drowsing off when there were footsteps on the stairs. Henry came into the room.

"Good night, Dad."

"Good night, old son. Sorry I shouted, but there are some things that I don't want to think about yet, let alone talk about. Even to you… two."

"That's Ok, Dad. We decided that we wanted to know what there was to know, but if you don't want to say then it's up to you. But…" he gulped, knowing the reaction there'd been when he last tried to say it. "If you do decide to get married again, we'd prefer it to be Susan rather than anyone else."

195

His father looked at him, no expression on his face at all. Stephen wondered what was coming. Henry bent down, kissed his forehead, and went soundlessly out of the room.

"I didn't get one then," said a voice by his side.

"He thought you were asleep, I should think," said the diplomat. "But I think you deserve half of that one, don't you?" And he leant over to kiss her forehead.

"That wasn't a half," she said.

"Hmm…perhaps they grow quickly."

It was early when, the morning tasks done, they set off with the milk churns. A fine rain was falling, and they were glad to reach the shelter of the milk staithe. They told Henry they'd be fine and told him to get back to the Island. The platform was too low to stand under really, so they passed the time by doing a paperless design of some seats they could fit inside. When at last the lorry arrived they were surprised to see red ribbons tied round the mirrors and the headlight stalks.

"Welcome back!" was the first greeting they heard from the two men.

"Thank you!" they replied, as one. "What're the red ribbons for?" asked Mary.

"You! To welcome you back!"

"Us? But that's lovely! Thank you."

"It's good to see you both. Now then, hop in, or we'll miss the bus."

By lorry it was a short haul up the hill toward the little village, but had they walked the rain would have driven into every crevice of their clothing as they panted their way up the steep hills of the valley. They sheltered, as always before, in the porch of Mrs Luscombe's store and they waved their friends off with shouts of thanks.

"Here he comes," said Stephen, as a green roof showed over the hedgerows on the crest of the next southernmost hill. "Any minute now."

But it seemed to take ages. Nothing appeared. "It must have been a van roof," said Mary.

Just when they had imagined that they were late at the stop and that Stan had gone without them there was a loud, persistent hooting from round the corner and their old friendly bus – as Mary always described it – panted into sight. And from every window, from the mirrors, from the headlights, there hung a red balloon.

The two just stood and watched the apparition draw to a halt by them. And not only did the door open, but Stan came out, followed by all the contingent from Salcombe and those whose homes lay to the south. There was a cheer, and they found themselves being ushered onto the bus like VIP's.

It was a day full of surprises. Those who weren't in on Stan's secret were astonished and delighted to see them, even some of those who weren't normally liked by one or other of them. And when they arrived at the school there were more red balloons, and a cheer went up from all those in the playground. Miss Armitage was there to greet them and to take them to her office for a pep talk.

"It's not much," she said, "but I want you to know that I am here to help if you need it. And I mean in *any* way. Don't regard coming to my office as a visit to the Headmistress, but as coming to chat to a friend. There may be times when I'm talking to someone else, but my Secretary will make you welcome and get you in to me as soon as is humanly possible. She might even make you a cup of tea." They both laughed politely. "I think – I know – that you'll find people are kind and friendly, but I know sometimes they're *too* kind, and I imagine what you need is just to get back to normal. Don't be afraid to tell them so. Any problems, I say again, come and see me. As a human being, a *friend*. Now, off you go, or I'll have to give you lines for being late to assembly." But her eyes were twinkling, and they knew she really was on their side.

The day settled down. They found at break that people were avoiding talking about the flood, and Mary's parents, and all the other things they thought would hurt. All, that is, except the friends of Stephen who had carried the coffin. Break found Stephen and Mary together, and surrounded by all the bearers, anxious to know how they'd settled down. Stephen acted as spokesman.

"Ok, thanks. We've had a lot to do, what with deciding what to do about the farm and so on. Oh, and renewing rigging on the boat, and learning to sail."

"You've learnt, have you? You looked as if you were doing all right when we came down to…to…" He trailed off into embarrassment.

"Learn how to be a coffin bearer? Yes, we weren't doing too bad. And look, it's all right to talk about it, isn't it, Mary? I mean, we all know it happened, and it's Ok to remember it. And…and I'm sorry I made a fool of myself at the funeral." How that stumbled out he didn't know. But even in his misery at the time he realised he was doing that thing that never happens to a fourteen year old. Crying in front of his peers.

Another of them looked uncomfortable. "Reckon there wasn't one of them who didn't join you. Never bin to a funeral before, never want to again, much less carry a coffin. But I'll admit to crying like a baby, too." This was from one of those who Stephen always regarded as one of the school's tough guys. He was the sort who could hold his own in a fight with most of the sixteen year olds who had left the school. It made him feel better. There was a silence. Each of them was thinking the same, that he'd wept, despite everything.

"Hey," said Stephen, after a long silence. "That's all right then. We're all pansies and cry-babies, and we'll fight anyone who says otherwise."

He got six astonished looks, then someone chuckled, the bubble burst and they were all in hysterics. The comment may have been only just about amusing but it was the stark contrast in mood that caused the reaction.

# 20 – Doctor

All in all they enjoyed the day and the return to normality. Having no rain on the journey home would have made it better, but they were still cheerful despite it. The bus dropped them at Blanksmill where they had boarded it that morning. The walk downhill to Lincombe was wet but easy: it was downwards and homewards. Henry was waiting for them in the launch, hunched up against the weather. Getting home was welcome, and they found that the Aga had heated enough water for a bath each. With that, and a cup of tea inside them they felt better and changed mental gear back into home life.

"I've been busy," said Henry after a while. "Come and look." He took them out to the cowshed. And there was a heap of sawn timber of all lengths and widths, some smooth and prepared, some just rough cut.

"What's it for, dad?"

"For my new bedroom, that's what! It's time I actually got on with it, and the first day I have to do it, it rains. But at least it's given me time to take some measurements and draw plans. And cut some wood. I know what I'm going to do and how I'm going to do it, and now I just hope I've got it right."

They were suitably impressed. Stephen felt a pang of regret he didn't understand.

A change of routine is always tiring, even when welcome. The day had gone well for them both, and they were secretly glad to be back in school with their friends and doing mundane things like learning. They seemed to have spent such a long time recovering from tragedy, in practical and spiritual ways, that home life had become the norm, as it did in the long holidays. They were more ready for an early night than normal, and went up without argument or comment when Henry accused Mary of falling asleep in front of the fire.

Upstairs, after the usual routines, Stephen slipped into bed and lay looking up at the ceiling, the moon providing enough light to see it.

"How did it go for you, today?" he asked Mary, hoping she was still awake.

"All right. Better than I thought it would. They'd listened to what Miss Armitage had said and just talked about it when I did, and didn't when I didn't."

"Same here. All except one idiot who kept asking what it felt like, being in the storm."

"What did you tell him?"

"I ignored him, mostly. Then when he kept on I told him it was wet and windy, just like him."

She laughed. "What did he say about that?"

"He just said 'Huh!' and walked off."

There was a long silence. He thought she'd gone to sleep.

"What was it like, Steve?"

She rarely called him Steve. His father did, of course, or occasionally someone made a mistake. He had always been Steve to his mother, and when she died it was more or less understood that, from then, everyone would use his full name. It started off that way because people thought it was better not to remind him of his mother's pet contraction, obvious and common though it was. But 'Stephen' stuck, and now when people used the contraction it was by accident, or else it was someone who meant a lot to him and knew it.

As it was Mary, he knew it was the latter, and she was being serious. He thought hard. How could he describe his thoughts of that night, without disturbing her too much?

"You know when you read a scary book," he started slowly. "And it's a good book that gets you really into it, and then things start to happen? Well, it was like that. I mean, the rain and normal flooding was the background and we were all really fed up with that. But then there was the radio message, then Dad going out, then that awful crash and the lights going out and the water, and I thought that Dad wasn't coming back..."

He stopped. To have told it in court was one thing, but to lie here and tell it to another of the victims, someone who had come out of it so much worse than himself, was quite another.

He gulped. "And then to hear his truck come towards me....well." He paused again.

"But the worst part of it was finding Greg, then getting his breathing back, then him just saying what he did before... before..."

The strength left him again, and he could feel the tears on his cheeks as the mental agony and helplessness hit him again. This time it was Mary's turn to comfort him.

"It wasn't your fault," she said, moving towards him and putting an arm over his shoulders. "You did all that anybody could."

But he shook his head angrily. "There must have been something. I just didn't do it."

"What?"

"If I knew that, I'd have done it."

"But then, you can't be to blame. I'm his sister, and I'm not blaming you."

"That's not the point."

"Then what is?"

He shook his head again, as if trying to dislodge the blame from it. It was good, what she'd said, he thought, but there must have been something he should have done. It was typical of adults to say that he'd done everything possible, just to make him feel all right, but there must have been something....

His desperation was interrupted by a light kiss on his forehead.

What? What was this? Oh. Mary saying good night. He sought the warmth, gave it a kiss in return and settled his body down as best he could. If Mary didn't hold out any blame to him it shouldn't be too bad. But then, did she know either? What was there he could have done? People were saved with worse injuries than that – just think of the war. He vowed that he'd find out. He'd have to find out just what the damage to Greg was, so he could describe it to someone who'd give him an honest answer. No good asking Dad – no medical training, and he'd try to fob him off, save his feelings...but he'd get an answer somewhere. Must be something. Field bandages. Morphine...

Funnily, he'd never had nightmares before. Not even the night of the storm.

The next day at school Stephen, who could be quite persistent when he wanted to be, asked Miss Armitage if he could talk to the school doctor when convenient. Much to his surprise and embarrassment he found himself provided with permission to leave lessons and an appointment with the man himself at his surgery.

"If *you* of all people say you need to see a doctor, then I know it's serious," she told him,

"It's not an emergency," he said.

"No. You know about emergencies, I know. If it was there'd be an ambulance on its way here now. If there's anything I can help with, you will ask, won't you?"

"Yes, Miss Armitage. It's just that you're... you're not the person who can give me the answer, that's all."

"I'm not going to pry. Go and see Dr. Theobald. He can do anything."

It was odd, being out of school and walking round Kingsbridge on his own. Usually he'd be with a crocodile of others, going somewhere on a nature study walk or a visit. But he knew the way to the surgery well enough.

"Yes?" said the forbidding looking receptionist at her window.

"I've got an appointment to see Doctor...er....Doctor..."

"Yes?"

"...Doctor Theobald."

"Then why didn't you say so? Name?"

"Doctor Theobald."

"Don't try and be clever with me or I'll have you out of here in two seconds. Name?"

"Mine?"

"Who else?"

"Stephen Loft."

"Age?"

"Fourteen."

"Address?"

"Loft Island, Salcombe."

"What street and number?"

"There are no streets. We're the only farm on the island."

She looked at him as if he was mad.

"Why do you want to see the Doctor?"

"I want some advice."

"What about?"

"It's er....it's....about what to do."

"What to do when? You haven't got a girl into trouble, have you?"

"Pardon?"

"No. You're probably too young. Well, you'd better sit down. Over there. And don't make a mess of the magazines."

Thankfully he escaped, wondering if she treated everyone like that.

Half way through a three-year-old edition of Woman's Realm a young woman came out, followed by a middle aged man in a white coat. The woman went out; the receptionist held a whispered conversation with the doctor.

"Hallo Stephen," the greeting was genuinely pleasant. "My temporary receptionist tells me we have a possible troublemaker in the surgery and pointed over here, but I think they must have gone. Come into the surgery."

He followed him in, the door shut and the doctor turned to him.

"You are the Stephen Loft who was involved in that tragedy in the flood, aren't you?"

"Yes sir."

He found a hand extended to him. In surprise he shook it. "I've read about it and heard about it, of course, and I've seen your picture in the paper. You did well, young man, very well. Circumstances like that would have rendered a lot of boys your age into gibbering wrecks, yet from everything I read and hear you kept your head and did everything you could. And it was your hearing that saved young Mary, wasn't it? I hope she's grateful to you."

"Er....yes, sir. We're looking after her... I mean she's part of our family now."

"I'd heard. Well, you sound to me like one of life's success stories. But what brings you here, eh?"

202

"I need to know, sir… was there anything else I could have done? To save Greg?"

"Greg's the youngster who died, isn't he? Tell me what you did."

"He was lying on his front and he wasn't breathing, so I did Holger Neilson and at last he started breathing again. I rolled him over and looked at his face. It was white. His eyes opened and he told me to 'look after them', then he stopped breathing again and his eyes stayed open. I was just going to roll him over again when I saw this hole in his chest, bleeding. And I could see bits of him in there and......." He stopped and covered his face with his hands as the horror hit him again.

The doctor waited patiently. At last Stephen recovered and looked at him. "Sorry," he said. "It's just that when I think of it again it's all so horrible."

"I'm not surprised," said the doctor. "You went through a lot that night. And since, come to that. It was an experience which would have defeated many other boys, as I said, and many adults too."

Stephen looked at him, unable to speak.

"And you want to know what else you could have done? Anything that would have saved his life?"

Stephen nodded.

"OK. Well, let me tell you that as well as reading the local papers and getting their version of it I also happen to know some of the medical people in Salcombe and around, and I know the extent of the injuries your friend suffered. And given that, yes, there were one or two things you could have done.

"You could have had a full scale operating theatre built in advance, with a hospital to support it. You could have undergone the six years of training it needs to become a junior doctor. That would have enabled you to assess the damage to his insides, perhaps to correct it, and certainly to sew up the wound. You could then have given him over to the care of qualified nursing staff to give him twenty-four hours a day care. And even if there was no irreversible damage caused by his injury, which would have been almost a miracle, the water he was floating in would certainly have infected the delicate organs inside him, so all your efforts would have been in vain."

He paused, looking at Stephen's expressionless face, and smiled grimly.

"Stephen, there is nothing I, nor the top surgeon in the world, could have done that you didn't do. If it had been me there, your friend would not have been happy to get over his last wish to you, his friend, that you and your family should look after the survivors. So you were by a miracle the best person to be there, who actually got the boy breathing again so he could speak, and so he could at the last die with someone he knew – his best friend – supporting him. And who can ask for more?"

By this time Stephen's eyes were unashamedly streaming. He was not sobbing, but the tears ran down his face for all that. The doctor went and stood behind him and gently rested his hands on the boy's shoulders until he had once again recovered. Stephen fished in his pocket for a handkerchief, wiped his face and blew his nose.

"Better now?"

He nodded.

"I wasn't lying to you either, Stephen. I meant every word. If it had to happen, you were the man for the job."

He nodded and eventually turned. "Thank you. I just had to know if I should have done anything else. You have no idea how much better that makes it."

"Yes I have, my friend. I'm a doctor. There are always times when I wonder the same things myself. But whatever I believe I may have done differently, nobody has yet invented a way of putting the clock back so I could try a different way. All any of us can do is the best we're able given the circumstances. You did."

This time it was Stephen's turn to extend his hand to be shaken, and turned wordlessly to the door.

"Oh, and Stephen..." He turned in the doorway. "Ask my receptionist to come into the surgery, would you?"

The journey back to the school found him walking automatically as his brain took in what he had been told. Gradually he began to feel lighter and lighter of spirit until as he re-entered the grounds his step was positively bouncing. He called first at Miss Armitage's office, but her secretary told him she was teaching.

"I've been to see the doctor," he told her. "Could you tell Miss Armitage that everything's all right, please?"

"Yes. Will she know what it's about?"

"Er....well....er....probably not. But if you just tell her, I'll see her later, please."

"Very well."

He waited in the school library for the lesson to end, and when it did sought out Mary. She detected something new about him, something lighter, more positive, although she could give it no name.

"Where've you been?"

"I've been to see a doctor."

She looked alarmed. "You don't look ill."

"I'm not."

"Then why..."

"You know last night? I wanted to know what I should have done for Greg to save his life? And you couldn't tell me?"

She nodded, eyes downcast.

"Well, there wasn't anything."

She looked up at him, puzzled.

"There was nothing else anyone could have done. The doctor said so. Not even if he was outside a hospital with all the life-saving stuff in the world could anyone have done anything for him."

"But why…what…what does it matter?"

"It means that it wasn't my fault."

"But we knew that."

"But *I* didn't."

"I've told you, so's Henry."

"But that might have been to make me feel all right about it. This was medical fact."

"Oh. So you feel better now."

"Yes. No. Greg's not alive, but I did what anyone could to save him. And the doctor said that it's just as well it was me 'cos he could tell me what he wanted."

She gave him a long look, and walked away. He looked after her in surprise, mouth open. At the other side of the room she looked at him.

"And that makes it all right, does it?"

"Er…no. But I needed to know there was nothing else I could have done. I know I can't bring him back – I wish I could – but *I'm not to blame.*"

She looked at him again, then nodded.

"See you later."

He watched her go, perplexed.

Miss Armitage was pleased to hear of the successful outcome of his visit once he had told her the reason for it. "I'm sure that's a weight off your mind, Stephen. It's as well to clear up these nagging little doubts, and no matter how many times well-meaning people tell you something, if you can get an unbiased opinion or facts from an expert then it's more meaningful for you. Have you told Mary?"

"Yes Ma'am. She's a bit…well….I don't know."

"Perhaps it's just that it's brought it back for her. Not just the loss, but that night. She'll get over it. Just tell her you're sorry if it upset her, and give her a hug or something, and she'll be all right. But try to understand her. Don't forget she's been through even more than you, and has lost almost everything."

He nodded. Perhaps that explained it.

She seemed normal enough on the bus home, which this time had to take them into Salcombe itself. Their normal mooring place at the end of the creek at Lincombe would be on the mud which, at low spring tide, now covered what had once been a solid road. The tides were wrong for them.

Over the weeks they had learnt quickly to realise that their lives would now be ruled by the tide's steady breathing. Although their own island was never inaccessible, and neither were Salcombe's main Hards and jetties, the creeks around them dried out almost completely at low water. What was once their own sweet grazing land would once again become visible, but gradually it was altering its appearance as the grass died off to be replaced by weed and mud. It was by contrast desolate, and the mournful beauty of wetland terrain was something they couldn't appreciate yet.

"Everything OK?" came Henry's greeting.

"Yes, thanks."

"I've started on the new room, so you might find some changes when we get back."

"Can you manage on your own, then?"

"Should do. I've done it before."

"When?"

"When we needed some more space for the cows. Some of that's my work."

They looked at him with new respect.

"I didn't know that," said his son.

"Ah, you don't know everything about me, not even you. I've had to do a lot in my time."

The old porch was cleared of all its usual clutter, and a new wall had been started to separate it from what would eventually become a much smaller entrance lobby. As a lobby it had extended along quite a bit of the front of the house, so would make a reasonable size bedroom. The roof had received the first attention, and Henry was almost looking forward to the next rain so as to ensure it was leak-free.

"So where's the new lobby going to be?" asked Mary.

"I'm going to extend from the door here, out and sideways the other way," he said. "That way we'll have a space between the kitchen and it to give us a more sheltered area for wood chopping. And it'll have a door to the side, not to the front, so we can stop the wind blowing straight in as it has in the past."

"How about a window at the end of the passageway from the kitchen, so we can see who's coming?" asked Mary.

Henry looked at her. "That's a very good idea, Mary. I should have thought of it. Anywhere else we should have windows? Not too many, 'cos they're difficult to build in, but say anyway."

Apart from an additional window in the main door into the new lobby there were no more suggestions, to Henry's relief. He was already thinking that he'd bitten off more than he could chew.

They ate, and then before the light failed completely they did what they could to help Henry with the building work. It was a very tired trio who at last faced the washing up, straggled upstairs and collapsed into bed.

That day set the pattern for the next few. Gradually – very slowly – the extension grew. Firstly the structure, the skeleton, was firmed up and attached to the existing outer wall. Then the planks were fixed to the inside to provide as flat a surface as possible for filling and painting. On the outside went long straight logs, split down the middle, flat surfaces inwards but showing a practical, weather-beating, rustic appearance to the outside.

Each Sunday saw the visit of Susan, and this was always a high point of the week. It wasn't that the three of them didn't get on or were tired of each other's company, but a change is, as they say, as good as a rest. And Henry was always somehow lighter of mood on a Sunday. The family's worsening financial situation was worrying him more than he was letting on, and being unwilling to discuss it with Stephen and Mary and so giving them worries, it meant that there was nobody else to talk to about it. Matters had not yet reached the state where he needed to take professional advice or even mention it to Susan, he believed. Yet something had to be done about their dwindling income from what was now a smallholding as opposed to a proper farm. True, there was a small income still from the Lofts' and Beales' combined herd of cows which were being looked after by friends, but it was less than they'd been able to realise when they had sole charge of the herd.

The burning question was, what to do about it? There was still no news from the Council or anyone else about compensation, nor any decision about rebuilding the reservoirs in the hills or the dams on the Estuary. Without that decision the insurance companies refused to pay out. As time went on it seemed they were being forgotten again.

Yet as summer approached there seemed to be more dinghies than usual on the lower estuary, many of which sailed up to look at the island and to explore even further north. In fact once or twice they found people who had landed on their property and were calmly walking around. They had to post signs at the obvious landing places to say it was a private farm with livestock and guard dogs.

Susan reported that Salcombe's few hotels were almost completely full, and that interest had been shown at last in one of the large properties which had been unoccupied for almost ten years. Her father's prospective clients wanted to turn it into a another hotel. It seemed that other people had heard about the area and its new attractions. Her own little café business had blossomed and she had taken on part time staff.

# 21 – The moment

At last spring turned to summer. The schools started thinking about exams and the end of term, which arrived with exultation from pupils and staff alike.

After that Mary and Stephen thought of little except sailing and exploring their new world, enjoying the freedom in contrast to the requirements of school. They were getting proficient with Mary's dinghy, and Henry trusted them more and more to go where they wanted. They wanted to go everywhere; everywhere they could explore by water, knowing that there was always the possibility that one day the works would be reinstated, the valley dried again and returned to pasture. And then would come the end of all those possibilities of adventure.

Every time they returned from the north of the estuary Mary wanted to land on her field, and would just stand looking round it, drinking in its secluded beauty, before they set sail again to cover the short distance home. Stephen also grew to love the little place, to start with just because his companion did, but later to love it because it was so quiet, so peaceful, so much *theirs*.

Work on Henry's new bedroom and the new entrance way continued and at last there came a day when they were able to move furniture into it. But a snag presented itself in that there was no bed for Henry to use – or, if he used his old double bed, there was no bed for Mary. Because of the indecision about the area's future there could still be neither compensation nor insurance settlements, and there was just no money in the bank account to allow a new bed to be bought for either man or girl. So despite the readiness of the room, sleeping arrangements had to remain unaltered until Henry had time and wood to build a bed – a job he baulked at since there was no spare mattress for it.

The weather became steadily warmer, and one weekend in mid-August there came a day of real heat. Mary and Stephen had tactfully gone sailing to be out of the way when Susan arrived at the island, and were sweltering their way to and from Southpool on the tide. It was one of their favourite sails, as most of the new visitors with their motor boats or badly sailed hired dinghies stuck to the main estuary. Southpool creek was peaceful, and safe, and they could turn into Watermill Creek if the wind wasn't in their favour for Southpool itself.

"I like Southpool," said Mary suddenly after one of their long periods of companionable silence. Stephen woke from his daydream with a start.

"Yes... yes, it's a nice little place. Nothing happens there. There's no visitors."

"Mmmm. Hot."

"Pardon?"

"It's hot. I'd like a swim."

"We need to keep going while the tide's in our favour. If we stop to swim here we'll be on the mud."

"Let's go to *our* place and swim."

"I was going there anyway. We always do."

"I know. But it's just the place for swimming."

"Yeah."

So they tacked on down the creek, being careful to avoid the places they knew were shallow. They'd somehow never become stuck fast yet in all the months they'd been sailing, although there were times when the centreboard had jerked upwards to tell them that the mud wasn't too far below them. Stephen rounded Scoble Point and turned up the estuary, the wind almost directly behind them. They hauled up the centreboard and despite her clinker build their little boat fairly creamed her way north east, past Loft Island and just beyond towards their own sheltered kingdom. Mary, who had taken over as they passed their home, skilfully gybed whilst they were still at full speed, bringing the sail over so they could reach in through the remnants of the kingdom's sheltering trees and toward the shore. Once inside, they were protected from the wind, and in a manoeuvre they had practised time and time again, Stephen struck sail as they glided through the calm water to their deserted shore. The dinghy grounded gently on the mud, and Stephen leapt ashore with the anchor.

"Phew, it's hot in here," he said as he stamped it in further up the field.

"Mmm. Very." Mary was just looking round, as she always did when they first arrived. Good. Nothing had changed, except the grass looked a bit more like summer grass and less like the rich, lush green of spring pasture. Ah…the farm….but she mustn't think of that. That way lay tears and unhappiness. Hot? Of course it was hot. Why did Stephen say that? And why was he looking at her like that?

"What's the matter?" she asked.

"You looked sort of lost."

"How can I be lost here?"

"No, I don't mean that sort of lost. I mean you were thinking about something else. Lost in thought."

"Oh." Silly boy. Why didn't he know what she was thinking. About how, one day, there'd be a house in here: hers and her family's, and they'd only be able to get to it by boat. By boat over the top of her parents' old farm….no! Not again! But it was there, for all that, and that presence meant that it was one of the reasons she loved this little kingdom. Their kingdom. Hers and Stephen's. Why was he taking off his shirt? Oh. The heat. Lucky boy. She couldn't do that. He's got some muscles. Funny. Never noticed that before. Gosh, he's right. It *is* hot. Why weren't girls allowed to take their shirts off too? After all, it's only Stephen. Would he laugh at her for not having breasts yet? But if she did, she'd never dare take off her shirt, even with him. Would she? Would it matter if she did? Now?

"Stephen?"

"Yeah?"

"Would you mind if I took my shirt off too?"

"No. Why should I?"

Well really! She might just as well be another boy! Why should he, indeed! She'd show him! So, mustering as much unconcern as she could, she took off her shirt, and laid back, facing the sun, as he was.

How odd, after all these years, to feel the breeze across her chest. How nice. How much cooler. Why had she ever bothered, with Stephen, to wear a top all the time? When they played together as young kids none of them had. Greg, Stephen, herself…. they'd all gone round just in shorts in the summer. And, early on, when still really infants, she remembered them all bathing completely naked in the river, too. What? What was Stephen saying now? Swim? Yes. Yes. Good idea. What would it be like without a top?

"Yes. Love to."

"Good. Where are your swimming things?"

"In the boat….aren't they?"

"I'll look."

He was fairly certain that they had both left in such a hurry that the chance of swimming hadn't occurred to either. But he wasn't going to admit that to Mary. He'd almost forgotten that she was a girl, so used was he to having her around, so used was he to her being as good a sailor as himself, so used was he to her being tough, physically and mentally, despite being a kid two years younger. It was a nuisance, really: if it had been Greg they'd both just have stripped off and jumped into the water as they had on those many occasions when the two of them had escaped from parents and kid sister for a while in the summer. There had been that sheltered backwater in the stream which just cried out to be swum in, and they'd done just that, oblivious to the farm workers in the fields that overlooked them who saw two boys swimming, or lying in the sun afterwards to dry, being boys, natural and unashamed.

But now here they were; he was with the 'kid sister', his old friend was dead, and all that was left was the memory and a friend to look after. But then, she was also his casual friend now, just as Greg had been. She was someone who it was natural to be with, who he wanted to be with, just as he had with Greg.

As he failed to find any hint of swimming things or towels in the dinghy Stephen shook his head impatiently with the quick movement that his father knew so well from his mother and now from him, and which Mary had also grown to know and find familiar. It cleared away the difficult, confusing thoughts,

He walked back. Mary looked up at him.

"No?"

"No. Didn't think we put them in."

He dropped back down to lie beside her. The peace and the heat were making them both lethargic, but at least he could think…

…back to the days when they had dived off into that backwater, he and Greg, bombing each other, climbing out of the steeply sloping sides, diving back in again, wrapped up in the game and each other, careless of anyone who might have thought it odd or unwise for two boys to wear nothing as they swam.

"Damn," he said suddenly.

She looked at him, a look he could feel.

"I was thinking back to the summers with Greg…" He tailed off, aware that he would upset her, probably.

"Tell me," she said quietly, almost eagerly. After her own thoughts it seemed fitting that Greg should be the subject.

"It's just… it's just that when you weren't around, we'd go off on our own to swim," he said. "I was just thinking back…"

"Where did you go?" She encouraged him, though she knew.

"You know where the river bent round, and there was that wide bit – a meander, I suppose." He remembered his Geography. "It was around there. There was a pool cut out that was deep enough to swim in even in midsummer. We'd go up there. Nobody could see us."

"I don't remember you ever taking your stuff to go swimming."

"We never bothered. We just went. Afterwards we'd just dry in the sun a bit until we could get dressed again."

"You never wore anything."

He failed to notice it was not a question.

"We never took anything. And anyway, what was the point? It was only Greg and me."

"Yes but… supposing someone saw you?"

"No one did."

"But supposing they did?"

"Well, I suppose we were in the water most of the time. It didn't seem to matter. And anyone else would have been a long way away. They'd probably think we had skin coloured trunks on."

She looked at him. Half of her wanted to laugh at him, at the thought of skin coloured trunks and the visual inconsistencies they would have presented, together with the possibility of discovery. How could they just do that? But she knew they had.

"I used to come and watch you."

He looked at her sharply. "You followed us?"

"Of course."

"And we never knew."

She had been envious then and was now. She wanted to throw off the rest of her clothes and just dive in the water, to get cool, and to pretend she was to him the close friend that Greg had been. But then, she was, wasn't she? They'd been family together for years… ages… months… surely that made her more than just 'friend'? She looked at him, sweating as heavily as she was herself, flopped back on the withering grass in an attempt to get the coolness from the earth against his back so that at least one side of him was comfortable. What would he think if… but she was a girl, and girls didn't do things like that.

And she remembered again the days when two young boys would give her the slip as they were playing some game and she would never see them again for the rest of the afternoon. The frustration, the misery at the loss of her only playmates, the tears to Mum, to Dad. And all she would be told was that they were boys and older, and needed time to themselves to do boyish things, and she couldn't rely on them all the time. And what now? What if Stephen were to invite some of the boys from school back here, boys of thirteen and fourteen, so much older than her own twelve years? Would the same happen? Would she be left behind again? She couldn't bear that, and the desperation mounted in her.

"Damn," she declared, unconsciously echoing his exclamation of five minutes before. He looked at her sharply.

"I'm too hot," she said, suddenly standing up. He watched, mouth open comically, as she appeared, in his eyes, to have thrown caution to the winds, and momentarily stood there, bare chested, looking down at him, before summoning up the remainder of her courage and pulling down her shorts, her knickers, and bending to take off her shoes. In seconds she was running down to the water's edge, conscious of his surprised eyes on her naked back, her exposed skin clenching all its muscles in apprehension, suddenly wishing she hadn't been so adventurous.

She made herself stop at the water's edge, and look back to where he was grinning at her. Damn him! She wanted so much to be accepted as Greg, as a friend and not just an adjunct to his family, and here he was, laughing at her.

She turned with all the dignity that a naked twelve year old girl can muster and waded fast into the water. Ahhhh… it was cold. After sitting in the heat for so long the shock of it made her gasp, almost shout. But she made herself go deeper, to spite him and to get herself away from his

212

surprised gaze. Although she wanted only to scream and turn back to the shore she made herself duck her head below the surface and start swimming. The shock of the cold made her draw in breath involuntarily and she thought she was going to drown, but swallowed instead and a supreme effort made her recover. Gradually the feeling of numbing cold wore off, and her strokes through the water gained more style and less splash.

She headed for the gap they had sailed through into the lagoon, although it was some way off still. She slowed down to conserve her strength. At length she was aware of sounds behind her and realised that, hoped that, it must be Stephen. She stopped and trod water, looking back. He was swimming fast after her, and as he came to her she could see that there was something in his eyes apart from the smile she had seen as she dived into the water.

"Bloody cold, isn't it?" He'd never used any swear words to her before, not even when they were having problems sailing. Why? Why now? But it was.

"Bloody cold," she said. He grinned wider.

"Warmer where it's shallow. Over there by the trees. I'll race you."

Somehow, despite the two years and gender differences, they both reached them at the same time. He was right, it *was* warmer there. She trod water again, and hit a tree root with her calf.

"Oww."

"What's the matter?"

"My leg hit something."

"Probably a bit of tree. You OK?"

She found something she could stand on, and hoisted herself up on it, only to fall off the other side and surfaced, gasping again. He laughed, then stopped. "Sorry."

"Ok. I can stand on the mud here."

"Can you?"

"Yes, look." And her chest appeared out of the water. He tried to do the same, and found that he could too.

"Better?" he asked.

"Mmmm. It's fun. I like the feel of the water over me."

"Yes. We do too. I mean…"

Yes, she thought, Greg and him.

He continued. "I mean, when we first did this we found how good it felt, and we'd have liked you with us too. But you were young and… and a girl, and your parents would never have allowed it."

"But now it's all right, is it?"

"It was you who did it! I didn't make you."

"But you looked so surprised."

"Well, I didn't expect it. You never warned me. If you had I'd have gone away until you were in the water, then stripped off…"

"So I could see you?"

"Er… no. I mean…. Well, we're here now, aren't we? What happens now?

"I'm going back to the beach to see if I've got a bruise."

"A bruise? Oh yes, the branch. What d'you want me to do?"

"Don't mind." And she launched herself into the water and swam away from him.

He watched her body bobbing up and down in the water more intently than he ever had with Greg. Odd. With him you just swam, then stopped, climbed out, chatted, swam again… And all you were looking for was to see where your friend was. With Mary, he was conscious of a need to look at her, to watch her for some reason. He put it down to his being responsible for her, not to the fact that her body was different from his, although as she swam away from him her bottom looked much the same as Greg's had done, so far as he could remember. But he'd not seen her from the front. And she'd not seen him naked at all. Oh.

He shook himself. He remembered how he'd stripped off as she swam away from the beach and had dived after her, how freezing the water had felt, how it had occurred to him that she was being very brave, how suddenly it had felt as if he were once again swimming with Greg, his old friend, on equal terms; how it had suddenly dawned on him that this was Mary, his family, a girl, who he was being so free and easy with. What would happen if he just followed her out of the water when they got to the beach? Would he have the nerve? What would she think? Would she tell her friends, or Dad?

Worried, he launched himself after her just as she was climbing out of the water, walking up the beach. She was lying face upwards in the sun – forgetting about the bruise, he noticed – and had her hands behind her head to tip it towards him. He stopped just in his depth, now quite anxious.

"Mary?"

"What?"

"This is between us alone, yes?"

"Ok."

Feeling himself going red in the face despite the water's coldness, he made his legs push him out of the shallows, and with only a momentary pause as the wavelets dipped below his waist he walked up the muddy grass and quickly turned to lie face down.

So that was what older boys looked like, thought Mary. Odd.

Why?

Not horrible. Not attractive. But somehow, well, strong. She must ask one of the girls at school who had hinted that she knew more than she'd said so far. To see if she could find out more.

She turned over onto her stomach, her head looking towards him. She smiled, and got a sheepish smile back. Looking at him like this, he did look strong. The muscles on his arms were quite pronounced. She remembered small boys at school holding their arms out to show off non-existent muscles and was suddenly quite proud that his showed naturally, even now. Once again she noticed the broader shoulders. He looked years older than he did in their silly school uniform, complete with cap. Someone to depend on. Like Henry. She smiled again.

"What's the matter?" came the question.

"Nothing. Just thinking."

"Oh. What?"

"How different you look like that compared with going to school."

He looked at her. What did she mean? Of course it was different from going to school. He'd never go to school naked. And a vision of them both, standing at the bus stop carrying the regulation school satchel and headgear each, but wearing nothing besides, came into his imagination, and immediately took off from there to the laughter they'd get, to the comments, to the ridicule... And over it all rose one huge belly laugh that scared two seagulls scavenging at the water's edge so that they flapped hastily away. To ease his cramped stomach muscles he turned over on his back to laugh. Mary looked at him, grinning widely herself, not at what he was laughing at, nor at his body, but just at the unexpected, infectious laugh.

When he had recovered and wiped the tears away from his eyes he turned on his side to look at her.

"What was that about?" she asked.

"I was imagining waiting for the bus on Monday morning, satchel over my shoulder, cap on my head, but wearing nothing else. And what people would say as they passed us, and what old Stan's face would look like, and what the others on the bus would say..." He chuckled again. She shuddered.

"I wouldn't like it."

"Nor would I. But it was funny to imagine."

She said nothing. It took him some time to realise he was facing her, exposed, and he quickly turned over again despite the fact that she was on *her* side facing *him*.

"Are we going back in the water, then?" she asked, as it was obvious he was content to lie there. Or was it that he didn't want to show off his front to her?

"Come on, then. We'll find somewhere we can dive from. How about by the entrance? It must be deep there."

"And cold," she reminded him.

"True. There must be somewhere else. How about outside this pool? What about the shore there?"

"People could see us."

"No. Nobody comes up here."

"I bet they do. Besides, we'd be seen from the other side of the creek."

"S'pose so. Where is there, then?"

"Must be a branch or something…" By this time he had risen to his feet and was scanning the shoreline around their small empire. "Look! Look over there. That tree trunk that's fallen into the water. I wonder if it's deep enough there?"

He had half turned round to engage her attention, careless for the moment that he was still naked, yet still aware of it in the back of his mind. She smiled at him.

"Let's go and find out, shall we?"

He set off at a run, anxious to explore, and subconsciously enjoying the feel of the breeze and the freedom on the normally clothed parts of his body. Mary ran after him, glad to be doing something, and glad that embarrassment seemed at last to be evaporating. They found that to get to the tree they would have to swim. The undergrowth was too thick to enable them to walk to it. For the first time Stephen turned to face her without being shy of his nakedness and allowed her to come close enough to talk.

"We'll have to swim from here. D'you want me to see if it's ok first, or are you coming too?"

For some reason she had no qualms about facing him like this, none at all. She felt at ease despite her nakedness, and once again exulted in the caress of the warmth and the airflow over her. She hesitated a moment before answering, feeling closer to her new brother than at any time before, even when they were having to share his bed. This must be what it was like between him and Greg.

"No," she answered. "I'm with you."

It was, of course, the best thing she could have said. It eased her up many notches in his estimation. He knew she wasn't a hothouse plant by any means. He'd found learning to sail quite easy and automatically expected her to take to it easily too. He was now pretty competent, and wasn't surprised that she was too.

But to be in the front line of exploration, even something as minor as this, that took the spirit of another boy. He hadn't realised that's what she had, and revelled in the knowledge and the possibilities in adventure it opened up, perhaps even to the level that Greg and he had enjoyed.

Once again the cold took them by surprise and their shouts as two sun warmed bodies were doused by the cold water made them each laugh. They struck out for the tree trunk determinedly, each aware that the other would think the worse of them if they didn't. Near the end of the tree, where it disappeared below the water, Mary took a dive, just as Stephen was hauling himself out to sit and, he thought, wait for her. She kicked her legs into the air as she disappeared below the surface and pushed with all her strength to find the bottom before her breath gave out. There were branches a-plenty, and she realised they would have to dive very wide to avoid them. She shot to the surface, just in time to surprise Stephen, and swam to join him on his perch. She hauled herself out and they sat side by side, mermaid and merman, talking in the sun. That neither of them had clothes didn't matter any more between them. They were both aware, and found it strange and adventurous, but there was no longer any embarrassment.

Stephen made some cautious entrances into the water, having been told about the spreading branches, and found a place where it was not only clear of them but deep too, deep enough for diving and bombing, and swimming underwater to grab the other's legs.

For nearly half an hour Stephen turned the clock back to the times when he and Greg had played these very games, and not all that far from this very spot. And gradually, between boy and girl as originally with the two boys, play was all that mattered. Having fun. The excitement of ducking and splashing and diving. There was no time for shyness, just acceptance; no hesitation, just play; no chill because of the water, just the glow of healthy innocent exercise. There became no 'her and me', just 'us'.

But at last the chill did make itself felt. "I'm going in," Stephen called. "Coming?"

"Yes. I'm getting cold too." And they launched themselves toward the beach and swam lazily, onto the dead grass, coming to rest like beached seals. Stephen tried swimming up the shallow bank, but found it didn't work. Even with breast stroke the ground was too hard to be comfortable when he dragged himself up it. Mary laughed at him.

"Seal!"

He barked like a sea-lion, then "Ow!"

"What?"

"It's not very comfortable."

"Doesn't look it. Why not try walking?"

"Seals don't walk."

"Ever seen one?"

"No."

"How d'you know, then?"

He had no answer to that, but got to his feet and walked up the beach to their untidy piles of clothes and flopped down, as did she. It was still hot. They lay there, uncaring still about their nakedness, rolling over from time to time as one side became uncomfortable. At last Mary sat up.

"I'm dry."

"Hmmm? Yes, I think I am too."

"And I'm hot."

"Mmm."

"Can we get back on the water? It might be cooler."

He looked at her. She did have a really nice face. And it was good to be, well, trusted by her. Without meaning to, he started to look forward to a time when...

"Good idea," he sighed, lazy, not really wanting to move, yet still too hot. She saw a look in his eyes she'd never noticed before. It seemed as if he was looking at her, through her, at something far away.

"Are we going like this?" he asked, snapping back to the here and now, with mischief in his eyes.

"Certainly not..." she started, then saw his eyes and swiftly dug him in the side. He rolled away laughing. She reached for her clothes and started pulling them on. He rolled back, saw he was in danger of being naked on his own, and swiftly pulled his shorts on.

"I'm dressed," he said.

"It's all right for you. You don't have to wear a top."

"Nor do you."

"I do."

"Why?"

"'Cos I'm a girl."

"So? They don't show yet."

She didn't reply. He didn't see the look of scorn she gave him. Couldn't feel the stab of pain she felt at his lack of understanding.

In silence they put the remainder of their clothes in the dinghy and pushed and pulled her down to the water. Once in they set sail, navigated carefully out of their kingdom, and reached across the estuary. It was mercifully cooler out there, as Mary had thought.

"What now?" she asked him.

"Dunno. Back to the island? Or down into Salcombe?"

"'Spose it's getting late. Better get back to the island."

He hauled in at the mainsheet. Mary took his cue and adjusted the jib and they tacked their way slowly in the failing wind back down to Lofts', helped more than they liked to admit by the ebbing tide. Mooring was particularly difficult. Because of their tiredness and the heat they were both a little fractious, Mary especially, and it took several frustrating, temper-shortening attempts to judge the current speed and the wind strength to make anything like an accurate approach to the old road. Finally they moored her, silently tidied her, and silently walked home.

Back at the house they found Susan and Henry making tea, with Henry appearing only to be allowing Susan to help under protest, on the usual basis of her having to make her living from catering. But the atmosphere was friendly, and the hot, silent ones found it relaxing.

"Good day?" asked Henry casually.

"Mmm," they said in unison.

And that was the only exchange of information about their day's activities.

# 22 - Disappearance

The weather continued to be kind over the next few weeks as the new term grew nearer and Stephen was finally persuaded by Henry that he had to revise in order to put in a reasonable showing in his new form.

Leaving for the bus and home after the first day back he was delayed by one of the teachers who wanted to impress on him that he was actually on a GCE course and he had to make himself work in order to be able to progress. No matter how many times he said "I know, Miss. My father and I have talked about it" she just kept going. Freed at last from her lecture he hurried out to find Mary and to climb into the bus, but she was nowhere to be seen. Assuming she'd already boarded and was probably chatting to Stan he hurried over.

"Mary poorly?" asked the driver. Stephen looked at him, puzzled.

"Isn't she here?"

"Ent seen her. Thought she might've been took home early."

"No...well, I don't think so. Nobody's said. Shall I go and find her?"

"You'd best. Got to start off and get the others back soon-ish."

He hurried into the school again and sought out the Secretary.

"Has anything happened to Mary Beale, please? She's not on the bus."

"Mary... Mary Beale... oh, I know, of course. Well, I saw her go earlier."

"But when?"

"About an hour ago."

"But why, please? Was she ill?"

"No. She left with an elderly gentleman."

"But who? We don't know any elderly gentlemen."

"I don't know. He asked to speak to Miss Armitage. I showed him in, but never got a name. Is there something wrong?"

"I don't know... but I don't know what's happened either. Can I speak to Miss Armitage, please?"

She looked at him, then disappeared into the Head's office. In a moment the lady in question appeared.

"Stephen...what is all this? Miss Trimm tells me you know nothing about Mary going with your uncle."

"My...*uncle*? But I haven't got an uncle!"

Stephen could feel a constriction in his throat, rising up from his chest somewhere...the sort of feeling that usually heralded something he was sure he would dread. Miss Armitage had paused.

"Stephen....I'm sorry, but are you sure? Is there even nobody who you've called uncle Jack, who might just be a friend of your parents?"

It wasn't the time to remind her that his mother was dead.

"No, Miss Armitage, really. And I don't know any elderly gentlemen."

"I beg your pardon?"

"Miss Trimm said she left with an elderly gentleman."

"I see....well, he was about my age, so I suppose.... Anyway, the man was taking her home specially, he said, because there was some important news."

"But why didn't she come for me?"

"I suppose the news didn't concern you."

"But she's my family now. If it concerns her and Dad it concerns me."

"It seems that the best you can do is to catch the bus and get home as quickly as possible."

"Yes... yes... I just hope she's all right."

"She's bound to be. He was a very *nice* gentleman."

"Thank you Miss Armitage." It was a polite, not really a heartfelt farewell.

He was still worried, despite the teacher's reassurances. It seemed unlikely that Mary would go off without him, without even leaving a message. And if she had done so he would find it difficult to understand and to forgive her. All through the journey down the hot Devon lanes he fidgeted in his seat, willing the bus along, impatient at anything that delayed them. Even the cows crossing the road, a regular feature of the journey, were a source of annoyance to him, not the meeting of old friends as they usually were. They were Loft family cattle.

He rushed off the bus at his stop, barely saying goodbye to the friendly driver, and scurried down the lane as fast as he could. Henry was waiting in the launch, as usual.

"Where's Mary?" The questions were simultaneous.

"Come on Stephen, stop mucking about. Tell her to come out of wherever she's hiding, I'm tired."

"But Dad, isn't she with you? She was brought home early by someone who called himself my uncle Jack... er....Loft."

"Who? No, she's not here. And you haven't got an uncle Jack Loft, or any uncle at all. You know that."

"I do, but Miss Armitage said that's who collected her, and was bringing her here to be told some important information."

"WHAT? And Mary went off with this man?"

"Yes. Miss Armitage said he was very pleasant." It was hardly a reason, but he had to give some sort of explanation.

"We must phone....damn, it still doesn't work. There's a call box up the road, isn't there?"

"Yes, just near the shop. Is she going to be all right, Dad?"

"How do I know? I don't know where she is."

Stephen's silence must have said something to him, because as he started up the hill he turned to his son. "Sorry, Steve. I'm worried, and we must find out what's happened quickly."

Stephen ran down to the launch and dumped his school bag into it, then turned and ran back up the lane after his hurrying father.

By the time they reached the phone box they were both out of breath. It was a steep lane, and each had been tired when they started. Fortunately the phone book was intact, and Henry turned the pages impatiently to find the school's number. He dialled, the fourpence went in and it wasn't long before he was able to press the button which connected the call.

"Hallo? Miss Armitage, please... Oh... gone... er, when? I see. Look, it's important. It's Henry Loft here, you know, Stephen's father and Mary Beale's guardian, and she's gone missing. I'm...what? Yes I know. But he has no uncles, nor any elderly friends called Jack, and neither have I. And she's not come home. I need to talk to Miss Armitage now. Can you give me her number, please?"

There was a longer pause. "Look, I know that's the case normally, but this is an emergency. If the school's let her go with someone she doesn't know who they haven't checked out it's wrong. If you have no idea where this person could have taken her or who he is then it's a Police matter. I think Miss Armitage needs to talk to me, don't you?"

Another pause. "Yes. Let me write it down. Stephen...pen and paper. What?"

"I haven't got any."

"Damn. Look, can you ask her to phone me? I'm in a call box – our phone's still out of order after the flood. And I haven't got any more money anyway... yes, yes, we'll stay here. As soon as you can, please." He gave the number and put the phone down.

"What's happening, Dad?"

"They wouldn't give me her number at first, but then I realised I'd got no more money anyway – I couldn't phone her. They're going to call, and she'll phone me back."

"Don't they know any more?"

"No. The woman I spoke to only knows what you told me – that's all. God only knows what's happening."

"Are you worried about her, Dad?"

A pause.

"Yes."

There was silence for some time, and they both jumped as the instrument jangled into life.

"Hallo... Yes it is... No, no idea at all. Stephen said we have no relatives or friends of that name and I can confirm it. No, nobody at all. No one's been near the island so far as I'm aware. I've been there all afternoon, apart from going to Salcombe at lunchtime... No, nobody odd I don't know... neither do I. I need to find out exactly what's going on, and quickly. I think we need to call the Police... Yes... No, I can't. The truck's on the island. I'm at Blanksmill near the shop and the school bus stop... Yes...Yes... Thank you, that would be kind. We'll wait here. 'Bye." He rang off.

"She's good, that woman. She's going to call the Police and get someone to the school in case she comes back there, then she's going... "

"Is she going to call 999?"

"Well... yes... I suppose so. Why?"

"'Cos it's something I always wanted to do."

Henry looked at him, anger darkening his face. "If that's all you can think of at a time like this, Stephen, then just keep your mouth shut."

Stephen, mature enough to realise suddenly how his comment must have appeared to his father, mumbled an apology. "But what were you saying, Dad?"

"She's coming down here to collect us and take us there."

"What, to school?"

"Yes. Where else? We need to talk to the Police, and fast."

They had only about fifteen minutes to wait before Miss Armitage's little car appeared. Hurriedly, wordlessly, they clambered in, and for one of the few times in his life that Stephen had been in a car, he found little joy in the journey.

At the school they found Miss Trimm flustering around two large policemen. The appearance of her employer calmed her.

"Miss Armitage – I'm sorry, but these Policemen won't tell me what's happening."

"It's all right, Miss Trimm. We'll take over now. But they'll probably come and see you later."

"But what is happening, please?"

"We think Mary Beale has been taken."

"Yes, but surely if she went with Stephen's uncle..."

"I told you on the phone: there is no uncle. Whoever it was had no right to take her."

The secretary's hand flew to her mouth theatrically, and she squeaked. "So it is true?"

"What is true?"

"What Stephen said, and what you said on the phone."

"Well, of course it is. Just because it's a telephone it doesn't mean it's not true."

She was silent, but dutifully followed Miss Armitage, Henry, Stephen and the policemen into the school.

The questions were asked slowly, methodically and repeatedly until Stephen could hardly sit still in his impatience to do something, or at least to see something done. It took about fifteen minutes, but to him it seemed hours. When at last they seemed to draw breath as if they had enough details all he could think about was how efficient Superintendent Birch had been. Why couldn't he be called?

"Could Superintendent Birch, in Exeter, help us?" he blurted out suddenly in one of the growing pauses.

The stolid Policeman looked gravely at him. "Sort out our own problems, we do, boy. No need to get foreigners involved unless we have to, stands to reason."

"But surely he can move quicker than this... er, sir..." he gulped, realising that he was being rude, and to a Policeman.

"We got to have the facts, boy, 'fore we can do anything."

"Yes... but... I mean, would they have gone by train?"

"Maybe, maybe. That's one of the lines of enquiry..." he puffed himself out "...that we'll be following."

"But couldn't Inspector Birch get someone to look for them at Exeter?"

"We don't want to jump the gun. Let's start by finding which way they've gone, if it is by train."

"Have you sent anyone up to the Railway Station?" asked Henry.

"How can I, Sir? I'm here talking to you!"

"Officer, I realise that, but for God's sake let's all *do* something. I can't stand any more of this. I don't know enough about Police procedure to know whether all this has been absolutely necessary immediately, but what I do know is that unless we start searching soon she may well be miles away before we even find anyone who saw them. We all know what both she and this man were wearing, so let's get going. I'm going to the Station."

"We-ell now, sir, what we usually asks for is that the family go home and stay there, 'case the missing person turns up. Then they can phone us to tell us..."

"Officer, we live on an island. Since the flood we have no phone. So she can't get there without a boat, and if she did I couldn't phone you. So I'm going to start the search myself. You do what you think you have to, but I warn you that if we have no news by nightfall I'm phoning your people in Exeter and asking Superintendent Birch to intervene."

He didn't look to see the expression on the policeman's face but just stood and turned angrily towards the door. Stephen caught a glimpse, though, and would have laughed at the angry astonishment and the dropped jaw had not the situation been so serious.

Kingsbridge's station was a terminus, if terminus isn't too grand a word for a small station at the end of a quiet branch line. Its only claim to fame was that once a week a carriage from the Cornwall Express was shunted on or off the fast train at South Brent, attached to a tiny engine, and carried a few people down the line stopping at every village station on its way there. Any minor thing that went on at the station was the subject of any gossip that circulated amongst the staff. Henry found the place more or less asleep, and only roused the booking office clerk from his comfortable chair with difficulty.

"Now, sir, there's no trains from here 'til seven, see…" The man began.

"I don't want a train. I need to know if you saw a man, an elderly man with a young girl get on a train this afternoon, about two and a half hours ago. She was in school uniform."

"Ah, there's a lot of school children catch the train home, sir, but it's the 4.27, not the 3.42…"

"No, I mean they would have got on the 3.42."

"But the school kids don't, see. They don't get out of school in time."

"But this one did. She was with an older man."

"Well…there was an old gentleman got on it, and in a bit of a hurry he were, too. But I didn't see no one with him…"

"Are you sure he was alone?"

"He must have had a ticket, see, 'cos he never got one from me."

"Would someone else have seen them get on the train?"

"Important, is it, sir?"

"Yes. I think so, and the Police think so."

This was news to Stephen, but he said nothing.

"We-ell, I could get on to the Station Master. He might of seen 'em."

"Would you, please?"

After a good deal of whirring of phones and muttering in the background the man reappeared. "Seems he did see a bit of a girl get on the train with a man…"

"Where were they going?"

"Oh, dunno, sir. Like I said, they had tickets."

"What about the ticket inspector?"

"He's on his tea break now, sir. Be back at 'bout quarter to seven."

"But look, this is urgent, man. My… daughter's been taken by this man against her and my wishes, and we need to find out what we can, quickly."

"Taken, is it? Ahh… well, p'raps I'd better get on the phone again then."

Moving quicker this time he disappeared, and there were more mutterings in the background before he once again filled the ticket window.

"Seems he just showed Bill the two tickets, a bit quick, like, and then pushed on through to the train. A bit late, they were; the train was about to go when they arrived and we had to get it to wait. Might have even delayed the connection a bit."

"What does it connect with?"

"Well, there's two; the stopper to Plymouth and the semi to Exeter. That's at Brent, but there's other trains off too, to Buckfastleigh from Totnes, Dartmouth or Moretonhampstead from Newton Abbott, and…"

"Yes, yes, I know…and if they go through to Exeter they could go anywhere….when does it reach there?"

"Where, sir?"

"Exeter."

"Ahh, just one minute, sir… where are we…. one minute…. yes, no that's the wrong one….er….just here…. yes…. er, 5.36 sir."

Henry looked at his watch and said a very rude word that made his son jump. Stephen looked at his own watch.

Ten to six.

Just then the policeman came puffing up and seemed put out to see the two of them there. Henry cut short his questions.

"They could have gone to Plymouth, or they could have ended up in Exeter. Or they could have got onto a branch line. We need your help to check at all possible stations, including Exeter. If it's there, we missed them by a quarter of an hour, about the time it took you to ask all those questions."

# 23 - Journey

It was the opening of the door that broke Mary's reverie from the heat of the afternoon and the French verbs she was trying to learn. The school secretary whispered something to her teacher. Mary jumped as the latter looked straight at her.

"Mary Beale, please will you collect your things together and accompany Miss Trimm. It seems there is someone here on an urgent errand for you."

The interruption to the normal run of things, coupled with the word 'urgent' made Mary feel suddenly apprehensive. What was so important that it couldn't wait until lessons were over in…what…another hour? Three-quarters? But the woman was waiting for her, so she pushed her way through the desks, not daring to say anything to her friends who were watching open-mouthed.

Miss Armitage was waiting, talking to a man. As Mary approached he looked at her, a piercing stare, and then, just too late, the mouth switched to a smile. Something made her feel uncomfortable, as if she didn't trust him. But Miss Armitage spoke.

"Mary, this is Mr Loft, who is Stephen Loft's Uncle Jack. He has asked if we'd be good enough to let you go early today, as he has something important to tell you. Although we don't make a habit of doing so, I'm making an exception, as he lives some way away."

Mary nodded. Well, if the man was a relative of Stephen's he must be all right. Perhaps she was wrong about him.

"Hallo Mary." He sounded pleasant enough. Yes, she must have made a mistake. "I have some important news for you, and I need to speak to you before I see Stephen, or Harry."

Harry? Who was Harry?

"Er…sorry, but who is Harry?"

The man looked nonplussed and, she thought, worried. "Er…Harry. You know, Mr Loft."

"Oh, *Henry*. His name's Henry."

"Ahh…." His face cleared. "Of course that's what he was christened, but we used to call him Harry at home."

"You were at home with him?"

"Well yes. He's my brother."

"I never knew he had any brothers or sisters."

"Only me. And I've been out of the… country for years, so he probably never thought to mention me. Anyway…" This to Miss Armitage… "I won't take up any more of your time. You've been most considerate, and thank you so much for your help. Thank you both, in fact. Now then, come along, Mary, or we'll be late."

"Late?"

"Yes. We have to go on a short train ride first, then I'll be able to tell you all about it. It's a surprise. You like surprises, don't you?"

Mary nodded dutifully. She didn't say much as they hurried up to the station, but was about to ask about their destination when Uncle Jack pulled two tickets from his pocket and pushed her in front of him past the ticket collector. The whistle was just being blown as they ran onto the platform. The guard put his red flag up again and the man flung open a door, ushered her in, and slammed it again. The whistle blew again and a moment later clouds of smoke and steam billowed past the window as the engine started its long climb towards Dartmoor.

"Er....Uncle Jack....er....do I call you Uncle Jack?"

"Yes, I think that would be suitable."

"Uncle Jack, where are we going?"

"I told you, it's a surprise. If I tell you where we're going it'll spoil it."

"But can't you give me a clue?"

"Well....it's to do with your parents."

The eyes widened, the face turned full beam to him. For a moment she couldn't speak, and when she did it was in a whisper.

"My parents?"

"Yes. Look, I'm sorry, but you asked for a clue. That's all I'm going to say at the moment." And despite all her questions all he would do was to smile at her with his lips and say nothing. Surely he didn't mean that they were still alive? That one of them was still alive? That sort of thing only happened in books. Her mind went round in circles as the slow train chuffed through the spring Devon countryside that normally she would have watched with delight for its novelty and its beauty. But all she could see now were three faces....no, two faces. She had seen Greg's body.

They changed trains at South Brent. By the size of the engine Mary knew that this was no branch line train but an express, or near-express, and that it was no short journey they were on. And still Uncle Jack would answer no questions.

"D'you want a drink?" he asked about an hour later as they were passing a housing estate, ugly to a girl brought up with the attractive, haphazard buildings of Salcombe and Kingsbridge.

"Yes, please." She was suddenly aware of how hungry she was, too.

"Stay there, then, and I'll bring you...what? Tea? A soft drink?"

"Orange squash, please," she said, decisively.

When he came back he was swaying as the train clattered over some points, and as he gave it to her he told her she'd better drink it quickly because they had to change again in a few minutes. The buildings around

228

them were certainly more crowded together now, and more grimy, and she thought they were probably in a big town. Obediently she took a gulp of the drink. It tasted funny.

"Come on," he said. "Drink it down. We have to get ready to get off or we'll end up in London."

Obediently she drank, shuddering a bit at the odd taste, then stood and watched as he took down the little holdall he'd been carrying.

As they climbed off the train she staggered, almost losing her balance. As they walked up the platform towards the barriers she felt peculiar, light headed, and hoped she wasn't going to be sick. As they approached the other train the announcements over the loudspeakers seemed to be coming from the next room. She saw bits of train, people's feet, a door handle, the cloth of a seat. And then there was a muffled roaring in her ears and she fell asleep.

The train must be coming out of a tunnel. There was a disc of daylight approaching. But why was she in the front of the train? Was she tied on to the engine? In a panic she struggled against the constrictions that held her, turning wildly this way and that, trying to break free. She shouted, and there was an answering sound like a hiss, as if the train was letting off steam, or was it the brakes going on? And why was her head so heavy, and why was it light… so light… it was never as light as this in bed on the island. Ah… bed. That was where she was. But why? She was on a train journey; how could she be in bed?

Slowly the senses returned, the eyes opened. A window. Light. Why? Aware now that her bonds were no more than bed sheets and blankets she tried to push them away, but either they were too heavy or she was too weak. Too weak? Why? She was as fit as a fiddle. She tried again, but all her efforts succeeded in moving them only an inch or so before they fell back.

"Don't try and move yet," said a voice. A female voice. Familiar, kind sounding, but with unpleasant memories behind it. A voice she didn't recognise… yet she must recognise it. She knew that she didn't like it despite its kindness.

"It's all right now. You're safe, Mary. Safe with your family."

Family? What? She remembered then what the man had said. There was something about her parents… but this wasn't one of them. Family? Family?

And then the recognition struck her.

"Great-Aunt…"

She flopped back onto the pillow, confused beyond words.

When she awoke next, it was dark. The air was warm, and scented. She found that her head ached, and wished it would stop. Stretching out her hands she explored the bed and found it narrow, and somewhat lumpy. Despite her continued confusion she was beginning to piece together what must have happened. The man who had collected her must have been a friend of her great-aunt, and it was she who had arranged for her to be brought here, wherever 'here' was. She couldn't think why she had suddenly fallen asleep in the train, or why she had been – still was – so confused. But she could think a little clearer now, and realised that her elderly relative had arranged the very thing that she feared. She had been removed from Lofts' and brought here, wherever that was, and was now to live away from her beloved, familiar people and surroundings.

"I won't... I won't," she said out loud to herself, yet even to her the voice sounded thick, as if she had a mouth full of porridge. She made an effort and rolled over, feeling beyond the edge of the bed. Nothing. Already tired again she rolled the other way, felt the lumpy edge of the bed, and beyond, and this time found something solid. She felt her way up it, and discovered it was a table or something. Feeling along the top she met a book, quite a thick book with a thick cover, and then felt a flex. Good. A flex meant electricity, and they had been without electricity since the flood...

But she wasn't at Lofts'. Stephen wasn't next to her... funny old Stephen... so serious and grown-up sometimes, and at other times so... what... like her? Like her brother? Like they'd always been? Yes. That was it; like they'd all always been.

But he wasn't here. Nobody was here. He and Henry were probably miles away. And as she thought more about what had become her home until that train ride, the tears ran down her cheeks, unchecked. Her head touched the pillow again and she let them flow until they became uncomfortable and she decided to sniff and continue her exploration.

But what if her great-aunt had somehow put traps in the room?

What if the bed was actually on top of a mountain, with a drop on every side that she could fall down? Well, the side of it with the table couldn't be like that, even if it dropped away the other side of the table. And there wasn't likely to be a drop between it and the bed where she lay. So she found the flex again, and, with some worries lest it too should be dangerous and electrocute her, followed it. She found the lamp it fed. Up the stem her hand felt... up... and there was the switch, just like those at home. She remembered her father calling it a toggle switch, and smiled despite her predicament.

Now what? Should she switch it on, and risk seeing the drops either side of the mountain the bed was on? That would be worse than just imagining

230

they were there. What happened if there were no walls, and the floor just went on for ever in all directions?

And then her brain kicked into gear. If there was a mountain, then there would be no floor. If there was a floor, then there would be no mountain. She shook her head, told herself not to be a silly little girl, and nervously pushed the switch.

The room was small. It had some very odd looking pictures on the wall, mainly of gloomy people in gloomy buildings. Brown seemed to be the room's main colour. There was also a table and two chairs, a bookcase filled with books she couldn't see properly, a chest of drawers with a mirror, the bed and the table. And that was it. No mountains. Four walls. Even a carpet, with the sort of pattern she used to see in the homes of elderly relatives when she was young. With her brother and parents. Mostly they had been told to play in the garden, not in the house, so as to keep the noise down. The aunt and uncle weren't strong. But when it had been raining they had played quietly – fairly quietly – in the house, and Greg had used the carpet's pattern as a roadway.

But soon after they'd been told that the aunt and uncle had gone to be with Jesus, and they never went to the house again.

But the carpet was the same, even if it had gone all misty as she remembered those happier times. She lay back for a moment to let her eyes clear, and the next thing she knew it was morning.

"Good morning Mary."

There was the voice again, but she didn't recognise it. Eyes firmly shut, she pulled together the cords of memory, and at last came up with her great-aunt. Should she open them, or should she feign sleep so the horrible woman would leave her in peace? She tried, but a hand was put on her shoulder and shook her to and fro.

"Mary! Wake up. It's gone seven o'clock."

Damn. And there were cows to milk and chickens to feed... no, wait. This wasn't the farm. This was... where? Somewhere she didn't want to be, and somewhere she vowed she would never stay. The eyes opened, and focussed with difficulty; difficulty which came from the headache that had once again attacked her.

"Why am I here?" she asked with difficulty, her voice somehow thick and indistinct.

"Because you belong here, Mary. I told you that when we were at that ridiculous court."

That was too difficult for now. But she could feel her blood starting to boil.

"Why did you bring me here? Who was that man?"

231

"You know why you are here. I am your family now. I have rescued you from penury and a dubious household in a flooded valley. As to the man, Mr Cade is a specialist who can bring families back together."

"He told me he was Mr Jack Loft. Uncle Jack. Anyway, my home and family are in Salcombe"

"No, they are not. *We* are family, you and I. The man and the boy with whom you were staying are not family. They were neighbours, maybe, but it would be quite unsuitable for you to stay with them or to think of them as your family."

"But they are. Greg wanted them to look after me."

"Greg is dead. What he wanted is of no consequence. He was only a child..."

The voice droned on. In Mary's mind she heard Stephen's voice, riven with emotion, telling the court the words Greg had uttered as his last: "Stephen, look after them for me..." Unbidden, tears came to her eyes as she relived those few moments, feeling again her dying brother's presence in Stephen's voice. How dare she? How dare this woman, whom she hardly knew, rubbish sentiments such as his which had been voiced at such a time....the moment of Greg's death? And reported by his best friend in all the difficulties of a coroner's court?

She interrupted. "How DARE you say that Greg is of no consequence! He is my brother. He asked my best friend to look after me and he and his father are doing so. I don't want to be here. I want to be at home in Salcombe. On Loft Island. And that is what HE asked Stephen to do, and that is what I want."

"Don't interrupt. And don't contradict. We can't all have everything we want. It is not appropriate for you to live in a house with two strangers – two men."

"Henry and Stephen..."

"You don't refer to an adult with their Christian name!"

"I do Henry. All right, then, *Dad...*"

"He is not your father. It is wrong to think he is."

"You don't know how he treats me."

"Don't be impertinent. They are strangers, in any case."

"They aren't strangers. They are my friends, my new family."

The old woman paused. "You have to realise that if they said you could live with them, it was only because they were trying to be kind, to keep you happy until after the funeral. They are happy now you have gone to live away with a relation and will be going to one of the best schools in the country. This is your home now."

"No...NO! They want me there."

"That is not what they have said."

"They DID. They DID! Many times!"

"Well, they seem to have changed their minds now."

"When?"

"I have a letter."

She was sure they wouldn't have done this, that they never meant it.

"I don't believe you."

"It's private, so you may not see it. But they say they would prefer me to look after you."

"You're lying!" She had never in her twelve years come across something so obviously wrong, said by an adult.

The woman stood. "I am not going to be talked to like that. You will stay here until you have calmed down. And then you will apologise, and we will speak again."

She crossed swiftly to the door.

The tears came then. Since that dreadful night she had never felt so powerless. Slowly she pieced together what she could remember of the journey, but apart from the man who collected her...

*Kidnapped* her. She mulled that over for a while.

...apart from him she could remember very little. Not until her hated great-aunt had appeared.

An hour later the door opened again.

"You will now apologise."

She swallowed, hard, and in a brittle voice said the words she had schooled herself to say.

"You have *kidnapped* me."

"I have not. Mr Cade had to collect you from school and bring you here. That is all."

"He gave me something which made me sleep."

"Every girl should sleep on a journey. It prevents boredom. And besides, we needed you to have a good rest after all that... *stuff* you were made to do at that *place*. You go to your new school tomorrow, you see."

"There's nothing wrong with my school in Kingsbridge where my friends are. And I want to be at home on Loft Island'."

"You will not be returning to that... *place*. You will tomorrow travel to your new school. You will settle down there, forget... Devon, and learn things more appropriate for genteel little girls to know."

"I will NOT! I will run away and go back to them."

"As I said, you would find them unwelcoming now. Even if you could find your way back to Devon from Scotland you would have no home there."

"Scotland?"

"That is where you will go to school. It is all arranged. And in the holidays you will go to a governess in the area. She will make up for the desperately bad schooling as a lady that you have received so far."

The effects of the drug she had been given had still not worn off fully. The fight against the lies and senseless arguments she had been given didn't evaporate but she could no longer think of the words to counter such injustice.

The woman left again. She slept.

Around midday she woke, feeling better. She got out of bed and crossed to the door. It was locked.

She was reduced to using the chamber pot which she found, not under the bed as she'd experienced when a very young child, at home, but behind a screen.

She dressed herself, then knocked at the door. No one came. She grew more and more angry, but after about fifteen minutes gave up and looked around the room. There was a window, but it was locked, and shuttered from the outside. She wondered if she could break it open but had no idea whether she was at ground level. She listened. No clues there.

A meal was brought to her, nearly wordlessly, by her hated relative. She picked at it. Later, when it had grown dim outside, she found she was still tired – presumably from the previous day – and returned to bed.

Breakfast the next morning was brought to her again and it seemed still to be dark outside. She drank the tea and ate the cereal, and once again started to feel disorientated, cursing herself for accepting any food or drink again from the woman.

As intended, she was unconscious again by the time her great-aunt's employee carried her downstairs to the waiting car. She was driven to the station and only started waking at midday.

She was aware that her great-aunt and the 'specialist' were opposite her, and that she was on a train.

"She's awake," the woman remarked.

"Where am I?" Mary slurred.

"On a train, going to school."

"What… why? School is in Kingsbridge."

"It is in Scotland from now on."

She remembered the angry conversations of the previous day. "I don't want to be in Scotland. I want to be with my family."

"I am your family, and I have decided it is best for you to attend a school in Scotland."

"But…"

"No buts. We need you to behave. We shall have to change trains again soon. Fortunately we could cope at Leeds but you need to walk to the

234

platform with us. Following your refusal to accept what I said to you yesterday I think it is likely that you might try to run away like a silly little girl, so let me remind you that no one will believe anything you tell them at your age, and you have no money to buy a ticket, nor do you know how to get anywhere. So you will just hold my hand and do what you are told. If you do not, Mr Cade will hold your hand.

She saw, or thought she saw, the flash of annoyance on the man's face. Why, she wondered. He had said his name was Jack Loft. *Uncle* Jack Loft. Then she remembered the earlier conversation when she had been so muzzy. His real name was Cade.

"Is that understood?"

She just looked at her relative, mutiny flashing from her eyes.

"Your great-aunt asked you a question, Mary." Mr Cade's voice snapped at her like a whip. "You will answer her."

He scared her. Gone was the gentle mannered man at Kingsbridge and Exeter stations. This seemed to her to be openly evil.

There seemed to be nothing she could do except nod. She did not want to speak to either of them.

At Carlisle they changed, and again at Glasgow. She knew she could not escape. The two things her great-aunt had been honest about was that she had no clue about how to get back, all that way back to Devon, nor did she have any money at all. She had to accept what was going on and act, if possible, once these two had left her.

It occurred to her that this must be a boarding school they were sending her to. Her misery settled round her, broken only by the thought that she would have to see neither of them again once they reached their destination.

# 24 - Confusions

They had returned to the Island as there seemed little point in doing anything else. Exeter Police had finally been persuaded to let them speak to Superintendent Birch, and he was as concerned as they were, as Henry knew he would be. But he was in the middle of a major trial and had no option but to be in Court. "I know you wouldn't want me to involve Inspector Moffatt," he had said, "but that's all I could do at the moment. I hope this trial is going to be over soon, and I'll keep tabs on what the local men are doing when I can. But although they're slow, they're thorough, and beneath it all they're as concerned as you are. They can start things going and I'll catch up with it as soon as I'm out of Court. But she'll be found by then, mark my words."

They'd had to be content with that. Enquiries had been made, but as there were so many trains leaving Exeter and heading in all sorts of directions, the Police had had a lot of questions to ask. "And if as 'ow," said one of the Exeter men, "it's London they've gorn to, 't'll be a miracle iffen anyone remembers them." Henry could have hit him had he not been on the end of a telephone.

The phone! Of all the times they needed their phone line on the Island, this was it. Henry spent a frustrating fifteen minutes talking (on the school's phone) to the Post Office, trying to find the right person – any person – who knew about the loss of their phone line. He had spoken to a man who had answered round in circles: yes, it was still in the name of Henry Loft; no, in view of the circumstances they would be making no rental charges; no, there were no plans to lay a cable under the water to reinstate the line as they had no official view about whether the water would be allowed to stay or not. And no, he had no suggestions about what the family should do, even in the present emergency. "We aren't charging you line rental sir," said the clerk again, as if that made it all right. Henry put the phone down.

Mr Merryweather proved quite positive. "I am so sorry to hear that. One cannot but wonder if she has been abducted by her great-aunt."

"Her great-aunt?" Henry exclaimed. "Surely she wouldn't do such a thing? Mary wouldn't go with her, anyway."

The Solicitor bowed, as if to recognise the point. "It is possible that she had no choice. Her great-aunt is a very determined woman, and there is a great deal of money at stake."

Henry looked at him aghast. "Money? What do you mean? I know she is due the value of the estate, and there was something about insurance, but it can't amount to that much."

For once Mr Merryweather looked uncomfortable. "The trouble is that I may only discuss it with the client himself or herself, or with the parent or *legally authorised...*" he paused to give the word stress "...Guardian. No matter what Mary may wish, and no matter what you wish, and disregarding the fact that you have effectively been her guardian since the incident, the court does not yet regard you as her guardian. It is one of the matters that we have in hand, but unfortunately things are moving very slowly at the moment."

Henry snorted, as if that would make things right. "So you mean that this wretched relative of hers may have a better idea than I do of the amount of money that is coming from the estate and from the insurance than even Mary does."

"That is a very distinct possibility, of course. In the eyes of the law also, the lady is Mary's next of kin, and to an unenlightened Court she may be seen as the most appropriate adult to look after the girl."

"But that mustn't happen!" Stephen had found his voice at last. "Mary would hate that. And I – we want her here. And she wants to be here."

"Stephen, I most fully realise that. Yet we have to face the notion that what a Court sees and what others see and want are often two different things, especially where there is a next-of-kin present. And in this case it may be that the hearing is scheduled to be wherever Mary is, if she is with her relative."

Henry's mind suddenly saw the risk. If Mary was living with her great-aunt, no matter how reluctantly, it was only a matter of time before the woman's solicitor could arrange a Court hearing. To a Court where she lived it would surely be just a matter of course. There was the girl, there was the female relative. That was where the girl should live. Much better than living in poverty with a strange man and his son. He slumped in the chair. "What do we do, please?"

"I suggest that you tell the Police of your fears. You had a good rapport with Superintendent Birch, I gather. Present the entire problem to him, by all means informing him of our discussions. He will be able at least to discover the situation. If it appears that Mary has been abducted against her will then we have a better chance when the case does come to Court."

"You mean there is nothing we can do in the meantime? That could take ages!"

"Remember we would be dealing with a Court remotely. If it appears because Mary's presence there was obtained illegally that her relative is not, after all, a suitable person, and they are unwilling to see that what Mary wants is valid, then they may think it best to place her in an orphanage."

Henry's jaw dropped.

"An orphanage! But that would be criminal and inhumane when we want her here and she wants to be here."

"It could be a problem if a Court which knows nothing about the circumstances of a child's life has to make provision for her. Little credibility is given to the wishes of the child, I fear. Not as a matter of course. I am sorry to have to say this.

"Of course, should it be found legally that there was to be no compensation forthcoming, then Mary's expectations could be less attractive to her relative. And if it was regarded eventually as an "Act of God" against the findings of the inquest, which I sincerely hope is not the case, then the insurance companies will not pay any claims either. So she – and her great-aunt – would receive nothing. But then, of course, neither would the Loft family."

Father and son each put his head in his hands.

After the Exeter case was over, Superintendent Birch asked some questions of the Harrogate Force who undertook to visit Miss Marriatt. With reluctance they did so, knowing her of old. They received a cold reception, a terse denial that any young person was in the house, a denial that she had removed her great-niece from school, and an accusation that the Police should mount a proper case if her relative had gone missing.

All of which was, of course, true, as far as it went. The Police retired, hurt.

On the island it was quiet, and depressed.
Stephen, in bed later, felt cold and lonely.

In Scotland, there had been a strange meeting with the Headmistress. Mary found that she couldn't bring herself to say or do anything, to tell the truth or complain, until after Miss Marriatt had left. The leaving was a relief. She declined the kiss, which earned her a glare. She was told by the Headmistress, that she was sorry to hear about the accident and was aware that Mary was likely to have some unusual flashbacks to an imagined past, and promised to keep a careful eye on her so these problems would not let her down. Mary was so shocked that she found herself tongue-tied.

She was taken into the care of other girls and kept so busy she had little chance to say much. She was in a whirlwind of activity until well after their meal, and shortly after was told it was her Year's bed time – far earlier than it would have been at either Beales' or Lofts'.

Lying in the cold bed, she missed Henry's good-night, and, more, Stephen's strong presence beside her.

"Dad, we've got to do *something*," Stephen said the next Saturday morning.
"What?"

"Go to Exeter? See if anyone there saw them? Saw what train they got on?"

"But if they do, what can you do? How will you know where they got off?"

"If it's a train up north we can see if it goes through Harrogate."

"The Police have talked to her wretched relative. She knows nothing about it."

"Huh! Don't believe her. They can't have asked the right questions. Can't we go to Harrogate and ask her ourselves?"

"Firstly we can't afford it. Secondly she wouldn't give us house room. You know that by what we all three have said to her after the inquest. No, Steve, all we can do is let the Police do their job. They'll find her eventually."


That Saturday night, Mary wrote a long letter to Stephen telling him where she was and saying she wanted to come back to Devon. Did they want her or had they changed their minds?

On the Monday evening she was called to the Headmistress who told her that the letter had not been sent as it was an address connected to her imagined past. Mary tried to bluster but the more detailed she made the information, the more the Headmistress became annoyed. She was sent away with instructions never to write to the address again, otherwise she would receive a punishment.

Mary retreated to her dormitory bed and wept in frustration.

Over the week, the term's activities started properly and Mary found that one of the encouraged activities was sailing. To the instructor's surprise, she soon proved that she knew exactly what she was doing. That, and other activities that her school in Kingsbridge could never offer, attracted her and took some of the sting out of the situation.


Stephen had no such distractions. The extra work he had to face at the start of the exam year sloshed around his psyche but little knowledge seemed to be retained from it. The understanding Miss Armitage cajoled him the best she could, but it was obvious to everyone that his heart wasn't in his studies.

At home the routine of farm work – the little that it now was – didn't really fulfil either of them very much. It was only Susan's quite regular visits that added welcome variety. Stephen found that he was rather out of sorts at times and realised how much he was missing Mary – kid though she still was, as he told himself. What he didn't realise because the word didn't occur to him, was that he was jealous. Though Susan and his father were happy together and friendly, there seemed to be no advancement of that friendship. Mainly it was the Lofts' parlous financial situation. Henry could not bring himself to hint at any permanency until he was more secure.

A message was sent from Miss Armitage to Henry telling him of Stephen's lethargy in studying.

Knowing his son, Henry knew that the usual sort of lecture would not just have no effect, it would put the boy's back up. After a near-sleepless night, and a boring day where there was no longer enough work to go round, he sat down with Stephen after their sparse meal.

"Steve, we're in trouble."

He felt himself stirred. Trouble was something that had ended with the funerals, wasn't it?

"Financial trouble. If we don't get recompense from somewhere, water board, council or insurance before Christmas, we shall run out of money. I never, ever, expected it all to go on this long."

"Why doesn't someone pay out?"

"The water people think it isn't down to them. The council say that as it wasn't their dam, they aren't responsible, and the insurance company won't release any money until the situation between them is resolved."

"But that's not fair!"

"We know that, and I've phoned all three from the vicarage whilst you've been at school. They persist that's the case at the moment."

"But what about the insurers? If they know they'll be paying out eventually – which they must, or why do we bother with insurance? Why can't they give us enough to live on now?"

"They won't do that. I've tried."

"Do you want me to?"

Henry looked at him, and played an ace.

"Is your English good enough?"

"You mean, I should write?"

"I've been as persuasive and patient as I can on the phone. They're used to me. If someone else wrote a really good letter, and gave them mathematical facts too, it might just start someone thinking."

"Do *you* think it's good enough, Dad?"

"I don't know, old son. I know, because I've been told, that you're still depressed and that's affected how you go about things. But whether it means your skills aren't good enough, I don't know."

He let the thought hang. Then the second ace.

"They'll find Mary eventually, you know. It may be a long time. Or it may be that once she is more aware of where she is and what she can do, that she escapes and makes her way back. But she will almost certainly have been to some sort of school, wherever she is."

Another pause.

240

"What would happen if the bright, intelligent friend she once had, the one she lived closely with, turned out to be not as well educated as her?"

This time he let the minutes drag on, hoping against hope for the response he wanted.

"Has Miss Armitage talked to you, Dad?"

"She wrote."

"What did she say?"

Fortunately the lady was wise and had been as tactful on Stephen's behalf as she knew how. Henry showed him the letter. He read and re-read it.

"It's so difficult when she's not here."

"I know, I know. But you are such friends. It would be a tragedy if she thought you'd avoided the chance of a good education and weren't the man she thought you were."

This time Stephen's mouth dropped open.

"You don't really think...?"

"Neither of us knows. But she will have changed a bit because of the experiences she's had and because she'll be older. And you will have got older too – people do change, you know. Whether you prove not to be the friend she once knew, when she gets back ... only one person can decide that."

"You?"

"No, Stephen! *You*! If I tell you to study harder it won't have any affect. Not at fourteen. I was as obstinate at times as a teenager and you're probably little different. If you decide you want to be an educated young man by the time she comes back, and can have the sort of intelligent conversations with her that your Mother and I used to have together, then it's got to be your decision. Simple."

Another long silence.

"No, not simple. But I will try."

Half term came for each of them, though at opposite ends of the country. Henry had decided that he just had to find a job and talked to some trawlermen in Salcombe. After discussing it with Stephen, who asked if he could go as well, Henry had to tell him it was a hard full job and he'd be away for days on end. It wasn't a job just for the holidays.

"But would you be able to look after the animals whilst I'm away? Also..." and he knew this wouldn't be popular "... we need to put the rest of the cows with the others, on the hills. We just don't have enough pasture for them in the winter, here."

"But..."

"And one man can't manage full churns on his own," he finished tactfully. "They'll leave us some milk every other day. It should be at reduced prices – after all, they're still our cows. You'll need the boat and you'll have to travel to and from Salcombe where the moorings are more reliable."

That was a responsibility he could rise to, thought Stephen, regretful as he was to see the last of the cows go. But then it would only be until they had some pasture again, and surely the water people must get on with it soon?

*I am asking your Headmistress to arrange for a suitable place away from the school where you will spend the holiday,* Mary's great-aunt wrote, the coldness oozing from the ink. *You will be taught how to behave as a young lady befitting the station in life to which you may now aspire.* There was more, not much more, but it was all in the same, cold vein.

'If she doesn't want to see me,' thought Mary, 'why did she bother to kidnap me? Though I don't want to see her. Well, at least I might be able to write to Henry and Stephen from wherever it is, and tell them where I am.'

The new school had been less daunting than she had imagined and, she was almost reluctant to admit, was almost enjoyable once she'd got rid of a little of the anger and the homesickness that had dogged her first weeks. There were certainly more activities available than at her Kingsbridge school, including the sailing where she had quickly become one of the stars of the show. She was reading the letter in the Headmistress's office.

"Your great-aunt seems to want you to become a Victorian," the woman smiled at her. "I don't know why, but from what I know of you now it would not be in your character. I can certainly find someone who would fit the requirements that Miss Marriatt has outlined, or I could just ask some friends of mine who have a farm locally if they would like a visitor for a week."

Mary's eyes grew large. "The farm, please! I was…"

She stopped herself. Quite a number of times she had told teachers and other girls about her true home, but they had all smiled and obviously just humoured her. They had been 'warned'. News was given to the Headmistress that she was still fantasising about Devonshire and there had been one or two meaningful discussions on the subject with Mary. Everyone refused to believe what she knew as the truth.

The farm and the family proved to be so similar to Beales' that she could hardly believe it. True, the nights were longer than in the south and the weather colder and wetter. But the activities were so similar that she felt at home immediately, much to the McTavish's surprise and pleasure.

But they too had been warned about Mary's fixation on the Devon estuary where she was sure she had been brought up and where her family was. They couldn't equate her familiarity with farm animals, farming ways and the country life generally with town life in Harrogate, but nevertheless guided her away from trying to make contact with an apparently mythical address. It caused some bad feeling at times, but Mary eventually decided there was no point in trying to pursue it. They had been too well schooled by her headmistress.

They invited her back to spend Christmas with them.


It was odd returning from school to an empty house for the first time. Henry had told Stephen that he would be away overnight; he was sorry but that's how the job had turned out. He knew Stephen would be happy to cope – something to give him more responsibility.

It was still odd...

He fed the hens and geese, and made sure their pigs were securely in and as clean as pigs like to be, then returned to the farmhouse. By that time it was almost dark, being November. He wondered, not for the first time, where Mary was settling down as dark fell, and longed just to chat to her. Having cooked and eaten a basic meal he wondered what else to do. It would be nice just to nip down to Salcombe and be with people, he thought.

Later, the final check of the livestock, then shutting down the farmhouse on his own, was another first experience. He still found, even after all this time, that going to bed with no one else there was – odd?

Lonely, said a voice in his head. He tried to ignore it.

He was once again seeing to the animals the next morning when a shadow crossed the byre door. He looked up in some alarm.

"Is your Mum at home, sonny?" asked a man in overalls.

He shook his head. "What do you need?"

"Well, cuppa'd be nice, but we're laying a cable to you and want to know where the old one came in."

"Oh, that's easy," said Stephen, and led the way to the back wall of the house where the line of posts across the low ground had once deposited its cable.

"Easy for you," grinned the man. "We've got to lay a cable 'cross there and connect it. Dunno why – the water'll be gone soon, surely?"

"Who knows? But does that mean we'll have electricity back soon?"

"Mebbe tomorrow. Mebbe next day. Gotta start somewhere. Anyroad, we'll be coming and going so if your Mum is in we can talk to her about it."

"She's dead," Stephen told him shortly. "Dad'll be back later when he's back from fishing. Can you come back then?"

"Sorry, son. Okay. We'll work on the mainland end today and keep an eye out for him when he gets back. Okay?"

"Okay," said Stephen, "and thanks."

"You're welcome. Sounds like you've had a rough time of it."

He nodded. "Just a bit. Anyway, sorry, but I've got to go."

He made his way to Salcombe's Town Hard and left the boat in place so that Henry could find it later.

The return of electric power two days later was welcomed by them both, not least because it banished another memory of that night of storm and tragedy.

"Perhaps things are starting to return to normal," said Henry cheerfully. "I just hope our finances do too."

The following weekend brought the usual visit from Susan, who had taken to bringing leftovers (as she described them) from the café 'in case they're useful'. They always were. She was pleased to hear they now had power but in other respects seemed a little on edge, Henry thought. In a quiet moment – they were both with her – she asked what they were doing for Christmas.

Father and son looked at each other. "Haven't thought about it," admitted Henry.

"Well, my father has asked me if I could ask you to come and spend it with us," she said cautiously.

"I'd love to," Stephen blurted out. She smiled.

"It's…it's very kind, but…well…"

He paused. "Look, I'm not in a financial position to be able to return the favour, that's all. I know it's not a nice thing to admit, and I'm sorry to have to. But that's the position." He stopped, red faced.

Not since the incident with the reporters had Stephen seen Susan's face change so quickly. There was a moment's strained silence.

"Henry Loft, you are the most aggravating man I have ever come across. We didn't invite your money for Christmas, we invited you. You and Stephen. And he has given his answer honestly. Will you please do the same?"

She swept out from the living room into the kitchen. The two Lofts exchanged glances.

"Oh dear," said Henry. "I suppose we'd better, then."

"Don't you want to?"

"Yes, but…"

"Well then. Tell her. Go on. You don't need me there."

Henry looked sharply at him. Had he not seen the look of strength, of challenge, of adult knowledge, on his son's near fifteen-year-old face he might well have bawled him out for interfering. As it was he meekly followed Susan into the kitchen.

They sent very few cards that year. One that Stephen bought himself he wrote privately, and posted it to *Miss Mary Beale, c/o Miss Marriatt, Harrogate.* He had almost no hope it would find its target but nevertheless was bitterly disappointed when it was returned some ten days later with very precise lettering on it: *not known here – return to sender.*

# 25 – The arrest, and Martin

Christmas was enjoyed at both ends of the country, although each of the younger participants desperately wanted news of the other. Stephen knew that writing to the only place he knew as a possibility was pointless, having tried. The McTavish farm was so far from a pillar box that Mary had no chance of posting anything without her hosts' knowledge.

How Miss Marriatt felt about it, despite feeling she should really invite her relative to stay with her, is not recorded.

School resumed. Henry's fishing trips resumed. Life continued. If Susan and her father were worried for the sake of the Lofts, they said nothing to the subjects. Mr Merryweather quietly kept pressing the water authorities, who just as quietly declined to mention anything specific. He had dropped any idea of starting an adoption process, knowing that it would be held wherever Mary was and was therefore unlikely to be in Mary's or the Lofts' best interests. It was academic anyway, since the Police had drawn a blank with their investigations into her disappearance and all seemed quiet.

"I could leave school and get a job" said Stephen, out of the blue, on his fifteenth birthday. Henry and Susan looked at him in horror.

"There's more in you than that, Stephen! I know we are a partnership, you and I, but you really, *really* need to prove that you can get some of these new GCE exams. Without them you have nothing to prove your capabilities to anyone. We will never be so... so down on our uppers that you have to give up that."

Susan had been going to add something but clamped her mouth shut. Despite her and Henry's strong and growing friendship she knew that Family still meant Henry and Stephen. Not yet, not perhaps ever, could she interfere.

There were times both on sea and on estuary when Henry and Stephen respectively had close calls in the rough winter weather and in the March gales. Not once did any of their experiences come anywhere near the violence of the previous year's dangers, though.

On three occasions that year between the fishing trips, came voyages that needed Henry to be away for over a week. He was non-committal about these with both Stephen and Susan, just telling them that they were longer trips than usual but would bring in better income. Stephen didn't read any local press, so failed to see a Customs notice after the third such voyage, asking for information leading to the apprehension of anyone connected with a group of smugglers in the area.

Susan did. She said nothing to her father.

As the weather improved into spring and summer it appeared that the

Lofts' finances had improved a little. One weekday, with Stephen at school Henry was surprised to find a visitor on the island. He was about to ask him to leave when the man identified himself as a GPO engineer who had come to look at reconnecting their phone. The following evening Stephen was startled out of his skin to hear it ring again. He rushed to it, thinking "*Mary*", but it proved to be Susan for his father. After Henry had rung off he grinned at his son.

"Gave you a shock, didn't it?"

He failed at first to notice the downcast expression. When he did he just said quietly "Did you think it was her?" He was answered just by a nod.

Susan became an even more regular visitor that year. Sometimes she was transported in the launch by Henry but a few times Stephen took the dinghy and sailed her back. Eventually she resurrected an elderly but solid dinghy with a new outboard engine.

"I need to be able to get here to see my men," she said. "It's good to arrive and give them a shock sometimes."

Stephen had seen the sense of the conversation with his father about studying; he was, after all, no fool. This made him emerge from his self-imposed loneliness at school and he once again became 'one of the crowd'. He and another lad called Martin, who had lost his mother to tuberculosis, got chatting and compared notes. Martin had asked if he could come and see where the family lived, had done so and had fallen in love with it. As he was of farming stock too, and could sail, he quickly became a good friend of Stephen's. Young male laughter was once again heard on the island, a tonic to Henry and Susan. They knew his friendship would soften the loss not only of Greg, but of Mary too, even though the latter was likely not to be permanent.

Christmas that year was spent on the island with Susan and her father, along with Martin whose home life in a small, crowded farm-worker's cottage just outside Kingsbridge was in his word, "hell". His father had taken the loss of the wife badly and was not in tune with a son who had surprised him by suddenly appearing obviously more adult and questioning, less the automatically obedient boy he was used to. Stephen and Henry's relationship of mutual trust and respect was refreshingly at odds with his own life.

"I can relax here," was all he said.

On Christmas Day the phone rang. Stephen jumped, sudden hope in his throat as always. But it was his brother, in a call box. Henry, pleased, phoned him back and they had a long chat.

And so once again life returned to what seemed now to be normal.

In Devon: life surrounded by water instead of pasture, few animals to care for, a father away for a few days a week, Susan visiting regularly and knowing she was always welcome.

In Scotland: a school which, although remote, was a good school and provided sport and leisure activities, many of which Miss Marriatt would have disapproved of. Fortunately the termly reports had detailed only the academic subjects and matters like Domestic Science. Miss Marriatt disapproved of Domestic Science as being unnecessary for a Young Lady who would of course be waited upon by servants once the shortage of candidates for such posts had been cured. Sport she could endure, thinking Lacrosse and Hockey. Had she heard of cross-country running, long walking expeditions in the wild, local uplands, and of course the sailing, she would have been horrified and probably have removed her Young Lady immediately.


In March, Henry went on one of his longer voyages. He expected, he told Stephen, to return the following Saturday morning. There had been no sign of him. The same afternoon a disappointed and slightly concerned Stephen was helping in the café, more for company and for something to do than because he was needed. The phone rang. Susan answered it.

There was a long pause whilst she listened, then: "Oh, the silly, silly, *stupid* man! Where is he again?"

Pause.

"He's here, thank goodness. Are you coming down?"

Stephen knew this was to do with him, and by the sound of it, his father. When Susan put the phone down and looked round he could see she was shocked.

"What's happened?"

"I need to sit down. So do you," she said tersely, and did so.

She took a deep breath.

"Your *stupid* father…" It was said in a way which was horrified, concerned and caring; not the dismissive way which the word is usually used. "…has been smuggling and has got himself arrested in France."

It was Stephen's turn to sit down with a bump. "*What?*" he said faintly.

"I was worried that's what he was doing on these long trips of his. Not the fishing, that's separate, I think; but using the same boat. I've been watching her leave the estuary. Hadn't you seen the stuff in the local paper?"

Stephen shook his head. "Where is he? When is he coming back?"

She shook her head. "Dad just had a call from the *Gendarmerie* in Cherbourg. That's where he is. He's coming down now."

For a moment Stephen thought she meant his father, but then realised that she'd meant her own.

"Now what do we do?" he asked after a long silence, and put his head in his hands. Hadn't life been horrible enough recently, not to be made worse by his father's…*stupidity*? He had come up with the same word that Susan had used.

"Wait until Dad has told us more," she said simply. "He's more used to this sort of thing than I am."

When Mr Merryweather arrived he looked round at his two charges, as he regarded them, immediately put the 'closed' notice on the door and locked it, then poured three cups of tea.

"I think it's time to be honest," he said, having slipped from solicitor mode to that of Dad. "I may be a stuffy old fool at times, but that is professional training and designed to make some people think that I am just a buffoon of a country solicitor. It does not stop me from noticing, deducing, asking questions, observing and coming to conclusions. It surprises people that those conclusions are most often correct.

"Susan: you know, I hope, that Henry loves you. I believe that you love him too. I also believe that you, Stephen, know this. As you are here now, and as you are a welcome regular visitor, I believe that you approve."

He paused. Susan looked embarrassed but was silent. Despite the situation Stephen gave a small smile.

"Henry is the sort of high-principled man who believes he should have a solid financial foundation before he offers his hand in marriage."

"Dad! Really!"

Her father held up his hand. "I said we are being honest. That means not beating around the bush. That is the situation as I read it. At the moment, since the flooding, many families' finances are in limbo. Savings are running out. The Lofts are no exception. I believe that Henry's standards mean that he must do anything, *anything*, to regain that financial stability which would in his eyes enable him to do what he really wants. Which is, of course, to ask my daughter to marry him and then ensure that his son has a stable foundation on which to build his life.

"I understand exactly Susan's sentiments when she spoke to me by telephone just now. On the face of it, it was a stupid thing to do. But given an incentive such as he sees, it is perhaps a measure of desperation and not the stupidity which was our first thought.

"Is it criminal? Yes. But the logic that perhaps he sees is that the authorities in England have been responsible for not acting quickly enough to avoid impoverishing your family. Smuggling is the purchase of goods in one country – France – and the transport of them to another – England – without paying customs duty. And that duty should be payable, of course, to the authorities.

"It is faulty logic, but it is a logic; desperate people with families are inclined to do things like that."

They digested this for a moment.

"But what's going to happen?" Stephen asked. "What can we do?"

"The *Gendarmerie* believe that the English will bring them all back to Britain, but they are vague about when."

It was Susan's turn. "But if all they have done in France is to buy... what? Goods, you said, whatever that means. Then that is not illegal. Why are the French keeping them there?"

"We liberated France, and it was just nine years ago. There are loyalties which were born out of that, between individuals and customs men. To start with it was to trace the more criminal Nazis who were trying to escape, but it developed into unofficial cooperation. That is what we are seeing."

"So what can we do?" asked Stephen again.

"We can talk to the *Gendarmerie* from time to time and perhaps befriend one of them. He can perhaps tell what they intend, and whom they are dealing with in England. That will give us a start. But we must do it carefully so as not to incriminate Henry and the others on this side of the Channel."

"Would it help if the *Gendarmerie* received a letter from the young son of one of the men being held?" asked Susan suddenly. "He could explain what has happened and how no one is making a decision about responsibility for the flooding, and how that has affected us?"

He considered that carefully.

"You know, my dear, it might be the right thing to do. In any case, I cannot see that it would cause any risk or any harm. They know Henry's identity and address; it is he who has quoted me as his legal representative. You are very astute, my dear. Stephen, how good is your French?"

He gave another small smile. "Okay, maybe, sir. But surely this means that I've got to leave school and get a job?"

"Stephen, on my daughter's behalf I have an interest in the Loft family, whether..." He held up his hand to stop her protest. "Whether she likes it or not. Finances will improve when the various authorities start actually making decisions. Do not throw away your abilities and the chances of improving them because of a temporary hiatus in your life. At least for the moment that side of things can be dealt with.

"I know that you and your father increasingly act together in making decisions. For the moment, though, I am going to try and direct some decisions knowing how he would work, and I hope Susan and you will accept them. Susan, will you, once you have closed the café every night, go to Lofts' and help Stephen with the running of the house? I know he copes with the livestock. You could perhaps sleep there too, returning with Stephen when he comes to catch the school bus.

250

"Stephen, in return, could you come and help Susan in the café on Saturdays?"

The feeling of relief that swept over Stephen surprised even him. He nodded, temporarily unable to speak, then looked at Susan. She was smiling, but at her father. She crossed to him and kissed the top of his head.

"You wise old owl," she told him.

In desperation the final of the many failed attempts of the letter to the *Gendarmerie* was taken to Henry's school. He felt he had to take his French teacher into his confidence so as to ensure the translation was as good as it could be. The man read it.

"This is a joke, I take it?"

Stephen's eyebrows lifted.

"No, sir, it isn't. It's not the sort of thing I'd do."

It was the teacher's turn to raise his eyebrows.

"This is serious. Very well. Go into the library now and do as good a job on it as you can yourself. Miss as much of my lesson as you need. Come back when you've finished it and we'll go through it in Break."

"Sir... wouldn't it be better if... if you just did it?"

"I would hope so, Stephen. But if they read perfect French they might think an adult had written it. I will correct it if necessary, but I will make sure they realise I've done so. That way they know it's genuine. And you need the English version on it too."

Stephen looked puzzled again.

"... So they can see it *is* a translation from the English"

In fact Stephen's translation was not too bad. Some less usual words had not been in his vocabulary, so corrections were neatly written in. At the end the teacher had written, in French, "composed and translated by Stephen Loft, aged 15, and corrected by M DUVAL Jaques, teacher of French."

It was posted that afternoon.

Returning to the island and finding Susan there was a tonic, especially as he didn't have to cook. Shared experiences and the knowledge of the person they had in common made their time together relaxed, although Stephen never referred directly to the feelings he believed might exist between the two.

Two weeks later a letter arrived from France. Stephen had given Susan's address as the postal contact since otherwise it meant collecting mail from the Post Office. There were no deliveries to the island. Susan brought it with her to await Stephen's return from school.

Trembling, he tore it open.

It started, after the usual pleasantries: *"Nous sommes desolés...."*

They struggled through the translation. It appeared that Henry and the remainder of the crew had been the victim of a swindle by those in France who provided the goods for transport. The *Gendarmerie* had discovered the intended trade, had watched, and had investigated. The goods, paid for by the Devon skipper in good faith, turned out to have been stolen from warehouses in France.

The crew was being detained, not for smuggling, but for receiving stolen goods. Of the suppliers there was no trace. There was no way for the crew to prove their innocence. Even at the addresses they had used to make contact there was no knowledge of the names of the French vendors whom the Englishmen had identified.

Mr Merryweather was called and given the news. He was silent for so long that Susan wondered if the phone line had failed again.

"That does put a different complexion on things," he said at last. "The French will not let them go until they have more information, or so I believe. They can hold them in the meantime on the basis that they are still investigating – whether or not they actually are doing so.

Another pause.

"I'm very much afraid that unless there are some developments in France we are in for a long wait."

Stephen took the letter to M Duval who confirmed their translation. With his knowledge of French law and *Gendarmerie* procedures he confirmed what Mr Merryweather had stated, too.

None of it encouraged Stephen. Or Susan, come to that. All they could do was to write to Henry, which they each did weekly, independently; though using the same envelope to save money. Peter in Torquay had been informed, just as he had been earlier about Mary's disappearance, and was naturally shocked, though realised that none of them could help. They had no option but to play the waiting game.


As summer approached, Salcombe became busier with tourists again. Edgar's boatyard was busier, fishermen who owned Salcombe's famous motor boats had commissioned even more from him and from other local builders. They hired them out by the hour to keen visitors who used them to explore the estuary.

That included Loft Island. Often now Susan's return there would find people wandering around, wondering why there were no humans where there were two friendly dogs but no people. The dogs were now used to visitors and, unless indoors, would welcome them instead of barking at them. They also wondered about the pigs and chickens. Susan explained time and time again. They made sure that doors were locked.

One Sunday, after a particularly busy week, she sat Stephen down and told him they were being silly.

"We have all these people visiting the island and they don't realise it's private…" she started.

"We need to put notices up to keep them away," he said flatly.

"But why don't we try and cater for them? Why don't we have a small café there? It could make quite good money. Mine does, now all the tourists are here. And don't forget that Edgar has started running a ferry up to Kingsbridge. We could ask if he'd want to call in here on the journeys to and from."

"But the island's a farm. It's always been private."

"But it's never been an island before. It's never had water all round it. And we… Henry needs to have an income when he comes back."

That floored Stephen.

"But he's a farmer, not a café… er… runner."

"No. But I am."

The cogs in Stephen's brain started working, slowly, but gathering momentum. So if they had a café on the island, Mary would run it. He could help. The farm – what was left of it – could provide fresh ham, chicken, eggs – even milk, maybe. And there would be an income, and Susan would stay, and his father would be there, and who knows?

"What would Dad say?"

She pulled a face. "I don't know. I think I could talk him round. But we could do it as a try-out this year if we're quick. Then when we tell him what it's made – if it does – then it'll help persuade him. But what about us talking to *my* father this weekend? Or now, on the phone?"

"Well…"

"It won't hurt to try him out, will it? We're not deciding anything."

"S'pose not."

It was a long phone call, but at the end of it the old man was positive. He'd even said that if it proved a success in the first year, using whatever temporary measures they decided on, he might invest some money in it to provide some more permanent facilities.

"Blimey," said Stephen when all this had been relayed to him. "What on earth is Dad going to say?"

"We need to write about it to him. Give the background. Tell him that if it just doesn't work it'll be easy to go backwards… yes, that's a good phrase. He won't like that."

Stephen looked puzzled.

"It would make him look like someone who won't change. He'd hate that, I think."

He nodded. "He might hate that our grazing land is under water, but he'd want to make the best of a bad job. That's one of his pet phrases."

She smiled. "I know."

The next two weeks were hectic. Susan had to find staff for her Salcombe café and talk to builders about a temporary shelter to act as a café, accessible from the house whose kitchen would be used for the preparations. Just to make matters even more chaotic, one Saturday in the middle of all the planning Stephen's school friend Martin called and asked if he could please, please come and stay as he had been told to leave home by his father.

Stephen said he'd phone back but was sure he could, if only for a night or two. He and Susan talked about it and the difficulty of accommodation. "You wouldn't want to share with him," she said with a lift to her eyes.

He bit back any comments about preferring to share with Mary and just shook his head. "But he could have the new extension until Dad gets back," he reminded her.

"Or until Mary gets back."

That left him straight faced, though at sixteen he was very aware that sharing with her, as he had when they were both children, was not going to be allowed.

"We'll need to build on again," he muttered.

So Martin received the call he was hoping for and found his way to Salcombe to which Stephen had rushed in the launch. He seemed to have very little luggage.

"Most of my clothes were kept by Da... by my father to use for my brothers," he said tersely when Stephen mentioned the fact. He was grateful to Stephen for agreeing to offer him sanctuary, as he put it, but otherwise almost silent until they were finally on the island and Susan had welcomed him. They sat him down with the inevitable cup of tea.

"What happened?" asked Susan bluntly.

He took a deep breath. "You know he's been on at me for ages, and nothing I ever do is right? Well, now he wants me to leave school, not even take 'O' Levels, and get a job. We had a row. I told him that the exams were only next month and he said he didn't care. He never got any exams. He needed me to get some money in because there wasn't enough to go round. I said that in that case, why don't I leave home so it was cheaper for everyone? He was so angry with me that he just said 'Great. Go. See how you get on. And don't come running back when you're hungry.'

"So I just rushed out of the room, packed two suitcases and came down. He asked me what was in them and I told him it was my stuff. He made me open them and took a lot of my clothes out, saying they would do for Ted when he grew up. Then he just told me to go."

He stopped, looking down at the floor, trying not to let his emotions get the better of him. There was a silence.

254

"And did you not manage to get anything else? Things you'd grown up with?"

He shook his head, unable to speak. Susan crossed to him, knelt on the floor and just put her arm round him. Stephen watched the floor, comparing Martin's experiences with his own recent emotional past.

"Sorry," Martin sniffed.

"Don't be."

The words came simultaneously from two mouths. Susan looked at Stephen, who continued: "If you knew the state I was in after all we've been through, you'd realise there's no shame."

Martin looked at him shakily. "Thank you."

Stephen nodded.

Susan sat down again. "I think I need to talk to my father about this, Martin. There are some things that you are entitled to, I'm sure…"

"Your father?"

"He's a solicitor in Salcombe. He will know what else you can take from… bring with you. Parents have duties to their children, you know."

"He doesn't think he has," Martin said shakily, yet with anger now returning to his voice.

Susan made the phone call.

The next Wednesday Martin left school early one day; Susan had seen to it that he was reinstated there, to Miss Armitage's relief. The Merryweathers, father and daughter, and Martin met with his aunt who, Martin remembered, held a key and who had been appalled when presented with what her brother had done. With Mr Merryweather and Susan they drove to his previous home. The aunt unlocked the door. Together they removed Martin's personal property from his old room which he'd shared with his two brothers, together with his clothes. Mr Merryweather listed the items and attached it to a letter which he left with the aunt, explaining the legal background to what they had done.

Martin had a last look round and just nodded.

"Sixteen years…"

"Best to come away now, Martin," said the aunt. "But keep in touch. You are always welcome. Tell me when you're coming and I'll get your brothers here too."

He smiled at her and nodded again. "I'd like that."

# 26 – Café, return, Peter, Dot

A local building company came to look at the site on the island and amazingly quickly drew up sketches for a temporary café built of wood – effectively a large, though pleasant, shed. It would have a counter area at one end and an extra door leading towards the farmhouse kitchen.

Mr Merryweather footed the bill temporarily, despite Stephen's misgivings. The wood was delivered and construction started a fortnight later. "We know your story," the foreman told Stephen and Susan, "and you need this more than many of the others we're doing jobs for. So if the two lads can help us on Saturdays we'll get it done in two shakes of a lamb's tail."

The lamb shook its tail to great effect. Stephen and Martin were quietly surprised that sixteen year old muscles were quite effective compared with the same muscles at fifteen years old, and there were times when the seasoned workmen had to tell them to "slow down a bit, lads!" Back at school the following Monday with the finishing touches being put to their GCE courses, the two were seen squirming in their seats, trying to ease the aches in those muscles, sixteen or not.

Henry's response to the original idea had been one of horror. Both of his correspondents had been persuasive. Eventually it was in particular their arguments on the money front that made him grudgingly give his blessing. But by that point the plans were well afoot anyway.

In mid-May the café opened. Signs had been installed on the sloping shore to advertise it. Susan had also advertised it in her Salcombe café and had talked to the people hiring out dinghies at the Hard and wherever else she could think of. There was some comment, but she ignored it.

The first day, a Monday, there were a few customers, but after that the numbers seemed to grow daily, though dependant on the weather. The return of the boys on Friday afternoon saw her almost on her knees.

"You need help," said Stephen. "It's us tomorrow. You have a day off."

Martin nodded his agreement. "I met up with someone today," he started diffidently, "who gave up school last year. She's done a bit of café work. She's looking for something at the moment. How about getting her here during the week?"

Susan looked hopeful. "What's she like?"

"Anyone I know?" asked Stephen.

"Alice Luscombe. She's nice…" he paused, and Susan could almost hear the blush.

"She's old Mrs Luscombe's granddaughter – you know, she has the village shop in Blanksmill. She could stay at Blanksmill during the week, perhaps, and come over here each day."

"Well, we've got no room to put her up," said Susan firmly. "Do you think she'd come?"

"We could ask her Gran," he said.

Alice appeared, was liked, and proved efficient. Martin took charge of her and seemed to be with her whenever possible. Susan wasn't surprised, having seen that blush. Stephen was a little put out, feeling for a time that Martin had just engineered her employment so he could enjoy being with her. For a reason he could still not really identify it made him think of Mary's absence. Or, he thought in a flash of inspiration, was he just jealous that Martin was 'with someone' whilst he wasn't?

The café throve. It was so much of a novelty that visitors' imaginations were fired up by having a Devon Cream Tea on a real island, one they had to get to by boat. The dismissive comments Susan had encountered at first were never repeated. Edgar, running the Ferry, operator liked them and offered to divert to serve the island.

The boys sat their exams and were non-committal about the possible results. They were relieved to be done with them. Martin had said his farewells to his school friends as he was leaving early, but Stephen, though in one way envious of him, knew he was going to continue to A-Levels. He had to restart at the school at the beginning of September.

At the end of September they closed the café for the winter. Martin wondered what he was going to do now. There was nothing on the island; not enough work to do, even with the extra chickens they'd bought for eggs for the cafes, and the growing family of pigs. He moped around, depressed that Alice had now returned home to Kingsbridge, although he knew he could meet her there at times.

The foreman of the building company came to look at how their work had stood up to the months of work. Martin made him a tea.

"So what are you two going to do over the winter if this is shut?" he asked.

Martin shrugged. "Stephen's back at school, doing A-Levels," he said. "Susan… Miss Merryweather has gone back to working in Salcombe. I'm just a spare part really."

"Is that so? Now then, do you like being a spare part or do you want a job now and again? Just labouring, to start with, and hard work. But seeing how you did when you were helping with the shed that doesn't seem to bother you much."

"Please…could you tell me more?"

When the other two returned he discussed it with them.

"Are you sure that's what you want to do, Martin? It's hard and dirty work."

257

"I don't know. But it's a job and will get some money in now the café's shut."

"You mean you're thinking of earning it for our income here?" asked Stephen incredulously. "No. If you earn money, it's yours."

"But there are expenses here…"

"But Martin…" Susan this time. "You worked hard all through the summer to get this going and got nothing from it. It wouldn't be right if you used your wages to support the Lofts."

He looked at them, eyebrows raised.

"I thought I was one of the Lofts. Like you are, Susan.

"You are… Well, if Stephen says you are, you are. But you need your independence sometimes. Perhaps Stephen will fly the nest at some point and he wouldn't be expected to pay into the farm, just like Peter doesn't."

"Who's Peter?"

"My brother. He left when he was about seventeen."

A long pause.

"And by the way," said Stephen, "the way you've just worked over this summer means that you're definitely one of us, whether you like it or not."

"Well…"

Martin made a phone call.

Gradually autumn and winter set in. Martin excused himself from returning on a few occasions, quoting appointments with Alice in Kingsbridge or an over-running job. His answer to the inevitable question from Susan: "Where are you sleeping?" was always answered by "Oh, on a mate's floor." She had to accept he was all right – he was nearly seventeen, after all.

On a wet, depressing day in November, when Martin was working late, Stephen stepped off the school bus at Salcombe into a puddle, soaking a trouser leg. Annoyed, and not looking forward to the journey back to the island in the open boat, he was not at his best as he walked down the Hard. He was even less at his best when someone put a finger against his spine and pushed.

Swinging round, he saw a dishevelled, pale man with nevertheless bight eyes and a cautious smile. It took him a moment.

"DAD!!!"

The bag was dropped into another puddle and the two embraced for what seemed ages. As they pulled apart they both knew that the wetness in four eyes was not caused solely by the rain.

"What…? I mean when did you get here? Why didn't you tell us? Oh, it's so good to see you! Have you been home yet?"

Henry paused to swallow, to get his voice under control, and to take in the sight of this noticeably taller, sharper featured, more confident looking boy... No, not 'boy'; this young man he had last seen eight months previously.

"I docked in Plymouth early this morning and have been hitch-hiking here since then. No, I haven't been home yet. Good God, but it's so wonderful to see you. And you look... a year older. Are you all right?"

"I'm fine. Just wet. And fed up – well, until just now. Are *you* all right?"

He looked ashamed. "It's such a long time since I was outside, *really* outside, that I was seasick on the voyage. I felt dreadful then. But I've had a tonic since."

"What – in the Shipwrights?"

"No – not a liquid tonic, but it's a good idea. I meant just seeing you."

He found arms around him again.

"Do you want a drink?"

"No. I want to get home and get dry. So do you, by the look of you."

"And you'll want to see Susan."

"What?"

"To see Susan. She'll be there, and there'll be a meal waiting."

For once he didn't object, but his eyes said a lot. Stephen picked up both his school bag and his father's heavy kitbag and carried them both down to the boat. Henry kept shaking his head, wondering about all this breadth in the shoulders that preceded him, and all this casual strength.

Once Stephen had steered clear of the moored boats he relaxed. "Sorry – do you want to take her?"

His father shook his head. "I just want to see everything again. Even if the trees are nearly bare, it's raining and cold, and I still feel a bit ill, I just want to see Home again."

Stephen smiled. "Apart from the season, nothing much has changed. We're still a real island."

"Still no news?"

"No. You'd have been the first to know. Well, the second."

They smiled.

"So how did you get released?"

It was a question out of the blue. Henry should have been expecting it, but wasn't.

"They were getting nowhere with tracing the bas... the men who swindled us. Someone felt that six months was enough to make the point, I suppose, then it took another month to get the paperwork through."

Silence. Then: "Well, I'm bloody glad you're back."

Henry looked at him and decided this was not the time to criticise.

"And I'm bloody glad to be back!"

They both grinned instead.

On the island, with the boat moored, Henry seemed reluctant to do more than look round. "So that's the temporary café, is it?" he said. "It's not as bad as I'd thought. Hmmm…"

"Dad, if you don't get in there and give Susan she shock of her life, I'm going to have to stay out here and carry on getting wet. Please go, then when you think I won't be embarrassed please will someone come out and tell me? I'll be talking to the pigs."

His father looked at him, for once unsure whether to laugh or be annoyed. What won him over was that this was the new, self-confident Stephen he'd glimpsed at the Hard; whilst he was still his son he was subtly not the usually biddable boy he had left behind.

He put a hand on Stephen's shoulder and set off for the house. Stephen waited for the scream, but there was only a shout.

That was enough. He shouldered the kitbag and school bag again and wandered round to the pigsty. At least it was dry in the nearby shed.

They both came to find him. He found himself hugged by both of them simultaneously. Once free, he smiled widely at them both, suddenly ridiculously, light-headedly happy.

"Has she told you about the café? What a success it's been?"

"I've only seen Susan for fifteen minutes! Give the girl a chance!" He sounded better already, Stephen thought.

"Food first," said Susan. "I hope there's enough to go round. But if you will keep secrets, Henry Loft…"

He grinned. "I wasn't very well on the way over, so I'm not sure about the appetite still. So I can fill up on bread and butter if need be…"

"I can do you a cream tea," said Stephen airily.

Henry chuckled. "I think that should wait until it's sunnier, don't you? But some time soon… to sit in the café with my feet up, being served by my son, with my fian… friend by my side…"

He looked round nervously, seeing two wide eyed stares on him like searchlights.

The silence spread.

"Daaaad… what was that word you were going to use?"

"Shut up, Stephen."

"Yes, Henry, what was that word? It was at the corner of your mouth."

They were both still looking at him. Slowly, he felt himself go red. There was a long pause and he knew, for once, that neither of them was going to break it. He couldn't tell Susan to shut up as he had Stephen, who nevertheless was smiling at him.

"It's no good," he blurted out. "I've been a fool and paid the price. Now I've got to get my good name back. We've got no money – well, I've got no income. I know what Stephen is prompting me to do, but it's totally unfair to ask me. At the moment."

"I don't think anyone's asking you, Henry. And if you really think that a French prison and money problems define you, then you are not the man I know you to be."

He looked at her, meeting her eyes full on. He looked at his son, who still wore an inscrutable smile.

"It wouldn't be fair," he almost whispered.

"It wouldn't be fair to say the words, or it wouldn't be fair for me to accept? I think that would be my decision, don't you?"

Silence.

"Stephen…" the voice was unsteady "…could you nip upstairs for a moment, please?"

His son was gone, still smiling, in an instant.

A very few moments later he crept down again and looked into the room. The two were still in their long embrace. Silently he crossed to them and, with some difficulty, put his arms around them both.

"Did she say yes?" The words were to his father but his eyes locked on to Susan's. The look in them, the happy tears, the smile, told him the answer.

And then, of course, came the phone calls. Firstly to Mr Merryweather to ask formal permission. It was quite a long conversation, with Henry constantly talking himself down about his recent shame and his doubtful future. But the resulting remarks he received could be summarised by "And about time too!" in an amused voice.

"Yes," Susan confirmed in an amused tone when asked by her father, "very happy. And yes, I thought he would never ask."

She listened again. "Yes, he's happy too. Well, I think so." Then to Stephen: "Dad wants to know if you approve too."

Stephen crossed to her and the phone and gave her a bear hug, nearly dislodging the receiver from her hand.

"Ow! … No, it's all right. He just hugged me. I think we can take that as approval." She smiled back at him.

Peter, when phoned, was ecstatic too.

Stephen's mood at school the next day was so light that all the teachers noticed and commented in the staff room. Miss Armitage, intrigued, made sure she bumped into him in the afternoon. He was still smiling.

"Did you realise that all the teachers you've dealt with today are pleased – if puzzled – that you look so happy, suddenly? That's not a criticism, it's just good to see after all you've been through."

He explained. She understood.

Martin's return after work later caught them all by surprise – including him. Henry had been told of the arrangement but in the euphoria of the preceding day, and its continuation, they had all forgotten. So it was a slightly bemused group of people who sat round, after greetings and introductions, wondering how the sleeping arrangements were going to work out.

At last Susan made her mind up. "Until we are actually married I think it would be better if I lived in Salcombe. People would talk otherwise."

"But that means I shan't see you," Henry complained.

"And it means that I'll have chased you out," said Martin, "and I wouldn't want that."

Susan smiled at him. "No, you won't have done. You see, in winter the café can't support staff. It's too quiet. So I really have to be there or it would close. If I'm going to start earlier to do breakfasts for local people it makes no sense to leave here when it's dark just to open up at 7.00 am.

"What I should do is to live there, run the café, and come over here in the late afternoons. Nothing happens in the café after 4.00 anyway. If Henry wants to come and help during the day, that'd be nice." She looked at him.

"There's something about wild horses," he smiled back. "So if I come over there with Stephen when he starts off for school, I can help, then come back with you later and start on our food. That means that there's the launch still there for Stephen's return, Martin has a home and makes his own way to and fro as usual, and we have enough room."

It was a happy, crowded Christmas on the Island that year. The café was heated, decorated and pressed into use to give space for everyone to eat. With seven people – Henry and Susan, Stephen, Martin and Alice, and Peter and Dot his girlfriend, there would have been no room for them to eat in the house in comfort. The boys and Henry slept there too, leaving the three bedrooms for the girls.

It was on the afternoon of Boxing Day that Peter dropped his own bombshell. They were still sitting over a late lunch when he shushed them all.

"I have something to announce," he started solemnly. The tone was so serious that he achieved silence instantly. "There must be something about this place, because I too have made a proposal to Dot, and she has accepted. So…" He was drowned out by exclamations and rewarded with astonished, but pleased, expressions.

"So," he continued when they let him, "I'm asking my Father for official permission to marry. And then may I use the phone to ask Mr & Mrs Cummins the same question?"

Henry looked at him, trying not to smile.

"Well, I don't really know, Peter…" He was rewarded by the sudden alteration in his son's face. "You see, in a few days time you will be twenty-one and so you don't need me to say 'yes'"

The relief on Peter's face made his own smile impossible to hide.

"But I'm still twenty *now*, Dad."

"Ah yes. Well in that case I'd better bow to the inevitable and say 'yes', hadn't I?" He held up his hand to stop any comments. "But even had you been still in your teens I would happily say 'yes' because you're both obviously so happy together and because Dot is such a lovely girl. Welcome to the growing Loft clan, Dot. He's not such a bad lad, and don't tell him, but I'm proud of what he's achieved."

"When are you thinking of tying the knot?" he asked them when all the hugging was finished.

"Probably not until the summer, Dad. We've got some planning to do first. And I've got my eye on a run-down place that we might be able to afford and do up, if I can find a builder."

Martin's ears pricked up.

"Where is it? In Torquay?" asked his father.

He cleared his throat. "Er...no... actually it's just east of Kingsbridge. An old farm cottage that the farmer doesn't need any more and wants to sell."

"Not near my old home?" asked Martin suddenly.

They discovered it had nothing to do with that farm or Martin's family.

"Have you tried the builders I work for?" asked Martin.

"Haven't tried anyone yet. We're still looking at how to afford it. But if we get near buying it, I'll contact you and see what they think. Unless..." He thought for a moment. "No, let's leave it like that for the moment. We're still too far off to plan."

"I'll do what I can," said Martin quietly.

Henry was quietly pleased that they would be living nearer and with any luck visiting more regularly. "I wish we had the capital to be able to help," he told Peter. "But since the flood – well, the farm's doing nearly nothing. If it hadn't been for Susan and Stephen getting this café going..." he waved his arm around "...we'd be begging on the streets. We have the water people to thank for that."

Peter nodded. "I know, I know. And I would neither ask nor expect. But thank you for mentioning it."

He's not such a bad lad, thought Henry; not for the first time.

# 27 - Flight

A tall girl with a naturally attractive face walked from a Scottish farmhouse down towards the nearby lake. It was cold. The long coat she wore was really too good for a farming life, but she had taken it with her so as to show respect to the McTavishes for their kindness and hospitality. She knew that after Boxing Day she would take it, and the smart skirt and blouse beneath, and pack them ready for the eventual return to school. Her usual garb around the farm was similar to that worn by a small girl in Devon a few years previously. Bigger in size maybe, and shaped differently, but still essentially practical as opposed to great-aunt- pleasing.

Devonshire! It seemed like a dream. Normal life had been school and the McTavishes since she was twelve. She knew without a shadow of doubt, even if she had to wait until her 21st birthday, that one day she would be returning south. At the moment Devon seemed so remote, geographically as well as in memory.

Her great aunt, rarely seen and never welcomed, had started to send her an allowance *'for suitable clothing so that she should be seen to be becoming a lady'*. In fact the clothes she had ordered by post from a catalogue were smart but functional and modern. Her teachers had an influence on her choices but she had been adamant that there was to be nothing bought that was even remotely as old fashioned as her relative would have wanted. She was still unable to persuade anyone, even the new girls, that she had a past on the south west coast, and had given up trying. A vague plan concerning the money saved from her allowance was starting to formulate in her head, but that would take a lot more nerve and planning than she could muster then.

After a stay that she enjoyed as always, she hugged her hosts and thanked them, and was taken back to school.

Staff seldom changed there. Retirements were few, resignations even fewer. But over these holidays, they learnt, one of the sports coaches had very suddenly lost a relative and had to take a sabbatical in order to take on the administration of an estate and a family home. They were both shocked and intrigued to learn that their new coach was to be a man.

"I'm Angus Gordon," he told them in a deep voice when asked to introduce himself. "In the war I was a major in the Sutherland Highlanders, quite a young major. I'm here to bring some teamwork skills to you, as well as skills in the sports you play. I play hard but fair, and I shall expect each of you to do the same." He sat down. The girls looked searchingly at him and decided that despite his age he was not bad looking.

Term started. Sports opportunities found Mary playing netball, lacrosse and hockey as before. Sailing was held to be out of the question until the weather had improved. That was always the case as it was a long job removing dinghies from storage and rigging them only to be unable to use them because of high winds and rain.

All the activities she took part in Angus Gordon helped to staff and sometimes run. Many times he would single one of the girls out to lecture them quietly on their performance. Mary was one such, and she decided from early on that Mr Gordon was not a man she liked, though if asked why she would not have had a ready answer.

There were a few girls who seemed to be the subject of his lectures or encouragement, whilst others were apparently ignored.

One day, just before the Easter break, he summoned some of the girls together, including Mary. She noticed that they were mainly those he had given individual time to.

"Over Easter I want to run a special course to introduce rounders to the school," he told them. "It will be a residential course near Perth and I want each of you to attend. This is a privilege, as the experience you gain there will help us introduce the sport here. You will need to contact your parents, of course, and make sure they realise what a chance this is.

"Please will you make arrangements to make contact and get permission as soon as possible."

He mentioned a fee but Mary was too confused to take in any more details. She was sporty, but the prospect of a fortnight with Angus Gordon didn't attract her, and she badly wanted the continuity with her earlier farming life at the warm-spirited McTavish home. She hesitated, then had a brainwave.

"I…I don't think my great-aunt would approve of that," she said slowly. "She doesn't really believe in girls playing sport and doesn't even realise what I *do* do."

He looked at her. "What does your great-aunt have to do with it?"

"She pays the fees."

"Stay behind once the others have gone, please, and we'll sort it out."

The others seemed to be more accepting. Perhaps they like the man, and I don't, thought Mary. Once they had gone he moved to sit next to her, half facing her so their knees touched.

"Don't you want to learn a new sport and teach others in the school, Mary? It would be a feather in your cap. And the course itself will be great fun, and a lot less formal than here. We can have fun." There was more, and despite her feelings Mary felt almost enthusiastic – at least about the course and the sport. She found herself agreeing to write to her great-aunt, and indeed did so that evening.

The answer two days later caused her both anger and an element of relief. *'Certainly you may not attend a course to learn such an unladylike game. And a course organised by a single man, too. The very thought fills me with horror. You will continue to attend the governess whom you have been visiting during the holidays up to now.'*

So that was that, thought Mary angrily. Her relative still treated her like a little girl who was to be brought up to become a delicate ornament. The school at least knew her character and abilities. She went to see the sport coach and once again found him move to sit too close to her for comfort. She showed him the letter.

"That is a great shame, Mary, But I wonder, would you come if there was no fee?"

"But she has forbidden me to go, Mr Gordon."

"She has no idea that you play all the other sports. I'm told also that you waste your time sailing, too. It would be a shame if she were to find that out, wouldn't it?"

"What do you mean... sir?"

"Well, I feel that I should write to her to explain that rounders is just another sport, similar to those you already play, and that she might also want to consider what a privilege it would be for her great-niece to pioneer a new sport at her school."

"No... please! If you do that she will stop me doing *anything!*"

"But you understand that I have to try, as this is so important. But of course, if you were to accept that you could just come with us, without telling her, then there would be no fee, I would make sure that no reference was made to the course or the sport on your report."

Mary thought fast. Part of her wanted to try rounders. Part of her wanted to defy her hated relative. Part of her was still wary of the coach. She still didn't understand why as he was obviously good at his job. But then, she thought, there will be all the others with her and she didn't have to see him except on the sports pitch. And at meals.

"And another thing," he was saying, putting a hand on her shoulder. "We shall have at least two days off to go shopping in Perth. So if you want to refresh your wardrobe, like so many girls seem to enjoy doing, that would be a really good opportunity. Shops in Perth are really good, I'm told."

The hand stayed.

More to get away than to agree, she said "Okay, then. I'll come. But please – don't say anything to my great-aunt."

He stood, much to her relief. "I won't. And I'm glad you're coming because you will be an asset to the group. Don't forget to ensure you have some money to go shopping, now!"

It was the Monday of the second week in April when they left for Perth in a hired coach. Mary was looking forward to the unaccustomed variety in

266

routine and surroundings, and the different spirit there seemed to be within the group. They were all excited, obviously, but there was something else; a sense of freedom, perhaps.

The journey was just over two hours. The hubbub of unaccustomed free talk and gossip had quietened by then. They were shown into the hostel and asked to choose beds and sort clothes out, then were taken into the city in the coach. An unexpected visit to a restaurant increased their excitement again. The coach took them on a short tour with the driver giving a guided tour, and then they returned. Games were played, bed time arrived and they retired.

Mary was surprised when, just as the majority of them were settling down, the door opened and the coach came and stood in the centre of the dormitory. Quietly he gave them instructions for the following day, asking them to ensure they were in sports wear at breakfast as they would be starting almost immediately afterwards. He waited, watching as the last few of the girls climbed into the beds, called good night, switched out the light and left.

Rounders proved to be a simpler game than she had imagined. Simpler if your coordination was good and you could get the bat and the ball connecting. It seemed that for many of the girls this was a problem, and the coach seemed to have to stand behind each girl at a time, hold her arm and guide it. Mary was no exception, despite being sure that she was able to hit the ball to good effect.

The personal approach continued into the afternoon, and Mary was starting to dread the warmth approaching her from behind and the hand grasping hers. At least, later, they were able to have a match without his physical interference.

After their evening meal at the hostel there was time for games again, then they were allowed reading time in the common room. But Mary was intercepted by the coach.

"I think it would be nice to get to know each other better, Mary," he said quietly. "Would you join me in the common room later, when the others have gone up to the dormitory? It would be good to chat, and maybe have a drink."

She didn't want to, but how could she refuse? He had waived the fee for the course; he had a hold over her with her great-aunt. So it was that later on she found herself sitting on one of the settees in the common room holding, to her surprise and slight alarm, a glass of wine.

It was not a happy situation. He was sitting too close, and asking questions which she sometimes had difficulty in answering. It was foreign to her now to mention growing up in Devon, and she didn't want to hear him scoff if she mentioned it, as she was sure he would just as all the others had. Doubtless he would have been warned by the school authorities. So she had to invent a life in Harrogate, and parents who had died.

At this he looked shocked and worked an arm around her shoulders. "It must have been hard," he said.

All she could do was nod, wishing she could just get up and go. The arm stayed there.

"So how long have you been at the school?"

"About three years," she answered truthfully.

"So you only see your great-aunt in the holidays?"

"Not even then. I stay on a farm by one of the northern lochs with a really nice couple."

"What are their names?"

Why did he want to know? "Mr and Mrs McTavish."

"So they teach you the sort of thing your great-aunt would want."

She had to smile. "No. They run a farm. I help."

"And does your great-aunt know this?"

"No," she admitted, "she would probably stop it if she did."

"So that is something else you wouldn't want her to know?"

She just looked at him.

"You see, I need to keep all this to myself, just as you do. And it would be nice to be given a little reward for doing so. What do you say?"

"A...a reward? What do you mean...sir?"

"You are an attractive young woman. We enjoy each other's company. I think it might be acceptable if we were...to kiss, perhaps?"

She was looking straight ahead, trying not to believe that a teacher at her school could be saying these words. There was only one person she wanted to kiss her, and he was in Devon.

It was a sudden revelation to her. It came from nowhere apart from her memory and her slow maturing over the three years she had been at the school. Why, oh why had she not tried harder to contact Stephen? She had been so feeble just to give up.

Returning with a start to the present she was aware that the coach's face was near hers, that his breath was uncomfortably hot, and that the arm not around her shoulders was moving towards her. The face closed in and contacted, the hand came up to touch her breast.

With a convulsive jerk she tore herself free, her right hand with the wine glass coming round to maintain her balance and depositing the contents into the man's face. She rose and ran out of the room. Quick! Where to go? Toilets? No, too obvious, too close. Outside? No, she might get locked out. Dormitory? The only place. And that was where everything was. Was there a lock on the door? She couldn't remember. She ran up the stairs, half listening for footsteps following but could hear none – yet. The door opened and she almost staggered inside. The lights were still on. Heads lifted from pillows to look at her.

"What's happened?" asked the nearest girl, seeing her face.

"Angus Gordon," she said as clearly as she could. "Tried to kiss me and... and..." She couldn't say the words.

"Lucky you!" said another girl.

Mary looked at her. "All right then, you go down and let him sit next to you. I won't."

No one said anything to that.

Mary marched to her bed and sat on it, then got up and returned to the door. There was no key. In a panic she grabbed the nearest chair and wedged it under the handle, then returned to her bed.

"What are you going to do?" asked the first girl.

Mary shook her head dismally. "I don't know," she said. "I can't stay here. Not with him..."

"But there's nowhere to go."

Silence.

"There's the town. The city."

"It's miles away."

"I can walk."

"Where can you go in the town?"

Silence. The door handle rattled. There were gasps.

Wild eyed, Mary looked round and a plan started in her mind.

Angus Gordon's voice told them to stop messing about and to open the door quickly. Mary hurriedly bundled all her clothes into her case, except the coat she had worn the previous day, and slid the case under the next bed along. Then she went to the furthest bed away from her own and dived under it.

"Tell him I've taken my case and gone," she said.

"Who is it?" the girl next to the door asked in a sleepy voice.

"Mr Gordon."

"Oh, Mr Gordon, we were nearly asleep. Did you see Mary Beale pass you?"

"No, of course not. Please can you unlock the door!"

"But you must have done. It was about five minutes ago. She was in a hurry and said she had to go somewhere else, another room."

"Another room?"

"Yes."

"Very well. I will check. Unlock the door, please, and I'll come back later."

His footsteps receded. Mary scooted out of hiding and padded softly to the door, thankful that all the money she had brought with her was still in her coat pocket – and that the coat was dark so as to be acceptable for the great-aunt's standards.

"Thank you," she said to the girl by the door, and meant it.

"Shall I come with you? Perhaps I can help."

Mary blinked. "Yes please. Don't you like him either?"

"Don't know," she said hesitantly. "But you're in trouble. Keep behind me. If I see him I'll distract him."

They tiptoed downstairs. Nothing could be heard apart from the normal sounds of the night. Fortunately it was only when they were near the front door that they heard an upstairs door close and footsteps cross the first floor landing. A male voice asked questions in another room. Quietly Mary opened the door and stole out into the night, gripping her helper's shoulder on the way, afraid to say anything by way of thanks or farewell. Once in the cool of the night she ran, remembering that the way to the city was the road the previous day's coach had taken.

Her thoughts had been that she must just get away from the sports teacher. But as she ran there was a growing realisation that this could be her chance to travel all the way to Devon and home. Home on Loft Island. She had the freedom, more or less. She had the money – she thought it would be enough for travel. And increasingly she had the urgent *need* to resume her real life.

She heard an engine behind her. Alarmed, she turned. A bus. She waved her arms wildly. It stopped.

"Dinna fash yersel," said the conductor. "We'll not leave ye tae run. Where to?"

"Oh…thank you," she gasped. "The station, please."

He reeled off a ticket, she passed over the money and went to sit. It was certainly more pleasant than running all the way, and considerably quicker.

At the station, where they arrived fifteen minutes later, she wondered what trains there were. She knew she needed to travel south, that was obvious, but where to? She decided to tell the bemused booking clerk where she wanted to end up – Kingsbridge – and had to tell him where it was.

"Bristol," he said suddenly. "Thirty-two minutes time there's the Inverness sleeper to Bristol. You can get to Exeter from there, then it's a short hop. You're lucky you got here in time. Emergency, is it? Platform 1. You'll have to ask if they have room."

"How much, please?" she asked, suddenly anxious.

"Child?"

"Er…I'm 15."

She was able to pay. Fortunately the school had not baulked at the amount she had asked for in order to restock her wardrobe.

The wait on the platform seemed to last forever. She looked up nervously at every sound, every footstep, certain that the man would have guessed her intentions and come looking for her. But only one couple actually appeared on the platform, fully equipped with luggage, and waited nearby. Their presence comforted her a little.

At last there were the unmistakeable sounds of a steam engine approaching. Waves of relief washed over her. The train stopped and stewards appeared. She surprised the one nearest her by waving her ticket and asking if there was room.

"Why yes, miss. We're not busy. The crowds going south travelled last Thursday and they won't be back until Tuesday."

She boarded, escorted by him.

"Where's your luggage, miss?"

"I don't have anything else." Thankful for the clerk's chance remark earlier, she told him "It's a last minute emergency."

He nodded, slamming the door behind them. A loud whistle sounded outside. He led her to a cabin, told her about breakfast, and left her to her own devices. She heaved a sigh of relief and locked the door.

It was not a very good night's sleep. There seemed to be very many stops. At last they were in a vast, echoing, noisy place where there seemed to be a long wait. Mary cautiously pulled back the blind and looked out: Edinburgh. Oh well. She was on her way. At last they started off again, and this time, without further stops with their attendant noise and whistling, Mary slept.

"Second seating for breakfast, please. Second seating for breakfast…" The voice was a few cabins away, then her door was knocked and the mantra repeated before the steward's voice retreated down the train. Mary stretched luxuriously. This was better than the school dorm with its strident prefect waking you in the morning and chivvying you to wash, dress and get to breakfast quickly. It was certainly better than the roving eyes – and hands – of Angus Gordon. She shuddered.

A quick wash later and after dressing in the only clothes she had, she went to enjoy a good breakfast, dreaming as she ate of being able to be free, of travelling home, and at last seeing Henry and Stephen again. Stephen! It had been three years! She knew she had grown and looked different. In fact she had been increasingly quite pleased with what she saw in the mirror. But what would Stephen look like? Whispered, giggly talks with other girls at school had told her a little about the changes to expect, and she blushed furiously as she thought about it. Not that she would ever witness those changes. The days of bathing without clothes would be well over.

The comments from her great-aunt years ago crossed her mind: *"Well, they seem to have changed their minds now. I have a letter."* That cannot have been true. She was sure it wasn't. It had been her wretched, lying relative making it up.

Hadn't it?

The words had hurt her at the time, and the scars were still raw after three years. They had accepted her as a family member. All that they had both said in the inquest backed that up. But there was still that nagging doubt.

"Bristol in half an hour, miss. More coffee?"

She shook her head, partly declining and partly to get rid of the negative thoughts. "No thank you," she said hurriedly lest the steward should think that she was being rude.

At Bristol she discovered that there was a connection to Exeter with little delay, so bought a ticket and sat, glad at last to be stationary for a while. The next part of the journey passed without incident and she arrived in Exeter just before 11.00 am.

Exeter, Sunday, morning. Church bells ringing. Having been so regularly to services in the school's Chapel for so long she had become used to the comfort in the words and the music. On the spur of the moment she left the station, having checked for a train westwards and discovered one that called at South Brent, but which didn't leave until well after midday.

The church bells welcomed her as she entered cautiously, to receive curious looks from people handing out prayer books. She took a seat near the back, intrigued to be able to see the bellringers at work in a partly screened-off area under the tower. She watched, mesmerised at their smooth, regular movements as the ropes rose and fell, paying little attention to the rest of the church. At last a voice called "Stand!". Hurriedly she complied.

"Thass for the ringers, m'dear. Not us." A diminutive lady had arrived in the pew whilst she was watching and was confiding the information. Mary realised that she was the only one standing. The bells stopped. She sat again, embarrassed, but smiling her thanks at her companion..

It was Easter Sunday. She found she was at a Communion service and was pleased to be able to take a full part in it, having been confirmed at school the previous autumn. It made her feel more at ease, to be a part of something familiar as an adult.

"I publish the banns of marriage..." It was immediately after the main service had finished. She switched off her brain again – at least until she heard "...Loft, batchelor of the Parish of Holy Trinity Salcombe..." Furiously she scanned her recollection of the full wording...

"Peter Loft."

The relief was overwhelming. But common sense took over. A boy couldn't get married.

Afterwards her companion spoke to her. "New in the neighbourhood, m'dear?"

Mary, disarmed, shook her head. "No, I live near Salcombe and I'm travelling home."

"Late for Easter! But then mebbe it's a surprise?"

She laughed, her first genuine laugh, she thought, for ages. "It will certainly be that!"

"Terrible the changes they've had down there. But I expect you know about them?"

"Do you mean the floods?"

"Yes, and still nobody's saying who's to blame. But it must be the water people, surely. They were their dams."

"I'm sure you're right."

"And did you know, one of the new islands has opened up a cafe? And it's doing well. The new ferry calls there now."

"New ferry? I didn't know about that."

"Been away some time, then. Yes, it goes either from the town Hard or from Crabtree Quay – wherever the tide lets it. Now that'd be a good way to go home! All down the estuary! Oh, hallo love..."

This was to another lady. She eased herself out of the pew and started talking to her, giving Mary an opportunity to look at the time and to decide that she needed to return to the station. She said her farewells and walked back there.

A cafe. On an island. She knew of only one 'new island' that was big enough to have a cafe, and she was going to it. She wondered about that ferry.

The through fare to Kingsbridge used up all her remaining money except for two-and-thruppence and she was glad she had enough.

South Brent station, when she reached it, seemed all but deserted, but she asked in the booking office about the times.

"Ah... that's the carriage comes off the Riviera. She'll come down at about 3.30, so you've a wait."

"What is the 'Riviera', please?"

"Riviera Express. Comes from Waterloo and goes down west, but there's a carriage separates here and an old engine takes her down to Kingsbridge, see?"

"Thank you... I suppose you don't know about the new ferry to Salcombe, do you?"

"Ah... you want that, do you? Well now..." He rummaged around at the back of his office and found a duplicated sheet.

"Today's Sunday 21st April... well, they're running, and it's low tide so they're going from Crabtree, seemingly. Last one's at 5.00pm, so you'll get that one easily."

She thanked him and went out into the small town to see if there was a shop open selling snacks. The only place open seemed to be a small hotel and she had to make herself go into it, so foreign was it to her to visit anything like a pub. But then, it did describe itself as an hotel.

Her question to a man who appeared at a hatch in the small hallway was answered with no, there was no shop open in the town, but he could sell her a sausage roll for sixpence or a pie for ninepence.

She had both. She was hungry. That left her a shilling and she hoped the fare to the Island would be less than that.

Feeling better, she slowly explored South Brent and then with plenty of time made her way back to the station and sat on a bench.

Devon. Dear old sleepy Devon. Now it was Scotland, the school and even the McTavishes that seemed remote and part of another life. She was home. Nearly home. Dreaming of the island, she suffered a pang of loss of her home farm and family; such a feeling had been almost foreign to her for such a long time. But it was bearable now she was here, so close.

Finally the impressive London train puffed into sight, as did the booking clerk who seemed to double as a porter.

"It'll be the last carriage," he said as he passed. She made her way to it and found that it was almost empty.

Whistles from the guard and a scream from the engine... there was a noise of a moving train but her carriage never budged. She watched as the back of it disappeared west, bound for more exotic places than South Brent. The carriage dozed. Mary was tempted to do the same but was anxious that nothing was happening. She kept checking the platform and finally there was a sound that sounded more like a wheezy old man than a steam engine. It rumbled and panted into sight and closed up on her carriage with a bump.

After several minutes of clanging and some choice language from somewhere below, there was another whistle that sounded horrifyingly like Angus Gordon's referee whistle, followed by a surprisingly low pitched response from the old engine, and they started off.

Mary was now excited.

She counted off the stations as they passed them: mostly strange names she had seen only once before. She shuddered at the puzzling journey with the man who had introduced himself as Loft and turned out to be called Cade. But now she was undoing that journey. She was going home.

If the Lofts wanted her.

She shook her head to rid the memory of that scar on her psyche.

At last she saw they were entering a town and saw to her delight and relief that it was Kingsbridge.

Thrusting her ticket into the hands of the only man on the station she almost ran down Fore Street towards the old Hard, the Hard that was now repaired and in use again, to her surprise. She wasn't to know that the same tourists who had caused the ferry to start had also needed a proper embarkation point.

Leaving that to her right, she continued south and at last found The Crabtree with its landing stage nearby. She checked her watch. Half past four. A poster nearby confirmed that the last ferry of the day was indeed due to leave there today, at 5.00. Impatiently she waited, alone, walking up and down like a caged lion.

A white shape appeared where the river swung to the west. It was keeping to the centre of the channel, and for a heart-sinking moment she thought it must be a fishing boat. But almost at the last moment she saw a board which proclaimed 'FERRY' on the typical pillbox style wheelhouse. It altered course towards the quay, following the deeper channel. Mary stood, watching with impatient interest as the two crew casually made fast, then swung the gangway across and down to the boat. The few people on board, obviously tourists, climbed carefully up it, helped by the men who hoped for, and often received, a tip.

Mary approached after the last person had left and did a double-take. She recognised the crew man as old Charlie, the man from Edgar's boatyard who had given them his marlinspike.

"Hallo, miss, Salcombe, is it?"

"Hallo, Charlie. No, it's home to Lofts', please."

"But they stop serving at 5.00 m'dear... just hang on now: you said *home* to Lofts'. Who'm you, then?"

She smiled cautiously. "Don't you recognise me, Charlie? Not even when you gave Stephen and me your old marlinspike?"

He looked closer, then closer still. "It's not...it's not miss Mary, wot got took all those years ago? But you was... you was twelve or so..." He trailed off, still looking closely at her.

She continued smiling, more confidently this time. "Yes, three years ago I was twelve. Now I'm fifteen."

"But you'm not a girl, you'm a young woman. And a beauty, too! Cor, bless my soul but there's a lucky young man on Loft Island who doesn't know what's coming to him. By heavens, lass but it's good to see you back, and looking so well. Come aboard now, come aboard and take a seat. Looks like it's just you..."

"I've only got a shilling left," Mary admitted, suddenly worried. "Is that enough for the fare, please?"

"A shilling, is it? A shilling? Here's Mary Beale back where she belongs and she hasn't got the fare! Bert!" he shouted. "It's Mary Beale, wot

275

disappeared three years since and she's only got a shilling! Should we chuck her overboard for her cheek?"

He bent down to Mary again. "Miss Mary, if you had offered me a tenner to take you back home where you belong, I'd refuse it. We look after our own here. You should know that. A shilling, indeed!"

Mary smiled at him and went to sit down, suddenly relieved. Not relieved about the fare, but that it sounded as if the Lofts weren't the only people who knew she'd gone – and were pleased to see her back. Now she just had that nagging mental scar to think of, and the nearer she got to the Island the more it weighed on her.

"You all right, miss?" asked Bert, seemingly out of the blue,

He had blue eyes, faded, but bright and somehow piercing. Eyes you could trust. Like you could trust Charlie.

"It's just, it's just that they haven't seen me for so long. I just hope...hope they still want me there."

"I was at sea when it all happened," Bert admitted. "Came as a bit of shock to find water all over the place and lots of farms under water. And to hear the stories, and what people went though... poor things. And then when it was all back to... well, not normal, but things had settled down, and they say there was all this fuss about a lass going missing. And how they Lofts went near crazy trying to find her – find you. But they couldn't. Nor could Police.

"So I'd say that they want you back very much."

"Come on, Bert, you old slouch! Stop a'yacking! 'Tis time, and we've got a precious cargo to deliver – and fast. And I want to see their faces on Loft Island when we drop them another customer for that cafe of theirs at half past five! And as a second helping I want to see their faces when they realise who it is! Come *on* now, will you?"

276

# 28 - Return

The first year, the cafe hadn't opened on Sundays. People still came in their hired boats, though; like some people do, they ignored the 'cafe closed' signs that had been carefully prepared, and expected refreshments.

Eventually Susan and Henry had weakened and started opening late on Sunday mornings. That year, Easter Day after church had been their first Sunday opening, and the cafe had been hectic. Hectic in a good way. The last few had boarded the ferry back to Kingsbridge at about 4.00. Five on the island had collapsed onto chairs in the kitchen, unwilling to attack the washing up until they had rested weary muscles.

Idle chat ensued. It was close on 5.00 that Stephen jumped up. "We can't just leave all this. Come on. We open again in eighteen hours time and I want to do something before we have to go to bed!"

The rest of them groaned.

"What are you going to do?" asked Henry.

"I don't know... go sailing or something."

"It's low tide. The dinghy's going to be high and dry, even with running moorings."

He frowned. "There's always something... Oh, I don't know then. Tiddleywinks or anything!"

They had to laugh at that. All through the washing up he seemed somehow agitated, never keeping still, always around.

"Stephen, what's wrong?" asked his father. "You're like a seven year old with ants in his pants."

"I don't know... I just feel... I don't know."


She could see the island. Excitement overtook her and she shivered. Much of the apprehension about the reception she would find had evaporated with the sight of her old home but still there were twinges of worry. What would happen? Would she see Stephen first? Or Henry? Or perhaps Susan? Was Susan still helping them? But as the boat neared she felt almost light-headed and had to tell herself not to be so stupid. It was home, that's all.

Home.

The Ferry touched land. Mary saw the old road was still being used as a landing, the road that used to lead to... No. Not that, not today. She hadn't even looked at the bones of her old house as they passed. It was indeed a low tide.

Charlie and Bert were making fast, not bothering with the gangplank on the island – an addition, she noticed – and she leapt ashore after them. There seemed to be no one around. The path, the well-trodden path, as Mary noticed, led to a new building that seemed to be a sort of solid shed-type affair, though very much bigger than the word 'shed' would have you think. It had 'Cafe' above the wide double doors.

Still nobody around. The house, then.

Charlie wasted no time, but marched up to the door and knocked on it, then, without being asked, opened it.

"You got a customer here! Can't a body get a tea nowadays?"

A girl came to the door. Mary's eyes widened. Who...?

"Charlie, you know we shut after the last ferry, and that was ages ago... what are you doing back here? And who's this?"

Charlie put his finger to his lips. Then shouted as if in a storm: "Come on, Henry, come on Stephen! Show a leg there, mates!"

There was a muttering from inside and a clatter of crockery. A figure appeared at the door, his eyes sweeping round in an arc, taking in the two boatmen and the stranger and past her...

...and back again. He frowned. Who was this tall girl waiting there with an expectant look on her face.

The face. That face. His eyes fixed on it.

His mouth opened. He took a step forward. Then stopped.

"Stephen," he said in a voice quite unlike his own; almost choked, almost a whisper. "Stephen..."

Another figure appeared. She gasped. This wasn't Stephen! This tall, broad, *man* wasn't Stephen... And she looked again at the face, now with its mouth open like his father's had been, looking, wondering, looking. And now *really* looking.

He saw a girl, a young woman; tall, shapely, an expression on her face of wonder, almost of fear. And that face... could it be? It *must* be. Please let it be...

There was a shout, and this young giant was bounding across at her. Alarmed, she stepped back. He almost skidded to a halt.

"Mary?" The voice was ragged. She knew by now that she would have difficulty talking too. "Mary? It *is* you? Please say it's you?"

"It's me." The voice dropped at the end. And all the pent up agony of three years, and the pain of separation from everything she knew, and the frustrations of her relative and the disgust at the recent events all stopped her thinking straight. She took a step forward and would have stumbled, but those widespread arms just enveloped her and would not let her go.

She had not expected tears from Stephen, not from this giant who seemed to be him. She hadn't expected to cry for so long and so uncontrollably herself. She knew that the other strong arms that embraced them both were Henry's but she didn't expect tears from him as well.

But they came anyway.

278

They didn't see Susan come to stand by them, smiling. They didn't see Martin and Alice talk to the ferrymen and take them into the house.

At last three pairs of red eyes looked around. Susan, not unaffected, said "is it my turn now?" and came to embrace Mary.

Breathing calmed: eyes cleared.

"I think we need a walk before we go in, all four of us," said Henry unsteadily. He wanted their initial exchange of news to be private and easier for them all.

They walked all round the island, twice. Mary explained where she had been, and why, and why she had been unable to make contact. That information lit a long fuse of anger in both of the men.

They and Susan explained what they and the Police had done to try and find her, including the Harrogate Police's visit to her great-aunt. "And I sent you a Christmas card at her address. She returned it 'Unknown, Return to Sender'." That lit a fuse in Mary...

"We must expose her, once and for all," said Henry suddenly. "All this has got to go to the Police. We need your father, Susan."

Mary, now more bitter against her relative than at any time since she found herself at school in Scotland, said with a tremor in her voice: "She told me... She said that you had changed your mind about wanting me here. She said you had put it in a letter but it was private so I couldn't read it."

They looked horrified at her.

"You didn't believe it, did you?"

She paused. "I... I didn't know. I thought you'd find me, that someone would discover where I was. When nothing happened, and everyone at the school said I had some sort of mental fixation about a mythical childhood in Devon, and I was forbidden to try and contact you – well, I just didn't know any more."

The tears were pouring down her face as the last terrible hurt was purged from her.

Stephen hugged her again, more gently this time. "Every minute of every day I – we – have wanted you back here. I was as miserable as hell at school for ages. Until..." he laughed "...until Dad said that you'd be at school somewhere and if I didn't study I'd find myself left behind when you *did* come back."

He paused, remembering. Bitter.

"Look: I don't know how we'll do it, but we have to make sure you're adopted, or something, as Greg wanted. Then that bloody cow can't ever do anything like that ever again."

It was a measure of Henry's agreement that he had no criticism of his son's wording.

At last, part talked out, they went indoors and told the others. There were exclamations of surprise and disgust at what had been done, and done by a relative too.

"And who's this bloke who took you in the first place?" demanded Charlie.

"He called himself Jack Loft – Uncle Jack…"

"And I have no brothers."

"… but when the great aunt was talking she called him Mr Cade. You know, I think that annoyed him. He looked angry for a moment."

"And you said he gave you something on the train and you slept all the way?" Henry had latched onto that.

"Yes. He offered me a drink of some kind and it tasted peculiar. But I drank it anyway 'cos I was thirsty. And then I just got sleepier and sleepier."

A silence.

"He drugged you," said Susan calmly.

"Yes, I suppose he must have done. I'm sorry."

"Sorry?" asked Stephen, "what have you got to be sorry about?"

"I should have refused the drink, then got off at the first station."

"You were twelve, Mary. Twelve year olds do what they're told. Even by strangers. You could have done nothing else. Don't be sorry, be *furious!*"

They all had to laugh at that. Stephen, when not talking, was just watching her, seeing her face move and change, seeing the similarities and three-year differences in expression compared with the child Mary he remembered. And taking in, too, her figure, her looks, her poise…

"'Ere, talking about being furious, Edgar's going to be! We're that late it's nearly tomorrow. Come on, Bert, and face the music. Not that he won't understand when he hears why."

"Just a moment, Charlie, Bert: please tell Edgar, but please ask him not to say anything to anyone else. And please could you do the same? Not a word to anyone, yet. We need to surprise Mr Cade. And when we do, we might end up surprising Miss Marriatt too. Will you do that for us?"

They agreed readily enough, and hurried off giving wishes of good luck to all of them.

Once they had gone, Mary found herself looking at Alice and Martin, who smiled back.

"I'm Martin – I was in Stephen's form at school. My father told me to leave home, and Henry and Stephen took me in until I could sort myself out. I've been here ever since."

"And I'm Alice. Martin and I met ages ago now, and we're… what did they used to say? Walking out together. We're helping in the café at weekends until they can get some more staff in. It looks like Martin may be helping Peter – Stephen's brother – with a house he's hoping to do up. Martin's working at a builders. The same people who built the café."

Mary nodded, suddenly relieved. When the girl had appeared first she thought for a gut-wrenching moment that Stephen had a girlfriend.

"And that prompts me," Henry said. "We have two announcements to make to you, things that have happened recently. Firstly, Peter has asked Dot, his long-term girlfriend to marry him, and she has accepted."

Mary nodded. "I know."

He stopped. "What?"

"I know." She smiled. "I didn't tell you but I went to church in Exeter this morning. They read the banns. It gave me a shock because I wasn't really listening until I heard the name 'Loft' and for a moment thought it must be you. Or Stephen." She didn't mention the turmoil in the few seconds between hearing it and recalling the Christian name, followed by Dot's. She laughed. "Bachelor of the Parish of Holy Trinity, Salcombe" sounds very grand."

"Ah yes," laughed Henry. "And maybe the next banns you hear will be in Salcombe. He'll say: 'I publish the banns of marriage between Susan Merryweather, spinster, and Heny Loft, widower, both of this parish.'"

It took her a moment and then her mouth dropped open again. "But you... you never said! We spent all that time walking outside and you never said! Oh Susan..."

She crossed and gave her a hug, once again almost weeping in happiness; then to Henry who also had a hug.

"Do you approve? Really?"

"I do. I do very much, if Stephen does."

"I do," said Stephen.

"Then I definitely do. Not that it's my business, really."

Henry held her away from him. "But of course it's your business. You're Family too. Remember?"

And once again she broke down and shook, quietly crying, in his arms. "I always believed, always hoped..."

They phoned Peter and he too was ecstatic. Horrified, angry but ecstatic.

"She heard your banns read in Exeter," Henry told him, so she knew about you two before we told her."

"Yes, Dot was brought up in Exeter – until the family was bombed out," he told his father. "Hope she approves!"

After a few more exchanges Peter ended with: "Tell Stephen to behave himself now!" Henry didn't pass that on, but there was a worry in his mind.

Susan phoned her father whose first comment was: "I prayed for her to come home, just this morning. Is she all right?"

Susan assured him that she was happy but said there were aspects of her abduction that they all felt should be shared with the Police before her return was made public, and would he advise them?

"Come down tomorrow, at 9.00, even if it is bank holiday. The school vacations are still in progress, I believe, so they will not miss out."

"Would it be best for Stephen and her to come down alone?" Henry suggested. "Too many might stifle her – she has been through a lot. And, of course, we have the café to run."

"Yes, yes. I think that is an excellent idea. I shall enjoy their company, too. I shall provide lunch."

"What was the school like?" asked Martin eventually, "apart from them all believing the headmistress over you, that is."

"To start with, it was like any new school. And of course I was angry and confused and felt beaten by that woman." She meant her great-aunt. "But when I stopped trying to persuade the girls that I really, *really* had been brought up in Devon and wanted to go back, they treated me as one of them. And it's a good school. We did lots of sports...but...well, I'll come back to that." She had remembered she hadn't told them the reason for her sudden decision to escape.

"There was a lot of sailing. They were surprised that I knew what to do as not many girls sail, it seems. So I think that now I could even win a race or two. I did up there!"

"Different from our school?" Alice asked.

"There's a lot more room. And sport..." again that cloud came over her face. "But most of the girls are just normal. One or two are stuck up, but the others are okay."

"Just a minute," Stephen asked, "what about the holidays? Did she drag you back to Harrogate?"

"No fear! That would have been worse still. I think she wanted me to go to a governess somewhere, and be taught how to be a lady. In other words, to be like her. But the headmistress said that I could if I wanted, but from what she knew I'd prefer to go and stay with a couple on a farm."

She paused, smiling. "the McTavishes are lovely, and I really felt at home there. It was nearly like being back home. Really back home. They were farming the same way we were in summer and autumn, but the winter and spring were freezing."

"And didn't you get a chance to write then? Or tell them you were from Devon?"

"They had been warned too. They were good about it, but had to do what the headmistress told them. And there was no post box anywhere near them! I think it confused them that I knew what to do on their farm without having to be told, though."

"So what was it that made you suddenly escape?" asked Martin bluntly.

There was a long silence. She gave a sigh, and started to tell the tale of that final saga. They listened with mounting concern.

When she reached the part where Angus Gordon had tried to fondle her, Stephen had had enough. With a force that surprised him and hurt his hand his fist crashed down on the family dining table. He bit back some words that he'd learnt at school and jumped up, running out of the house. Mary watched him go, then rose herself.

"May I?" she asked Henry. He just nodded.

Day was drawing to a close. In the twilight she could hear a crashing, and headed towards the noise.

He had started off kicking a tree, but that had hurt his foot. Now he was pulling and pushing two saplings, trying to wrest them from the ground. She hurried over to him.

"Stephen, please?"

He froze. Cautiously she put her hands on his shoulders and gradually could feel the muscles relax.

"Stephen, he didn't do anything, you know. I escaped."

"But he could have." The voice was rasping, nearly panting with the effort he had put in to the innocent saplings.

"But he didn't. And one thing made me want – need – *have* to escape, above all else."

Now he turned. His face still grim, though not at her.

"What?"

"You. All the things you've said. What you've done to support me. Maybe what I've done to try and support you. Having all that fun, even after what had happened. Sailing. Landing." She blushed, but he couldn't see. "Swimming naked that time. Perhaps especially that. And after the flood, sleeping and waking alongside you when we were kids. ..."

Mary was not surprised once again to find herself in a bear hug. But this time a hand came up to lift her face from his shoulder. Cautiously Stephen closed the gap, and for the first time ever kissed another human being with more than just a polite peck. Considerably more than just a polite peck.

"All those odd feelings, all those years ago," he said shakily. "I kissed you goodnight then. And it was just two kids. And we had fun. Like kids do. And all I knew was that I wanted us like that, together, friends, for ever.

"And then you weren't there and I panicked. Then life settled down again, sort of. But I felt as if you'd died, and that I was left alone again. I was grieving all over again. But this time it was different."

He stopped and cleared his throat. "I don't talk like this. I don't do emotions. But today – for only the last few hours – well, it feels like a fairground. A happy, dizzy, nearly sick feeling, but happy, happy as hell. Oh God, I'm *so* glad you're back. And here. And can we do that again?"

This time it was Mary who started the approach. They were still together when footsteps were heard in the distance.

"Stephen."

A pause. They parted. "Dad."

He sighed. "From when Mary was here last I was afraid... no, I *thought* this would happen eventually. And no, I'm not against it, not at all. After all, this island seems to breed love. Dot and Peter. Alice and Martin. Susan and me. And now Mary and Stephen. And we shall all have to be careful we don't do anything stupid. For all sorts of reasons. Two more in your case: firstly Mary is still fifteen, and secondly she has a great-aunt on her case who would be delighted to point at any 'impropriety', real or imagined, to ensure she gets custody and gets her hands on the compensation when or if it arrives. Because that is all she really wants, I'm absolutely convinced. So's Susan's father."

Brought down to earth with a bump, they nodded. Stephen wanted to point out with pride that his and Mary's relationship had started first, even before his father's and Susan's, but didn't.

They returned to the house. Mary continued her story and surprised everyone with her confidence in what she had achieved.

"When your mind is set on escaping someone and getting back home, you can do anything," she said.

Stephen, still watching her closely, half unable to believe she was really there, nodded grimly.

"You must have had a lot of money with you," said Henry. "Did she give you an allowance?"

"She gave me a little to start with. Most of it I hid. But when I needed new clothes she increased that, thinking I would be buying 'suitable' clothes. But as she never saw me, I didn't, and it was sort of 'banked' by the headmistress. Then when we were going to Perth with its clothing shops and were encouraged to 'refresh our wardrobes' as they called it, all the girls latched on to the idea of being able to buy what they wanted. I didn't care. I might buy a few things, necessities, but I took as much money as they did anyway. And of course I also took what I'd hidden away for months, all in a good dark coat. Perhaps it was in my mind that this was going to be my opportunity to get away. Whether I'd have dared just to take off like I did, I'm not sure, I don't know. Then along came Angus Gordon who at least gave me something to run *from*."

She laughed. "And do you know what I'm left with? A shilling! It wasn't enough for the ferry back from Kingsbridge. But they refused to accept it, anyway."

Next day they arrived at Mr Merryweather's house at 9 a.m. as agreed.

He was in informal mode and refused to discuss any of Mary's story to start with. "Better left until I can make notes and get the story straight in my own mind all at once," he told them. Carefully, tactfully, he asked their real views on Henry and Susan's engagement. "It's difficult when you're with them, you know; knowing you wouldn't want to upset them. But tell me, please. The truth."

They started together and then both stopped, each waiting for the other. Stephen gave way.

"I think it's wonderful. I love Susan. I love Henry too – and have done ever since he was a sort of uncle to me when I was really young. They're happy together and each of them seems brighter when the other one is around."

"And you, Stephen? How do you feel about having a replacement mother?" It was deliberately phrased, and took Stephen aback.

"I'll only ever have one Mother," he said slowly, "and she died years ago. But Susan is a friend. She talks good sense and is... comfortable to be with." He paused, embarrassed. "And Mary is right. She makes Dad happy and he does love her. I'm very happy that they will be together."

"And that they marry?"

"That's what I meant."

"And will that make you call her 'Mum'? Either of you?"

They looked at each other.

"I don't know," said Stephen honestly. "When we met properly she told us to use her Christian name and we always have. And Mary uses Dad's Christian name too. It's almost become habit. But do you think we should?"

The old man looked at them with twinkling eyes. "That response serves me right for asking you both such a question, because the answer to your question is not mine to give. If I said 'yes' it would result in a forced response and neither of them would want to think you were forced into calling them something. If I said 'no' it would confuse you into thinking that it wasn't the right thing to do. That would be wrong too.

"Draw from my question this: that the decision is yours and yours alone, and no one should influence you. Not even them."

Neither expected an answer like that. Mary had spent the previous three years at school where making a decision on what to call an adult had been made for her. Stephen, like all children, had been guided on how to react to different people, and how to address them. It was only recently that he realised how he reacted with adults was now his own responsibility. Mr Merryweather, a product of a strict upbringing, had forced himself not to bring up his daughter in the same restrictive way. He was certainly intent on trusting these two young people to steer their own course.

They considered his reply. Mary, accustomed to formality, realised how fair was his response, and how different from most other adults.

She smiled, then crossed to him and planted a kiss on his head. "I don't know about Susan and Henry, but I've never had a grandad. Would you take that on?"

He looked up at her astonished, and blinked.

"I must go and check on lunch," he said abruptly, and was gone before they could say anything.

"Did I say something wrong?" Mary asked.

"I'd say the opposite. I think you just affected him a bit."

She grinned. "Well, I meant it."

"Count me in on that, too." She sat again and touched his hand.

It was a few minutes before he returned to the room.

"I think we had better start hearing your story, Mary, before this old man reacts to what you just said. But I will do so, afterwards, but for now I need to be a Solicitor first and foremost." He gave a small bow in her direction, but she glimpsed the very slight traces of pinkness around his eyes – as well as the smile around them.

"Where shall I start?" she asked.

"At the beginning, please. We know that you were interrupted in class by someone telling you there was a relative to see you."

"Yes... he said he was Mr Loft, Mr Jack Loft..."

With questions from the old man and occasionally from Stephen she told the story from beginning to end, hesitating only over the matter of the sports coach. As she struggled with it she looked at Stephen's face; it was grim and she could see he was still angry. She put her hand on his again and was relieved to see the expression replaced by a smile. A somewhat grim smile, but still a welcome expression.

The story of the journey south was rather rushed as she forgot that her main listener hadn't been present when she'd told those on the island the previous evening. But with additions from Stephen she managed to get it straight.

When she had finished there was a long pause. Mr Merryweather nodded, asked a few questions, then paused again.

"There are things we must do," he said. "Firstly the school in Scotland needs to know that you are safe and that there is a very good reason why you left the Perth hostel. Gordon has done nothing illegal, unfortunately... no, let me rephrase that. What he *did* was not illegal. Distasteful, disturbing but not illegal. He is not a suitable person to serve in a girls' school, however, and that needs to be brought to the headmistress's attention. However, it may be that if I were to do the obvious thing and write or telephone to the school, the information would be passed to your relative, Mary. That might cause a reaction we want to avoid.

"I think it best if you wrote, giving no address, saying you are safe and giving the information about the sports coach. Tell her, too, that more information will be forthcoming when it is appropriate – use those words.

"Separately we must give the police your statement. Are you content for that, and prepared to answer their questions? I shall be there too as your legal adviser."

She nodded. "If I can make sure that no one will try and get me away from here I will do whatever is necessary."

"That is indeed what we must avoid. I shall be laying a complaint against this Mr Cade and the police are in duty bound to investigate. It will lead to Miss Marriatt as well of course. With evidence from your headmistress, from the McTavishes, and from some of the senior girls in the school with whom you tried to share details of your home and upbringing, we shall persuade a Court that this was a kidnapping. A kidnapping with the aggravation of the deliberate administration of some kind of drug. Twice.

"What we *might* still have difficulty in discovering is the likelihood of any meaningful recompense being made by the water authority, whether or not under pressure from a higher authority. Until that is known, there can be no movement from the other possible source of compensation, the insurers for each of the two families.

"It might be that this case itself could give the Member of Parliament a push to insist that three years is too long a time for all the affected families to be impoverished. As he is a member of the government it means that he could have more influence than otherwise might be the case."

This last comment was all but lost on both of the younger people. Mary was just glad that someone else, someone she trusted to be effective, had taken over her problems.

"And now, early it might be, but I think a celebratory lunch is indicated." In a blink he had switched from Solicitor to friend.

"Celebration?" asked Stephen.

"Celebration," he said firmly. "It is not every day that a dusty old solicitor is entrusted with the title of Grandad. And this Grandad wants to celebrate that, and would be glad if his honorary grand-daughter and her friend would please join him."

"I think..." said Stephen, "that both she, as well as her friend and your honorary grandson would be delighted to join him."

The look on the old man's face was a sight to behold.

# 29 - Injury

Mary wrote her letter after lunch with their new grandad's input and it was posted as they returned to the boat later.

On the island they found the farmhouse full of people; Peter and Dot had arrived and were hoping to welcome Mary back. Martin and Alice were already there. Fortunately Henry had already given the former couple the full story, as Peter said after he'd given her a hug.

"I know Cade," he said, dropping a bombshell to Susan, Mary and Stephen who were in the kitchen at the time (the rest were serving in the cafe). "At least, I know *of* him. He's a private detective who works out of a crummy little house near where I live."

"We need to tell Dad," said Susan. "I was waiting until you two returned before phoning. Shall I do that now?"

This last was a general question, but Mary answered it. "Yes, please. He or the police will need to know."

Susan made the call. Her father asked to speak to Peter who gave the road name but couldn't remember the number. It was later, when the cafe had closed, that he gave his second piece of news.

"I've been keeping the best bit until last," he said, "so I'm glad everyone's here. That old farmworker's cottage we're looking, well, it turns out that the price the old chap quoted was for the two of them. So we could live in one – when we're married..." He shot a look at his father "...and let the other one out to help pay off the loan. So it looks like we might be living there sooner than you think, Dad."

Henry smiled. "That is a stroke of luck. But are you sure you're going to be able to get a loan, or a mortgage?"

"Well, this has only just happened, so I've not started looking into it."

"Well, don't forget that although I still can't do what I'd like and give you the money or even lend it to you, I'm still a landowner, with a business, and the only black mark I have against me is safely hidden in France." He winced. "So if you need a guarantor, you can put me down – if they accept me."

"I'll second that," said a quiet voice.

He turned sharply. "Susan... I'm sorry. We should have talked it over first. Sorry... I'm still not used to... to..."

"Being nearly married? No, nor am I. But still I'll second that."

He rose and kissed her.

"Er..."

Martin almost withered at being fixed by so many eyes.

"Er... if you want a tenant, Peter, and if I can manage the rent, would you consider me? And..." His voice dropped almost to a whisper. "And

Alice, if she'll say yes?"

None of the Lofts felt they could answer that implied proposal so silence reigned for a few seconds. It was broken by a clear, glad voice.

"Yes."

As so often before in that house, and for similar reasons, pandemonium broke loose. In the middle of it all Stephen lifted his eyebrows at Mary and they sidled out and walked down to the shore.

"Looks like it's just us left now," he said.

She looked at him quizzically.

"Well, *I* still think that actually we were the first."

His turn to look at her.

"We knew each other before any of the others got together. We – and Greg – were together since we were big enough to know what was going on."

He remembered himself and Greg, at eight, running fast from Greg's little sister, so they could play together. And years after that trying to do the same, only to find that her ten year old legs were almost as fast as their twelve year old legs. And the frequent occasions – when younger even than that – when the boys had decided it was time to swim, and had emerged embarrassed to find Mary swimming with them. All with nothing on.

And he remembered that last summer they had been together when she, aged twelve and still a child, had thrown caution to the winds and done the same, showing that actually she was now his best friend; replacing Greg yet not replacing him. And he remembered those nights when they had, in all childhood innocence, kept each other warm.

And he remembered how he wanted their companionship never to end.

"Do you think we should?" he whispered.

"They'd never let us," she said. "Not until I'm sixteen."

He calculated quickly. "Eight months. If I asked you on your birthday, what would you say?"

She opened her mouth, then shut it.

"D'you remember what Grandad said?"

He smiled to hear the reference to Mr Merryweather. "What about?"

"About us not letting anyone else influence our decisions to do some things?"

He nodded.

"Well... you'll just have to ask on my birthday and see what the answer is."

His eyebrows lifted. "You're teasing me!"

She nodded. "But..."

He waited.

"Please don't forget to ask."

He just had to kiss her.

When you are used to boats passing the whole day, some of which come to your island to visit your café, you acclimatise to the sound of small petrol motors. Stephen didn't notice it: Mary did, once their embrace had parted and they were walking arm in arm back to the house.

"That's a bit close, isn't it? They're not coming here, surely?"

He realised what she was talking about and looked at the launch with its three passengers approaching the old roadway that they now used as a landing stage.

"We'll go and tell them we're closed," he said.

But Mary had frozen. He turned to her.

"It's Cade!" she whispered.

Stephen's head whipped round. Suddenly he almost shouted: "Run! Get them to come down! Call the police!"

She needed no second bidding and fled.

A voice cried "That's her! Must be!"

Stephen ran to the landing place.

"Here – take this rope and hold it. This is urgent!"

Stephen took the rope, and with his not inconsiderable strength put a foot against the stem of the launch and pushed it out into the estuary again, throwing the rope after it. The man about to jump ashore fell into the shallow water and splashed about, finally regaining his feet and staggering ashore.

"You lout! You absolute fiend! Why did you do that?"

"We're closed. And we don't like people who try and chase others on our property." Stephen was being as calm as he knew, despite shaking with anger.

"You don't understand, and you have no right to interfere with an investigation."

"This is our land, and I have every right."

The dripping man was nearer him now. Stephen held his ground.

"You're nothing but a boy! Out of my way."

Stephen grabbed his arm as he tried to push him aside, and held on to it, turning the wrist so the man almost put himself into an arm-lock.

"I said that this is private property. We are closed. You are not welcome here."

"Let me go! This is assault!"

"It is self defence and preventing trespassing having asked you to leave... Ow!"

He hadn't realised that the other two had jumped ashore and had come to the aid of Cade. One of them had grabbed Stephen's arm and then put a foot out for him to trip over. He overbalanced and fell, letting go of the man's arm. As the man was facing him, ready to stop him rising again he raised both legs and managed to thrust against the man's chest, causing him to stagger back at speed. Since he was quite near the water he fell in.

There were shouts from the house. Stephen saw his father, brother and Martin running towards the melee. He was about to try getting up but received a kick to his side which took the wind out of him and made him feel sick. A pain shot through his chest, the sort of pain that tells you quite categorically that trying to move would be a bad idea. He lay where he fell, listening as some interesting cracks and thumps came from near his side. Then, after a confusing break interrupted only by some very bad language there was heavy breathing approaching him and a welcome, scared voice said "Stephen…"

Mary was with him all the time it took the fast launch to arrive. To Stephen, agonised and breathing with difficulty, it seemed to take for ever. The two ambulance men from the boat checked him over, causing him to shout aloud when they felt his side. "Fractured rib," one said immediately. "Hospital for you, m'lad. Are these okay?"

"Bruised and tied up, but otherwise okay," said the other one. "Police on their way?"

"Hope so," came Henry's voice. "We asked for them."

"And you people – any injuries?"

"Bruised knuckles." That was Martin's voice. "But worth it."

"We heard the rest of the story. So they can wait for the police. This one will be in Kingsbridge hospital soon."

"I've got a name," said Stephen faintly, trying not to breathe too deeply.

"We know, son" said the first one. "And you're going to be all right. Anyone coming with him?"

There was a chorus of 'yes' from Mary, Henry, Peter and Dot.

"Blimey! Well, I suppose we can. But don't know about the ambulance from the Hard to the hospital. We'll see."

"Actually… shouldn't you stay behind, sir? You've got four unpleasant characters here and the police probably want to talk to someone over twenty-one."

Henry swore, then apologised.

"It's all right, Dad," said Peter. "We'll have to go anyway because we've got work tomorrow, and you running us back to Kingsbridge to the bike isn't going to work now, is it? We'll hold his hand on the way – that is, if Mary gets tired of doing it."

She smiled faintly, and carried on holding his hand.

The police arrived about a quarter of an hour after the launch had left, by which time the carefully trussed three had started complaining and were making noises about false imprisonment. Henry stood just out of reach with Martin and just smiled at them.

Henry looked at the approaching blue uniforms and his heart sank. Inspector Moffat was one of them.

"Hallo, sir; we meet again."

"We do indeed. And I need to bring information against these three. The first" – he pointed – "is name of Cade. I hear he has a private investigation business in Torquay. He arrived on the island and attacked my son…"

"I'm on an investigation and that lout…"

"…Who had told him that we are closed and that by insisting on landing he was trespassing. He had expressed the intent to chase after my foster-daughter. Stephen stopped him, then the other two came up and attacked *him*. Fortunately we had been warned, so managed to intercept them and, er, persuade them not to take further action. Before we were able to do that, one of them kicked my son in the ribs when he was on the ground, breaking one of them and endangering his life. Yes, I wish to press charges. Shall we start with attempted murder?

The complaining from the three stopped suddenly, to be replaced by an even stronger chorus of denials. Henry led the Inspector away.

"Separately," he said quietly, "my son Stephen, with Mary who went missing three years ago but who returned yesterday, have laid information with my solicitor in Salcombe, and he will be presenting statements to the local police tomorrow, I believe. She identified Cade as the man who kidnapped and drugged her three years ago. However, I don't want these men knowing that we have that case against them as well, please. Not until a formal investigation has been started. Are you able to ensure that is the case?"

"Well, what we should do is to arrest them for whatever crime we believe they've committed, and that includes the original one if that's the case. But if the information has only been laid by two children…"

He left the sentence hanging.

"My son is seventeen, Inspector; Mary is fifteen. The Head and secretary of their Kingsbridge school will be able to identify Cade in due course. There is other evidence given by adults that will also be available. So I think it best if any reluctance to rely on the sworn testimony of two 'children' as you call them is left to these people's defence lawyers, not to the police who are public guardians. Would you not agree? I'm sure your Superintendent would.

A look of pain crossed the Inspector's face.

They formally arrested the three, handcuffed them and secured the handcuffs to rings on the police boat – a safeguard that intrigued Henry,

Martin and Alice. And then they were gone, towing the men's hired launch by the same painter that had just been used as the prisoners' bonds.

The Cottage Hospital introduced Stephen to ice packs and aspirin. "It's not dangerous," the doctor told them, "but it'll hurt for a bit. We'll keep him under observation overnight, and in the morning put a dressing round him. But it'll take six weeks before it's mended, and he'll have to be careful after that."

"Excuse me," said Stephen, "but how long will I need to stay here?"

"Oh, just overnight. You can take him home afterwards, I'm sure."

"Er… well, no," said Peter. "We have a bike, but firstly we're at work during the day and live in Torquay anyway. And I can't believe a bike is the best way of transporting someone with a rib injury."

The doctor nodded. "There's bus, or a taxi, I suppose."

"I live on an island, down the estuary," Stephen told him.

"I see," he said slowly. "Then he'll need to go by boat."

"Exactly. And to do that we need to get to the quay. Can someone take us there?"

"We'll see tomorrow," said the doctor. "He must sit up in bed tonight and not lie on the injury. They'll check him at intervals."

And with that he was gone to the next patient.

"That's helpful," said Peter.

"Why couldn't he talk to me? It's my rib!" Stephen spoke rather too vehemently and with a wince held the ice pack tighter to his chest.

"What are you doing tonight?" Peter asked Mary.

"Staying here."

"What, at the hospital? They won't let you."

"Well, where else can I go? I don't want to leave him on his own."

Stephen carefully turned his head and smiled at her. "It's all right, really. I can look after myself. It'd be nice if you could, but very uncomfortable for you. No, go and phone Dad before it gets too dark."

"I could come up in the morning and get you home…"

"I don't think I could walk down to the Ferry."

"Well, the hospital could help with that, as the doctor said. We'll worry about that in the morning. Are you sure you'll be all right?"

"I'll be fine. And if that doctor wants to say anything when none of you is there, he'll actually have to talk *to* me!"

Mary went to phone. Dot said to Stephen: "She seems so much older than fifteen."

"I know," he said, "and now I just want both of us to be older."

"We need to make sure that woman can't get hold of her first," Peter growled.

Dot nodded. So did Stephen, and wished he hadn't.

Mary returned. "He'll be at Crabtree in about half an hour. If I go now I should be in plenty of time."

Stephen looked alarmed and tried to move. "No, either he needs to come here, or Peter and Dot should walk down with you. I'm not risking that woman grabbing you again – maybe she's come down to direct those men." He stopped, breathing shallowly, worried.

"We'll go down, Stephen. We've got to anyway 'cos the bike's down there by the ferry. We'll leave you to rest. Don't forget to call a nurse if it hurts too much."

"It's all right unless I move. Or breathe too deeply. You go, and I'll see you in the morning, Mary. But don't come on your own, please. Not until this lot's over and that woman's in gaol or something."

He lay back on the pillow, looking tired and grey. Swiftly Mary went to kiss him. He smiled.

"I feel better already. Can we do that again?"

She put her tongue out but kissed him anyway, then turned and walked swiftly to the door. The other two said their goodbyes and joined her.

Henry, Susan and Mary collected him the next day. Stephen was taken aback to find a taxi waiting for them.

"We thought about going all the way in it," Susan told him. "But Mary reminded me you'd have to get in a boat at some point, and out again. So the launch it is.

By the time he reached the island he had had enough, and once again looked grey. He slept for most of the rest of the day, which meant he was wide awake at night. In his mind he only managed to rest properly as the hills to the east were dimly outlined by dawn's first light.

It was mid-morning when Sergeant Franks and a colleague arrived from Salcombe. Fortunately the café had yet to start being busy, so Susan volunteered to run it whilst Mary, Stephen and Henry answered questions. It was a relief to all of them that the annoying Inspector wasn't involved.

"We've had a deposition from your Solicitor which mentions a man called Cade. To your knowledge is that the same man we arrested yesterday?"

"Too much of a coincidence for it not to be," said Henry.

"Yes. It definitely was," said Mary. "I recognised him. It was the same man who made me go with him on the train and who drugged me." She was positive about it.

"So we need to combine these two cases into one, and that might involve Miss Marriatt again. Have you heard from her?"

"No," said Henry, "but the appearance of those three, including Cade, is hardly likely to be coincidence, is it?"

"We need to discover that formally. The three men are still in custody and we'll be talking to them this afternoon. It's to be hoped one of them will mention your beloved relative, Mary."

She tossed her head.

"Now then, young man: your injuries. What are they and how did you get them?"

Stephen tried to draw a deep breath, then winced in pain. "I have a broken rib and bruising. It hurts to move and even to talk or breathe sometimes. I got it when one of your prisoners pulled me to the ground and then kicked my side."

"It was the dark haired man," said Henry. "I saw him do it."

"Is there anyone who witnessed that?"

"My other son, Peter."

"Is he here?"

"No, he works in Torquay."

"How can we contact him?"

"He's not on the phone, but I can give you his address."

"Please."

"Are you going to release these men?" asked Mary.

"We'll have to eventually, but probably on bail. Don't worry though, they wouldn't be so stupid as to come back here."

"It's not that. But as soon as Cade gets free he will contact my great aunt and tell her. What she might do then scares me."

The sergeant thought for a moment. "Well, once we've talked to them all there are bound to be matters we need to check on, so that should mean we can keep them for a little longer. And once Cade realises we know the connection between Mary, him and Miss Marriatt, chances are he will sing like a bird. That will mean that we can get our colleagues in Harrogate to arrest the woman, and who knows, she might spend a night in their cells."

"That would be good," said Mary quietly. "*She* held *me* prisoner."

"Do we really have anything to worry about after that?" asked Henry. "She'll know that you've caught up with her. And when the case goes to court we can get people down from Scotland, presumably, to give evidence."

"Probably done first by statement, sir, then get them down if need be. It's an expensive business, travelling from Scotland."

"As I know too well," Mary muttered.

"So when can we expect the case to come to court?" asked Henry.

"Early days, early days. If we need to keep Cade and his cronies we'll have to get them to Torquay for a hearing, but that won't actually hear any facts. Let's see what happens first."

Life settled down – if settling down is an appropriate phrase for a café business which grew busier as the weeks passed. More staff had to be employed to ensure it kept open seven days a week – there had been some heart-searching about that, but all agreed that by providing a service for those at leisure it was acceptable within their church-led beliefs.

To great rejoicing and very many remarks about the physical and mental changes to Mary that had taken place since her friends had last seen her, she returned to school. Henry made it very clear that absolutely no strangers were to be introduced to her, nor was she to be expected to travel anywhere unaccompanied. Stephen, more tactfully than his father, also did his best to insist with all the staff that this should be the case. Unbeknown to Mary, he organised a militia of friends who would keep tabs on her and make sure she was safe from outside influence when he wasn't around himself.

There were no incidents.

At Loft Island and in a small flat in Torquay, weddings were planned.

One day, rejoicing in the mending of the relationship with his eldest son Henry jokingly said that they could all save money by combining the two services and wedding breakfasts. He was expecting a polite laugh, but instead there was silence from both Dot and Peter. He looked at them.

Peter was looking at him strangely. "Dad... where do I start? Dot and I were talking about that possibility last night. But we thought it wouldn't be the sort of thing you wanted. And certainly we didn't want to ask you and make you embarrassed by having to say no!"

Henry looked equally surprised. "It never occurred to *me* that you'd even contemplate it. But...well, are you serious?"

Peter and Dot exchanged glances; she nodded. "We'd love it. It'd be a proper family affair and somehow I think it would make the day complete. But then, what would Susan say?"

"I don't know. I do know she likes you both, and I'll most certainly ask her. Not just at the moment though, when she's serving and I'm meant to be preparing stuff!"

In the short break between the café closing and the last ferry, Henry put a cautious feeler out to Susan. She gave a gasp and smiled delightedly and immediately rushed to tell the other two she'd love that.

"And another thing; Susan's father will give her away, and Mr Cummins will give Dot away. But Peter needs a best man, unless he's asked someone, and so do I. I've given my choice some thought."

He looked round, grinning. "Stephen...?"

His son looked up quizzically. "Who do you want me to ask?"

"I don't want you to ask anybody. I want you to be my best man."

Stephen coughed, and held his side. Five weeks after the injury and it was still a little painful. "*Me?* But I'm your son. I can't be your best man too!"

"You can if you agree."

"But... but are you sure?"

"I wouldn't ask otherwise."

"What do you think, Susan?" Stephen asked her.

"The best man is the groom's responsibility. But I think it's a really wonderful idea. And I'd like Mary to be my bridesmaid, please."

Mary blushed and smiled, and just nodded.

"Well..." Stephen started.

"Just a minute," Peter interrupted. "I was wondering who I should ask and was wondering who at work could do it without it being a complete disaster. But if Stephen is acting for Dad, I wonder... would you be my best man as well?"

Now Stephen was speechless. But smiling broadly. "Well, yes..." he said hesitantly, "I'm just so surprised that either of you would think I could do it. But really, really happy; so yes, if one person can do both, I will give it my best shot."

He was almost overcome when both bridegrooms firstly shook his hand and then – very carefully – hugged him.

"Scotch all round," announced Henry, turning to fetch the bottle. The resulting glasses were met with a variety of expressions: Henry and Peter downed theirs and grinned at each other; Stephen's, well watered, was sipped warily and with something of a grimace, Susan and Dot sipped theirs and smiled at the others; Mary looked at the glass suspiciously, took a sip and screwed up her face, handing it back to Henry.

"Congratulations to all," she said. "Thank you for asking me to be bridesmaid and good luck to Stephen. But please may we have something different to drink at the wedding?"

That was the start of a period of planning which to start with drove almost everything else from their minds. It seemed the first opportunity for the double celebration would be September, so they all worked towards that.

At their busiest time, mid-July, with schools on holiday, a letter arrived to say that the first day of the case of The Crown v Cade, Marriatt and others would take place at Torquay Crown Court on Thursday 1st August.

"I hope it's over by September 14th," Henry remarked. That was the date for the weddings.

"Can we get enough staff in?" asked Susan.

"I'm sure we can. People are waking up to the money there is in the tourists. So long as we get the right people we'll be fine."

They had been lucky so far. There had been a lot of interest in working on an island and each time an announcement appeared in the local paper there were plenty of people, mainly young-ish, who were attracted by the idea of having to travel to work by boat.

"If only we had the space to keep a herd of cows," Henry was heard to say each time he paid for all the café's milk and butter. "We could use almost all the milk for ourselves, what with butter and cream and all."

# 30 – Court case

Inevitably there were more meetings with Mr Merryweather who, with the Police, had arranged a full range of witnesses. Both the Head and the Secretary of Mary's school were required to attend. There were written affidavits from the Headmistress at the boarding school at Rannoch and from the McTavishes. Interestingly there had been no mention of Angus Gordon from that quarter, a fact that the sharp eyed old solicitor had noted. Peter and Dot, Martin and Alice, Henry and Susan would all be called to give evidence about the assault.

To their surprise, once they were in the court room, only Cade appeared in the dock. The charge that was read out concerned just the kidnap and drugging of Mary, "a child then aged twelve". The man blanched, and pleaded guilty.

He was asked for whom he had been acting and to the relief of the families watching he named Miss Ethel Marriatt as his client. Swiftly he then detailed how he had been engaged, the actions he had taken, all of which agreed with Mary's statements, but naturally continued past her remembrance of the strange tasting drink. He detailed the address where he took his charge and carried her upstairs.

Mary's great aunt was called to the dock. She appeared frail, and spoke in almost a whisper. She was accused of arranging the kidnap by employing a private detective, Cade. When asked to plead, she replied "not guilty."

That started a prickly question and answer session which led to her stating that she could not have arranged a kidnap since Mary Beale was her nearest relative and she was merely bringing her home.

Mr Merryweather explained that the term kidnap meant the taking away of a person, in this case a child, without their consent.

"No consent was necessary," the old lady almost whispered, "Since her home is with me, her nearest relative."

"Have you been claiming a child allowance for her?" asked Mr Merryweather.

She paused. "What does that have to do with it?"

"It is part of the material gain that the word kidnap entails. Please will you answer the question?"

"Yes," she said, almost inaudibly.

"Do you know the situation with the Beale family land?"

"What do you mean?"

"You are aware that the house and farm are completely inundated by water, are you not?"

"Yes."

"And do you join with all the local people in hoping that soon there will

299

be some financial relief to be made available by the Council or the Water Board?"

"I don't see…"

"Answer the question, please," barked the judge, "and kindly speak so that the Court is able to hear your answers."

She glared at him.

"Will you answer my question, please?" Said Mr Merryweather again.

"Yes," she said a little louder.

"And if you were the nearest relative would you expect that relief, or restitution, to come to you?"

"As Mary's Guardian so I might keep it safe for her, yes."

"But as her nearest relative rather than her Guardian? Would you then?"

"I… I don't know."

"Are you acquainted with the contents of Mary Beale's parents' will?"

"No."

"No, indeed. With the Court's permission I will read it out."

Each was a simple will. All possessions and property were to be left to the other parent or, should they be already deceased, to the two children.

"So you see, it is no third party to whom this would be left. In the sad loss of not just the two parents but the brother as well, it would pass to Mary. If the beneficiary was a minor then it would be held by the executor in trust with any interest being payable to the guardian at the executor's behest. My firm was appointed executor. Do you understand that?"

"As her nearest living relative I would honour that of course. As it was I intended to advise Mary and keep her inheritance safe, allowing her access to it appropriately until she attains majority at twenty-one. That is why I had to have her brought to me."

"So are you saying that Mary asked to come and live with you?"

"She would have done so had she been given a chance to recognise her own best interests."

Mary gasped.

"You were at the inquest into the deaths of her parents and brother, were you not?"

"I was."

"Do you recollect her brother's dying words, reported by his best friend who is sitting in this Court today?"

"Hearsay! Nothing but hearsay from one child to another. And the Loft boy had his eye to the main chance."

It was Stephen's turn to gasp. He coughed, and held his side. Henry put a hand on his.

"So to extrapolate from what you have just said, this child, Stephen Loft, who had just witnessed a death, the first he had ever witnessed and which was the death of his closest friend, immediately realised that at some future point there would certainly be restitution or compensation coming Mary's way and that he might benefit from it if he made up a story that the dying brother wanted the Lofts to look after his sister. Have I got that right?"

"Yes. Something like that."

"Yet this is also the child whose word you have refused to accept on the basis that he is a minor, whereas the Coroner at the inquest not only accepted his evidence without difficulty but complimented him on his courage under the incredible events of that storm. Remember, this is a lad who did his very best to save his friend's life, and who found Mary on the island, thereby saving her life. Can you explain to the Court how you balance such courage and selflessness with what is apparently his cynical desire to share in the disbursements of a will of whose existence and contents he had no prior knowledge?"

"I... I'm not sure what you mean."

"I put it to you that you are accusing him of an avarice which was premeditated and cynical. The situation that night was one of havoc, of chaos. I believe you are asking this Court to accept that this plot was dreamed up by him in the extreme confusion of a violent storm compounded by the catastrophic inundation of his neighbours' farm which led to the deaths of all but one of the family. And this was a minor of thirteen years. Is that what you are asking the Court to believe?"

"I believe it is, yes."

"You only believe it, you are not certain."

"I am certain."

"And yet apart from once, you have never met Stephen Loft, much less conversed with him. You have no idea of his character or personal standards. Is that true?"

"It is. I do not need to meet him. It is obvious what was in his mind."

Stephen tensed again.

"I put it to you that a plot to make a financial gain from the contents of wills whose existence and contents were unknown to everyone except the Beale parents was much more likely to have been hatched by an older, more mature, more selfish and more cynical brain. Does it not occur to you that had you known his character, your plot to use the 'saving' of Mary Beale by trying to discredit him would be bound to fail?"

"I just wanted to provide a home for her and ensure she was safe, and that any compensation that might be forthcoming would be cared for too."

"So the possibility of compensation had occurred to you?"

"Naturally."

"Would you not consider it odd that it had not occurred to Stephen Loft?"

"You only have his word for that, and he is only a boy."

"I would remind you yet again that he was a boy who had discovered his friend Greg Beale as he lay dying and did his best in that chaos to save his life. He had already discovered his other friend Mary Beale and ensured she was taken to shelter, thereby saving her life. The Inquest accepted those facts. Do you?"

A long pause. "I have to."

"I think you also have to accept that as a thirteen year old minor, in the midst of a calamity, with death and destruction all around him, Stephen would not have had the mental capacity to think of compensation from whatever source, and even less how Mary Beale's parents would will away their money. I am sure you agree?"

"I cannot say."

"You cannot say. Yet that is precisely what you have been saying, have you not?"

No answer.

"Please answer the question, madam."

"If you say so," she said sulkily.

"I take it that was a 'yes' and should be recorded as such. Your honour, is that the case, please?"

"I shall direct it so."

"Turning to your attempt to have Mary Beale kidnapped…"

"I did not kidnap her, as you put it. I asked for her to be brought to me."

"I did not ask you a question. But turning to your comment, do you admit that you employed Mr Joseph Cade, Private Investigator of Torquay, to bring her to you."

"Yes."

"Why did you not come yourself?"

Another hesitation.

"Harrogate is a long way for a lady to travel."

"It is indeed a long way. It was a very long journey from Kingsbridge, via South Brent and Exeter, to Harrogate, is it not?"

"It is. I said so."

"Yet that is precisely what you expected a twelve year old girl to do, in the company of a man she didn't know. Do you regard that as 'proper'?"

"Needs must when the devil drives."

"So, as the prime mover of this journey, the driver if you like, you are equating your behaviour with that of the devil, are you?"

There was a laugh in the court.

"That is an impertinent question, young man."

"Madam, thank you; it is many years since I have been honoured with that epithet. Nevertheless it is a question and, as this is a Court of Law, you

302

are bound to answer it."

"I merely did what I deemed necessary."

"And did you consider Mary Beale's welfare on the journey? After all, she was with a stranger, and a male one at that."

"I was sure she would pass the time by reading or looking out of the window."

"Or sleeping, perhaps."

"Maybe."

"Perhaps you hinted that Cade should offer Mary something to help her sleep?"

"I cannot say."

"There is quite a lot you seem unable to say, may I observe. Very well, we will ask him later if it was his idea to administer a drug, or yours. We shall discover, in any case, unless you wish to enlighten us?"

"I do not."

"You do not, or you cannot?"

"I cannot."

"In that case, would you not say it was strange that you are not saying forthrightly that you did *not* suggest a sleeping draught?"

"Very well, I did not suggest a sleeping draught."

"Thank you. We will nevertheless ask Cade later, and discover from where it was bought. Turning now to Mary's treatment at your house, we know that she was locked in a bedroom – have you any wish to deny that?"

"She was confused and may have come to harm had she been allowed out."

"Confused by the drug, I take it you mean?"

She paused. "Maybe."

"So you were aware that a drug had been administered."

A longer pause. "Yes."

"And when did you learn of this? Would it have been when you suggested it or did Cade tell you when he arrived?"

"It was obvious from her behaviour."

"Can you describe that behaviour?"

"She was asleep."

"Asleep or unconscious?"

"Is there a difference?"

"You were proposing to look after a twelve year old girl and you are unaware of the difference? A naturally sleeping twelve year old will waken if spoken to and persuaded to wake. Anyone unconscious will be unable to. Are you saying there was no response whatsoever, that she had to be carried to the bedroom?"

Another pause.

"That is so."

"And did you ask Cade what drug had been used?"

"No."

"So you had no idea whether she had actually been poisoned and needed urgent treatment. Is that not somewhat careless?"

"The drug wouldn't have been poisonous. That would have defeated the object."

"So you made sure that a suitable drug was used?"

"Yes."

"How?"

"I beg your pardon?"

"How did you make sure what drug was used?"

"I... I..."

"Either you told him what to use or you *did* actually ask him. Which?"

Silence.

"Answer the question, please," the Judge barked again, "and make sure it is a truthful answer. Remember you have sworn upon the Bible."

"I... I provided it."

"You provided it. Finally we have the truth, despite your earlier prevarication. Well, that lets Cade off the hook. Or rather, it doesn't, since he was the only one who could administer it. Do we assume from that answer that the drug administered to Mary Beale, presumably in her breakfast, on the first part of the journey to Scotland was also your decision?"

Silence. The judge was about to bark again when there was a quiet "Yes."

"So twice you arranged for a drug to be administered to a twelve year old girl who was under your control?"

Another pause. "Yes."

"Turning now to your decision to send Mary to one of the most remote boarding schools in the country, please can you tell the Court the reasons for your decision?"

"It was obvious from her behaviour towards me that she would not be happy living with me in Harrogate. The school is a very good one, and attracts a good class of family."

"Its remoteness was another benefit to you, was it not, since it ensured Mary Beale would not be capable of escaping back to where she wanted to be?"

"It would mean that she could receive a good education, suitable for a young lady, without distractions."

"Distractions?"

"Distractions from the ridiculous notion that she could be some kind of

304

farmer on an island in Devon."

"Are you aware that, at the age of twelve, a child is capable of choosing between a number of options for her after the death of her parents?"

"The law will give the nearest blood relative custody."

"That is not an answer to the question. Are you aware of the importance of the child's choice?"

"It is up to relatives to choose who is best suited to provide for the child."

"Even against the child's express wishes?"

"If necessary, yes."

"And was it necessary in this case?"

"In my estimation, yes."

"Did you ask Mary Beale her wishes?"

"For some ridiculous reason she wanted to stay in Devon."

"So you asked her, and then rode roughshod over her wishes. Is that so?"

"I did what was best for her."

"If it was best for her, why did she voluntarily, and with considerable difficulty and expense, return to her old life in Devon three years later when mature enough to decide how to do so?"

"I don't know what you mean."

"It is a simple question. You decided what you thought was best for her without taking her wishes into consideration. Years later she decides to return to the life she wished for all along. Is that not the case?"

"She has proved that despite all I have done for her, all the money I have spent on her education and her allowance, she would defy me."

"Is it not more the case that by paying no heed at all to her wishes, that you defied her? And that she merely reacted against your doing so?"

"She is a minor."

"Minors have wishes too and, increasingly these days, rights. While Mary Beale was enduring her sojourn in Scotland, Harrogate Police were asked to visit you to discover if you knew her whereabouts. Is that so?"

"Yes."

"And what was your reply?"

"I told them that she was not in the house."

"Did you also tell them that you had not removed her from her Kingsbridge school?"

"I did, because I had not done so."

"Miss Marriatt, you are an educated woman. I imagine that English comprehension is one of the subjects you covered in school. Are you aware that the words "Did you" also mean "Were you responsible for?""

"You do not make yourself clear."

"I think I do, to an *educated* person. You knew what the Police wanted to know, did you not?"

"They were asking if I removed the girl from school. I did not."

"But as we have discovered, you made arrangements for her to be removed by an employee, did you not?"

Another long pause. "I did."

"And you, as an educated woman, knew exactly what the Police wanted to know. But, against the provisions of the law, you prevaricated."

"I answered the question they asked."

"I put it to you that either you are not as educated as I believe, or that you deliberately misled the authorities. Which would you admit to?"

"Perhaps I misunderstood the question."

"Would that be in the same way that you misunderstood the Christmas card sent to your address for Mary Beale? The one you returned as "Not known, return to sender?"

"That was obviously a trap from the Loft child to try and get me to acknowledge that Mary Beale was with me."

Stephen stiffened again, and held his side.

"How did you know it was from Stephen Loft?"

"Because of the address."

"Which was inside the card. So you admit to opening someone else's personal mail against the provisions of the law?"

"I needed to return it."

"Despite your knowing that it was not addressed to you personally and that you could easily have forwarded it to Mary Beale's school? Despite knowing it was from her friend who must have been desperately anxious about her welfare?"

"I needed to ensure that the child was not encouraged to try and corres… to return to Devonshire."

"Despite the fact that your actions were illegal?"

"Sometimes the end justifies the means."

"Even when the means are themselves illegal?"

"Maybe."

"I think, since you are an *educated* woman we must regard that as a "yes," don't you?

"If you wish."

"It is not as I wish, Miss Marriatt, it is as the jury sees it. I am sure they have taken note. Is it true that you falsely told the headmistress of Mary Beale's new school that she had an illogical fixation and belief in a previous life in Devon?"

"I wished to ensure that she was safe there and would not be allowed to wander."

"That does not answer my direct question. I will put it to you more bluntly: did you provide a story that was a tissue of lies to her headmistress?"

A long pause. "Yes. To ensure she did not leave, and that no one assisted her to leave."

"Did it occur to you how distressed, embarrassed and frustrated Mary Beale felt when even the prefects and her contemporaries at the school regarded her insistence on the truth of her previous life as a fiction?"

"No."

"Were you aware that the headmistress realised how active and sporty Mary was, and that during the school holidays when you presumably didn't want her to return to you at Harrogate, she was sent to a farm and not to the governess you had requested?"

Miss Marriatt sat up. "No. I most certainly was not. How dare she?"

"I imagine she dared because she, at least, wanted what was best for the girl. And were you also aware that the reason she returned home to Devon when she did was that a sports coach made a physical pass at her?"

There was a gasp in the Court. This time Miss Marriatt's astonishment was complete. The woman may also have gasped, but it would have been inaudible under the voices within the chamber.

"Silence in Court," the usher bellowed.

When all was silent again Mr Merryweather asked again. "You recollect the question, Miss Marriatt. How could you forget it? Were you aware of that?"

For the first time the old woman's voice was clear. "No. I had not been told that. And I am horrified that it should have been so."

"So, had you known, can we take it as read that you would not have engaged Cade's business again to remove Mary Beale for the second time, so as to return her to the same school with its danger?"

"I most certainly would not have done. I would have found another school."

"And then arranged for her to be kidnapped – sorry: 'collected' – again?"

"Yes... no... I don't know." She put her head in her hands.

"Let me just put this to you, Miss Marriatt. You are a spinster, living half way up the country from where Mary Beale has been brought up, attends school, and has close friends. We hear that no closeness developed between you and the Beale children on the occasion you visited. Nevertheless when the parents and brother are killed you decide that there would be a large amount of compensation coming Mary's way and that if you brought her up you believe you could bend her to live the sort of life you do, including persuading her to spend that large inheritance as you willed it.

"To accomplish that, you have her abducted, drugged, imprisoned and sent to Scotland where a fabrication of lies that you concoct prevents any chance of escape. I suggest that as you hardly ever saw her from the day she went to Scotland until now that there was never any love between you, and will remind you that love is an absolute essential in the growing up process.

"On the other hand, in Devon there is a man and his son who have been friends with the Beales since they were each themselves young. Gregory Beale's last words to Stephen, his best friend, were "Stephen, look after them for me. That is a fact that has been accepted as such in court, at the inquest. You heard it for yourself, I believe."

The Court was silent as he paused and looked her straight in the eyes.

"And from the day of that disaster until the day you removed Mary Beale to the other end of the country, the Lofts, father and son, looked after her with love, respect and consideration, including the tremendous support they gave her at the inquest and the funeral.

"Now, all that is not really a question. But I will ask you this: by way of the natural love as one friend to another, and by way of the support Mary has received, whom do you now regard as the more appropriate person, or people, to offer Mary a home? Is it you, who have admitted to the court that you have lied throughout your dealings with her, and whom she frequently and eloquently expressed her dislike both before and since you arranged for her abduction? Or is it the Loft family with their love and total happiness with her presence? I should tell you also that Henry Loft is engaged to marry, with the ceremony taking place next month."

The crafted questions, the pauses, the difficulties in finding answers; all came together in the old lady's mind. She thought, then nodded and looked at the Judge.

"I need to change my plea."

The judge called for a recess whilst he considered the case, looked at his watch and decided to resume after lunch.

The conviction of the other two men for attempted abduction and grievous bodily harm, and the second charge of attempted abduction for Cade, were now almost academic. Mary was called as a witness first to describe how she had recognised Cade. Stephen described his actions, then Peter, Martin and Henry were called and had to identify the man who had kicked Stephen when he had been brought to the ground and while he was still down. They were delighted to do so, and even more delighted that they all picked out the same person.

Their defence solicitor was almost defeated before he started. All he could really offer was that the men were working for Mr Cade's business and doing as they were bidden. He tried to brush away Stephen's broken rib as a mere scratch, exaggerated by a young boy who had deliberately put himself in the way.

The jury, when set to decide guilt, took just fifteen minutes from dismissal. The foreman announced they were agreed, and the accused were guilty on all counts. All, including the old woman, were remanded in custody. The judge decided that sentencing would be in a week's time.

Having left the court room in a surprisingly sombre mood they waited for Susan's father, who appeared after a delay, unusually flustered. With him they retreated from the newspaper reporters and Peter and Dot took them to their flat for tea. It was the first time Henry had seen where his elder son was living and was taken aback that it was so small.

"Any news on the house yet?" he asked.

"Not really. The old farmer's dragging his feet a bit. And I can't do anything about money until I get a firm acceptance from him."

Henry nodded, wishing he could help.

"Any news on the council or the water board?" Peter asked in turn. It was Henry's turn to shake his head.

The old solicitor interjected. "It is probably just as well the decision has not been made, not before the case. If Miss Marriatt knew the likely extent of such compensation her arguments may well have been more prolonged."

Stephen jumped up.

"We're forgetting Mary's and my grandad," he announced. There were looks of surprise from all apart from the two concerned. "He has done a really wonderful job for us all and we've never even thanked him. So I will now. Please will you raise your...er... teacups to the best solicitor in Devon, our friend, Susan's Dad, and as I said, our Grandad. Without you, sir, this would never, ever have happened. We owe you a big debt, not just for this and all the work you did in advance, but for all the things you've done for us over... well, three years. One day we will be able to repay you."

"That was really my speech to make," said Henry, "but Steve got in before me and said everything that I would want to say. Thank you, more than I can really say."

The old man looked embarrassed. "I was honoured to have been adopted by these two, and I'm very proud to be able to say that. So everything that was done was actually done for my extended family. But that aside, I bumped into someone in the Court building I knew, someone who happens to be one of the Children's Officers."

They looked puzzled.

"How does that affect us, please?" asked Mary. A smile started on Susan's face.

"I told her about today and... well... also told her what I was able to say to summarise what Mary wants, where she actually wants to live. She looked interested and I persuaded her to ask for a transcript of the trial. If she agrees, and the committee backs her up, she should be able to arrange for Mary to be properly adopted by you two as their daughter." He nodded to Henry and Susan. "Once you're married, of course."

Henry looked astonished. "I never imagined in my wildest dreams that it could be that easy. I thought there would be forms and investigations and all sorts of things we had to do first."

"Well really, the investigations have taken place. We have the evidence from the inquest as well as from today. I *believe* that no Children's Officer in their right mind would still regard Miss Marriatt as a suitable person to bring up a child. And by child, I refer to the technical term of 'minor' which we all are until we're twenty-one. She also agrees with me and will use those proven facts to sway the committee. Forms are, in contrast, a minor matter, albeit necessary."

Several conversations broke out. Stephen's hand reached out to Mary and she clasped it. But his thoughts were in turmoil, a rapidly worsening turmoil as facts coincided in his brain.

"Just a minute," he said loudly, interrupting everyone. "Just a minute, please: if Mary becomes my sister, and we were to...well... want to... to... get engaged, won't that mean that we can't? You know, as brother and sister?"

"No," his adopted grandfather put in quickly. "That applies only to blood relatives, not to adopted ones."

The relief on Stephen's face was a picture.

"Of course, there will be something of a delay, as the transcript will not be available until after sentencing. But I will give her some time, then make contact again. I can't promise anything, and I can't influence anything and nor should I, since I am now rather emotionally involved. In fact" – he cleared his throat – "I was relieved that no one picked up on our personal ties today. It might have skewed the whole case."

"But all you did was bring out the truth," said Henry.

"But I did so knowing more of the family situation than would normally have been the case. I believe it was only because Salcombe people outnumbered Torquay people there, and so obviously showed their goodwill, that nobody else picked up on it."

"Did they? Outnumber local people, I mean?"

"Oh yes. It may have had something to do with something the vicar mentioned in church last week."

Another pause. Henry rose and approached him. "Could you just stand a moment, please?"

The old man did. Henry was about to shake his hand but instead put his arms round him with a bear hug. "Susan said you were a wise old owl," he whispered. "I think we've found out today just how wise."

Conversations restarted. "Just you wait until your birthday," Stephen said in a low tone to Mary, who just wriggled beside him.

They decided not to attend the sentencing. "To me it feels too much like revelling in misery," said Henry to Susan when they were preparing for the first customers on the day it was to take place. "We'll hear about it from your father, anyway. I'd prefer to be here, not in a stuffy Court room."

"What, you'd prefer to be in a stuffy café?"

"If it's with you, yes." He pulled her close and kissed her. They didn't hear the door opening.

"Oh Dad, Mum! For goodness sake…" And a gasp.

They wheeled round. Stephen had a deep blush on his face and dipped out of the room in a hurry.

They looked at each other. And kissed. There were tears in her eyes.

"Are you okay for a moment?" he asked. "I probably should talk to him."

She nodded. He went outside, down to the shore where his son's tall figure was standing, alone for a change. As his father appeared at his shoulder Stephen looked round sharply, then nodded.

"It just came out," he said.

"Why did it worry you?"

"I… it's…it was always… you know, Mum… Mum's name…" he broke off, wretchedly.

"And do you think sharing it with someone else is somehow disloyal?"

He shook his head, not in disagreement but to try and clear it. "I don't know."

"Well, I knew her pretty well, you won't be surprised to know. And I think that if she wasn't around, and there was someone else who you felt almost as comfortable with as to call her Mum accidentally, she'd just be pleased that you've found such a person. Because that would mean to her that someone else can help pick up the pieces if your spirit breaks. And that would be a tremendous relief.

"And it doesn't mean that Susan is a substitute for her. The two are different people and we love them, their characters, for all sorts of different reasons. Your mother, whom you called Mum, will still be with us, in there" – he tapped Stephen's head – "whatever else happens. So don't let that worry you. And no, you haven't offended Susan – rather the reverse. I think she was just – well – surprised, but honoured."

"Should I call her Mum?" he asked suddenly.

"You're not six. It's not something I can or should instruct you on. I wouldn't even try because whatever I said might alienate you. It's a personal thing to you. You just go on how you feel. And perhaps there'll be times when it's Susan, and other times it might be Mum. Who knows?"

Stephen, comforted, told him about what the old solicitor had said on the subject.

"Ah well, we know he's a wise old owl. Perhaps I might be a bit, as well. And you know you astonished a lot of people when you christened him 'Grandad' at Peter's."

"All except him. We told him that Bank Holiday Monday when he was writing up the statements for the Police. I think he was a bit emotional. Pleased, but emotional."

Henry smiled. "I'm sure he was. It's a big compliment."

# 31 - Weddings

It rained early in the morning of the wedding day. They were wet when they arrived at the Town Hard and moored the boat, but fortunately their finery was safely in suitcases.

They changed at Susan's house – the café below having been closed for the day, with its blinds down and an explanation on the door. Mary was worried about the rain on her simple dress. They had decided against the more traditional – and expensive – wedding dress; neither couple was well off. As they opened the door again the sky seemed brighter – it had stopped raining and looked more promising. The nine of them set off with plenty of time to spare, hoping to welcome guests outside before the service.

Although Dot and her parents were strangers in the town, people recognised Peter and welcomed him. Henry and Susan, Stephen and Mary were now very well known. Mr Merryweather was now positively famous. So there were a number of delays in their walk along Fore Street and very many calls of good luck, some from complete strangers. They learnt afterwards that the vicar had been busy telling people about the double wedding, a rarity anywhere.

Fortunately there were fewer well-wishers on the way up to the church, a steep climb which they took at a steady pace, mainly for Mr Merryweather's sake.

If they had received a welcome on Fore Street, it was nothing compared to the crowd that cheered as they entered the church yard. They all dispersed, meeting up with friends. Mary and Stephen were astonished to see that a good number of their school had come down, and were particularly pleased that every one of Greg's coffin bearers was there.

Fifteen minutes before the service was due to start, as arranged, the bells started ringing. That was the sign for everyone to take their places and for the fathers and the brides and bridesmaids to remove themselves to the church hall "so they can be conventionally late," as Henry had put it. He, Peter and Stephen were now thoroughly nervous, Stephen particularly so; he had a double duty to perform, and two rings to take care of. For the umpteenth time he checked both jacket pockets: yes, there was a pair of rings in each and they corresponded with which side each groom would be. He relaxed a little.

The double ceremony went without a hitch except that they had all forgotten to mark on the cases which was the groom's ring and which the bride's. But with a little sleight of hand by the vicar no one noticed, and all at the altar steps just smiled to each other. Nervously, maybe, but they still smiled.

Finally they were able to retreat up the nave to the sound of organ and bells, and congregate outside where a friend of Peter's was waiting with a camera. He took control for a few moments, then they led close friends and relatives up the hill to the Knowle hotel and the reception.

Stephen felt a weight lift from his shoulders, until he remembered he had to deliver the speech that he and Mary had spent hours perfecting over the previous few days. He was about to dig it out of his pocket when the first of his school colleagues started talking to him.

After drinks and talk which seemed to Stephen to be never-ending, they were called to sit for the celebration wedding breakfast. Not for the first time did Stephen wonder why a meal starting after midday was termed breakfast but he said nothing, just dreading the moment when he had to stand up and speak. Once again he fumbled in his pocket but was immediately grabbed by Mary who had seen where they were to sit.

No sooner had they all sat down, waiting presumably for food to appear, than Henry stood again. Silence gathered.

"I'm speaking not as a bridegroom at the moment, but as head of the Loft family. I think it unfair to hold rigidly to tradition and leave speeches until after we have eaten. Those who have the duty of speech-making, and I'm referring to myself, would like to eat without the strain of knowing we have to stand up later and talk. Speeches first would aid our digestion and enjoyment. So if I may, could I ask my very efficient best man to speak now, rather than later?"

A round of applause and some supportive comments rang out. Stephen, shocked, and with his heart suddenly beating faster, was finally able to dig in his pocket for the carefully prepared speech.

It was not there.

His eyes grew wide. He dug in all his other pockets. Nothing apart from the empty ring boxes.

He breathed deeply, making himself somehow calm down. He bent to speak to Mary, finding her already looking at him in shock. "Prompt me when I dry up," he pleaded. She nodded.

He stood again, aware the room was silent. All eyes were on him. He looked around, and finally latched on to the kindly, twinkling face of his honorary grandfather, who winked and nodded.

"It would appear..." he paused "that the very efficient best man has efficiently left his carefully prepared speech somewhere."

To his surprise there was a roar of laughter and some scattered applause.

"So... what follows will be short, to the point, wandering from what Mary and I concocted, and maybe end up as rubbish."

"As they are the elder... er... senior, I'll talk about Mr and Mrs Henry and Susan Loft first." More applause.

"As you know, their story started in tragedy." That at least he

314

remembered from the written version. He also remembered their agreement that he should pause after the words. He did so, but so as to remember what had come next in the written speech, not for effect. He realised that all he could do was to think back.

"Whilst we were trying to sort out – well, everything – we visited a café in the town. It was the first time we met Susan, and..." he smiled "...the first salvo of words threatened to blow any conversation at all out of the water."

He was glad to have remembered that phrase. There was a chuckle.

"But before long we had started to realise that we could help each other. Mary, Dad and I helped that day in her café and she helped us with just about everything else that we have needed since. I suppose," he said, only just now aware of it, "that it was very one sided."

To his surprise there was another chuckle.

"But it seemed that the more we did for each other, the easier it all became, and Dad and I started to regard Susan as a part of our lives. Obviously Dad was feeling that more than me, because..." he smiled at the memories "...every time Mary or I mentioned anything about it we got our heads bitten off."

This time there was a roar of laughter. Stephen realised he had gone well off course, and tried to steer back to it.

"Then, of course, Mary was... taken." Unconsciously he paused again. He felt his hand held, and looked down, meeting smile with smile.

"The strain of that left us both feeling as if something was missing.

"She was."

This time the face was grim. "And I felt that, I think, even more than Dad. But Susan has a calming presence and although there were many times when it hurt I was persuaded that life had to go on. With the help of both of them, it did. They persuaded me that I should carry on with the exam course I was on... Hang on! This is meant to be about them, not me! Sorry."

He took a deep breath. "I'll not say that the next period was easy. But again, Susan took charge, made things happen and helped a forlorn fourteen year old become an obstinate fifteen year old, started the café on the island – with help from her father who Mary and I are now proud to call our grandfather..."

There was a gasp from some and warm applause as everyone turned to look at the old man. He seemed to be wiping his eyes.

"And when Dad returned and saw what had happened he had to swallow his own obstinacy..."

"Here, steady on..." came from his right.

"...as he realised that until everyone in this estuary receives financial compensation we had to find an income from nothing. And that was the start of a growing reliance on each other. That's something else we're celebrating today."

At this there was another burst of applause. Stephen knew he was back on track. He remembered that year when they were all working as a team, with help from friends and staff. Peter...

"And this is where Peter and Dot come in. You'll know that my elder brother, who was usually on my side when we were kids but left Mary, Greg and me alone to get on with it most of the time, wasn't attracted by farming. He moved to Torquay, found a good job and an even better friend, who became his fiancée. The friend, not the job."

Chuckles.

"There were times when the first job started to feel as if I was getting married to it!" Peter called. More laughter.

"When we were starting the café, Peter and Dot, and Martin from school, and Alice *his* girlfriend, joined the café and made it what it is. And it was during this time that both Dad and I realised that, even if relations between Peter and Dad had been strained at times, Peter is still a Loft, and a good person. I'm proud to have him as a brother."

He was again interrupted by applause.

"Dot is another lovely person and we all like and respect her. We're thrilled to have got to know her properly and now to welcome her to the Loft family."

More applause.

"So surrounded by all these people rallying round to help get that café going, it's hardly surprising that we all started taking things for granted. But we are all so very, very grateful for every bit of help that people have given.

"It was when Mary and I were writing the speech... well something like this one..." Laughter "...that I started to realise something. And here I'm going off track completely."

He stopped, screwed his eyes up and took a deep breath.

"Susan has been the lynch pin – I think that's the term – for what we have today, for our being here. Oh, Dad asked her to marry him. After a lot of prompting from me, but..."

"Stephen..." from his right hand side again.

"You always told me to tell the truth, Dad, no matter what. Anyway, he asked, she agreed. I was so really, really happy. And have been since. And...well, it sort of slipped out the other day, for the first time."

He could feel his throat constricting. He kept silent trying to stop it. Eventually he felt confident enough to continue. "I called her "Mum.""

Fortunately the chorus of "Ahhh" and the long applause enabled him to regain an even keel. Mary grabbed his hand. Again they exchanged smiles.

"Now I'm going to stop. I want to wish Dot and Peter, and Susan and Henry, the Loft clan, every happiness and success in the future. I'm sorry this has been so – well – bitty, and I'm sorry Dot and Peter hardly got a mention in the end, but I wish them both so well. And I hope everyone else will do the same by drinking a number of toasts. The first is to Mary's and my new grandad who has done more to help us all than anyone will ever know. To Mr Merryweather!"

They complied. Stephen started to feel that it was nearly over and the relief washed over him. But Mr Merryweather was standing. This was in no script. Not in his current, extemporised one; nor in the lost original.

The buzz of conversation died swiftly. The old man looked round carefully.

"I am not in the general habit of interrupting wedding celebrations," he said, "and would not dare do so even when I have been honoured so many times by this truly remarkable young man." He bowed at Stephen, who just blinked stupidly and smiled back. "But as this is a family celebration first and foremost I feel it would be unfair if I did not act on this piece of paper immediately."

He held up a large, brown, official looking envelope.

"As it would take me longer to carry it to its recipients as it would to pass it round the table, I propose to do the latter. Please could it be given to Miss Mary Beale?"

Mary stiffened. Stephen looked down and took her hand. The envelope arrived. It was blank. She looked at the old solicitor.

"It needs opening," he said.

Wondering what could be so important, and for her on this day of all days, she pulled back the flap. With a hand that trembled slightly – she knew that every eye in the room was on her – she drew out the sheaf of papers and looked at it.

"Application to adopt a minor," it was headed. Shocked, she looked back at Mr Merryweather.

"That is a form which Mr and Mrs Henry Loft will have to sign, with your signature too, all witnessed properly. Once it has been returned to the Children's Committee and accepted, you will become legally the adopted daughter in the Loft family."

Silence, a gasp from her, and then thunderous applause. She felt Stephen sit at her side and slide his arm around her back. She looked at him with shining eyes, then past him at Henry and Susan.

"Did you know about this?" she asked. Henry shook his head. She passed it to Stephen, who passed it to his father, who put it in front of himself and Susan. He turned to Mary again.

"Are you sure?" Henry asked.

"Of *course!*" she responded. "You know I do."

He nodded, then looked back at Stephen, who stood again and waited for silence.

"I told you we had so much to thank him for. This is just one more thing. But I must finish. The next person I want you to toast, please, is Mary. I just want to say, without any blasphemy intended, 'Thank God you're back here, and safe.' Will you drink to that?"

This time there was a lot of chinking of glasses, and a pause while they drank.

"Now please will you stand and raise your glasses again, and this time to Dot and Peter, Mr and Mrs Loft the younger; brother and sister in law to Mary and me."

They did.

"And finally to the heads of the family: Susan and Henry Loft, now *our...*" he put an arm round Mary's waist "...Mum and Dad."

More applause, this time prolonged as he and Mary finally sat down. She squeezed his hand.

Peter's turn.

"I don't do speeches. I didn't even prepare one, let alone lose it."

A roar of laughter.

"Dad will do all the talking that's needed. But I'll say this. When my brother stood up and announced he'd lost his speech my heart sank. I knew how I'd have felt at seventeen if I had to talk to a room full of people with nothing to read from. But now I can see that my annoying little brother has become a ... well... thoughtful, intelligent, really rather nice, young man. And as he's now as tall as me, and probably broader, I suppose I'd better start being nice to him.

"Stephen, I never thought I'd say this, but I have tremendous respect for you. Thank you for saying what you did, and with no notes too. And..."

He was drowned out by applause again.

"And..." he said forcefully, "I want to thank Dad. I know that I made him very unhappy when I went to live away from Lofts'. If one good thing has come out of the disaster it is that we have at last come to an understanding. I do have a tremendous respect for him, as well as still loving him. And thank you and Susan for asking us to share our wedding day with yours.

"Lastly I want to thank Dot for finding something in me that she liked well enough to agree to marry me. You have made me very happy, and very proud, and I love you very much."

Yet more applause. At last Henry stood.

"Fortunately I warned the poor Knowle hotel staff that there was a chance the speeches might take a time. I'm now hungry, and I'm sure you all are.

"I think I've come out of all this really well. I have a café whose income partly replaces that from the farm. I have my freedom..." He smiled grimly. "I have a friend whom my son and my new daughter have adopted as a grandad though I'm still not sure how I should address him. In accordance with Mary's, Susan's, my and Stephen's wishes I have a daughter. I have my elder son back, something else that makes me extremely happy. I have discovered that not only has my younger son become a man – except in law – but that people – including me – respect him, and that he has the ability to talk sincerely, from the heart, in front of a lot of people, scripted or not. And most of all, I have a friend, a confidante, someone who laughs with me, someone who is dependable, full of ideas and who, for reasons best known to herself said 'yes' even if it did take some prompting from my best man."

He waited whilst the laughter diminished.

"I count myself lucky beyond expression that I have all these people who I love in so many different ways. And now I want you, please, once again to toast and thank my best man and son, Stephen; my other 'best man' and son, Peter and his wife Dot; and not least my wife, Susan."

As the applause calmed and the conversations started, food appeared, and at last they were able to eat.

Many hours later, as they changed for the boat back to the island, the speech was found carefully buttoned into the back pocket of Stephen's old trousers. They gave it to Henry and Susan, who read it through.

"Good," said Henry, "very good."

"I prefer the one you actually gave," said Susan. "It was more 'you'."

Their newly appointed Grandad was a regular visitor at the island and took a quiet delight in going there for many reasons. Firstly he was always invited, yet knew he could just appear when he felt like it and receive the same, genuine welcome – even though there might be a teatowel involved if the cafe was busy. Secondly going there was a complete break from the town. Thirdly he was interested to watch the reactions between his daughter and Henry, and particularly between Mary and Stephen.

He knew, from bitter personal experience, that childhood friendships rarely last as adult relationships. It worried him that the two of them had been thrown together twice in their short lives. The three years between those two episodes were also a time of great change in human beings. He wanted to observe at first hand whether the two were still so obviously attached to each other as they had so far demonstrated.

But each time he saw them he saw mutual respect and care for each other, and those little touches that he knew from his own marriage and from elsewhere were natural expressions that mutual love and care engender.

Quietly, over a few months, he asked each of them to say whether they felt stifled by the near-constant presence of the other.

Stephen shook his head. "It's like the sun's behind a cloud when she's not there," he said. "Even if we're on opposite sides of the room I just want to know she's there and all right. But it's better when she's next to me."

Mary smiled and said "It's like being with someone who's just making you complete somehow. I just think I'm so lucky."

Cautiously he hinted at the character differences that people experience through their late youth and that sometimes they go unnoticed until it's too late. He told them that they would be rare, and lucky, if they experienced no times when things between them grated, caused rifts. He hinted how important it was to be completely honest, individually and together.

Mary smiled and nodded. Stephen looked at him and just said that they talked about everything, honestly.

He was comforted. Later the two of them talked about what he had said, and understood.

Dot and Peter, on their motorbike, stopped off at Kingsbridge one Saturday at the beginning of October. They still had heard nothing from the old farmer whose unused cottages they wanted to do up. Peter stopped first at the newsagents and bought, through habit, a copy of the local paper. Trapping it between himself and his jacket he continued to the farmhouse.

"I'm glad to see you," the farmer started. "That lawyer of mine has finally done the paperwork. He tells me I'm being a vule, that my sons'll need the cottages as part of the farm once I'm gone. But they don't know me, or farming, or the future, and I need some money now. Things aren't like they were…"

He carried on in the same vein for some time. All the junior Lofts wanted to do was to look at the bottom line, make sure it was still as they agreed, then try and find a way of affording it. Finally the envelope was handed over, hands shaken, and a promise given that they would tell him how things were going in their search for a loan.

With the envelope lying next to the newspaper in Peter's jacket they made their way down to the ferry and parked the bike. There was no time to do what Peter was intending, read at least the headlines as they waited for the boat, as it was already on its way towards them. Boarding, they found themselves chatting to Charlie and Bert all the way to the island.

"Got something to show you, at last," said Peter when with their family. He unzipped the leather jacket. The newspaper fell on the floor, disregarded whilst he carefully opened the envelope.

"Look, got it at last. Let's see if it agrees with what we shook hands on."

They scanned the document. Mary, finding no room to see it properly, picked up the paper and glanced idly at it. Then she frowned and looked harder, ignoring the muttering behind the piece of paper the others were holding. She read, and read…

"Well, that looks quite hopeful." Her voice rang out over the conversation that was in progress about the houses.

Henry looked up. "What, the price, or Dot and Peter being able to get a loan?"

"No. What the government are forcing the water board to do."

There was sudden silence. Henry almost grabbed the paper from her but stopped himself in time and joined her in reading it. The others craned over their necks.

By the time Stephen returned from clearing a table in the café there was hubbub in the kitchen. Mary noticed him and went to help him.

"The government has told the water board that they have to admit responsibility for the flood and compensate people," she said simply. He looked shocked and they once again picked up Peter's newspaper. It said little more than that, apart from stressing that the board had been told to do so without further delay.

"There aren't actually that many farmers who lost out," he said thoughtfully. "And no one else who… who…" He stopped.

"Who lost the rest of their family," she said.

He nodded. "We should tell grandad." They got the attention of the others. Henry went to the phone.

"I need to get busy," said the old man when presented with the news. "There's still the matter of Mary's parents' insurance. That couldn't be paid out until liability was proved. And this, of course, proves it. I will find a formal notification of the decision and contact the company directly."

There was a pause as this was relayed to the family.

"What it means," said Mary's quiet voice, "is that it provides the price for your cottage, Dot and Peter."

Silence. A look of hope shot between the couple.

"Mary… that shouldn't be," said Henry reluctantly. "When I get compensation for the land that Loft's farm lost, I can, and will, pay for the cottages. But that insurance money will be yours, for the loss of the house and… and everything."

"What's the difference?" she asked. "We're all in this together, aren't we? It's what you've said all along and I agree."

"But with money, it's different," Henry told her. "I know you want to help them, and thank you, but it's your money for your future, not mine to give."

She thought. "But if I have money which I can't use, and there's people in my family who need it, how do you think I would feel in my future if those people had to go back to living in a small flat? Just because I didn't make it possible for them to take their chance when it was available?"

"But it's just not right." Peter this time. "We can't just take money from you. How would that make us feel? Dad's right, I'm afraid."

"But if he already had the money for the farm, and offered some of it to you, would you say the same?"

"That's different."

"No. It's not. It's family money. If you really want, Henry can pay me back when he *does* get the farm money. What's the point in it sitting in a bank or something for years when it's needed *now*?"

Stephen kept quiet. He could see both sides.

"And…" she continued, "how much money is going to come to me to compensate for the farm, the buildings, for three lives…" she choked on the words and Stephen was holding her before anyone else moved.

"It'll be *thousands*," she said fiercely. "Grandad will make sure of that. For both of us.

There was a silence.

"Please," she said at last. "Make me feel better. Agree to take it and use it for something *useful*. And don't forget that you'll be providing a place for Martin and Alice too, away from that father of his, or him having to sleep on the floor at her house."

Henry was about to make another call to Mr Merryweather when he phoned.

"I really apologise: I forgot to say in the excitement of hearing the news. Since you all signed that paperwork and it was accepted I've been working on the Court to get the child allowance back from her relative – it was, after all, part of the sentencing. The authorities have diverted it to you, and that takes effect from the date of the acceptance of the adoption paperwork. What you don't know is that at the sentencing the old lady was directed to repay three years worth of allowance in view of the fact that Mary was forcibly abducted. I now have a cheque for £300 for you which arrived yesterday."

"Three hundred?" Henry almost spluttered. "But that's… that's…"

"That's quite a lot of money." He could hear the smile in the old man's voice.

"What I meant was that… that it will go a good way to Dot and Peter's house." Henry looked round at the rest of them. Mary and Stephen nodded.

"I have to make the cheque payable to you as my client. Just a moment… yes, I can actually assign this to Mr Henry Loft, and you can assign it to Mr Peter Loft. That means it only goes to the bank once, when

Peter presents it for payment. That will save weeks."

"You are wonderful to us," said Henry thankfully. "Come to tea?"

"I could get the ferry, I think. Yes, if I'm quick. Would you like me to bring the cheque with me?"

"That would be kind," Henry laughed.

"Dad, are you sure?" asked Peter when Henry had put the phone down.

"My daughter has just voted to help Dot and Peter. This money is, I suppose, also hers, but if it had been paid to me as the person who wanted to provide a home for her, it would have gone in general expenses. So as it comes in a lump, after the event, it's part hers, part Family, and that includes her. But I would really like to do what any father would want to do, and that's give a son a good start in life."

"Then use whatever money is coming to me to make up the rest," Mary urged. "It really is what I want, and I really would feel awful if it wasn't used when it's needed."

"Should we vote?" asked Stephen.

Henry looked at him and grinned. "Hands up if you believe this windfall and some of Mary's insurance money should buy Dot and Peter's house."

Peter called in to the old farmer on the way home and gave him the news, telling him that as soon as the cheque cleared, Mr Merryeather would very quickly draw up the documents and transfer the money to him as a deposit.

"Old Merryweather... Is he still working?" the old man asked. "Haven't heard from him for years! Oh, he'll be good. He's honest as the day is long."

"He is," said Peter. "My Dad called him a wise old owl."

The farmer laughed. "We used to have fun together playing cricket – we weren't so wise then! But that was a long time ago."

"You played cricket together?"

"Yes. He was really good. There had been some talk of him playing for the County, but he never did. Too busy with his business."

Peter nodded. His mind was jogged back to playing cricket at school, and not for the first time he wondered what would have happened if he had stayed at home and continued on through the Higher School Certificate. University? Well, it had been his choice, and had he not made it he and Dot would never have met.

"But who's your Dad?" asked the farmer suddenly. "He's not the chap on Loft Farm, is he, who's had all that trouble over the last years?"

"He is. But most of the troubles have been sorted out now. We've got Mary Beale back..."

"Ah yes. That was disgraceful. I heard about that."

"...and they started the café which is doing well. And now it looks like the water people have got to pay out…"

"Does it? Since when?"

Peter explained, and the conversation continued. At last the farmer said he really should carry on. "Farms don't run themselves," he said. "But now I know you better, and who you come from, whenever you want to start work on those cottages, you do. No need to wait for all the paperwork and the rest of the money.. You get stuck in."

They were so pleased that Dot hugged him and Peter pumped his hand. They found a phone box and told Henry the developments.

"Does Martin know all this?" Henry asked.

"That's a thought… Haven't seen him for some time. I hope he still wants to come in with us."

"Actually, we've not seen him either… Steve – seen Martin recently?"

A pause.

"No, he hasn't seen him either. And we don't know where Alice lives."

"What's the name of the building firm he works at?" asked Peter.

Henry told him.

"Okay, I'll call them on Monday, see what's happening."

He called the Salcombe company early on Monday morning and was surprised to be put straight through to the owner, who was brusque almost to the point of rudeness.

"And who are you, may I ask?" came the terse question.

"Peter Loft. Son of Henry Loft, who you built the café for."

A pause. "Oh, that's all right then. I thought you were young Martin's father."

"Wrong age. What's happened, please?"

The man sighed. "It should be Martin telling you this, but he and his fiancée have split up. He was so upset he started being careless, though we didn't notice at first. Last week he fell off a ladder and broke his collar bone."

"Oh no… Is he all right?"

"Well, fairly. The hospital discharged him, and as they knew his father that's who they sent him to. He says he was so muzzy when the man came to get him that he didn't resist. But the day after, when he'd had his life story told to him so many times he was sick of it, he walked down to the ferry and came here. We've given him an old army camp bed and he's been here since."

Peter put another 4d in the slot.

"Do you know why he didn't go to the Lofts?"

"He thought that he'd not be welcome any more. He thinks you'd be ashamed of him – or that you wouldn't have room."

Peter was speechless. "I'm going to phone Dad and get him to come and sort it out. He'll have Martin back there today, if I know him, and once he's well enough to look after himself he's going to rent one of the cottages in Kingsbridge that I'm buying. We arranged that months ago."

"Well, it'd be good to know he's going to be properly looked after. Painful business, a broken collar bone."

Peter nodded. "Don't tell him, please. Let Dad do that. I don't want him vanishing, being too proud or something."

The man promised.

Peter called Henry, who had some choice words to say about Martin being a little idiot and of course he should have gone there. "It's his home, after all," he said.

Later that day Martin was almost dragged from the firm's offices, protesting he didn't need charity, that he'd be all right. Henry had to be firm with him.

"Months ago we told you that you had a home at Lofts'. Why did you think that we'd go back on that? My family doesn't work that way. Oh, you have your freedom, and you'll continue to have it. But only once that collar bone's mended. Then you can either stay at Loft Island, or you can move into the other one of the cottages Peter's buying. Or you can do whatever you think's best. But right now, my lad, you're coming back home with me and you're going to be fussed over. Just stop anyone from hugging you – for the moment."

It was the first grin on Martin's face for days.

They looked after him for the next several weeks whilst the bone and muscles healed. Henry made him be careful and almost insisted he didn't go back to work. "It's a tough job, what you do," he said. "If that's not back to full strength you'll break it again and that could be more serious in the long run. You don't want to end up being a crock, do you?"

So he stayed, using Stephen's room whilst its owner cheerfully slept in the café, until Christmas. Dot and Peter were dividing themselves between their jobs and the start of renovating the cottages. The parts that were habitable were cleaned and decorated, but they knew that the structural repairs would need experienced builders with proper equipment.

Martin begged leave to go and help them, and even with his limited experience was able to suggest improvements he'd seen done elsewhere, on other jobs. He tried physical help too, but a combination of the December cold and trying to use his arm properly for the first time in ages made Peter tell him not to be a fool.

"Your time will come, when we get your firm in to do the work. That'll be next year."

He argued, but this time it was Peter being firm. He stopped the conversation by asking what had happened with Alice.

"She found someone else," he said bitterly, and would say no more.

"More fool her," said Dot, and almost got a smile in return.

Christmas was spent on the island, as usual. Mr Merryweather had invited his sister and great niece to stay before receiving his invitation, so asked if there was enough room for them as well.

"The more the merrier," said Susan and Henry. "We have a café to fill! And they'll stay the night, of course."

Susan and Henry, Dot and Peter, Stephen and Mary, Martin, Mr Merryweather (now called Dad or Grandad universally by everyone), his sister Dolly and great niece Bronwen did their best to fill the place and succeeded. Martin found Bronwen's soft Welsh accent musical and shyly told her so. She, a year his senior, smiled and told him she had always loved the Devon burr and please could he talk more?

Increasingly they were found together, doing just that, and laughing. At various points of the day it was noticed. The other younger people were happy for them. The elders couldn't help but wonder what would happen when it was time for her to return to Wales.

By the end of January Dot and Peter had engaged Martin's employers to restore the parts of the cottages that were beyond the scope of their own abilities. To keep costs down they agreed that the work should be done when they had time between other jobs. Martin, now just about using his arm – carefully, was an early volunteer for the job. As well as pulling his weight with the actual work he cautiously started making practical suggestions about design and even methods. At various times he was told by his colleagues that he wasn't the foreman and was pushing his luck.

"But I am going to rent this one," he told them, "So I should be able to ask for it to be done like I want, surely."

It was done so nicely that they laughed. The foreman jokingly appointed him his assistant. Encouraged, he continued his input until the man had to admit he was right on many occasions. He also proved a useful 'night watchman', a task he enjoyed as it meant he could stay overnight in the cottage that would become his home. Having grown up in a tied cottage he had no fears of using an outside toilet, necessary until the cottages were connected to the main sewage system.

Mary's birthday fell at the end of January. As the family had missed so many of them, Henry was determined that this would be special. It turned into a weekend affair with all the people there who had stayed at Christmas. When Martin heard that Dolly and Bronwen were coming back his grin was so wide that he was accused of being the Cheshire Cat.

"We need to build onto this place again," said Susan, when she and

Henry were alone in the kitchen, planning for the festivities.

"Do we? It's a lot of expense for the occasional influx. And we can use the café and camp beds, can't we?"

"I can see a time when we'll be grandparents and need somewhere for babies to be. And when we're parents again ourselves we'll need the space anyway."

It took a few moments for the penny to drop.

"You're not trying to tell me something, are you," he asked, half in disbelief.

"No. Not *trying*, Henry Loft, *telling.*"

He waltzed her round the kitchen, then wondered if he should have.

# 32 – Christmas and more

Early on the Saturday morning, Mary's birthday, Henry vanished in the launch to Kingsbridge and wouldn't tell anyone why. Susan knew already as it had been a part of their plans.

Mary casually watched the boat's return, then screwed up her face in puzzlement to find three people on board. The launch landed; she walked down to help.

"Well hallo, lassie. So you're home at last, and happy I hope?"

Her mouth opened comically. The McTavishes, secretly invited soon after Christmas, had arrived.

"My, but it's a long way you came, Mary," said Mrs McTavish when they were indoors and all the introductions to family and friends were complete. "But I can see why. Not just the place, but your people, your family." Mrs McTavish's face straightened. "And it's guilty we are that we were taken in by that headmistress of yours who said all this was imagination. And you being so natural as a farmer too – we should have realised. She has a lot to answer for, that woman, and I hope she's had to."

They explained that it was actually Mary's great-aunt who had been responsible for the deception, and that the headmistress had felt as guilty as them. Mary mentioned, without rancour, that her relative had been punished for what she had done.

Susan and Henry announced the eventual arrival of a new Loft at the beginning of the main meal and, as usual, there was pandemonium. Privately Stephen wondered how a baby in the house would affect their life, but was nevertheless thrilled at the prospect of another sibling, as was Mary.

"It'll be good practice," she said incautiously. Stephen looked at her with the far-away look in his eyes she had seen from time to time when they were on their own.

He waited his time until it was dusk and then whisked her outside. For a change the sky was clear. They walked round the island until they could look up the estuary, over the Beales' drowned farm. Stephen stopped, holding her around the waist.

"I can't ask your parents, or Greg," he said quietly, hesitantly, wondering how such a reminder would be taken, considering that they were looking directly over the old homestead. "But I think that they would all approve. I think that Greg would be saying 'about time too!' like Grandad did to Dad. He'd probably already be calling me 'brother-in-law."

She gripped his hand.

"You know what I'm going to ask, don't you? I promised, months ago."

No response.

He knelt, and did it properly.

She turned and looked him in the face.

"Yes."

There was a long gap, a long and intense embrace. Their emotions were once again settling before she spoke again.

"And I know what is going to happen with that compensation money, if there's enough," she said. "If you agree I want to use it to build a house. A new house, with land we can farm. And…"

She held up her hand to stop him talking.

"I know where I want it."

He looked at her, waiting.

"Do you remember that last summer, when we were just two children on our own? When we took the dinghy and sailed up to our special place?"

He smiled.

"I remember it. I've held that memory for the last three years."

She caught her lower lip in her upper, surprised.

"What do you remember?"

"How hot it was."

"Anything else?"

"We went swimming."

"And?"

"Like Greg and I used to. No swim things. It was the first time I realised that you weren't Greg's little sister who was now my family, but that you had become… become…"

She waited.

"My closest friend. Like he had been." He gulped. "But more, somehow. In a way I didn't understand."

"You were rude to me. You said I was flat chested."

"I did not!"

"Not those words, but that's what you meant."

"I… I don't know what I said, now. I don't even know if it was true at the time. But…"

She waited.

"I'm sorry to have upset you. Sorry to have been rude. And…"

He gulped again.

"It's not true now."

She had to laugh.

"Anyway, that's where I want to build it. Near that land, overlooking the Creek. To remember that day when…"

His turn to wait.

"When I saw a boy who I suddenly realised was almost not a boy any more. And I never noticed it happening."

He didn't know what to say.

She laughed again at a linked memory, then to his surprise blushed. "At the time, when we seemed to be happy to be naked with each other I looked you over and wondered to myself "*why?*". She blushed and laughed again. "School taught me why. And I don't mean in lessons. But girls talk, and some of them were very... knowledgeable. At first I was appalled, then as the years passed I thought again, and then held that memory for years, and wondered..."

She blushed again.

"We've both got older, and grown, in all sorts of ways. And we've got all the time in the world to discover just how."

Stephen looked at her again with that far-away expression that she now realised came when he was becoming emotional. And at that moment it seemed right that they should hold each other and sway in time to a music that was solely within them. They stood, as so often before, by the water's edge, in that close, swaying embrace, with the winter moon's silver tracing a path from the living island to the drowned homestead, linking their childhood homes.

At last, even they had to stop and spend time looking at each other. The beauty of the night struck them and they watched the stillness.

At last Mary said: "Should we tell the others?"

"I suppose we'd better... hey, how about getting them all out here before we do?"

She looked again. The drowned area was bathed in light, but the sight no longer held any horrors for her. She just saw its mystical, silvered beauty.

"I'd like that. And I suppose we've each got to ask permission, too."

He nodded. "Like Dad did, and like Peter did. What do you think your parents and Greg would have said?"

"I know what they'd say. They'd be thrilled. And you're right; they'd say "About time too" but they'd be so, so happy. And Greg would say something soppy, or rude. But he'd be shaking your hand and hugging you."

Silence again as they looked over the Beales' part of the estuary.

"Shall we get them?"

"Mmm."

They walked back, hand in hand and opened the cafe door. There was a burst of applause. The younger contingent started making some slightly raucous remarks but were shushed by Henry and Susan when they saw the happy faces which seemed shocked at the reception. Stephen waited for calm to reign.

"Please will you come with us, outside? You might need coats because

330

it's cold."

This time the murmurs were of surprise, tinged with reluctance at the thought of leaving the warmth. But they all dressed as requested and followed the two down to the water's edge.

The sight silenced them all. Susan and Henry knew how special this flooded area was for Mary, and how previously it had held memories of traumatic events. The moon over it made it special for them all.

Stephen looked at Mary. "I seem to have done all the talking so far. How about you this time?"

She gulped. "Well..." She paused, facing them all. "This is quite difficult. You see..." Another pause while she gathered her thoughts.

"When I got off the ferry, after escaping from Scotland... no...sorry...that's not right..."

"It's all right, lassie," Mr McTavish called, "we know what you mean!"

She nodded. "When I'd escaped from *that* life, and arrived here, Stephen was the first person I saw. I was... was so surprised to realise that the good friend... but that's wrong too. He'd always been more than just a good friend really. It's just that I hadn't realised it. I do now. The good friend I'd left behind had become.. had become..." she searched for words which would embarrass neither of them. "Had become the person you see now. But he was – is – still Stephen. But he's more than that.

"And he just swept me off my feet then. Not by doing anything, just by being *him*. And I've not really come down again since. I think Susan and Henry know that."

She waited for one of them to say something, but they were just looking at her, gravely.

She gave a sigh. "It was the day after I'd come back. So many people seemed to have got together and it struck both of us that, actually, we'd been friends for the longest of all of you. Steve asked me what I'd say if he asked me something on my sixteenth birthday. I told him he'd have to wait and see, but please not to forget to ask."

She wondered if this would cause a laugh, but everyone was silent. It seemed that the view and the moment had their own magic.

"He didn't forget. He asked me here, on this spot, just now, looking over the land where we played as children, where we shared our lives with both sets of parents and Greg. And just look at it."

By now she was becoming emotional, not at the old memories but at the beauty of that moment and at the moment of proposal from earlier. Stephen looked at her. She looked hopelessly back and just nodded at him, willing him to finish the story. He lifted his hand from hers and put it around her waist protectively.

"Yes," he said in a soft voice. That far-away look was back. "Yes, I asked Mary to marry me. To spend the rest of her life with me. And she said 'yes.' She – we – believe that her parents and Greg would be pleased and would have given their permission. We must now ask our own Mum and Dad for permission."

He stopped and almost gulped with nerves. Though he knew there was goodwill from the two adults, he knew that he and Mary were both young. And there was no cast-iron guarantee what the reaction to their question would be. And on the answer would hinge their futures together, at least until Mary was twenty-one in five long years time.

He looked out over the silver water again, unwilling to meet anyone else's eyes until he knew. Mary put her arm round his waist too.

Henry and Susan looked at each other, still grave.

"Well?" Henry said in an undertone that no one else could hear. Susan looked back and now a smile was appearing.

"You know, I don't think it would be right to stop them, do you?"

"I'm inclined to agree. But I'm not sure about a married schoolgirl."

"I don't think they'd want to endure that complication either."

"Agreed, then?"

"Agreed."

"You or me?"

"You."

They joined the two at the water's edge. Henry could now see the tension in his son's frame, and wondered at it. They stood at the young couple's backs.

"We think... please turn round?"

Hesitantly the arms dropped, and they turned. Stephen's eyes couldn't meet his father's.

"Stephen? Mary? We're not ogres, you know. Please?"

Stephen dragged his eyes up to look directly at these two, one of whom he had known since birth and the other whose arrival with the family and whose near-constant presence he welcomed so warmly. There was compassion and understanding and a gentle smile on each face. His spirit started to lift with hope.

"We think that it might complicate things for you both if you got married whilst still at school, especially if you started a family. But you'll have thought of that, I'm sure. We both knew Stephen's unhappiness when Mary couldn't be found, and the immense happiness of you both when she returned. We've seen that happiness deepen ever since, and it seemed more than likely that this was going to be the result. And we both really welcome it. So the answer is obviously 'yes'. And we wish you both so well."

There were cheers and congratulations from everyone. The couple's misgivings flew away. Strained expressions were replaced by smiles of happiness.

Bronwen and Martin were to be seen holding hands, looking alternately at the engaged couple and at each other.

After the round of hugs that seemed to have been almost the norm on this island, at this home, recently, all except two drifted off back to the cafe and warmth.

Mary and Stephen stood again alone, looking silently at the silver path. This would forever be their time. Their place.

# The End

Continued in *The Island and the Town*

## ABOUT THE AUTHOR

Richard Wright has been, or in some cases still is, a transport enthusiast, church bell ringer, Bluebell Railway guard, Scout Leader, IT enthusiast, narrowboat part-owner, NCI Watchkeeper. He has dabbled in local politics and spends too much time on Facebook. He has earned a living running buses and coaches, later becoming a school security manager and theatre manager. In 2013 he saw the light and retired – at least technically.

He and his wife live in Sussex.

*The Suspects* was his first published book, followed by *Loft Island*, *Change at Tide Mills* and now *The Island and the Town*. He believes in setting his books in real or very plausible places, and most certainly in crediting his younger subjects with intelligence, self-reliance and innate common sense.

He welcomes contact about the books at richard@rw2.co.uk

# Other books by Richard Wright

## The Suspects

A lighthearted book with spikes. Faced with little to do over the summer, six mid-teen mates camp illegally. Evicted back to their home town, they soon find they have to return to camp to keep out of the way. A dog, a Dutch recluse, a town gang of adults, parents, maps and a hospital all play their part. There are brambles, nettles, blackthorns, wild swimming, self-sufficiency, fires, friendships and of course the dog. And those truffles…

## Change at Tide Mills

Set near Seaford, Sussex in the 1960s. Owen persuades his parents to take on the dilapidated Tide Mills (which exists in real life but as a ruin).

During the improvements to the site one of the villagers engages Owen in the old Sussex trade of smuggling. How will it end?

## The Island and the Town

A continuation of Loft Island, centring (to start with) on Bronwen and Martin, but with the involvement of all the other characters in Loft Island.

## Make contact

It'd be great to hear your views – positive or negative:

Web page: rw2.co.uk. Here you'll find access to a mailing list so I can keep you updated with other titles. We could even end up chatting!

Email: richard@rw2.co.uk

Facebook: www.facebook.com/suspects

Printed in Great Britain
by Amazon